and Swashbucklers

Edited by Valerie Griswold-Ford

Spells
and Swashbucklers

Edited by Valerie Griswold-Ford

DRAGON
MOON
PRESS

Spells and Swashbucklers

ISBN 978-1-897492-46-8

Printed and bound in the United States

www.dragonmoonpress.com

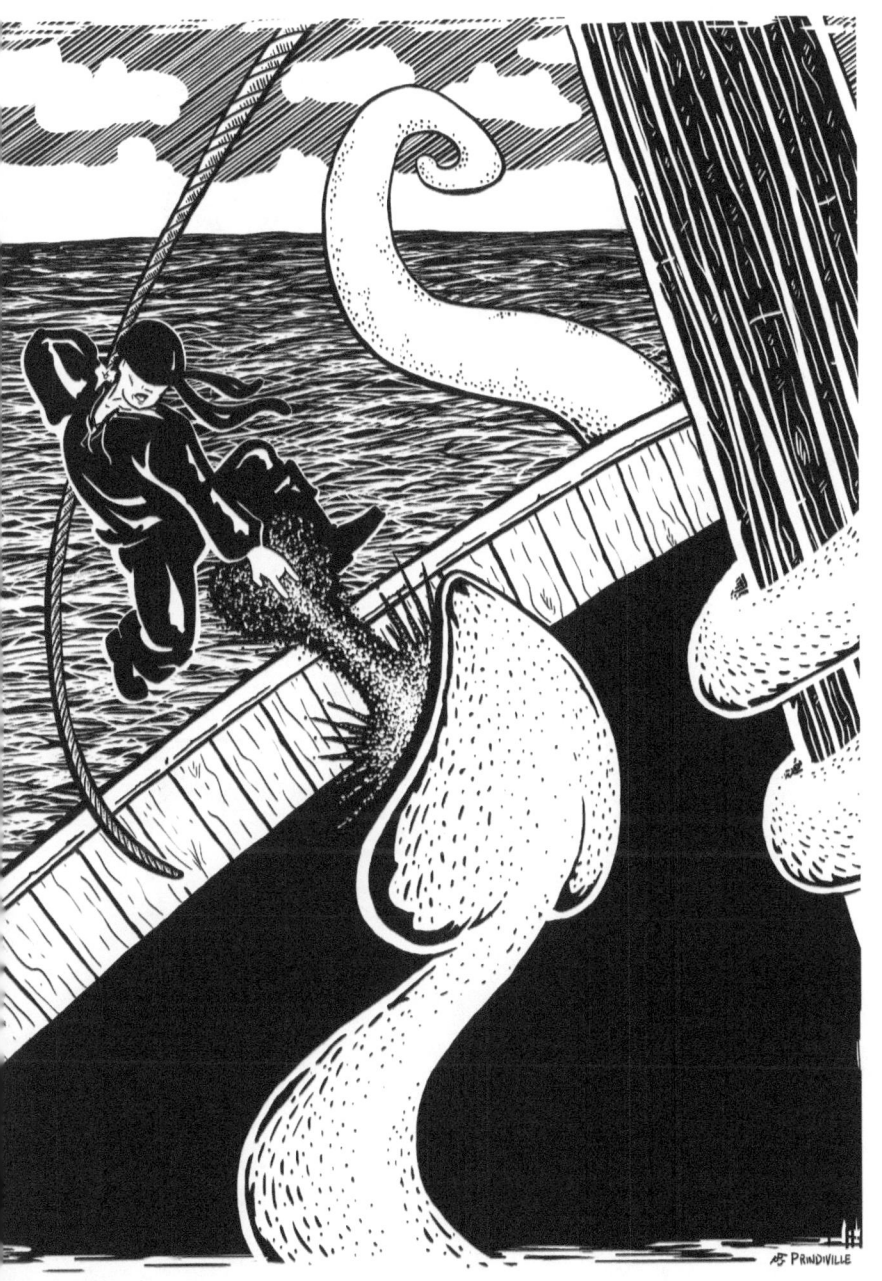

Table of Tales

Foreword

PG HOLYFIELD

Roberts was a gentleman
Drank his tea from an old tin can
Never touched a bottle kept a clean ship and
You'd never guess he was a pirate
He said, "Our ship was mighty as a sloop could be
Over four hundred vessels plundered we
With our sacks full of biscuits we'd return to the sea
Our jolly roger blowing proud and free
After Roberts robbed a vessel of it's prize
He'd return the ship to it's captain's sorry eyes
Never questioned any man's disguise
He followed the sabbath as he followed the sky.

                    –David Shepherd Grossman –
                    "Bartholomew Roberts" (song)

My favorite pirate from history has always been Bartholomew Roberts. During the Golden Age of Piracy, *Black Bart* Roberts was estimated to have captured over 470 vessels. He is one of the four pirates mentioned in *Treasure Island* and in my mind, anyway, is the inspiration for The Princess Bride's *Dread Pirate Roberts*.

Roberts would make a great character in pirate fiction, no matter the genre. He was taken prisoner by a Welsh pirate named Howell Davis. In a very short time Davis had taken to Roberts, as he was Welsh himself and an able navigator. Only a couple of months later Davis was dead after a failed kidnapping of a Portuguese governor, and the crew had elected the former prisoner Roberts as Captain. And in so doing Roberts is said to have stated a phrase that pretty much encompasses the romantic allure of pirates in history:

Since I have dipp'd my Hands in Muddy Water, and must be a Pyrate, it was better being a Commander than a common man.

Roberts was courageous and an inspirational commander. He avenged Captain Davis and captured two ships in his first action as captain. For three years he roamed the Caribbean and the seas off of South America and Africa, at one point capturing 42 Portuguese ships in a harbor without firing a shot. Eventually Roberts was killed in battle by the English Navy.

In addition to his reputation as a pirate, Roberts is a great *character* due to a personality that made him atypical among his peers:

- he drank tea instead of rum
- he disapproved of drunkenness in his crew (a good rule of thumb: ironically, his crew was mostly drunk during the attack that killed Roberts)
- he was clean-shaven and dressed in his finest clothes during battle
- he held church services on his ship, and the musicians he constantly had on board during his captaincy were given the Sabbath Day as a day of rest.
- he treated most (even most of his prisoners) with kindness and respect.

Character is one of the most important elements of a pirate story. And in this anthology, you have some great characters, whether it be the pirates who are the main viewpoint characters in several stories, or the viewpoint characters being hunted or captured by pirates, as is the case in other stories here.

Adding magic to the mix is the rope that ties these stories together. The question is, would Bartholomew Roberts succeed as a modern day pirate, in search of a woman with magical powers? Would he succeed in a world where magical weapons and defenses were the norm for sailing vessels? Would he have prospered in space where the ships moved in zero g with rockets rather than sails?

I think so. He was Black Bart, after all.

P.G. Holyfield is the author of *Murder at Avedon Hill*, available through Dragon Moon Press and through Amazon.com. P.G. manages the speculative fiction website SpecFicMedia.com, co-hosts the *Game of Thrones* podcast Beyond the Wall and organizes and emcees the yearly online speculative fiction live-streaming marathon called TuacaCon. P.G. is currently working on a multimedia fiction project that sadly has no pirates, but does have murder and possibly magic aboard a spaceship in search of New Earth. For more information on this project, please visit SpecFicMedia.com

Death Tide

JESSE L. CAIRNS

I raised the binoculars again, already knowing what I was going to see. There was a full moon tonight and I didn't need the starlight setting but I engaged it anyway. A cursory glance showed the other ship was still there off the stern about a mile or so back. No running lights, but I could still see it under the moonlight. It hadn't changed course and gone about its own business; if anything, it seemed to be closer. I took a few quick measurements and felt my stomach shift uncomfortably.

Damn. No question about it, the other ship *had* closed the distance. I let the binoculars fall back down, the brief burn from the strap lost amid the uncomfortable prickling on the back of my neck. Our charter yacht, the luxurious fifty-two-foot Bayliner 5288 model christened the *Tuscan Sunrise*, had been running on a course parallel to the Northern California coast for the past fifteen minutes. Before that, we had been headed due west, and before that, south. Not only was it still on our tail, now the mystery vessel was closing in. Bad news.

I ran a hand through my hair, then went to the wheel. After a quick consultation of the *Tuscan Sunrise's* GPS readout, I set us on a course back toward our launching point of San Francisco. As an afterthought, I opened up the throttle to full.

No point in trying to keep a low profile now; if we were indeed being pursued, it was time to beat a retreat to safer waters and not wait around to see if their intentions were friendly or not.

Besides, if push really came to shove and things got bad, there was always the .454 Cassul revolver hidden in the ship's galley. For last resorts.

I went below to the sleeping quarters and quietly opened the door. "Samantha," I whispered. "Wake up."

She rolled over on the bed, her black negligee slipping from one shoulder as she did. "Thomas. Are we back to port yet?" she asked, voice throaty from sleep.

"Not exactly. We're near the—"

"Oh, good. I'll have to remember to tell the company that you deserve a bonus for this charter." She grinned, her blue eyes sparkling wickedly. She plunged both hands into her mass of tightly-wound red curls that had reminded me so much of corkscrews when I'd first seen them a few delightful hours ago, then patted the mattress next to her. I seemed to remember her saying she'd gotten a perm to have her hair be like a girl she knew and admired. It was weird what thoughts could go through your head when you were trying to keep a lid on things. "We still have a bottle of champagne on ice left, care to join me... again?"

"Great thought, bad timing," I said. "Get dressed. We're in trouble."

I have to give her credit; Samantha didn't panic, her voice didn't go up and she didn't clutch at the sheets. Her eyes widened slightly, and then they hardened. That's all. Strangely, I wasn't sure whether I liked that better. "I see," she said after a moment. "What's going on?"

"Somebody is following us. I've spent the last forty minutes or so making a path that should have shook them off at some point, but they're gaining on us. I've opened the engines up to full for the push back to San Francisco, but I honestly don't know if that'll be enough," I answered.

She swung her perfectly-shaped legs out of the bed, reaching for her evening dress. "Give me a couple minutes and I'll be up," she said tersely. "Do we have any weapons?"

I thought of the pistol. "We're not exactly defenseless, if that's what you're wondering."

"We never were. All right, then." She slid the dress on over head, then stood and shimmied into it. Incredibly, the next thing she reached for was her makeup compact. Was she serious? Blush and mascara, at a time like this?

"Thomas?" Her voice was cool.

I swallowed. "Yes?"

"Was there anything else?"

"Ah... no, not that I can really think of right now."

"Good. Then take another view of our would-be pursuers and I will join you on deck shortly."

I left the room, going up the ten steps to the deck with my head shaking. Then again, considering how this evening had gone, maybe I shouldn't have been that surprised. Samantha Blackshear was a successful young businesswoman who had chartered the *Tuscan Sunrise* for an evening cruise off the coast of San Francisco, paid cash and brought along three magnum bottles of Roederer Estate Anderson Valley Brut champagne already chilling on ice. She had drank the first bottle in a kind of blissful silence, standing at the bow while the ship slowly made its way out to sea directly into an absolutely beautiful Pacific sunset, then invited me below to share the second with her in bed. It hadn't been the first time that a customer had requested this "additional service," and it just reinforced my long-held position that I had the best job in San Francisco. There was a reason why Louis booked the cruises and I was the one who displayed the company presence on the *Tuscan Sunrise*.

Standing at the stern, I sighed deeply and raised the binoculars again. Yeah, just my luck to be the point man when—

What the hell? I zoomed in for a better look, and felt the saliva in my mouth dry up.

There were three figures standing on the deck of the other ship, one of them pointing in our direction. There was no sail in evidence, meaning that the pursuing ship was running purely on engine power and, what was worse, I could visibly tell they were closing the gap. Even in the dim illumination provided by the starlight mode, I could see the eagerness on their rough, unshaven faces as the prow of their ship cut through the water toward us.

I swept the binoculars from fore to aft of the other boat. At the very stern I could see what looked like a black flag flying from a short pole attached to the edge of the railing, not the usual stars and stripes. Near the waterline there was something written, but it appeared that somebody had attempted to scuff the letters away. The vessel had absolutely no identifying marks whatsoever, as if the people piloting it were trying like hell not to—

I swallowed heavily. "Oh, Jesus," I said in a small voice. Just like that it fell together in a terrible jumble, like a sack of broken glass.

No name on the ship. Lack of running lights. Black flag. We might not have been anywhere near Somalia, but I definitely smelled piracy. That was impossible, though; this wasn't some third world dirt hole country with a military strongman in power and corruption as far as they eye could see. This was America. This was my home.

Pirates. No. No way.

I spared a glance at the speedometer. Forty-four nautical miles per hour. The engines were maxed, and it still wasn't enough. Dear Jesus, it wasn't nearly enough.

"Oh, shit," I said and was appalled by the watery weakness of my own voice. "This isn't happening, man, this is just *not* freaking happening. Not happening."

I drew in a deep breath. Focus. First things first; if we were able to get back to friendly waters, or at least be within hailing distance of a Coast Guard cutter, there was a chance that all this panic was for nothing. I went to the navigational station and saw that at our current rate of speed versus that of our pursuers, we'd be overtaken before we got within fifty miles of shore. Not good. I wasn't exactly sure how far their vessels patrolled from shore, but unless I threw up an emergency beacon and called for help, our chances of simply stumbling across one of them were dim at best.

I picked up the radio... and hesitated.

"Damnit. The Cassul," I growled. "What's possession of an unregistered, possibly illegal handgun get you in the state of California, anyway? What's the worst that could happen?"

Half a dozen cop shows flickered before my eyes, telling me it was anywhere from probation to ten years in some horrific bullpen like San Quentin. Bottom line, didn't know. However, the alternative was to keep my mouth shut and see what our new playmates wanted out of us instead. A bad choice was sometimes no choice at all. I pressed SEND on the unit and swallowed heavily.

"Distress, distress, this is the *Tuscan Sunrise*, calling from—"

A squeal of static ripped through the room and I dropped the handset. Grinding my teeth together, I picked it back up and tried again. "Distress, this is the *Tuscan*—"

Another blast of interference shrieked through the cabin and I let it tumble from my fingers with a moan. Jammed. The bastards were jumping on our signal as soon as it sounded. I switched channels and tried again, only to get the same result. That meant the could-be raiders were either using the mother of all scramblers that blotted out everything within a certain radius, or they were able to follow our frequencies just as easily as they could the ship itself.

Some sort of tracking device? Maybe, but where? The *Tuscan Sunrise* was fifty-two feet from bow to stern, and had been thoroughly detailed before Samantha's charter. If a bug had been placed, it could literally be anywhere. Hell, it might even be below the waterline. I didn't—

"What's going on?" Samantha asked from the deck.

I thought about playing it tough, then junked that idea in favor of brutal honesty. "We've got real trouble," I said. "The basics are this: another boat, looks like about a thirty-foot sailboat outfitted with some serious power in the engine department is on our tail and closing fast. I count three people on board, but there could be more below deck so I wouldn't count on that figure. Weapons unknown, but it looks like they're going to catch up with us before we get within fifty miles of San Francisco. And I definitely think they're not the local welcome wagon. Like I said, real trouble."

She nodded slightly. "Got it. What about calling for help?"

"Tried it already. They're using a very powerful jammer, and I can't get through." I spread my hands. "Is God returning your calls?"

"Hmm. Not really." She pursed her lips, steepling her fingers together in front of her face. "When you said we weren't defenseless, what *exactly* did you mean by that?"

"I have a heavy revolver in the galley," I said. "Six shots worth of high-impact ammunition."

"On a pleasure ship?"

"It was my partner's idea. He believes in being prepared. Unfortunately, that's all the ammo we have. So if it comes down to violence, we'd better hope that I'm a good shot and that they don't have any backup or assault rifles."

"All right." She nodded decisively and folded her arms. "Then let's pick the time and place to face them. Start slowing down."

I felt my eyes bulge. "Say *what?*"

"I don't think we should do it all at once," she advised. "It would probably be best to bring the speed down gradually, as though we're having engine trouble, so they can gradually catch up. What do you think?"

"Look, I'm really glad we had such a fun time earlier, but this seems like a really bad idea," I said. "I mean, one patch of the Pacific Ocean is pretty much like any other and we're lucky the water is so still tonight. We're not going to gain any kind of environmental advantage by meeting them in one place rather than another. We should go as hard as we can for shore and—"

"And then what?" she asked. "Like you already said, we're not going to make it to friendly waters before they catch up with us. The only thing we can really do is make the encounter happen at a time and place of our choosing, and therefore that gives us a bit of a psychological advantage. If they think they have us captured because the engines crapped out, they'll assume we'll be scared and frustrated, which might make them play things a little bit looser than they might ordinarily do so. That gives us at least one small advantage, and since it's likely the only one we're probably going to have, it's definitely in our best interest to try to take advantage of it."

Try as I might, I couldn't come up with a good reason to disagree with her. She was right; we were in a corner, and we only had one play left that could possibly swing things in our favor. Too bad it felt like volunteering to stick our heads in the guillotine. "Anything else we should do?" I asked, a slight edge to my voice.

"Get your gun and keep it someplace where you can easily get to it," she advised. "My guess would be to stash it in our—I mean, the *Tuscan Sunrise's*—sleeping quarters. It's the only place where you can really hold a prisoner and if they're not in a prisoner-taking mood..." She trailed off, then tried to smile. "Then hey, we don't have to really worry about it. On second thought, maybe you should have it on you."

I swallowed past a vast dryness in my throat. "Got it," I croaked.

She hesitated, then placed a hand on my shoulder. "I really enjoyed myself earlier," she said quietly. "I did. You're a good man, Thomas. I promise I will do whatever I can to protect you."

I eased back on the throttle and could have almost sworn I heard a whoop from the enemy ship. Who knows, maybe I had; sound carries in funny ways at night across water. "How exactly are you going to do that?" I asked.

"Every situation has its price for getting what you want," she said. "I'm worth a good piece of money, so perhaps we can buy them off."

"And if not?"

"Then we'll dynamite that bridge when we come to it," she said softly. "Better go hide that hand cannon, Thomas; it looks like we're about to run out of time."

I went below to the sleeping quarters and opened up the small safe next to the bed. The Cassul was a long-barreled heavy chrome revolver with a bore that looked almost big enough to fall into. For the first time since I'd become aware of its existence on the *Tuscan Sunrise*, I found myself wishing for an extra speed ring or two of ammo. Six shots. That's all I had. I wondered briefly if perhaps Samantha had a snub-nose stuck in her purse, then shook my head and jammed the Cassul down the back of my jeans and carefully settled my shirt over the handle. No sense in wishing upon stars or anything else; I had two shots maximum for each of the men I'd seen on deck.

I was no slouch on the firing range, sure, but this was real. This was for keeps.

God, if you're listening, help us out, I thought, closing my eyes briefly. *This is bad, worst trouble I've ever seen, and we could sure use your assistance.*

I rejoined Samantha on deck and now I could see the pursuing vessel with my naked eyes under the moonlight, barely a hundred yards off the stern. Jesus, they had closed quickly. There were two men standing at the bow of the boat and one man back amidships, cradling what looked like an assault rifle in his hands. That was bad.

"I only count three," Samantha said. "That makes things a little better."

"All right," I said, relieved. "How do you want to play this?"

"Follow my lead," she advised. "We'll see if we can buy them off, and if that doesn't work then I will—"

"Tuscan Sunrise!" an electronically amplified voice blared from across the water. "Kill your engine and prepare to be boarded! If you attempt to escape, we will shoot out your engines and take your vessel by force. This is your only warning!"

She inhaled deeply, then turned to face me. "Guess that's our signal," she said, squaring her shoulders. "How do I look?"

"Um, fine. Beautiful," I said, confused.

She kissed my cheek, leaving a swirling scent of jasmine and cinnamon. "You're sweet," she smiled. "Maybe when this is over we can go out again sometime, huh?"

"I think we better survive this little hurdle first," I said, with little bit more bite than I had intended.

"We'll survive. Do you trust me?" she asked.

After only a few hours, even if most of them had been pretty pleasurable? About as much as I could, I supposed. "Yes," I said aloud.

Samantha nodded, then straightened her back. "All right," she said. "Follow my lead, don't freak out over anything I say or do, and keep that pistol ready."

A pair of heavy flashlight beams came from the other vessel—which I now could read, just above the waterline, had letters scratched away which said the boat had used to be called the *Sea Horse*—and played over the structure of our vessel, momentarily blinding me. It began at the bow and moved methodically backward, being sure to spend a good amount of time around the cabin area, before finally coming to rest on the two of us. The lights pinned us to the deck like bugs before switching off, leaving me with a few seconds of swirling motes in my vision.

A grappling hook whistled out of the darkness and locked into place over the rail about halfway down the *Tuscan Sunrise's* length, drawing the two vessels closer together. Now I could see the men on deck: two white, one black, all with rough week-long growths of facial hair, hard faces and easy, even contemptuous, eyes. All wore black jackets and pants, and one of the white guys carried an assault rifle that reminded me of the ones the Germans used during World War Two; I think it was called an MP40. The other two had heavy semi-automatic pistols drawn, but were held loosely at their sides. They didn't think we were going to be any trouble. Maybe Samantha was right and we could use that to our advantage.

"Nice night for a boating trip, gentlemen," Samantha called, her voice strong and giving no hint of nervousness. "Can we help you with anything?"

The one with the assault rifle cocked his head. "Samantha Blackshear?"

Her face fell slightly for a moment, then reasserted itself. My bad feeling doubled. Oh, shit. This wasn't just some moonlight piracy; they knew who at least one person on the vessel was. It looked less like a robbery by the second and more like... like an abduction. Or maybe even a hit.

If they were here to put her down a hole, what would they do to me?

As surreptitiously as I could, I reached behind my back and flicked the safety off.

The man cocked his weapon and pointed it toward us. The sound was hideously loud over the waves lapping against the sides of the boat, barely five feet of space between us. "I'll say it one more time," he said quietly, the other two men moving into position behind him. "Are you Samantha Blackshear?"

"I am," she answered.

"Good." The boats bumped together and the assault rifle-wielding man crossed over onto our deck, followed by the black man with the pistol. The third man stayed behind, then went down below. Damnit. I didn't like the odds of being able to shoot both men on our ship and then target the third before he got us, so I continued to stand with my arms folded. Hey, they hadn't told me to put them up, so there was no point in following their script for them. Why make their jobs easier?

"May I ask what this is about?" she asked, a touch of frost to her voice.

"We'll ask the questions, if you don't mind," the second man said tersely. "You just keep your mind on the answers and maybe this doesn't have to get really unpleasant."

"But I wouldn't count on that," the first man snickered.

I saw Samantha's jaw tense and said a mental prayer. It was pretty evident that she wasn't used to being talked to in that sort of voice, and I just hoped that she could keep enough self-control until we knew what they wanted so we could—

"How much are you being paid for this?" she asked.

They glanced at each other; the one with the pistol shrugged. "Ten thousand dollars," he said after a few moments.

"I'll double that if you leave right now," she offered.

Now the stare between the two men was longer; the pistol-wielder made a go-on motion, which made the assault rifle thug shrug. "It's a nice idea, but no can do," he said with a sigh.

"Aaron, come on," his partner argued. "Twenty large doesn't come around every day."

"John, did you forget about the special cargo?" Aaron asked, his lip curling in contempt.

Now it was John's turn to look as partner as though he were stupid. "It has a two day shelf life, or did you forget about that part of the briefing?" he said acidly. "No big deal. We dump it over the side of the boat and the poor bastard expires long before it can get within spitting distance of the shore. More money than we were previously counting on gets collected. How is this a bad plan?"

The word clanged in my head over and over again. *It has a two day shelf life.* Oh, Jesus.

Samantha, for her part, was frowning. "What are you talking about?" she asked.

"Our insurance policy," Aaron said. "And the answer is no, John. We're not going back on the contract. I'm not crossing them, and neither are you. We're going to do this the way we were paid to do it, and that's the bottom line."

John opened his mouth to protest and the most blood-freezing moan I ever heard in my life drifted across from the other ship. Some of the color dropped out of John's face; Aaron, for his part, acted as though he hadn't heard. It was Samantha's reaction, however, that really threw me. A look of absolute horror came to her face, her eyes widening.

"Travis!" Aaron shouted to the other ship. "Let's do this. Get moving."

The third thug came back on deck again with a length of chain in his hand, leading a person whose hands were bound before them and had a burlap sack over its head. I took an involuntary step back. Samantha, for her part, took four. A look of revulsion was clearly stamped on her face, and her hand reached for mine.

Her fingers were cold. This was really happening. Oh Jesus, this was really happening.

"Our new friend Roger is here to make sure that things don't get out of hand," Aaron said, gesturing to the hooded man that was now making a series of wet snuffling sounds as though it were trying to scent the air. "He's been getting progressively more excited over the last hour or so. Can't imagine why."

Samantha swallowed heavily, the mask of her new-applied makeup now standing out sharply against her chalky skin. "Get that thing out of here," she whispered.

"Oh no, sweetcheeks. I've already got the rundown on you, and I know just what you're capable of," Aaron grinned as Travis slowly brought Roger across from the *Sea Horse* to the deck of the *Tuscan Sunrise*. "I also know that our buddy Roger here is something that you won't be able affect if you decide to try any of your tricks, so that should ensure your cooperation, since Travis and that length of chain is the only thing keeping him off your neck. Do we understand each other, Samantha?"

"I... yes. Yes, we do," she whispered.

As she said the words she took another step back and to the side so that she was slightly behind me, as if cowering... and firmly tapped the handle of the gun I'd shoved down the back of my pants.

My head was swimming with questions. Who were these guys? Who had hired them? Why did they want Samantha? What the hell *was* that thing under the burlap sack? What sort of tricks did she have up her sleeve that made them so cautious? But most of all, the question swirling around was *Am I going to survive the rest of the night?* I knew that if I had any chance of doing that, I was going to have to follow her lead.

I inhaled deeply, then slowly let it out. A prickling coldness settled into my scalp. Bizarrely, surrendering control cleared things up a little bit. In fact, it was a huge help. No time for pondering unthinkables or trying to figure out the full depths of what was happening here; there was only survival. For whatever reason, Roger was here to counter Samantha. All right. The Cassul would just have to counter him, too. Less than two shots apiece, now.

Sure. Nothing easier. I felt the cold touch of mortality on the back of my neck and shivered briefly.

Travis yanked the chain, causing Roger to stumble slightly before righting himself. "What do I do with this?" he demanded.

"Hold on to him like you've been doing," Aaron said. "He can go back down in the hold when we have the bitch tied up in the chair opposite his chaining post. Let's go."

My blood ran cold for two reasons; first, Travis had pulled the hood off of Roger. He had once been a man with a crew cut in his mid-twenties, and married to judge from the plain gold band on his left ring finger, but those days were long gone. I guessed him between twenty and twenty-five years old, roughly my own age, but there was what looked like a bullet hole in the middle of his forehead, a streamer of dried blood running down his nose and into the corner of his open mouth. The teeth inside were broken, jagged and crusted with dirt. His cheeks were sunken, skin gray and slack like uncooked dough. The creature's eyes were cloudy and vacant, unblinking and fixed with idiot concentration on Samantha. I could feel the full force of the unnaturalness of the monster even from ten feet away, would have sensed the thing's—because it was clearly no longer a man—presence from ten feet away, and I would have shrank away from it even had it been in a pitch-black room. This thing was clearly not of the natural world.

A kind of quiet fright settled into my bones, like fresh snow drifting through the branches of a dead tree. I'm not a complete dope; I took a couple years of junior college before deciding to go into the touring business, and something kept prodding at me over and over again. One of my philosophy professors had brought up a thing called Occam's Razor, which when plainly stated meant that when faced with a situation with two or more possible explanations, picking the one with the fewest assumptions usually resulted in the right answer.

This one was very simple. The raiders had brought a zombie. Unless it was an elaborate makeup job done for no other reason than to give us an extra scare, we were dealing with an honest-to-God member of the walking dead and all that was holding it back was a single length of chain.

My second reason for being frightened? Easy. They were

getting ready to leave and nothing yet had been said about me. Unless I did something soon, I was likely looking at a bullet to the temple, followed by being dumped over the side of the boat with cinder blocks attached to weigh me down. As surreptitiously as I could, I reached behind my back—

I paused for a moment, frowning. Was that whispering?

It was, and was more, it was coming from Samantha. I leaned in closer, trying to hear what she was saying, but I couldn't make it out. No; that wasn't quite right. I could hear what she was saying, but the words—if that was what they were—didn't make any sense. Like they had too many consonants and not enough vowels to them.

And at the same time, the gunmen began to scratch.

Aaron began to run his fingernails across his forearm. John rubbed his left foot against the inside of his right leg. And even though both hands were wrapped around the length of chain around Roger's neck as he continued to strain toward Samantha, it was obvious that Travis was similarly discomfited. His neck rolled first to the left, then right, rubbing against his shoulders but still keeping firmly focused on the zombie that was beginning to wrench the chain back and forth in its efforts to escape.

Samantha took two large steps backward to bring her alongside me, her lips continuing to move. She pinched my upper arm, hard, making me yelp in surprise.

Meanwhile, the itching was obviously getting much worse for our captors. John was leaning down to dig into his calf muscle, gritting his teeth as he did. The muzzle of his pistol pointed toward the deck of the *Tuscan Sunrise*, apparently forgotten in the torment of the moment. Somehow Travis had managed to drag his undead charge backward a few paces and was grinding his back against the rail of the ship, his eyes half-closed and groaning softly in pleasure. Roger didn't appear to have been affected at all by whatever malady was plaguing the raiders; he had unblinking, hungry eyes only for Samantha.

However, Aaron appeared to be suffering the worst. His MP40 clattered to the deck as he dug his fingernails into his flesh, making small whimpering noises while his ragged fingernails quickly punctured the skin and blood began to flow, then drip onto the deck. Roger stopped in his efforts for a few seconds and half-turned toward Aaron, making those wet snuffling noises again, then swung back toward Samantha almost regretfully. It was almost as if—

She's doing this, I thought wonderingly. *Whatever it is that's making them scratch hard enough to rip the skin from their own bodies, it's something she's doing. She's the one who is—*

She pinched me again, harder this time. "Stop that!" I shouted. "Damnit, that hurts!"

Aaron went to his knees, gasping in either relief or pain as his fingers dug further into the ruined meat of his forearm. "Travis!" he grated. "Do it now!"

Travis' eyes opened. They seemed dazed. "What? But the boss said he wanted her alive—"

"Do it! *Now*, dammit!"

I knew my cue when I heard it. A look of dazed incomprehension on his face, Travis didn't really seem to be in this act of piracy on the high seas any more, but he was still in the ballgame enough to know that he had a job to do. With a final fearful glance to Aaron—who had already gone back to tearing at his own flesh again—he opened his hands and let the rusted chain fall to the deck with a clank.

Roger lurched forward, halted for a moment as if surprised to find himself freed, then half-turned back toward his former handler. He bared his broken teeth in a snarl, then sniffed the air again. Almost reluctantly he swung back toward us again—

I shot him through the heart.

In the movies, when somebody takes a round in the chest they get knocked off their feet, fly backward and red stuff seemingly explodes out of the wound. In real life, the person simply goes down in a heap with blood squirting out of the hole; the stopping power of a .454 Cassul is impressive, granted, but no pistol is going to make real life look like a John Woo movie. Roger was even less impressed. He staggered backward one step as something plopped wetly to the ground behind him—most likely a chunk of his body—and then growled as if to say,

That's your one freebie, buddy. Now I'm coming for your ass.
He began to advance again.

This time my round took him right between the eyes, where the wound that in all likelihood had originally killed him had struck home. The impact was more spectacular this time because of the hollow-point round. Everything vanished above the middle of his nose in a gory explosion, leaving a jagged landscape of bone, clotted black blood and twisted meat in its wake. What it *didn't* do was put the monster down, because after stumbling in a full circle and getting its feet tangled in the length of chain still wrapped around its neck, Roger began to shamble forward toward us again. I think I peed myself; either that, or I had a wound that I hadn't been aware of on my inner thigh.

The raiders saw what was going on and went for their weapons, but Samantha raised both her hands in the air as though signaling that the extra point was good and with choked screams, they went back to tearing at their flesh again with renewed vigor. Except now, the areas being affected weren't just John's leg, Travis' back and Aaron's forearm. Now they went to work on their faces and throats with renewed energy, and their pain-soaked wails were something I knew I'd never forget.

I turned away from that grotesque scene to one of utter horror; while I'd been distracted, Roger hadn't given up the ghost. In fact, he was less than three feet from Samantha, who had shrunk back against the front wall of the *Tuscan Sunrise* while continuing her supernatural torment of our would-be captors. Though his hands were still bound the zombie could bite, and his jaws snapped steadily as he edged closer to the—

Sorceress. Jesus, she's a sorceress, just like Morgan LeFay, I thought dazedly.

Roger's hands reached for her and her eyes widened in terror.

The sorceress needed my help, and I was more than happy to provide. I shot him through the right knee from my position slightly behind them both. The slug embedded itself in the ship's wall, but more importantly, it absolutely shredded the hinge joint of Roger's knee. The zombie heeled over to that side as though a deflating balloon, continuing to reach for Samantha, but now his own inertia was carrying him away from her and, with a final, frustrated hiss, the monster hit the railing and flipped over into the dark Pacific Ocean with a horrid smacking sound. I ran over to the spot where he'd taken his swan dive, and saw the clutching hands still reaching upwards toward me as the zombie sank beneath the water.

I turned back from the railing and my feet nearly skidded out from under me. Blood from the three downed raiders was running across the deck toward us. John and Travis had evidently reached their carotid arteries because they were now lying on their sides twitching spasmodically, but Aaron was still sitting upright. His face was a bloody, flayed horror.

Samantha lowered her arms and his fingers fell away. I breathed a sigh of relief. Even though these men had surely meant to kill me and possibly Samantha as well, nobody deserved this fate.

"Who sent you?" she asked quietly.

Something shifted in his eyes and Aaron spat on the deck defiantly.

Samantha raised her arms again. "Would you like to begin with your balls this time?" she murmured.

The mercenary moaned, tried to stand and fell over again. His head smacked against the deck and left a ragged bloody print in its shape. "We're from the Triad," he hissed. "You've been overstepping your bounds. We were sent here to make sure that you didn't do so again."

"The Chinese gang?" I asked, frowning.

"No, the Triad of—"

Samantha closed one hand into a fist and Aaron gagged, spitting blood onto the deck. "That was a clever move, to bring the zombie," she told him. "That's the one creature my magic would not have affected, and it was almost a good enough plan to work. If we hadn't had the gun..." And now she smiled. It was a cold smile, and I found myself edging back. "But we *did* have it, and there's no use in considering things that might have been. Goodbye, whoever you are."

Samantha picked Aaron up by the lapels of his shirt and pushed him over the side of the yacht. Like Roger, he too sank beneath the water in seconds. Whatever he was wearing beneath his black duds, it certainly wasn't buoyant. The now-comatose Travis and a faintly moaning John followed him into the Pacific's dark and cold embrace. The terror was finally over.

She turned to me, and I had a sudden, horrible suspicion that perhaps it wasn't.

"Now, then," she said softly. "Those loose ends have been tied up, but there's still one left. What exactly am I going to do with *you* now that you know about us?"

"Don't kill me," I pleaded. "Please, don't kill me. I won't say anything, I won't tell anybody what happened—"

"Of course you won't say anything. Like my master often says, who would believe you?" she asked, then laughed. Samantha dusted off her hands, then looked around distastefully as if just noticing the blood for the first time. "I think we should clean this off, and then... then we still have that last bottle of champagne, don't we? Perhaps we should enjoy it on our way back to port." Her eyes flashed red for a moment, then returned to normal.

I swallowed heavily and said, for what I hoped would not be the last time, "Whatever you desire, mistress."

"Oh, good. Keep *that* mindset and things will work out just fine with us," she said with a soft chuckle, and left me alone under the full moon's light to clean up the mess.

Something told me the real horror might only now be beginning.

Jesse L. Cairns served at Chico State University as an award-winning columnist and magazine editor. He is the author of the *Ring Of Fire* urban fantasy series (where "Death Tide" is set) among other works. Visit him at facebook.com/jesselcairns for more information.

The Low Road

GAIL Z. MARTIN

Editor's note: This is a sequel to Steer A Pale Course,
which appeared in Rum and Runestones.

"It's so nice to see a young man like yourself takin' an interest in the pipes." The elderly woman smiled at me, and reached over to pat me on the knee like a favored grandchild. The gesture felt odd, largely because I was wearing a kilt.

"Well now, what can I say?" I murmured with a warm smile, and Mrs. Balfour sat back and picked up the knitting that she had temporarily set down in her lap. "When I heard, through friends, that you were planning to sell some of your late husband's things—God rest his soul—I knew what a piper he was and how he loved the old pipes, and I had to stop in."

"Oh, it's always nice to have company, no matter what the reason." The knitting needle in Mrs. Balfour's hands flew, with a sprightliness I wouldn't have imagined from the gnarled fingers. "But you're right; Edwin loved his bagpipes. He liked to listen to them, and he liked to play them, and he also liked to buy them." She leaned forward conspiratorially. "You wouldn't want to take the whole lot of them off my hands, would you? I loved my husband, but I never really cared for the sound of the pipes. Fifty years I heard his music, and I never did like the sound of it."

"I know your husband's collection was quite extensive, but there's one set of pipes in particular I'm interested in," I said, trying not to sound too eager. But when my patron sends me to obtain a particular set of bagpipes, I can't help it. "I'm looking for an old set, probably not even in good condition any more, but they have sentimental value, you see? He might have called them the Dow pipes."

Mrs. Balfour looked at the ceiling, thinking. "Dow pipes? Now let me think. Ah, yes. I think I know the set. Would you know them to see them? Come, I'll show you."

And at that invitation, I rose to follow Mrs. Balfour down a long, dim hallway. I shivered. Let me say that a kilt is not my normal attire, nor was I being won over as a convert in this drafty house. It was October in Philadelphia, and it was damn cold to my way of reckoning. Before I had a three-centuries-old vampire as a patron and mentor, I'd been a fisherman off the North Carolina coast. Now, I was a pirate in a kilt, doing my best to sweet talk an old lady out of a set of magical, and dangerous, bagpipes. Not exactly the future I would have foreseen for myself just a few years ago, but then again, water magic, not foresight, is my gift.

Mrs. Balfour narrated our whole journey down the long, narrow hallway. She pointed to the paintings on the walls, to small objects on tables and in nooks, even at the oriental rugs on the floor. Captain Balfour had been a very successful merchant, and the large old home overlooking the cold Atlantic was crammed full of the trinkets and collections he had gathered in forty years at sea.

At the end of the hallway, Mrs. Balfour pulled a jangle of keys from one of the pockets of her apron and turned the balky iron lock that secured a scarred oaken door. The door swung open into a dusty storage room lit dimly by one grimy window. The room was packed nearly floor to ceiling with all manner of goods: statues with many arms, a full suit of armor, baskets, trunks and tall wooden wardrobe boxes of every size. Mingled with the smell of dust and mildew was the faint odor of spices from places I would probably never see in my lifetime, and the unmistakable scent of old leather.

Mrs. Balfour knelt in front of a huge trunk and fingered her keys like a rosary until she found the right one. Funny how that one trunk seemed to sit by itself, while in every corner of the room, treasures were heaped one atop another. Even silenced, the Dow pipes seemed to demand caution and respect. Mrs. Balfour might not understand why her late husband saw fit to lock up this particular set of pipes, but I knew.

The Dow bagpipes were ghost pipes.

Sorren, my undead mentor and patron, had drilled me on the identification and careful handling of the pipes. They were one of two prizes my partner Coltt and I intended to bring home this trip. With luck, neither would require thieving on the high seas, a dangerous proposition as the Atlantic waters grew wild this time of year. No, I'd hoped that flattering an old lady and a little burglary might net us both trophies and let us sail home in peace.

I really should have known better.

As Mrs. Balfour worked the balky lock on the trunk, I remembered Sorren's instructions for this run.

"Know anything about bagpipes, Dante?" Sorren had asked me as we sat in the back room of my uncle's curio shop.

"Heard them at festivals. My grandfather tried to teach me to play them, but it sounded like I was trying to squeeze a cat out of a big plaid bag through those tiny little pipes."

Sorren chuckled, and I could see the tips of his long eye teeth. When he was mortal, Sorren had been one of the best jewel thieves in Europe. While three hundred years hadn't blunted his agility one bit, Sorren now preferred to stay behind the scenes whenever possible. That's why he took Coltt and me under his wing, taught us how to blend into any level of society or social situation, made us master thieves as well as damn fine pirates.

"Well, don't play these. The Dow pipes are half of the reason you're going to Philadelphia. In the hands of a piper who's of Scottish blood and has some magic, these pipes call forth the spirits."

"Ghost pipes?"

Sorren had nodded. "They were made by a man named Ian Dow, a piper of renown two hundred years ago. When his only sons drowned off the Scottish coast, Dow went mad with grief. Legend has it he built a special set of pipes and made a deal with the Darkness so that the pipes would bring the spirits of his sons home to him again."

"I take it that his bargain was successful?"

Sorren's lips twitched upward in a predatory smile. "More than Dow intended. Dow went to a cliff overlooking the sea and began to play. But he forgot that his sons weren't the only ones to lose their lives to the dark water down below. His sons came home, all right, along with hundreds—maybe thousands—of drowned souls who heard the song of the pipes and followed it. They found him on the cliff, the pipes still in his hands, dead. Heart stopped."

"And the pipes?"

"One of my associates acquired them through family connections, knowing how dangerous they could be in the hands of a dark wizard. They've passed from caretaker to caretaker, until they reached Captain Balfour, who was supposed to bring them back from Scotland and deliver them to me. Unfortunately, he died of a fever before he could do that, which is why I need you and Coltt to retrieve them before someone else does."

Sorren was the silent partner behind the curio shop in Charleston run by my Uncle Evann. Three years ago, when Coltt and I had been the only survivors of a pirate raid on our small fishing village, we'd taken our stolen ship and fled to Charleston, hoping Uncle Evann could give us sanctuary. We'd killed the pirates who had murdered our families, and had a haunted necklace to show for it, one that I knew for a fact was evil. I thought Uncle Evann would know what to do with it.

As it turned out, Uncle Evann's shop, Trifles and Folly, was more than it appeared. Sorren was one of a small, secret group of mortals and immortals pledged to keeping dangerous magical objects out of the hands of those who might misuse them. Sorren and Evann kept an ear open whenever objects with unusual pasts came up at auction, or were part of an estate being distributed. One way or another, Sorren made it his business to take those objects out of circulation. Evann handled the legal acquisitions. Coltt and I now took care of the rest.

"And the other item?"

Sorren looked thoughtful. "I know who has it, but I'm not totally certain exactly what the item is that we're looking for. But I do know this—it's even more dangerous than the Dow pipes."

"If you don't know what I'm looking for, how are Coltt and I supposed to "acquire" it for you?"

Sorren frowned. "I've had my eye on a man named Galoshin Lawry for a while now. He comes from a family of minor magical talent and few scruples. On his own, Lawry is a bit player. But lately, there's been talk of him trying to acquire "soul cash" and that put him in my sights."

"Soul cash? Lawry's selling souls? To whom?"

"I don't know, and that worries me. By himself, Lawry doesn't have the magical power to raise the dead or tamper with spirits, so my hunch is that he's gotten his hands on a dark object, something that has power over souls."

"Like the Dow pipes."

Sorren shrugged. "There are more dark objects that tinker with souls than you want to know about. The Dow pipes are benign compared to most of them. Lawry is heading to Philadelphia on a ship from Scotland. I want you to be there when he arrives. He's connected to some wealthy people, so there'll be parties in his honor. I've arranged to get you into some of them, so you can try to get an idea of just how his "soul cash" works. Meanwhile, Coltt can search his rooms. Between the two of you, I expect that you'll make short work of it." He paused. "Oh, there is one more thing. Both Captain Dow's widow and Galoshin Lawry take extreme pride in their Scottish heritage. So of course, you'll wear a kilt when you're in their presence."

Which is why my knees were freezing. .

The lid to the old trunk creaked open, and Mrs. Down removed a protective sheet of muslin that had yellowed with age. Beneath it lay a finely crafted set of the most beautiful pipes I had ever seen. The bag was a black and red plaid, and the drone cords and their tassels were crimson. The chanters were a dark wood, and the slides were bone or ivory. Even at a distance, I could feel its magic, but Mrs. Balfour seemed completely oblivious to its power.

"It is a beauty, isn't it? Never could understand why my husband would never play them." She looked up at me. "Do you play? I'd love to hear these, just once."

No, Mrs. Balfour certainly couldn't feel the magic resonating from the pipes, or she'd have never asked me to play them. Pipes, I'd learned from my Scottish grandfather, are almost a living thing in the hands of a master piper. He fills them with his warm breath and holds them in his arms close to the warmth of his body, intimately, like his beloved. Those damned pipes held a residue of Ian Dow's spirit in them; even several paces away, I could sense his despair and overwhelming grief. No bloody way would I breathe life into to those pipes.

I hoped my weak smile looked appropriately contrite. "I'm sorry, but much to my grandfather's chagrin, I've no talent for the pipes myself. But I was a Dow on my mother's side, so there's a bit of sentimental value, if you know what I mean."

Mrs. Balfour sighed. "Ah well, I had to ask." Her eyes took on a harder glint. "Did you bring money to pay for them??"

I took a bag of gold coins from the fur sporran that hung from a chain around my waist and held the coins out to her. I waited as she counted them.

She smiled when she looked up at me. "As promised," she said with a nod. "They're yours now. Take them with you. And I hope your dreams are more peaceful than mine have been."

I looked at her and frowned. "I beg your pardon?"

"I've heard pipes playing in my dreams twice now. Once, the night my husband died, and then again last night. Woke up with the cold shivers, like someone was walking on my grave."

Ask not for whom the pipes play...they play for thee.

"I'm sure I'll sleep well, and so will you," I assured her with a confidence I did not feel. I had a bad feeling about what it might mean to hear the Dow pipes in one's dreams, and a suspicion it was a harbinger of death. From the look in her eyes, Mrs. Balfour thought the same.

"Well, off with you. I've enjoyed visiting with you, but there's work to do and potatoes to peel," Mrs. Balfour said, closing the trunk and dusting off her hands. She saw me to the door, and gave a last, mistrustful glance at the bundle in my arms.

"You'll see that the pipes are kept safe, won't you? My husband seemed to think they were quite valuable."

That, I could assure her in good conscience. "They'll be very safe. I promise you."

Coltt was waiting for me in a closed carriage down the lane from the Balfour home. "Did you get them?"

I nodded. "How about you?"

"Lawry is the toast of the town," Coltt replied. "I spent the day helping out with deliveries to two of the houses where he's going to be a guest at parties in his honor. Got inside, had a look around, and loosened up a back window to make going back in later all the easier," he said with a grin.

I had magic, and enough of a flair for schooling that Sorren made a gentleman of me, when circumstances required. I was passable at several accents and could blend in amid high or low society. As Sorren put it, I "cleaned up well."

Coltt, on the other hand, wasn't quite as versatile, but while he lacked magic, he had a natural agility I could never match, which made him the perfect choice for climbing into windows and scaling walls. Where I was Sorren's protégé when it came to smuggling and magic, Coltt was his apprentice thief.

"I want to get these pipes stowed aboard the *Vengeance* before we do anything else," I said. "I'll lock them up in my cabin. I won't feel right about storing them anywhere else."

I paused. "Any news to report?"

"I got a glimpse of Lawry."

"Not enough for him to recognize you, I hope."

"Doubt it. I was with the servants, and everyone knows servants are invisible."

"And?"

Coltt's eyes darkened. "I don't like him. I don't have a magical bone in my body, but Lawry gives me the creeps. Can't imagine how he got the society folks eating out of his hand."

I shrugged. "Don't underestimate magic. Sorren told me that some wizards can work an attraction spell that's very specific. Maybe his spell is focused on money or pedigree or connections."

"The question is, what is Lawry after? And where does the "soul cash" come in?"

I didn't have an answer, so I asked another question. "Did you find out where he's staying?"

Coltt nodded. "Lawry is staying with the different families that are hosting his parties. Normally, I'd say that was going to make it easy to break into his rooms, but he's got magic, so it's probably not going to be simple to get in and get out without being noticed."

"I thought you and Sorren worked something out on that."

"We did. But what it means is that I'll have to rely on some of Sorren's tools to do my spying rather than going in personally. More chance to overlook something, if you ask me." He paused. "Oh, I did overhear some talk as I was helping unload. Seems like our Mr. Lawry is soliciting contributions for an expedition he's heading up in a week. The families hosting him already have contributed to his cause, and he's hoping that their guests will be equally generous."

I rubbed my chin as I thought. From what Sorren had told me about Lawry, he didn't seem the scientific type. "What kind of expedition and what exactly is his expedition hoping to find?"

"Not sure. Maybe you'll find out at the party tonight. Whatever it is, Sorren must be pretty certain that it's connected to that "soul cash" Lawry's interested in."

I shrugged. "I'll see what I can do. Did you overhear anything else of value?"

Coltt thought for a moment. "Not sure whether or not this has anything to do with Lawry, but I heard the servants talking, and there've been a number of servants and day laborers who've turned up dead rather mysteriously."

"Oh?"

Coltt nodded. "Not the sort of folks whose deaths get a lot of attention. Scullery maids, dock workers, some vagrants. Oddest thing about it is, none of the dead had a mark on them."

"They had to die of something."

"That's just it though. It's quite the buzz below-stairs, and in the tavern where I took in some stew and ale for lunch. They weren't stabbed or strangled, and there's no sign of poison. Most were too young to have had a bad heart. The police are dismissing it as water from a bad well, but talk at the pub says they weren't all from the same area, so they would have gotten their water from more than one pump. And besides, if it were the water, more would be sick."

"Anything that ties the deaths to Lawry?"

Coltt met my eyes. "Only the fact that they began the night Lawry arrived in Philadelphia."

"Would you care for another brandy?"

"Thank you." I watched my host pour a measure of the dark liquor into my glass, and then returned my attention to the evening's gathering. Tonight, a group of about twenty of Philadelphia's captains of industry and pillars of society mingled at the home of Mr. Everston Willard Cummings, III. Cummings had made his fortune in the shipbuilding industry. I looked around the room. There was Robert Towars, whose glass furnace had risen right before the outbreak of war with England. Chatting with him was John Hewson Sr, famed for the calico and linen prints his company produced. There were others, wealthy men who had built fortunes copying English and French designs in porcelain, textiles, silver and fine furniture when the war cut off trade between the former colonies and the Continent. They were shrewd men, known for their eye for a good deal, and Lawry had their full attention.

"If you'll pardon my saying so, Mr. Lawry, I wonder about the soundness of your expedition." All eyes turned to Everston Cummings, the man whose deep, authoritative voice rang out over the small room. "You're asking for quite a tidy sum of money to fund your research in Bermuda, but I'd like to know why there and not somewhere closer?"

Lawry smiled, and I wondered if he had somehow planted the question with Cummings, because from the smug expression on Lawry's face, it was exactly the issue he'd been longing to raise.

"An excellent question, Mr. Cummings. You're correct that there are many stretches along the coast of this new United States of America that have been the sites of numerous shipwrecks. Indeed, there are no shortage of such sites all over the world, and my new invention has the potential to make us very rich from all of them," he said with a knowing wink that brought greedy chuckles from the assembly.

"But Bermuda has the enviable position on old, established trade routes to make the waters around it home to a most unique graveyard of ships. Merchant ships, galleons, ships laden with the treasures the Spaniards gathered in the darkest jungles of South America. Bermuda itself is divided on its loyalty to the crown. In fact, I'm sure I'm not alone in believing that, by proximity alone, it should belong to these United States rather than to a far-away monarch."

Lawry leaned into his crowd, and I saw that he fingered a mirrored cube that hung from a silver strand around his neck. The surface shimmered strangely in the light, as if it reflected and distorted the faces of the men clustered closely around Lawry. "The delicate instrumentation in this small cube, coupled with its larger mate that rests safely under lock and key in my room, enables me to calibrate changes in the wind and barometer as well as the temperature and currents of the sea, to find wrecks that have long evaded treasure hunters. Working with men like yourselves—in fact, with some of you in this room—I have hired a uniquely skilled group of divers from the orient who are used to deep dives, and outfitted them in special suits to protect them from cold and pressure. We have everything we need to take the lost gold of the Spaniards and the sunken treasures of the East India Company for ourselves: everything except the money necessary for a journey of the duration that would be most profitable."

Lawry leaned back. As a fisherman, I recognized the movement. He had them hooked, now he just needed to reel in the catch. "I have enough to mount a small scale expedition right now, but of course, once that happens and the results become known, there will be a clamor for investors to get in on the opportunity. I'd like to make this as profitable as possible for the people who had faith in my vision by limiting the number of investors."

I watched as the fat fish practically jumped out of the water and into his creel. The merchant princes of Philadelphia withdrew bank notes and vowed to have promissory notes delivered the next day. Only a few hung back with me at the fringe of the feeding frenzy. With the pretense of going to refill my brandy, I slipped from the room before I would be notable by my lack of sponsorship. I'd gotten what I wanted, although I didn't have any idea of what it meant. I could only hope that Coltt's night had been more illuminating.

I found Coltt waiting for me at our rooming house. "Were you able to get a look into Lawry's room?"

Coltt nodded. "Not in person, since he had the doors and windows spelled shut. But the magic telescope Sorren gave me worked perfectly. With it, I could see in the dark, and I got a good look around. I was also in a good position when Lawry came in a few hours before the big party."

"Came in from where?"

"Don't know. But he pulled a necklace of some sort out from under his shirt. It had a small box on a chain, and the box was glowing. He placed the small box on top of a larger box and then the big box picked up the glow. Damnedest thing was, I could have sworn something was flowing out of the small box into the big one, and for a moment, the light inside the big box seemed to swirl and move. Then they both faded and Lawry put the necklace back on and started to get changed for the party."

"I saw him wearing that necklace at the reception. But it wasn't glowing. I couldn't really tell what the small box was made of, but it had some kind of magic; that, I'm sure of."

"What do you reckon he's up to?"

I shrugged. "Well, what he told the men at the reception was that he'd developed a very delicate scientific instrument to help locate shipwrecks, and he was sailing for Bermuda with a crew of specialized divers to make a fortune bringing up sunken treasure. He also hinted that he'd like to see Bermuda break away from the crown, which played well to the audience."

"But where does the "soul cash" come in?"

I shook my head. "Don't know, but he took in enough hard cash to provision a nice expedition."

"Do you think it's possible that he's gone straight?"

"Doubt it. Sorren was sure Lawry was up to something, and Sorren's sources aren't wrong often. No, I think Lawry may be telling a half-truth at best. I'm sure he'd like to get his hands on some of Bermuda's lost treasure. But I doubt his investors will ever see any return on their money—or that Lawry will show his face in Philadelphia again."

I dressed for bed and yawned. "Tomorrow, I need to hire replacements for the crew that shipped out so that we're ready to sail on a moment's notice. I don't believe the timetable Lawry's given us. I think it's more likely that he'll skip town unexpectedly, and I want to be on his tail when it happens."

I spent the bulk of the next morning in the waterfront pubs looking for replacements for the crew members who decided to leave us in Philadelphia. I kept the crew of the *Vengeance* deliberately light at twenty-five men because most of our runs weren't the usual for smugglers and I wanted to keep portside talk to a minimum. I'd expected to replace eight men, and was none too happy to find myself hiring ten when two of my crew went missing.

Since nearly all of our runs were at Sorren's behest, the *Vengeance* worked a little differently than most pirate ships.

We often carried cargoes of tobacco or whiskey to cover expenses. When we raided a ship, we had a specific prize in mind, one of Sorren's missing magical objects. Sorren didn't mind if we helped ourselves to anything else of value that was easily carried off, but the crew had to be disciplined enough to understand that we weren't in the business of pillaging every ship we encountered. Sorren made sure that the crew was paid well and paid promptly, which kept the grumbling about not seeing enough "action" to a minimum.

In short, I needed a crew that could sail a Bermuda sloop and who didn't mind thievery, men who could hold their own in a fight but weren't bloodthirsty lunatics. It wasn't always an easy combination to find. I had no problem finding candidates who fit the first three requirements, but it could be difficult weeding out the lunatics.

It was the middle of the afternoon by the time I finished hiring crew. We'd given the *Vengeance* a fresh coat of paint and a new name for this trip, since our ship was becoming a little too well known. As far as Philadelphia was concerned, I was captain of the *Venture*. That suited me just fine. While a reputation as a dangerous pirate was a benefit in some circles, in the company I was keeping in the city, it was more likely to result in a trip to the gallows, something I preferred to avoid. Sorren even managed to provide letters of marque for the *Venture*, making us a more genteel sort of pirate, a privateer.

When I returned to the rooming house, I found that Coltt had packed all my things and was in the process of having them put aboard a wagon. "What the devil's going on?"

"Lawry's gone. He was supposed to move from the Cummings' house to the Hewsons, but that's not where his carriage went. He left an hour ago, and I followed him straight to the port. He's booked passage on a merchant ship there, the *Sea Lass*. Our ship is faster and better armed, but they're likely to have more crew. They looked like they'd be sailing pretty shortly, so I packed your things and hoped you'd had success hiring a crew or we'll lose Lawry once he heads out."

We had to scramble, but we were under sail shortly after

Lawry left port, putting us far enough behind him to hopefully evade his notice, but close enough that we could follow. I used my water magic to slow his progress, while keeping the sea friendly to the *Vengeance*. Yet every time I used my magic, something alien touched my power. Whatever Lawry had in those two boxes was strong magic, and it was dark. I didn't like its touch even at a distance. The touch of its magic gave me the shivers, and every time, the same image came to my mind. I had once passed the Half Moon Battery in Charleston late at night, and through the barred windows, I could hear the piteous wailing of those imprisoned within, criminals, debtors and the deeply unlucky who served their sentences. It was a chilling sound, made the more so since few if any who heard it were likely to be moved to compassion for the rogues inside.

Despite our quest, my mood lifted as we left the gray North Atlantic for the warmer waters of the Caribbean. We easily kept the merchant ship in our sights, with a plan to attack that night, before we reached Bermudian waters. Yet even the warmer temperature and bright sunlight couldn't drive away my sense of misgiving. And the nearer we came to Bermuda, the more my magic tingled in the back of my mind. There was something strange about these waters. Growing up along the coast, I'd heard stories of ships lost to pirates and to the treacherous reefs. There were dozens, maybe hundreds of ships that had gone down over the last few hundred years in the shipping lanes between Bermuda and the mainland. Some blamed it on reefs while others cursed fickle winds and dangerous currents. But as we sailed onward, I recognized another reason these waters had become a graveyard of ships. Magic.

I could feel the wild magic on my skin, making the hairs on my arms rise. It waxed and waned like the wind, swirled in eddies no one else could see, and slipped along the surface of the sea in places, racing the current. It was a tinderbox, waiting for a spark.

"Do you think he knows we're here?" Coltt asked.

"More to the point—if he did know, would he care?" I wasn't sure what the limits were for the magic of those confounded boxes, or what type of magic it was. The sooner they were off Lawry's ship and onto ours, the happier I'd be.

While the *Vengeance* couldn't outgun a warship, our guns were more than adequate for frightening a merchant ship into submission. Adjusting our sails, we quickly pulled up alongside the *Sea Lass*, and readied our guns for a shot across their bow. But as my men went to load the cannons, the *Sea Lass* slowed and came around, and as it did so, wooden panels in the sides opened up, baring the muzzles of twenty cannons. That was five more cannon than the *Vengeance* carried, which wasn't good. We looked up to see Lawry smirking at us from the deck, which now brimmed with heavily armed pirates, not the passive merchants we expected.

Shots fired, close at hand. I looked up to see that eight of the ten new sailors I had hired in Philadelphia stood armed, their flintlocks pointed at the rest of the crew. Grappling hooks flew through the air, pulling the *Vengeance* closer to the "merchant" ship as rope ladders were flung over the larger ship's sides and dozens of invaders scurried down the ropes to land on the *Vengeance's* deck.

"My sources were quick to tell me of your interest in my ship," Lawry taunted. "It didn't take much to buy the loyalty of your newest crewmen. You seemed quite fascinated with my expedition at the reception," he said, fixing his gaze on me. "You're just in time to see the real show."

Lawry's pirates and the turncoat sailors prodded the rest of us to climb the rope ladders that hung from the sides of Lawry's *Sea Lass*. We were badly outnumbered and while we would have given them a fight for their money had we the chance to draw our guns, as it was, we were outmatched.

"Where are your divers?" I challenged Lawry. "Is this really all about retrieving treasure from old shipwrecks?"

Lawry did not answer. He sent the majority of his sailors and the traitors from my crew back to their posts with a jerk of his head. Several armed guards herded most of my loyal crewmembers into the hold, while Lawry and three of his guards motioned for me, Colt and two of my crew into his cabin.

There on the desk in his cabin sat the mirrored cube Coltt had spotted in Lawry's room back in Charleston. And as Lawry entered the cabin and locked the door behind him, I saw the small cube on its chain around his neck. Lawry wore a triumphant smile, and the armed guards made him bold.

"Treasure is only part of it," he said. "Have you never heard the strange tales about these waters? Even the Spaniards whisper about the number of ships that have gone missing and the odd things they've seen if they were lucky to pass this way and leave alive. Some blame the currents and some say it's the winds, but I know the truth of it," Lawry said with a conspiratorial grin. "It's the magic."

I remembered how my own powers had sensed the oddness of the magic in this place, how my nerves jangled and my skin crawled. "Magic?" I said, wondering whether Lawry could sense my power. I clamped down my shielding, just in case.

Lawry lifted the small cube on its chain and caressed it with his fingers. "I intend to own these waters. I'll turn the wild magic to do my bidding, and when I am the master of this sea, I'll have the power to take Bermuda for my own. We'll control this shipping lane and all who want to pass will pay tribute or be destroyed. We'll have gold aplenty from the wrecks, and time enough to loot them when our men aren't waylaying ships."

"How do you plan to do that? There's a British fort on Bermuda. Magic or not, why would they just give up without a fight?"

Lawry's smile broadened. "Let me show you." He jerked his head, and two of his guards pushed one of my crewmen forward. Lawry removed the cube necklace from around his neck and held it out toward the frightened hostage. The mirrored surface of the cube began to shimmer and glow. It flared, and for an instant, I thought I saw a reflection of the crewman's terrified face reflected and distorted in its surface before the man fell down dead without a word.

Coltt and I surged forward to take Lawry, but the guards held us back. He turned his cube on the second crewman, who met the same fate as the first. This time, I was certain that I saw a reflection of his face on the small cube.

"What is that thing?"

Lawry fingered the cube fondly. "A tool. What matters more are the souls in my cache that amplify my magic, giving me the power to bend this region's wild magic to my will." He walked over to the large cube and held the small cube out toward it. Both cubes pulsed with a bright glow, and I felt a surge of old, strange magic as a flicker of light moved from the small cube to the large one. Worse than that, in my mind, I heard both of my crewmen scream, and I knew in every fiber of my body that it was their souls held prisoner within that awful cube.

Coltt and I exchanged glances as the realization struck us. Not soul *cash*. Soul *cache*. A hoarding place for stolen souls, kept prisoner for eternity, robbed of their final rest. A source of power that Lawry could draw upon at will to strengthen his power. In time, he would become invincible. Perhaps he already was.

Lawry seemed to tire of impressing us. He turned to the guards. "Go aboard their ship and disable their guns. Take their firearms, and leave the two of them tied up. Set a fuse in their munitions stores, and rig their sails to carry them into the shipping lanes." He looked back to Coltt and me. "I do so love a good fireworks show."

"And my crew?"

Lawry gave an exaggerated show of false remorse. "Unfortunately, they will not be joining you. They're much more valuable to me as fuel, so to speak. But the captain and first mate of the *Vengeance*, now that's a prize that lets me send a warning to the region."

Lawry clucked his tongue. "Oh yes, I learned the true name of your ship despite its hasty repainting and new name. You've made quite a reputation in a short time, and it will serve me well to let your ship explode where others will see it, where the wreck will bear witness that someone was able to best you." He nodded to his guards. "Get them out of here."

Coltt and I struggled, but Lawry's guards had us outgunned and outnumbered. I could see anger and defeat in Coltt's eyes. Lawry left us, and within a few minutes, as the guards bound us and began to make their way back to the *Vengeance*, I heard the silent screams of my crew in my mind as Lawry fed their souls into his soul cache.

How could Sorren have missed such a thing? Then again, unless he had ever seen the words actually written, there was no way for him to know that "cash" was "cache." But I had bigger worries. I had no idea how to keep Coltt and myself from being blown sky high, let alone stop Lawry from making himself master of some of the most valuable shipping lanes in the Atlantic and Caribbean.

Lawry's guards made short work of their assignment. They tied us hand and foot, and dropped us like luggage in my cabin aboard the *Vengeance*, taking care to lock us in and leave with the key. Before they left us, they clipped us both soundly on the head with the grip of their cutlasses. Coltt was knocked cold; I ended up with a hell of a headache, but I managed not to lose consciousness, though my vision blurred and I swore I could feel every beat of my heart like a drum in my head.

I could hear Lawry's men making their way into the cargo hold of the ship, looting our guns and setting the fuse in our munitions store. Once they cut our ship free, they'd probably leave a man aboard long enough to light the fuse, and the unfortunate man would have to jump ship and swim back as the *Vengeance* caught wind in its sails to carry it away.

We didn't have much time, but I wasn't about to lie back and wait for the ship to explode beneath me. I could still hear the echoes of my dying crew's screams, and the more I thought about it, the angrier I got. I rolled closer to my hammock and kicked with my bound feet until I sent a pair of boots flying from under the bed. I managed to get my bound hands inside the right boot, and with my fingers, nudged at the blade concealed in the toe until its tip peeked into view.

Bracing the boot and its knife as best I could, I sawed away at my bonds, having no idea how long it would take Lawry's men to complete their task. They had used good hemp rope, and it seemed to take forever to free my hands and feet. Coltt was still unconscious. I paused to check for a pulse and was relieved to find that he was breathing, but he would be no help to me. I tried the door and threw myself against it, but it was made of sturdy oak and held fast. I resolved to hide a spare key within my cabin should I—and the *Vengeance*—survive.

I heard the clatter of the grappling hooks as they were withdrawn, heard the creaking of the ropes and mast as the sails were hoisted. Lawry's men were ready to light the fuse and abandon us to the current. We were running out of time.

Desperately, I cast about the cabin for a weapon. Lawry's men had been efficient in tossing the contents of my drawers and chest onto the floor in search of firearms or swords, all of which were missing. I kicked at a bundle of clothing, and found it strangely solid. Curious, I bent down and moved the shirt and cloak aside. Beneath them were the Dow pipes.

I had told the captain's widow that I could not play well, but that was a lie. I had been afraid of the claim the pipes might place upon my soul if my magic woke them. I stared at the pipes, knowing that whether I was blown to bits or used the magic of the pipes, my soul appeared consigned to Perdition. I glanced back at Coltt's still form, and closed my eyes, hearing the desperate, anguished screams of my murdered crew. Rage filled me. I picked up the pipes and walked to the porthole as I felt the *Vengeance's* sails fill with wind and carry us away.

The sight of Lawry's ship receding was not what filled me with dread. A strange mist had risen from the water, and as far as the eye could see from side to side, the horizon glowed an eerie green color. I stole a glance at the compass on my desk. The needle had gone crazy, bouncing from side to side erratically, giving me no indication of our course, but confirming my suspicion. Lawry had begun to draw upon the soul cache to work his magic.

I took a deep breath, and called my magic to me. First, I reached out in my own power to the water, using my power to slow our progress, keeping us in sight of Lawry's ship. I sent a surge of power toward Lawry's vessel, giving it a sudden patch of rough sea to keep them occupied. Then I lifted the pipes and began to play.

I only knew one song for the pipes, "Loch Lomond". It seemed fitting to play a song written by a man about to be hanged, a man who expected to return to his beloved homeland by the "low road"— his spirit walking through the valley of the shadow of death. I saw no way to defeat the burning fuse amid our powder kegs, but I had every intention of taking Lawry and his infernal cubes with me. And as I played, my anger called up my magic, and my magic through the pipes called to the spirits.

With the screams of my crew still fresh in my mind, I swept the magic of the pipes toward Lawry and his cube. My anger fairly vibrated through the music, and I felt the pipes find the imprisoned spirits within the cube. There were many, many more than I had imagined. Not just my poor crew; oh no, there were hundreds of souls stored in Lawry's soul cache. I remembered the feckless vagrants and servants back in Charleston that had been found dead without a mark on them, and I knew where their souls had gone. I put everything I had into playing those damned pipes, trusting its magic would do as its doomed owner had original intended and free the spirits to go home.

All around me, I could feel the magic rising. Outside the porthole, a green glow now stretched from the sea into the heavens, but Heaven had nothing to do with this cursed phosphorescence. Above me, I could hear the winds howl, and the sea beneath us had begun to pitch with the frenzy of a storm. On and on I played, and I heard the howls of the imprisoned spirits grow to a maddening pitch, echoing the anger that moved my fingers over the chanters with more speed and skill than I had ever mustered on my own.

But the magic of the pipes was not selective, and too late I remembered what had doomed their maker. The seas of the Scottish coast were not the only ones filled with the wrecks of ships and the skeletons of the lost. These waters off the Bermuda coast held an untold number of ill-fated ships and their drowned crews and passengers. Some had gone to their watery graves by accident of fate, while many more had been sent there by treachery and murder. All had been cheated out of their full lifespan, and as they rose, I knew that they had one thing in common. They were very angry.

The spirits whipped around the *Vengeance* like hurricane winds, tattering its sails and stirring the sea to whitecapped fury. The winds blasted open the portholes and the door of the hold and set upon me with such power that I feared I might not keep my feet. They tore at my hammock and sent my papers flying, buffeting me. I heard the winds howl through the hatch and heard the spirits toss the contents of the hold as if the heavy casks were empty. With a crack, the lock on the door to my cabin split in two and the door swung open.

I had loosed the ghosts from the soul cache and summoned the spirits from the sea, but I had no idea of how to set them free. Yet as they whipped around me, plunging the cabin into an icy chill, I sensed...curiosity. Oh, there was malice aplenty, but not directed toward Colt and me.

Lawry was a different story.

I felt the spirits of the soul cache and the sea dead gather their forces, even as, across the waves of power and water, I felt Lawry summon his power. All along, I had played verse after verse of "Loch Lomond", over and over, until my fingers ached and my lungs felt as if they were on fire. I played with crazed speed, off key, a refrain of the damned. Lawry sent his power along the channels of magic in a blast he hoped would scatter the spirits. It was magic worked by a living mage, magic that took the high road. The spirits were ready for him, and they massed their power, aided by the Dow pipes, and the magic of a mage surrounded by the dead. The low road, the pathway of the dead, was faster.

Through the magic, I could feel when the cube prison exploded, knew it sent mirrored shards at lethal velocity all around as the tormented wraiths that had been held captive burst forth. Empowered by the magic, they did not rise as mere vapor; no, these revenants possessed the will and wherewithal to set themselves upon their captor and his guards. I heard their screams across the water even as my bond through the magic showed me the attack and I watched the enraged spirits strip skin from bone and suck the breath from their bloodied, terror-struck keeper.

I felt the shock of the magical impact in my body. It jarred every bone, sending an immediate, blinding headache from the base of my skull to the crown of my head. I felt the spirits rip away Lawry's magical protections, strip them from him like shears through silk, felt them leech the heat from his body and the breath from his lungs and finally the twisted magic from his fingers.

Their vengeance flowed through my veins, rose and fell with my breath as the pipes played their cursed tune. My rage had fueled theirs, and their hunger for justice had enraged me even further. They, and we, were avenged. I felt the spirits pull back, and then dissipate. They had what they came for.

As suddenly as it came, the storm ended. The *Vengeance* rocked on quiet waters. It was then I realized two things. The first was that Coltt was staring at me in wide-eyed horror, very much alive. The second was that we had not exploded.

My arms were shaking as I carefully laid aside the Dow pipes. The marks of the chanter's holes were imprinted—no, burned—into my fingertips, and my lungs ached. I freed Coltt, and together we ran to the hold. We found the partially burned fuse, but it was cold, extinguished by the mighty gust of wind the spirits had sent around and through the ship. We returned to the deck, and I looked skyward. The *Vengeance's* sails hung in tatters, and one of its masts had snapped.

"Look there!" Coltt pointed. Lawry's ship was listing badly to port. Its sails were in even worse shape than ours, and two of its masts had fallen, bringing the rigging with them. Bodies lay scattered across the deck and bobbed in the water. Later, we would go aboard, but our visit only confirmed what through my magic, I already knew. Lawry and his crew were dead, and his soul cache was shattered and useless.

"If we manage to get back to port, I don't know how we're going to explain this to Sorren," I said. We had reclaimed the Dow pipes and destroyed the soul cache, and Lawry along with it. I wasn't sure whether that made our mission half successful or a half failure.

Coltt still looked ashen from the shock of it all. "I opened my eyes to hear you playing those damned pipes, and I saw spirits weaving all around you. How did you do it?"

I thought about the rage and grief I had felt over my murdered crew, the anger that surged through me to be held captive on my own ship, threatened with my own munitions. It had been sheer, blinding rage, not courage, that had driven me. I was glad to be alive, but I wasn't particularly proud of myself.

"Easy," I said with a wan smile. "I just had to put the 'irate' back in 'pirate.'"

Gail Z. Martin is the author of The Summoner, The Blood King, Dark Haven and Dark Lady's Chosen (*The Chronicles of The Necromancer* series). She is also the author of *The Fallen Kings Cycle* from Orbit Books with *Book One: The Sworn* and *Book Two: The Dread*, and the upcoming *Ascendant Kingdoms Saga*. For book updates, tour information and contact details, visit www.ChroniclesoftheNecromancer.com

Gail is the host of the Ghost in the Machine Fantasy Podcast, and you can find her on Facebook, GoodReads, BookTour, BookMarketing.ning, Shelfari and Twitter. She blogs at www.DisquietingVisions.com. She is also the author two non-fiction series. *The Thrifty Author's Guide* series Comfort Publishing) includes *Launching Your Book Without Losing Your Mind* and *Selling and Promoting Your Book Online*. *The 30 Day Guide Series* (Career Press) includes *30 Days to Social Media Success* and *30 Days to Online PR & Marketing Success*. Gail's short fiction has been featured in two previous anthologies: *Rum and Runestones* from Dragon Moon Press and *The Bitten Word* from New Con Press.

Enemy of My Enemy

SUZAN BUTLER

The sunset marked the end of the day as Captain Brendon Chance leaned on the railing. It was the beginning of the day for him and his crew. They looked forward to this night every month, when the moon ran full, illuminating their one night to run free ashore.

His first mate's higher pitched voice cut through his crew's much deeper ones like a knife, shaking him from his thoughts. She snapped at the youngest of the crew, John, as he let one of the lines slacken unexpectedly, lecturing him in that way only she could.

Her blonde hair gave her face a fair look she didn't deserve. There was nothing *fair* about her. Her turquoise eyes didn't hide the fierceness she'd acquired from working with a crew full of men day in and day out, month after month, for the last five decades. Grey was no fragile being.

"You make a mistake like that during a storm and you'll get all of us killed!" she shouted at him as she made her way up the steps to the bridge, shaking her head.

She was still shaking her head as she came to stand by her captain. Chance couldn't resist a smile. "He's just a boy."

"Nonsense." She turned to him, placing her hands on her hips. "He was a boy fifty years ago, when this all started. Now, he's had

54

fifty years to learn his job. He's as much a man as the rest of us."
Grey glared at him through the corner of her eye as if expecting
the comment floating behind his mouth. "So to speak."

They stared down at the crew in silence for a few moments
before Chance finally broke the silence. "It'll do him good to
get some time away. Do us all good." He couldn't help but
think of his meeting later. If he succeeded, he and his crew
would go free of the curse that kept them tethered to the ship.
If he didn't... would he even be around to regret it?

"Do you really think that, Captain?" she asked tersely.
Obviously, from the look on her face, she did not agree.

"You do not?"

"John is nearly sixty-eight years old, and yet he looks like a
fresh-faced seventeen year old child. Why do you think he gets
into these bar fights every month?"

"I was sailing with my father when I was twelve." he pointed
out. "He'll be fine."

"Yes," she agreed. "But you were not a seventy-year-old
trapped in a twelve-year-old body."

"Seventeen," he corrected. She gave him The Look, the one
that made him feel like a boy instead of the captain of his own
damned ship. He sighed. It would have been easier if he hadn't
doomed her to this existence in the first place. "So, what will
you do with your twelve hours of freedom?" he asked her.

A small smile crept up on her lips as she watched the men
below, then it disappeared just as quickly as it came. He hated
that. He loved her smile. It was all soft where she was normally
hard and edgy. She didn't smile much, which was what made
it that much more precious. She let out a sigh. "I will probably
buy the men a round, then take a walk on the beach, on the
sand in my bare feet, and then... go to bed. Sunrise comes
awful early this time of year and we need to have a clear head.
I think there's a storm on its way."

He wasn't sure he agreed with that. The sky was clear, the
air dry. No sign of a storm, but Abigail Grey was rarely wrong
about such things. She had what she called an inner eye to
such things. He didn't pretend to understand it. He only took

advantage of her accuracy. But why she would have preferred to serve on board a pirate ship was beyond him.

She laughed suddenly, making him realize he'd said that last part out loud. "It might have been easier if I hadn't. I still think it would have been much more difficult for me if I hadn't joined this crew."

He nodded. "I see. Have a good evening, Miss Grey. We cast off at sunrise, as usual, barring your imminent storm. Make sure everyone knows not to miss ship's movement."

Grey nodded and turned to the crew as he walked away. There had been cheers from the crew when released during the first few years of full moons, but it had become routine now. Get supplies, stock the ship, go back into town, have their fun, and return before sunrise or risk certain death. They had lost a few over the years. Some by accidental tardiness, some because they were tired of living eternity on the sea. It was never easy when he lost one of his own.

Captain Chance sighed as he looked after his men. One stupid raid on the wrong ship and he'd cursed himself and his entire crew to an eternity of life on the sea. Damn that witch for being on that ship. Damn himself for getting so cocky, so sure of his invincibility, that he didn't realize the ship had been flying witch's colors. And damn himself again... just because it really was all his fault.

Chance sat at the table in the corner, an empty cup in front of him. The bar girl came by and filled it again; he flicked a few coins her way. Normally, this was how he spent his night free of the ship's chains. Pitiful. Tonight, though, he was waiting for someone, someone who could hopefully help him make this end. So, drinking had to wait, but he didn't have to be happy about it.

"This seat taken?" He looked up, seeing Grey standing there with a mug of beer in her hand. He shook his head and she slid into the seat across from him, leaning over the table. "You're wallowing... again."

Yes, he was. Which only made him feel worse. Grey didn't wallow. No, she was the epitome of strength.

"It seemed the thing to do," he replied as he took another swig from the cup. "I'm entitled."

"Really," she said flatly. "So let me get this straight. The curse is your fault, or so you believe, so it's okay to drown yourself in this swill they call beer here?"

He frowned drunkenly at her. "You don't understand. The curse *is* my fault." He sighed and looked at his first mate. She had that disapproving frown, wrinkling the fair complexion of her smooth skin. Or at least he assumed it was smooth. It looked smooth. He wanted to touch it. Touch her... Caress that smooth, pale skin...

Hell, he was drunk. There was nothing smooth or delicate about Abigail Grey. She was all hard edges and strength. Trying anything with her would get his arm broken. Not that he wanted to. It was the drink that made him think that way. There weren't many opportunities for time with women on board his ship, especially since she was the only one.

"Captain?" He focused on her, realizing he'd never answered her question, and gave her a smirk as she added, "The witch's colors should have been seen by several other people. You. Me. The lookouts in the crow's nest. I wish I could make you understand that it's not your fault."

He rolled his eyes, unable to contain himself emotionally. She did that to him. She made him vulnerable. But he couldn't be. He was the captain. He had to be infallible. He looked up at the door. The person he'd been waiting for wasn't coming. They should have been there already. Something must have happened.

He shook his head and stood up, dropping another couple of coins on the table. He drained the rest of his cup and stared at his first mate. "I am responsible for the lives and the decisions of my crew, including you. Regardless of how the events happened, I am responsible for all of it. So, yes, it is my fault. Entirely mine."

Before she could say another word, he slipped out of the bar and headed down the beach. In the distant harbor, he could see his ship floating on the rhythmic waves, reminding him that in a few hours, he and all his crew would be back onboard, cursed to be thrust together for another moon cycle.

"You're such an angsty fellow, Captain Chance." He whirled around at the sound of the familiar voice. The witch seemed to float as she walked, her hips swaying seductively. Behind her, her daughter trailed. He'd only seen the girl a few times before. "What? Did you expect I would not show myself on your one day of the month? That I would not remind you and yours that you belong to me?"

He glared at the witch.

"Sorry about your meeting with that old hag. I had to dispose of her. You understand I could not allow it. I will not be challenged, especially by weaker beings like that...harpy." She wrinkled her nose in distaste.

"What do you want, witch?" he snapped, with a roll of his eyes.

"To give you an offer." She smiled. "A fair one. One for which you will not need to betray me."

"Our last deal did not go well," he replied.

"No," she agreed. "But that was hardly a deal. You invaded my ship. I don't take kindly to pirates, Captain. But..." She paused. "I'm feeling generous today and your behavior since has been honorable...for a pirate. So I offer your crew freedom."

"What?" He stared at her, dumbfounded. It couldn't be what he thought. Freedom? He blinked in confusion then shook his head. "You wouldn't do that."

"Freedom, Captain," she repeated. "You get to leave that abomination you call a ship."

"My ship is not an abomination." he growled through clenched teeth. His face grew hot but he knew better than to make this witch angry. She held a grudge. He took a minute to breathe and said, "Freedom. In return for what?"

"You are a good, strong man, Captain. I need my family to continue."

He stared at her in shock. Was she seriously suggesting she and he— "What? You?!" Incredulous, he shook his head. "No way in hell, witch."

"My daughter, you twit." she grumbled. "Hopefully, the child will get her mother's intelligence." Her daughter stood silently behind her, no expression on her face at all. Her brown hair covered most of her face as she stood with the setting sun in the background.

"Why me?" he asked. "Surely you could choose anyone."

"You are the one I've chosen," she replied. "And for your service, your crew will be freed."

"Doesn't she have a say?"

"No," the witch replied. "Of course, you can stay aboard your ship, having your one night of freedom a month for eternity. How long will it be before your crew begins to resent their imprisonment? You've already lost several..." She trailed off, watching him expectantly. "Regardless of our differences, your strength, your willpower... They would be excellent qualities in my granddaughter. Unlike her would-be mother."

He growled and shook his head. "I'm a pirate. I raided your ship and you cursed me for it. And now you want to stud me? What about my crew?"

"They would be free, as I said."

"But I would be a prisoner?"

"Prisoner is an awful word. I'm giving you a choice. The decision is entirely yours. Think about it, Captain. Your crew would no longer be punished for your mistake. You would be able to touch land again in the light of day."

"It's not much of a choice, is it?"

"I never said it would be an easy decision." The witch smirked. "Think about my offer, Captain Chance. You have until sunrise to make your decision. After that, it will be too late. Be sure it's the right one." She flicked her wrist in the air, and light golden flakes appeared over both her body and her daughter's.

"Captain?" Grey approached them from behind the witch and her daughter. Her hand hovered close to her sword at her hip, and only relaxed when the witch and her daughter vanished completely in a whirl of golden flakes.

He blinked again, swallowed hard. Freedom. For his crew. It was everything he'd been looking for when he'd set up the meeting the witch had ended before it begun. But he would have to lay with a witch's daughter. One that would eventually be like her mother. Give them both another daughter to be like her grandmother? And what kind of freedom was being put out to stud? But to be able to walk the beach in the daytime for the first time in fifty years... to sleep in a real bed... To not be confined... Would it be worth it?

Grey's presence was almost suffocating.

"What did she want?" she whispered, like she was afraid the woman would return.

He chuckled. "Me, apparently."

"What?" Her face paled. "What do you mean?"

"She offered the crew freedom," he said.

"Are you serious?" Grey said. "How? Why?"

He looked at her, eyebrow arched. She looked panicked, which was not what he'd expected from her. He'd expected maybe curiosity, or maybe a little hopeful anticipation at the prospect of freedom.

"There were complications." He felt a little embarrassed about discussing this with Grey. She was the person he was closest to on his ship, and still, he didn't want to discuss the particulars of the offer with his first mate.

"Nothing is complicated about it. She can't be trusted. Don't take anything from her."

"Miss Grey—" He stopped, collecting his wits about him. "There's more to it than what you know."

She waved his comments aside. "Don't analyze it. Don't trust her." She sighed heavily. "If she offered freedom, then she has an ulterior motive. That woman would never do anything for anyone because she's nice." Her mouth curved up, gifting him with that smile he so loved, but he detected some hint of...what was that? Sadness? It disappeared before he could identify it. "We'll figure out what it is together."

He wanted to say something. Anything. But no words would come. How would she view him when she found out exactly what the witch's ulterior motive was? How would his crew view him?

He cleared his throat. "Miss Grey..." He sighed. "She wants a granddaughter."

His first mate's mouth parted in surprise. "What?"

"The crew's freedom in return for my...services." He looked away from her, feeling guilty for being so torn. He had the chance to free his crew now. So why was he hesitating? A good captain would just do it; sacrifice himself for his crew. Right?

But he wasn't a good captain; he was a pirate captain. That was why they were in this situation in the first place.

"We'll find another way," she stated. "You cannot give that witch another life to ruin!"

"This curse must be broken by the person who cast it. There is no other way."

She frowned and crossed her arms indignantly. "There has to be."

"There isn't! I thought I might have a way, but it didn't work out. The witch found out first."

"What will you do?" Her voice was uncharacteristically low. "Will you do as she wants?"

"I don't know. I honestly don't know, Miss Grey."

"Well, I do."

It took Chance a moment to realize that Grey had not spoken. He whirled around, and froze as the witch's daughter stood not five feet from them. He looked back at Grey, but was surprised to find her gone and his entire world faded into a dismal grey swirl.

He glared at the witch's daughter. "What did you do with her? Where are we?"

The girl sashayed toward him, not at all the meek girl he'd just seen behind her mother. "She's fine. I wanted to speak to you privately."

He growled out some expletives that would have made one of his own crew blush with its vulgarity.

She gave him a withering look.

"Take me back, now!"

She laughed. "You're not in a position to be demanding, Captain."

"You're as bad as your mother. Never asking, always demanding."

"I am nothing like my mother!" she yelled at him. She caught herself and pulled back. "That woman is evil."

"Yet right now, I almost wish I was dealing with her instead. I think her personal torture would be preferential at the moment." He glared at the girl. Damn witches. Always assuming everyone else would be on their time table. He had only a few precious hours left on land, and here he was, wasting them away with her and her mother.

"It's more about punishing you, you know." she replied.

"What is?"

"My mother's curse... You're the first to humiliate her," she replied. "My mother is a hard woman. She does not take insubordination well." She smiled ruefully, as if she spoke from experience. "She wanted to keep you under surveillance, to prevent you from doing any more harm than you already have. Not to mention she needs me to give her a granddaughter. This is her way of keeping you under her watch, so you can do no more harm to her."

"Harm? I have done nothing to her."

"You did not fear her," she said. "My mother powers her spells on fear. Her magic needs it to function. You took her punishment fifty years ago, did not cower in fear of her. As a result, the hold she has over you and your crew is weak. Breakable. I could do it, in return for a favor."

He didn't quite believe her, but it still interested in him. He knew better than to trust a witch, but he couldn't stop himself from saying, "Go on."

"I hate my mother," she continued. "She's a horrible harpy who can't help but force her will on people, including me." She paused. "I don't want to have your children. In fact, I don't even want a daughter. A son, maybe, because men cannot carry the magic, but I cannot take the chance that the child would be a girl. This stupid witch line will end with me." She glanced at Chance. "I need your help, though."

"With what? You just said men cannot carry magic."

"No, but you can distract her for me." She pursed her lips before speaking further. "My magic is rooted in...a different emotion. It's hard to focus on it for very long. I need someone to stall her, distract her so I can work from behind."

"I don't even know you." He shook his head, frowning. "For all I know, you're working with her to screw with my head."

"I promise you I am not."

"And how much is the promise of a witch worth?"

"What would you have me do to prove my sincerity?"

"Give me your name. Your true name, if you please."

She hesitated. He really did not like witches. He liked seeing a witch squirm with a tough decision for once.

"What are you afraid of, witch?" He smiled. "It's not as if I can use it."

"You—" she stopped herself. "You're right, of course."

"So?"

"Ariahlla," she replied, using intonation in each syllable that sent magic through the air. He blinked as the wave of power hit him. Chance hadn't expected her to actually give him her real name, the one that was tethered to her magic. Not that it really did much good. He could be affected by magic, but using it was another matter. Men just didn't carry magic. Her hesitation was unwarranted.

He met Ariahlla's grey eyes, which had been downcast while he'd talked to her mother. At the moment, they were so full of fire and promise; they almost reminded him of Grey's blue eyes.

He stiffened. "What happens to my crew if we do this?"

"The curse will break if my mother is killed. You and your crew would be free."

"How do I know that I can trust you?"

"I just gave you my name!" she protested.

"Which isn't worth a lick of an empty beer if you end up killing me!" he growled back. "Surrender yourself and talk with my first mate."

"Talk to Abigail Grey?" she asked. "She would snap me in two if she had half a chance."

He chuckled. "That's the one, darlin'. You prove yourself to her, and I'll help you." He nearly laughed again as the girl's face paled considerably. He really did like having such an advantage over a witch for once. He'd spent far too long having no control. Even the little battles meant so much. "That's the price, sweetheart. You want my help, you'll convince her too."

The girl stiffened, and pulled her shoulders back in outright defiance of his challenge. Her lips curled upwards in the corners as she met his eyes again. "Fine, my pirate friend. I'll talk to your wench."

He snorted. "You might want to avoid using that term in her presence, darlin'."

"Which term? Pirate? Or wench?"

He smiled, "Either. She's sensitive." He looked around at the grey fog then back at Ariahlla. "Well?"

"Oh, fine." She glared at him, irritated, and flicked her hand. Golden flakes fell from her hand as the fog began to dissipate around them. But the beach was gone, replaced by the wooden planks of his ship. Before they had fully formed, he counted twelve rapiers pointed at them.

Grey stood above them, her eyes hard and guarded. Chance felt a shiver go down his back and hoped that wasn't Grey walking on his grave in the near future.

"You brought a witch on board this ship, after what happened fifty years ago?" Grey's voice was shrill, making Chance grind his teeth together. Grey shook her head. "I can't believe this."

She crossed her arms and glared at him before resuming the pacing she'd been doing. Her nostrils flared, fury emanating from her as if she was leaking emotion from every orifice of her body. He'd never seen her like this before. In fact, he hadn't expected such a strong reaction to bringing Ariahlla aboard.

He rolled his eyes at his first mate and pulled her by the arm off to the side of the room, speaking almost inaudibly. "She can break the curse, Miss Grey." Grey froze. He continued renewed by her silence. "She hates her mother. She wants to stop her as much as we do."

Grey laughed coldly, "I highly doubt that, Captain. I know her kind." She shot Ariahlla a dirty look. "We cannot trust her. She will do anything just to get her way."

"Miss Grey—" He stopped as he heard the sudden whistle of high winds rolling in. He frowned as a hard mist rolled over them, sprinkling them with cold sea water. "Were we expecting bad weather soon?"

Grey shook her head. "Not exactly. I thought it might but that is no natural storm, Captain. I can feel it." She looked out beyond the sea where the sky had darkened to a black void in the night, the clouds blocking the moon's reflection on the water. Lightning lanced across the sky. "That is a magic storm."

He did not like this. Something wasn't right.

"It's her, Abigail," Ariahlla said. "Mother is coming."

They both stared at her. His frown deepened. "Recall the men, Miss Grey."

Grey glared at the witch's daughter as she crossed the room. She did not back away from the girl, even though Ariahlla could have cursed her. "If you have led the captain into a trap, I'll cut you to ribbons myself."

Then she left with heavy, angry steps, leaving him alone with Ariahlla.

She turned to face Captain Chance. "Do you believe I have tricked you?"

"A storm is building," he replied. "I can feel the pressure. We must leave dock before it hits or the ship will take damage." He pointed an accusing finger at her. "You will remain here until I can assess the situation."

"Do you believe I have tricked you?" she demanded, raising her voice.

"Make me believe it isn't true, Ariahlla." Speaking her name had no effect on her, as he'd expected. Men didn't carry magic. But he took pleasure in watching her flinch anyway.

Her mouth opened and shut. Lowering her head, she shook her head. "I cannot. There is nothing I can do that will convince you of the truth you cannot see, Captain." She met his eyes, tears beginning to glisten in the corners. "I should have known she would find out. My mother is coming for me, Captain. And she is angry."

What Chance didn't understand was why the witch wasn't there yet. An hour had passed since the wind began to pick up and the humidity had crept in. It hadn't started to rain yet, though he could see lightning in the distance. He'd recalled the men, and all were aboard. They were leaving port now, even with the strong winds that whipped the sails about. Ariahlla was still in his stateroom, with a guard posted at the door. She hadn't even tried to leave, even with her declaration that her mother was coming for her. He did not understand it.

If she was truly in cooperation with the witch, playing some strange game, why was she still there? Or was that why she was still there? Even if she wasn't, what was preventing her from leaving them alone? Maybe the witch was blocking her from leaving, and just biding her time before she made her appearance?

Chance watched his men through the darkness. Fifty years of dealing with leaving ports before dawn had given them experience at sailing in the dark. Even leaving so unexpectedly from port didn't faze them much, either. He was right proud of how well his men performed under the worst circumstances. Now, though, tension was rising on his ship, because the crew knew only bits and pieces of what was going on.

Perhaps he was wrong. His men weren't happy. Especially as they were only allowed twelve hours of leave, once a moon cycle. Perhaps he should have taken the deal, married the witch's daughter, and done his civic duty. Given the woman another daughter with whom to terrorize the world, and freed his men from their sea-faring prison.

"She's doing it to strike fear in the hearts of your men... and in you." He didn't turn as Ariahlla walked over to stand by him. It didn't surprise him that she was walking free. More than likely, the guard probably didn't even realize she had left.

He'd only posted one as a statement to her that he didn't trust her. He held no illusions that the guard would be able to stop her if she so desired to leave.

He didn't even look at her. He couldn't. He'd let her manipulate him. He knew that, but he wasn't quite sure of the extent of it yet. He was in the middle of a battle between mother and daughter, and he'd stuck himself right in it. Would he ever learn?

"Did you hear me?" she asked as she looked out at the crew. Her long brunette locks whipped about in the wind. "She wants you afraid. It gives her power. That's why she's waiting."

"You knew this would happen," he said.

"What?"

"You used us to lure your mother out." He turned to look at her. "Because once she came, and stomped her witch feet around, our fear, the same fear she'd spent hours cultivating in us, would turn to anger, rage at being bullied like that. And that's what your magic is rooted in, isn't it?"

She shook her head, her face pale. "No."

He growled as he took a step toward her. "You purposely started this mess so she would leave the safety of your damn world for ours."

"No," she insisted. "No, that's not true."

"This was never about you not wanting a child," he snarled. "This was about revenge. You wanted to catch Mother off guard."

Her face changed, growing angry. "I was trying to help you. I could free you."

"No, you couldn't," he snapped back, taking another step toward her. She instinctively stepped back, though if she wanted, she could have destroyed him with a flick of her wrist. That only made him bolder, knowing that she hadn't. Maybe that meant she *couldn't*. "There's no way. It didn't matter if the curse was weak, even though it really wasn't, was it, Ariahlla?"

She hesitated, studying his features, then shook her head. "No. Only she can break it. Unless she dies."

He demanded, "You wanted to kill Mother Dearest, but you needed her to be looking somewhere else when you plunged that dagger deep into her back."

"Now, Ariahlla." The feminine voice snaked its way through the whipping wind. "Is that true, my darling daughter?" Ariahlla froze at the sound of her name, and for the first time since he'd realized she'd been playing him, he felt guilty. He knew what kind of torture her mother could dole out. Did she deserve that? Ariahlla's face paled and she swallowed. Fear lit up her eyes as she focused on a point behind him. Chance turned slowly.

The witch descended from the clouds like an avenging angel, her flowing dress flittering like a canary in the wind. Gold flakes floated around her, giving her an ethereal presence. Her feet moved, as if walking, but her movements were smooth, like she was on moving steps. As she descended, the high winds dissipated almost instantly, leaving the ship in an eerie silence.

"I ask for sanctuary aboard your ship, Captain," Ariahlla said. "Please."

"Even if I felt like granting that request, Ariahlla, which by the way, I'm not, it would not help if she wanted you," he said.

Panic filled Ariahlla's eyes as her mother's bare feet touched the deck and walked over to them. The power behind her eyes flamed with fury that was just barely in check. She glared at her daughter, who shrunk down a few sizes in fear, then said, "Captain, I believe you have a pest problem aboard your ship."

He looked at the girl and then to her mother. "Well, I do have a couple of large pains in my ass aboard right now."

Her mother glared at Chance and then back to the daughter. "I will take my disobedient little wretch of a daughter off your hands now. I have decided we do not require your services any longer, not for Ariahlla, anyway. "

"What about my crew?" he shouted at her. "You said you would free them!"

"So I did, if you helped me." She didn't take her eyes off her daughter. "Now, I have to break a deal because of your foolishness, daughter. How rude."

"No!" Chance snarled and put himself between the two. "I'll do as you want. I give myself to your service, as long as you release my crew. They've been punished long enough. Let them go home."

Her eyebrow rose as her eyes searched his for something and he almost lost himself inside the black pools of power that whirled as she studied him. He wasn't afraid. It wasn't that. Or was he? Was she pulling fear from him for his crew?

"Don't be foolish, Captain," she laughed finally. "You'll live an eternity here. They'll live an eternity. If I free them, they'll grow old and die. What kind of life is that?"

"People do it all the time," Grey spoke for the first time. He glanced at her in surprise. Where had she come from? Grey didn't stop there. "They would be normal. Free to live again."

"This is not your concern, child. Trust my judgment and take what you've been given." He blinked at the softness in the woman's voice. Why was Grey being treated like she was one of them?

She was a woman, he realized. Witches didn't care much for men. In fact, they were little more than chattel to them because they couldn't carry magic. But a woman could. Especially if she was from a magic line...

He paused.

Grey had opposed him taking the deal earlier. She'd been against anything that got them closer to the crew being freed. Why wouldn't she want to be free of the bloody curse? Go home, have a family... Or did she already have a family?

"Is there something you'd like to tell me, Miss Grey?" Chance asked.

"No." She glanced at him and at the look on his face, she flinched. "Not really."

"Miss Grey?" he pressed.

"I can't."

"She has magic," Ariahlla said. Chance looked at Grey, whose guilty expression confirmed the truth.

"Of course she does," the witch said. "She's my child."

He looked at Grey. "That's why you came aboard? Because you're a witch? Why didn't you say anything?"

"Oh, I don't know," she said. "I was afraid you would resent me."

"You lied to me. You are my right hand on this ship, and you lied to me." Chance glared. His stomach flip-flopped as the revelation sunk in. Abigail Grey was a witch, the daughter of the crazed witch who did this to them. How could he ever trust her again? "Why are you even still here? Don't you have some men to torture?"

"That's not fair." She shook her head. "I've been nothing but loyal to you."

"Only because it's been convenient," he growled. "You could have left any time. Why are you even still here?"

"I like the damn ship, alright?" she snapped. "It was the first place I felt like I belonged." She glared at the witch and Ariahlla. "You two had to ruin everything with your damned feud." She turned back to her captain. "Living among humans, they would have realized what I was, especially when I didn't age, and they would have made it their mission to end me. No one likes witches. On board this ship, I didn't have to worry. Because of the curse, none of you aged..."

"So you would not be noticed," he finished. She nodded. He looked at the other two witches. "She is really your mother?"

"Unfortunately, yes." Grey said. "I have always been loyal to you, Captain. Forgive my lie."

The mother smirked. "I need new blood in my family. This one is obviously defective." She jerked her head toward Ariahlla, then glared at Grey. "And this one likes this bleeding ship too much. She's too damn nice to carry on my blood."

"Get the hell off my ship. Free my crew on your way out."

"Not without payment," the witch said. "That's the only way you'll get them released."

"No," Grey said, "You're done manipulating these men, Mother. It's over."

"It is not. And you cannot stop me, child," the witch snarled. "I will bury you if you attempt it. I've patronized your oddities for too long."

"You can try." Grey's voice echoed in the stillness of the air, like they were in an enormous cavern. The witch looked her over with half surprise and half disgust as Grey added, "I believe the captain said to get the hell off his ship."

The strike happened before it registered in his brain, as did the defense. Blue lightning bounced off Grey's now-crossed arms like nothing had happened. She uncrossed her arms and in that moment, with her blonde hair flying about and her blue eyes glowing from power, she was the most beautiful thing he'd ever seen.

The witch slammed another bolt at her. She crossed her arms again, fists clenched as the bolt absorbed itself into the shield Grey's crossed arms made. She looked the witch and smiled lazily, as if she were drunk. The witch screeched angrily and shot again. Grey sidestepped it, allowing the bolt to hit one of the dinghies hanging behind her. It burst into brilliant orange and red, the yellow tips of the flames threatening to devour the rest of its surroundings.

Grey spun quickly, a long slender icicle jumping out from her fingertips to encompass the burning dinghy. Just as she did, the witch readied another bolt. Grey didn't catch the power build up, but Chance saw it. As it leapt from the witch's fingertips, he tackled Grey to the deck as the bolt sailed overhead and hit her icicle-covered dinghy. The combination of magics proved too much. A boom assaulted Chance's ears as he covered Grey's body with his own. Ice and fire licked at his back and his ears rang loudly.

"Get off, you big lug!" Grey shouted at him. He rolled off her. She jumped to her feet, then took a running dive at the witch, who hadn't been expecting a physical attack. They both went over the side of the ship, a high screech from the witch's mouth echoing in the night.

Chance ran for the railing, just as Ariahlla grabbed his arm and jerked him back. She held fast as she said, "They're gone, Captain. Witches and water don't mix."

He stared at her, not comprehending what she'd said. No. Grey was a survivor. She couldn't die, much less die from falling overboard. He wouldn't allow it. She was a member of his crew. He tried to pull away with little success.

"Captain."

He growled at her, and she let go. He narrowed his eyes, searching out into the dark waters. That was his first mate. One of his crew. He was responsible. If she died, it was his fault. Ariahlla couldn't be right, anyway. If Grey was, in fact, a witch as well, she'd spent the last fifty years on board a pirate vessel. Obviously, she didn't mind water.

"Come on, Abigail," he whispered into the breeze. The silence stretched on, and still he waited, listening for that telling splash that meant his first mate was alive.

Splash. He blinked. A splash. He hadn't heard a splash when they'd gone overboard. There should have been one when the two women hit the water.

Unless they hadn't.

"John!" He yelled. The young man ran forward, stealing a nervous glance at Ariahlla, who had the good sense to stay quiet.

"Capt'n?"

"I need rope. Right now."

"Captain Chance—" Ariahlla started but he put up a hand in front of her face and gave her a very stern You-Better-Not-Say-A-Word look. "It can wait."

He wrapped the rope around his waist, dropped another line over the side, and climbed over the side himself, his boots flat on the hull. John held the rope, allowing his captain to lower himself carefully. About halfway to the waterline, he saw her.

Abigail held on to a rope that ran the length of the wooden railing with one hand. It was wrapped around her hand to prevent slipping, even as her feet dangled beneath her. There was no sign of the witch.

"Miss Grey!" he called to her.

Her blonde head swiveled to face him and she smiled. "Captain. I seem to be in a bit of a predicament."

He braced his feet on the hull of the ship. "Indeed. Where is the witch?"

"Disappeared," she replied as he began to step to the side one foot at a time, allowing John above to compensate for his movements. "We were both magically charged, and when I hit her, the magics combined and blew out. Don't know where she went but I couldn't bring myself back up alone. Was too drained."

He stopped, just outside of her reach. "You lied to me, Grey."

"Really, Captain." She glanced up at her hand holding the rope. "Is this really where we need to discuss this?"

"Yes, because I need to know if I can trust my first mate. For fifty-two years, you've been lying to me. To my crew."

"Captain." She frowned. "I could never be sure of your reaction. You hated the old crone. And she's my mother. You always cursed about the witches. What would you have done if you'd found out I was one?"

"I don't know," he replied honestly. "But you never gave me a chance."

"Therein lies my problem," she said. "I liked being your first mate. I liked being accepted, despite what I was, and what gender I was. I didn't want to destroy that, but you're right. I did lie. And as sorry as I am for lying to you, it doesn't make up for breaking your trust, Captain. I would take any punishment you wish of me. Even if you wish me off your ship."

He stared at her, the shadows being cast on her from the lights of the ship above. She didn't try to look repentant. She knew she was wrong, but she still wasn't apologetic of it. She'd done what she had to do to survive, and now she said she would take any punishment he wanted from her. Staying on the mainland would have been death for her if the regular population would have found out. People looked upon witches with even more hostility than he did. He could not fault her for being careful about telling him. But, at the same time, could he trust her now? She'd lied to him.

"It will take time," he said finally. "A long time."

She smiled ruefully. "Time, Captain, is something we have in abundance."

He nodded and held out his hand to her. "Come on, then. I need to rescue your ass so's we can deal with that bitch up there."

"Ariahlla won't trouble me. I was always stronger than her." Grey smiled dangerously as she took Chance's hand and allowed him to pull her in to him. She wrapped an arm around

Chance's neck and met his eyes. "I am sorry, Captain. Truly."

He didn't smile but he met her eyes as he handed her the extra rope. "The discussion is over, for now. Go on. We'll talk later." She frowned at him, still unwilling to leave it alone. "That's an order, Miss Grey."

Her frown deepened, but she took the rope in her hands and began the climb up the side of the ship, rappelling the side of the ship as if it were a rock face until she made it to the top. She glanced down, met his eyes for a moment, and then allowed one of the crew to pull her over.

Chance started back up himself, then froze as the hairs on the back of his neck prickled. He stopped and looked around, but saw nothing, yet he knew the witch was there. The chills that ran down his spine were familiar.

"It's too much to ask for you to die, isn't it, crone?"

"She'll turn on you, Captain Chance." He turned, facing the voice. The witch smiled at him as she sat on the ledge not too far from where Grey had been hanging. "She is a witch. She must be true to her own kind, even if she does not wish it."

"Is there a reason you're telling me this?"

"Only for your own well-being, my little captain. Take it as you will."

"You've never had my well-being in mind," he said, ignoring the strain of his muscles from hanging off the side of his ship. "You've imprisoned us on board our own ship, screwed so many of my men out of their lives, just so you could use me later."

She inclined her head in acknowledgement. "You would have made an excellent husband for my daughter. She really has made quite a mistake in crossing me." Her eyes glittered with dangerous intent. "She will find that out in time. I've removed her from your ship. She will trouble you no longer. In the meantime, I have decided to change the conditions of your sentence."

"What?"

"Oh, I realize how quickly your minds might degrade, being stuck on this ship day in and day out. You've already lost several of your crew."

"There is an easy fix. Let us go."

She smiled. "You are correct. But I must protect others like me from human persecution." The witch paused, then continued, "Abigail and I are polar opposites, Captain. Two sides of a single coin, even though we come from the same blood line. I must protect her because without her, magic is unbalanced. She is not like Ariahlla. She is my equal, or will be in time." She paused again. "That is my stipulation for freeing your men. You will protect her, keep her on board, and I will allow your freedom from the curse I bestowed upon you."

"That's it? You will impose no more on us?"

"That's right. And you'll keep your immortality, as long as you remain on board this ship. Those that leave the ship's service will relinquish their immortality to the sea."

He had not expected that. "Why would you do that?"

She smiled. "I told you, Captain. The balance must be maintained. She must be protected. And... if I cannot have a granddaughter by Ariahlla, Abigail will do just as well. I will trust you with her safety. But betray me, and allow her to be hurt, or killed, and I will tear apart every particle in your body." Then she was gone, enveloped in golden flakes until she'd vanished completely.

He let out a sigh. It was over. It was really over. And yet, it really wasn't. Not at all. He had no guarantees with the witch that she would allow them to continue on without her interference.

Grey's golden head peeked over the side. "Captain? Are you alright, sir?"

He nodded and began his ascent, allowing the rope to pull him the majority of the way before he latched on the side of the railing and pulled himself over. He collapsed on the deck, not realizing how much hanging from the side of the ship while he talked with the witch had exhausted him. His legs felt like the writhing tentacles of jellyfish and his shoulder muscles burned like fire.

"Sir?"

He looked up at Grey, realizing what the witch had said. *And if I cannot have a granddaughter by Ariahlla, Abigail will do just as well.* The witch hadn't given up, he realized.

She'd just adjusted her plan. And she was still interfering. "I am well, Miss Grey." She frowned, as if she were trying to figure out what had happened to him. He groaned as he rose to his feet, feeling the exhaustion take hold on him, "I think I will retire for a few hours."

He started to walk away when he heard her speak again. "Captain, are we good?"

He turned back to her. "We will be, Miss Grey. In time." Her face fell, and for the first time, she looked vulnerable. He'd never really seen her in such a way. "Walk with me." She followed him up the stairs. His legs protested with the movement. "I want to be back in port before dawn. Make it happen."

"Sir?"

He smiled broadly. "You're going to get your wish, Miss Grey. A walk on the beach in the sunshine." Her face twisted in confusion, her brow wrinkling, her eyes narrowing.

"Captain, that doesn't make any sense. The curse..." She trailed off. "I couldn't have broken it either."

"I know."

"After I came up... She was down there?"

He nodded. "She was. She promised me something. Will she keep her word?"

"What did she promise?" Grey asked.

"Does it matter?"

"No," she admitted. "She'll keep her word."

"That is good." He looked out at the darkness and the now calm sea. "Then let's go back to town. I need a beer."

Suzan Butler graduated from the University of North Texas with a BA in Creative Writing, and minors in Technical Writing and French. By day, she keeps herself busy doubling as workshop coordinator and freelance editor at Novelists at Work (www.novelistsatwork.com). By night, she writes romantic fiction and maintains a healthy online social life on Twitter (@SuzanButler), Google Plus, and Facebook. Visit her website, suzanbutler.com, for more information about her shenanigans.

Tarwell's Last Day

As a Pirate

STUART JAFFE

William Tarwell's stomach dropped as he gazed over the bay far below. From the temple's stone wall atop Mount Rototori, he watched the clouds wrap around his feet, but no amount of wondrous beauty could relieve his nerves this day. Three ships had anchored—each one alive in his memories as if he had walked on their wooden decks only the day before. The brigantines *Bloody Maria* and *Sea-Dragon,* and the frigate *Caesar.*

After all these years.

He heard Master Park's gentle tapping from behind like a morning greeting. The old Master always tapped a gnarled wooden staff to scare away all the little creatures he might otherwise step on by accident He walked in front of William and placed a bulky, brown paper package on the wall.

"They arrived just before dawn," Master Park said. His blue robes swayed with the breeze as another cloud drifted along beneath their feet.

William clicked his tongue several times while thinking — something he hadn't done since the pirate days he longed to forget. "They'll head straight for the temple. It'll just be the three captains. No one else'll be allowed. Not for this." He squinted at the rising sun. "Won't be long. We should go."

Master Park inclined his wrinkled head toward the package. "Open that."

"I'll take it with us. Open it on the way. Trust me. They've had too much of a lead. We must go now."

"Open it."

William knew better than to argue further. Five years had passed since he left all the evil of his past and made the arduous climb up Mount Rototori's steep side to reach the temple. On that day, Master Park Il Woo had greeted him and welcomed him to the brotherhood without question. William had been more hesitant about the decision — he had simply wanted a place to hide out for a short time.

"The choice is easy," Master Park had said, dismissing all objections with a wave of his stick. "After all, there's a reason so many monks atop mountains are old. If we ever gave up and climbed down, we'd never want to make the climb back up again. Everything we worked for, everything we believed in, would be over. So we stay."

William, too, had stayed.

Over the years, he had witnessed many trainee monks arrive, only to be disheartened by the firm, disciplined hand of Master Park. A strong crack across the back from that gnarled staff sent most back down the mountain within their first week. But William had served under harsh pirate captains for many years before getting his own ship and crew — one cranky old monk with a stick hardly compared.

Now, Master Park pointed that vicious stick at the package.

Out of respect, and knowing the Master would not be dissuaded, William pulled back the brown paper. Besides, the faster he appeased the man, the faster they'd get moving.

It was his old pirate garb. He stared at it as if laying eyes on some new sea creature. After so many years wearing thin robes and feeling nature against his skin, he couldn't imagine putting on the heavy, multi-layered costume again. How did they ever run a ship wearing such nonsense?

Except it was more than just a costume. Those clothes were part of all the terrible crimes he had committed, all the people he had injured, all the riches he had stolen, all the life of a pirate. And that life touched upon worse things — things like magic, things like curses.

"Get dressed," Master Park said.

"But Master," he said, but the old man stepped toward the main temple — a squat, rectangular building in the center of four courtyards — and snapped crisp orders to the three trainees emerging from morning prayers. They would sweep the west courtyard, prepare a strong tea, and set a small table for the approaching guests. Then they would go on a hike with the expectation of not returning until nightfall.

William untied the small knots on the side of his robe. His fingers trembled as he removed the thin clothing and slipped on the burgundy hose. They smelled of sweat, dust, and the ocean. Cold against his skin, he took a sharp breath and put on his velvet breeches. He shook his head — the extravagances of a pirate captain no longer felt right.

"Master Park," William said, despising the whine in his voice but unable to prevent it. "Please go. If you get hurt because of me, I couldn't live with that. I've enough to burden my soul. Please. Don't make me deal with worse."

Master Park folded his arms and sat on the stone wall like a petulant child. When he spoke, however, he took on the countenance of a disapproving parent. "In all the years you've been here, you refuse to let your troubles go. Tell me what you didn't want to tell me before."

"They're more than mere troubles. If I let things go, true evil will be upon us. I can't let that happen. Not here."

Master Park shook his head. "You are afraid. We all fear that which is inside us. Face your fears, and we'll find a way for you to atone and move forward."

William pulled out his favorite blue shirt, punched his arms through, and buttoned up. Though it lacked the ornate puffiness many captains wore on land, it did have fancy ruffles around the wrists. On one ruffle, he saw a dark stain — blood.

He clamped his eyes shut against the memory. He could still hear the sobbing and the screams and the wet, gurgling end to it all. He could smell the blood and the sea mixing like some witch's brew. Rubbing the ruffles between two fingers, he said, "See this? This is what's important to a pirate."

"Ruffles?"

"Wealth. It takes money to buy these clothes, money that's stolen or killed for... or worse. But there's one more driving force behind a pirate's actions, one that doesn't always occur but when it does, it can supplant all other senses. It's what drives the captains of those ships to pursue me right now." With a meager sigh, he glanced down at the anchored vessels. "Revenge."

Master Park's stoicism broke for an instant like a surge in the wind, only to return to an indecipherable breeze a second later. "What did you do that has angered them to this degree?"

A white and black bird circled overhead, swooped down, and perched on the wall just a foot away. William observed it as he added the waistcoat and baldric to his outfit. The bird cocked its head, pranced along the wall, and pecked at the stones.

William took a deep breath, trying to inhale the creature's peace, to preserve it within his body. He focused on the immediacy of the moment just as Master Park had taught him, to be free from his troubles and for just one flickering second, experience nothing but the simplicity of a bird at peace. But the bird shot off into the air.

With a mixture of regret for the bird's leaving and dread for having to face Master Park, William slipped on his land-doublet with its gold fringes and shiny buttons, and settled his leather tri-cornered hat firmly atop his head. The heavy clothing pressed on his shoulders, labored his breath, and obstructed his movement. Already he tasted sweat beading on his lips — salty like the ocean.

"Captain William Tarwell," a voice bellowed from the far end of the temple.

Master Park popped to his feet, scowling. "Stay here," he said, snapping the words with a familiar harshness that still struck William with tension.

William's shoulders drooped. He should have told Master Park. Instead, he had wasted time dressing and staring at birds. If anything happened to the Master, the old man would never know why.

William wrapped his wide-buckled belt around his waist and sheathed his cutlass in it, along with a small dagger. None of these clothes and accessories fit right anymore. It all hung awkwardly, like a child playing dress-up.

He watched as three men entered the temple grounds. They surrounded the table the trainees had prepared, each a perfect specimen of a real pirate captain.

Captain Reed, dressed in black and gold, wiped his brow with his wide sleeve. His shoulder-length black hair and his equally long beard were damp with perspiration. Captain Song stood to Reed's right. Bald and scarred, Song lacked the bulk of Reed but carried an off-kilter twinkle in his eyes. Last, Captain Crosswise stood at Reed's left, panting from the long climb and sweating through his red and brown silk shirt.

Master Park offered them hot tea. They looked at the delicate cups and laughed. Reed swept the table aside, shattering the cups on the ground. "We don't want none of your drinks, old man. We just want William Tarwell, and we know he's here. So bring him out."

"No need to be rude," William said, approaching the table with an overly-firm stride.

"Well, if 'taint that all," Song said. "Ol' William's lookin' just as spry as ever."

"Yeah," Crosswise said, wheezing for air in the high altitude. "It's as if nothing's happened to him in all this time. As if he ain't suffered once for what he done."

William and Reed locked eyes, and William could tell — Reed knew much of his shame. But nobody could know the full extent to which he had been ruined. William touched Master Park's shoulder and hoped his shaking hand did not betray him. "I'll handle this now."

Master Park bowed and stepped several paces back, his mouth set in a stern line. Park, no doubt, hated appearing subservient, but William silently thanked the old man. Pirate captains were sensitive toward such things. If they thought that Park was in charge, Reed and the others would have skipped revenge and simply torn William apart for weakness.

"Well, well," Reed said as William swept aside broken bits of teacup with his foot. "William Tarwell, the great thief, the scoundrel what brought a curse upon the heads of us all."

"We all took the same risks," William said, his voice soft even as his hand slid toward the hilt of his cutlass.

Reed pointed toward Master Park. "You watch yourself, old man. Don't believe this one. He's a liar."

"A liar, indeed," Song said.

"That's right," Crosswise said. "Do you know," he continued, walking around Park like a giant dog eyeing its prey, "what your Master here did to us? Did he ever tell you?"

Song made a chittering sound that William knew from experience to be a laugh. "Oh, look at that," Song said. "That's one confused face. Ol' William never told this one nothing."

Reed leaned his chair back and banged his feet onto the table. "Y'see, old man, years back, your Master here, he come to the three of us with an idea. There was this story he had heard about Zaqualia, the ocean goddess. You know this one?"

Park slowly moved his head from side to side. William opened his mouth to stop this from going any further, but Crosswise paused right next to Park and raised a dagger. His thirsty eyes promised that one wrong word, one wrong movement, and he would slit the old man's neck. William backed down, cringing at the disgust he expected to see when Master Park learned the truth.

"Story goes," Reed went on, "that there's a certain location in the ocean where Zaqualia can be summoned. It takes four men to do so — one stationed at each of the four main compass points. Being in the ocean, you really need four ships."

"That's why he come to us," Song said.

Reed grimaced. "Shut up. Just 'cause he's a servant don't make him stupid." To Park, he said, "William had come upon the right map with the right coordinates. He just needed some partners. See, if four men position their ships just right, and if each says the proper words, well then, ol' Zaqualia ain't got no choice but to rise on up."

Crosswise wiggled his dagger so it glinted in the sunlight. "Rise she did. Biggest sea monster I ever seen. Towered above all our ships, and the water dripping off her hit us like a heavy downpour."

Reed's face tightened and his mouth drew a grim line. "William said that Zaqualia would shower us with riches. We'd have all we'd ever wanted. But he forgot to mention that should any of us have the merest thoughts of betrayal, all that gold and gems and coin would go to those who stayed honest and the rest would be cursed."

Song laughed. "Slipped his mind, it must've."

"You're right, it must've. After all, we're pirates. Thoughts of betrayal are like breathing. William had to have known what would happen. He even made a point making sure none of us try to outwit him — as if daring us to betray him."

"Insisted on it, I recall," Crosswise said.

Reed nodded. "And while we fought off a right angry goddess, while we suffered injury to our vessels and watched strong men disappear into that beast's throat, dear William made off with our treasure."

William averted his eyes from Master Park. Crosswise yanked Park close and placed the dagger at his throat. "Took us many years to find him. But here we are."

William gripped his cutlass. His heart pounded and his stomach clenched. Like the sudden certainty he would feel when reading the waves and the weather, he knew he would not let Reed finish the story. Five years he had spent with Master Park. Five years. Building trust, friendship, a new life. He'd kill a thousand Reeds before he allowed all he had built to be destroyed.

Reed and Song had their weapons out fast. Eyes darted from one set to the next. Reed's lip curled up. "We don't have to do it this way. Just give us the treasure, all of it, then we'll go."

"Don't have it," William said. That was true enough. He had

hidden the riches in the praying statues. "Besides, some of it's spent. So if you're thinking of breaking the curse —"

"There is no breaking the curse," Reed said, growling out the last word. "We tried everything. The curse is forever."

William blanched for a moment. Forever. That couldn't be true. There had to be a way out.

"We want whatever you've got left," Reed went on. "We want to retire like you did. Give up this life and find some peace."

"I'm sorry, but I'm telling the truth." William wished he could give them the treasure, but they'd never believe he didn't have anything else hidden somewhere. And even if they did believe, they'd still kill him for what he had done. He remembered what it meant to be a pirate. In a matter like this, gold was just the excuse. They had no intention of leaving until William's blood spilled down the mountainside. "The treasure's all gone. Spent."

"Then we'll have to settle for revenge," Reed said and lunged forward.

William fumbled out his cutlass and parried the attack. Adrenaline shocked away his nerves and filled his muscles with long-forgotten strength. He swung into the area he expected Song to be. Song's sword clanged against his. William repositioned, keeping Song between him and Reed.

Crosswise said, "Sorry, old man, but now, you die." Before he finished uttering the final syllable, Master Park reached up, grabbed Crosswise's wrist, and twisted with enough force to release the dagger. Park ducked under the pirate's arm, stepped through, and came up behind, wrenching the arm upward against Crosswise's spine. Two sharp kicks to the back of the pirate's knees sent Crosswise to the ground. It happened so fast and smooth that Reed, Song, and William froze in befuddlement.

"William. This is your fight. Pay attention," Master Park said.

Swinging his cutlass upward, William sliced a thin line into Song's chest. Song jumped back, spit to the side, and yelled as he hurled a fresh attack. The lanky captain proved easy to parry away. William's confidence rose — he had once been good at this and his muscle memory knew it. Song came in low. William spun the cutlass around and smacked Song's forehead with the hilt.

Song's eyes rolled white. He stumbled backward. He lost his balance and hit the dirt hard. William didn't expect the pirate to awake anytime soon.

Like a shark, Reed slid into a firm stance and raised his cutlass. "You've always been a stubborn fool," he said.

William tried a reasonable tone. "I'd give you the gold, if I had it. I would. I just want to live here in peace. You say you want to retire, too, then do so. You don't need gold. I gave it all up to be here, and I've found my peace." All a lie, of course. He had hidden the gold just in case the monk's life didn't pan out. And he had yet to find any peace.

"Just give up the gold?" Reed said, his face scrunched, his knuckles white from his grip. "We got nothing else to live for but that gold. We been cursed for eternity, so we might as well enjoy what little bit a life we got left. We want good food and easy women and that takes the gold."

William shook his head. "Not me. I'm not a pirate anymore."

"Liar!" Red-faced and bellowing rage, Reed thrust forward. William stepped back, struggling to parry the onslaught of attacks. Reed attempted an overhead, ax-like cut. William dodged the sloppy move, repositioning with his back to the main prayer room.

"Leave me to suffer?" Reed said, overcoming his graceless attacks with sheer power. "Leave me to die at the hand of some sea bitch?" William edged back but the attacks kept coming. "I want my gold." *Slash.* "I want my power." *Slash.* "I want you dead."

Like a raging storm with no end in sight, Reed continued his furious assault. William tried to defend his way toward Master Park, but Reed blocked his path. The burly captain swept his weapon neck-high. If not for a quick duck, William's head would have rolled across the floor.

He could only evade Reed for so long. He would die if he didn't change the situation.

As he came back up, he made a fist and popped Reed in the chin. The jolt opened Reed's eyes wide and bought William a few seconds. Lacking Master Park's skill and grace, he could think of only one way to win this — brutal force.

Matching Reed's rage with his own, William fought back. Slashing and slicing, jabbing and cutting — he pushed Reed back across the courtyard.

Blocking attacks and stepping forward, William edged Reed toward the stone wall. Over his shoulder, he caught a glance of Song still unconscious and Crosswise still held tight by Master Park. Reed saw William's eyes shift and took advantage. He aimed for the gut. Fast reflexes deflected the cutlass but not far enough — Reed sliced across William's leg.

As white-hot pain seared through him, William let loose a barrage of screams and strikes. Reed locked swords, shoved William back, and dashed to the right. With blood dribbling down his leg, sticking his hose to his skin, William followed.

Reed faked a low strike and came around from high up. William saw the move as if it had been played out in his imagination. Instead of deflecting the weapon, though, William stepped into the attack and chopped through Reed's arm. A coarse sound erupted from Reed. He cradled his bleeding stub.

Panting but still standing, William pointed his cutlass at Reed. "This is over. You lose."

Reed scrunched his brow and turned his head toward Crosswise. "Is it possible he don't know?" Facing William, he stretched out his bloody half-arm like a red candle dribbling wax. "Is that right? We been talking about this the whole time and you don't know our curse? Well, it's time you see what that bastard sea monster did to us."

The pained look in Reed's eye shifted to a malicious joy. His skin rippled as if waves rolled just underneath. Five tendrils snaked out of his stump while Crosswise laughed.

William tightened his grip on the cutlass. He caught a glimpse of Master Park — horrified, confused, repulsed. Though he kept his focus on the transforming Reed, William felt darkness settle across his heart. He knew all about the curse. What would Master Park do, what would he think, when he learned the full truth?

The five tendrils hardened into a new hand. Reed's shoulder jerked and his right leg jittered. And he grew. His entire body reshaped.

Trying to take advantage of the moment, William swiped out with his cutlass, but despite the painful metamorphosis, Reed managed to block the attack. His strength increased with his size, and his block sent William sprawling in the dirt.

Crosswise let out a strangled yelp while his body transformed. Master Park jumped back as if he might be infected by touching the pirate. Crosswise's skin became smooth and his arms grew suckers. Two more arms emerged from his sides.

Though Song remained unconscious, his body changed, too. His skin darkened to a rich mahogany, as his body turned into a wooden version of itself.

Reed stepped closer, his lizard-like shadow covering William. "This is what we've had to live with because of your treachery. Many of our crew left. Even in our human form, people won't talk with us. They fear us, but not like they should fear a pirate. They fear us like monsters. We are monsters now."

William looked from one beast to the next. Struggling against the sadness brewing within him, his eyes rested on the old man. "I'm sorry, Master Park. I'm sorry for bringing this to you."

"Enough," Master Park said, snatching his staff from the stone wall and plunking it onto the dirt. "You're a thief. There are far worse crimes in the world. These men have had to pay for such crimes. Give them what you can and let them be on their way."

"But I have nothing. Not anymore. I gave up such possessions when I left the pirate's world."

"Do not lie to me," Master Park said, disgust flashing across his face.

William clambered to his feet, and Reed did nothing to stop him. "You're right. I did steal this treasure. And I hid it here."

In a guttural voice, Crosswise said, "I knew it."

William went on, "I hoped to escape the curse and keep the gold, and in a few years, I'd leave here and settle on some forgotten island."

Master Park folded his arms and smiled. "But you changed."

"You changed me. I want to be a better man."

"Then do so. Start today, here, now. Tell them and tell me what I've watched torture you every day for five years. You, too, have been cursed. Your guilt cursed you, plagued your conscience."

William rubbed away his tears. "You don't understand. It's more than that. I'm worse than a thief."

"Then tell us that. Voice your fear."

"I can't."

Reed shoved William. "The old man's right. You've got more to say, then say it."

Master Park pointed to the beasts with his staff. "They wear their fears. Crosswise is like the monsters of the sea that haunt him. Song is wooden — fear of ships, perhaps."

"The plank," Crosswise said. "Song always frets he'll one day have to walk the plank and drown."

Master Park nodded. "And Captain Reed fears reptiles, I suppose. If you wish to free yourself, then you must acknowledge what happened and what you fear. You weren't cursed like them, but —"

"But I was. I've hid it from you all these years. The goddess didn't care for blood magic calling her to the surface. She cursed me, too."

William inhaled deeply and as he let the breath go, his body grew. His muscles strengthened and his chest expanded. His bones cracked and reformed. He let out grunts as his nails extended. Then, the skin around his head began to split. Tears streamed down his bleeding cheeks. He dug his sharpened nails into his head and pulled apart the skin. In three quick strokes, his skin was removed and a breathing skull surveyed the courtyard.

Though his face remained stoic, Master Park held his staff in a defensive position, his grip whitening his hands. "I see," he said, a slight tremor to his voice. "You fear Death."

William, the skull-beast, tackled Reed. Reed cried out as he brought his arms up to protect his head. William slashed at the lizard with his claw-like nails, shredding the cursed pirate's skin into strands of flesh. He batted Reed's hands away. Saliva leaked from the skull's mouth and spattered against the pulp-mess that had become of Reed's face.

"You want to know?" William screamed. "You want to see how depraved and worthless I am?"

Master Park and Crosswise watched in shocked silence. But only for a moment. Crosswise stepped ahead to intervene. Master Park moved fast. With two fingers, he jabbed five key points on Crosswise's body. The monster fell, contorting against unseen, internal pains.

William's frenzied barbarism continued though Reed offered up little resistance. "You three were bait," he said. "You were supposed to die while I got away. But the worst was casting the spell." Breathing heavy and sweating through his thick garb, William stood. His skull-face turned toward Master Park. "Blood magic — it requires blood. I... I had to kidnap a virgin, just a teen, and I slit her neck on the deck of my ship and held her until her blood gushed over the side into the ocean. That's why I'm cursed."

William lifted Reed above his head. He carried the lizard to the stone wall. And he tossed him down the mountain. Without waiting to watch the results, he returned to the courtyard, wrangled Song's wooden form, and did the same.

When he came back for Crosswise, Master Park put out a single hand. "Stop. There's no need for further killing."

"Move away," William said, his voice scratchy and wet.

"Let this one live. Tap into your humanity and free yourself from this guilt and rage. Let this one live and I'll teach you more. You can overcome this curse."

"You said I should atone. That's what I'm doing. I'm cleaning the mess I made, and I'll atone."

Without any more resistance from Master Park, William took hold of Crosswise and tossed him over the stone wall. William returned to Master Park and knelt.

"You'll find the gold and all the treasure hidden in the statues in the praying room. You'll also find the map that I used to start this whole thing. I ask one favor. Burn it."

Master Park's eyes widened. "Will that end the curse?"

"Didn't you hear Captain Reed? There is no breaking the curse. It's forever. Only death can end it for me."

"You can learn to live with it. You can live here. Let me teach you. You —"

"Master Park, you've been a good man to me. More than anyone. More than I deserve. Far more. But I must face my crimes and end my pain. Every day is a struggle to fight against turning into this horrid figure. Every damned day. It's painful and exhausting. It warps my thoughts. Even now, I fight to control the rage so as not to harm you. One day, I'll be like Reed, and I just won't care anymore. Then you'll have the burden of having to kill me. I don't want that for you."

"But —"

"I'm tired."

Master Park reached out, his face locked in a dumbfounded expression. William Tarwell stood up and shook hands with the old man. Though his skull-head displayed little emotion, William could feel the tears on his bony cheek. He nodded once. Then he whirled around, sprinted toward the stone wall, and vaulted over.

As he dropped through the air, fast approaching his rocky demise below, his face dried in the wind. He watched the land soar by faster than he ever had experienced on a frigate in a strong wind. He recalled the stickiness that never left the deck after the sacrifice and hoped, somehow, this final act would gain him some forgiveness.

A white and black bird swooped by him, cocking its head in his direction. He closed his eyes and recalled the long hike the day he came to Mount Rototori. *No way will I ever climb up that again,* he thought and then thought no more.

Stuart Jaffe is the author of *The Malja Chronicles* (*The Way of the Black Beast, The Way of the Sword and Gun*), a post-apocalyptic fantasy series, as well as the short story collection, *10 Bits of My Brain*. Numerous other short stories have appeared in magazines and anthologies (including *Rum and Runestones*). He is the co-host of The Eclectic Review —a podcast about science, art, and well, everything. For those who keep count, the latest animal listing is as follows: five cats, one albino corn snake, one Brazilian black tarantula, three aquatic turtles, one tortoise, assorted fish, two lop-eared rabbits, eight chickens, and a horse. Thankfully, the chickens and the horse do not live inside the house.

The Vapor Rogues

M.J. BLEHART

Then – Below the Cloud

Over eight hundred years ago, war raged across Amasheer. In an act of unspeakable violence, a chemical agent was unleashed, poisoning the atmosphere. To hold the poison at bay, the magic wielding, dark skinned Maju-Orcericians created a perpetual cloud layer to hold the poison beneath it. The Maju-Orcericians took as many people as they could to the highest peaks of the world, above the dangerous atmosphere. The survivors constructed immense floating cities over the next eight centuries, starting new lives and rebuilding the population...and a new era was begun.

Now – Above the Cloud

He always thrilled to the feel of the wind on his face.

To protect his eyes, he wore his goggles down. His airship, the *Silver Huntress*, was accelerating, leaving the floating city of Ot-Daven behind. He and his crew had resupplied their ship, and taken on their next contract.

Captain Booth James Michael was standing before the

windows of the bridge, on the walkway that surrounded it. He wore his soft leather flight helmet, and was buttoned into his long charcoal pea coat with the chocolate brown leather shoulder pauldrons. It was a cool, but not cold wind, and the sky above was clear and blue.

Throughout his childhood he would often venture to the edges or bottom decks of his home city, Vi-Charn, and peer down at the perpetual clouds below. He would dream of soaring through, over, and into those clouds, and learned to fly a biplane before his teens. When he was old enough, he joined the crew of a dirigible, and began to see the world of Amasheer.

The *Silver Huntress* was a medium class airship. Her center was a long, lighter-than-air gas filled bladder. It was surrounded by a metal framework enclosed by titanium panels to protect the balloon. The ship was compartmentalized to house supplies, crew and passenger quarters, cargo, and the triple-expansion steam engine. Iron catwalks connected the compartments, the majority of the habitation at the top of the craft. A stacked trio of massive propellers spun astern before a huge rudder, pushing the ship across the skies. Booth loved his airship.

Highest up, towards the rear of the craft was the bridge. The helm and controls were on the inside, currently manned by his first officer.

Booth looked back into the bridge, and saw his dark-skinned Orcerician first mate, Paton Tarik Hanif, standing confidently at the wheel. His hair was black, thick dreadlocks, without a streak of white. Tarik did not practice sorcery, at least never intentionally. Those Orcericians who practiced the arte developed streaks of white in their hair. In time the hair turned shock white, and then it would fall out, revealing an intricate, silver tattoo embedded in the scalp from the use of the energies.

They would be marked now as Maju-Orcericians, wielders of immense power, identified by the tattoo as either Emissaries or Adepts, the most powerful users of their inherent sorcerous endowment.

Tarik had never been interested in the benefit he was born to. All Orcericians could use sorcery, and take on the mantle of Maju...but it was a choice.

The *Silver Huntress'* engineer, Morse Simon Ray, had just entered the bridge, and was clearly speaking to Tarik about the rate of acceleration, as per usual. Simon was often over-fussy, but a more than adequate engineer, keeping the airship a-flight and in good repair.

The other members of his crew would be going about their business, securing the items they acquired while in port.

The *Silver Huntress* was a transport and prospector craft. Sometimes they would take cargo from one city to another, but other times they would seek and explore the lost cities, hunting treasures and other unclaimed valuables from abandoned platforms from the beginning of life above the cloud. This particular business was the latter.

Booth thought back on the man they had met. He had been wearing a long duster, and a cowl and hood that left his face in shadow. His hands were gloved, and his voice had a wet, gravelly quality to it. He had been seated, so his height was indeterminate. But he had an odd, damp, musty smell to him.

"The city," he had said, "is long forgotten. To the southwest, positioned just atop the clouds. It was called Cy-Ondon, and has been abandoned for nearly seven hundred years."

"So what makes this lost city so special?" Captain Booth had asked.

"The elevator...to the surface."

Few who attempted to venture below the cloud were ever seen again. The descent through the cloud itself was treacherous, between the rumors of living creatures in the cloud and the intense electricity. That was before you even reached the perpetual rains feeding and cycling the cloud. A means to the surface such as an elevator was greatly intriguing.

There were legends of cities below the clouds, long ago abandoned, that might still have untold treasures. The air below the clouds may have been poisoned over eight centuries ago, but it was believed possible that after so much time the surface may have been cleansed by the rains. The history of life below the cloud was mostly lost, but the legends were plentiful.

Booth felt the *Silver Huntress* lurch beneath him, and was thrown against the rail. He righted himself, and felt the wind lessening. The airship was slowing. He looked into the bridge, saw his engineer go racing back, and his first mate gesturing for him to come inside. And behind them...smoke.

He stepped to the side, and saw that the trio of propellers were gone. Only one thing could do that: cannon fire.

Leaning over the railing, Booth caught a glimpse of something below them, in the distance. He reached up, and lowered first one, then two of the magnifiers over the right eye of his goggles – and saw an armed and armored craft ascending towards them.

Booth ran into the bridge, raising his goggles to the top of his head on the way.

"We've lost main propulsion and the engines," Tarik said.

"Incoming attackers," Booth informed him calmly. "They must've gotten off a clean shot at the propellers – they're gone. Use maneuvering fans to turn us...they're approaching from our lower port quadrant at about five o'clock."

Tarik began to turn knobs and adjust switches. "Turning the *Huntress* is not going to be easy without the main rudder! Radar didn't detect a thing!"

Booth shook his head. "They probably were in the cloud. They have what looked to me like a warship of some sort. Our four forward cannons and biplane will be hard pressed against that."

Tarik looked frustrated as he spun a small wheel. "I think they may have damaged some of our maneuvering fans, too. I wonder how..."

Booth suddenly felt his whole body light on fire. The sensation was just becoming unbearable, his bones vibrating and his skin tingling uncontrollably, when it stopped. He caught his breath...and dropped to the deck, twitching.

His last thought as he blacked out was *how are we going to get out of this one?*

A splash of cold water on his face brought him around.

Booth found himself leaning against a wall, his hands tied behind his back. A number of guttural noises, which he guessed were voices, soon became clearer. He opened his eyes.

There were six men and a woman standing there, chuckling. The largest man, dressed in pin-striped pants and a leather vest, had in his hand a water hose attached to a pipe above. Everyone else was armed with various guns.

Looking past the armed rabble, Booth saw his airship through a viewport, looking none-the-worse for wear, save the ruined propellers.

He looked to either side, and saw the other five members of his crew, looking unharmed, but similarly bound and leaning against the grey titanium bulkhead.

His attention returned to their captors, in particular the woman. She was slender, with long dark hair pulled back in a braid. She wore a deep green corset covered by a leather coat with brass accents, and a porkpie hat with goggles atop her head.

"Welcome aboard the *Warbird*," she said, almost pleasantly.

Booth didn't move, but his heart skipped a beat. Everyone had heard of the *Warbird*. An old warship that had fallen into the hands of devious pirates, notorious for destroying ships and abandoning their crews in old, lost cities.

"Why did you attack us?" Booth asked.

"Straight to the point, then," she commented. The others chuckled. "Very well. I am Captain Childs Elspeth Rachel... and you have something we want."

"So take it, and let us go back to our ship," Tarik said.

She smiled sweetly at him. "Sorry, Orcerician, we can't do that. You will need to come along."

Someone with a heavy footfall walked into the compartment. The pirates stepped aside, save the captain and the man with the hose. An even larger man, wearing heavy leather boots and black pants, stepped forward. His head was shaved, and he had a long scar across one side of his face. But his most distinguishing feature was his right arm. It was entirely cybernetic.

The cyborg had a wide gait, and his slightly oversized mechanical right arm showed brass and copper and numerous exposed cogs and gears. It must have had a small power cell within. There was a pinscher hook, and clearly weapons of varying kinds attached to it.

"My first officer... Lynch Kenneth Howard," Childs introduced. Booth noted that the large man who had remained with the captain placed himself between her and the cyborg.

"You are wasting time, Captain," Lynch said. "We have searched that bag of gas and found nothing. We should start to tear off limbs until they tell us who has it."

"Easy, Lynch," Childs said. "I've not yet tried to ask politely."

Lynch made no further move, except to open and close the pinscher a couple times, the mechanics of it whirring.

"I presume you are the captain?" Childs addressed Booth.

"I am."

"You just left Ot-Daven after meeting an unusual man," she stated. "You purchased a map from him."

"I have no idea what you are talking about," Booth replied.

Childs cocked her gun, and pointed it at Booth's head.

"Oh, that map. It's in the inside pocket of my coat."

Childs gestured to the large man at her side. "Wat?"

He moved forward, opened up Booth's coat, and reached into the pocket. He withdrew the map, and returned to his captain.

"Now that you have the map, let us go," Tarik stated.

"You wish to be dropped into the cloud?" Lynch asked.

"Just let us go back to our ship," Simon requested. "We're dead in the wind. It's going to take a lot of work to get the *Huntress* flying again...so we're no threat to you."

"You are mistaken," Lynch said, sneering. "Your ship is beyond repair." He reached to a wall panel and opened it, pulling out a microphone. Flipping a switch, he ordered "Fire."

The *Warbird* shuddered as a barrage of cannon fired at the *Silver Huntress*. Booth watched with a sinking feeling in his chest as a dozen shells, a mix of balls and bullets, accelerated towards his beloved airship. They all made contact, shattering compartments and framework where they connected, and clearly piercing the inner balloon.

The *Silver Huntress*, crippled and bashed, began to roll onto her side, and sink towards the clouds.

"You bastard!" Simon shouted, somehow rising up and rushing at the cyborg, his hands still tied behind his back.

"Simon, stop!" Booth ordered.

The cyborg reached out his mechanical right arm towards the rushing engineer.

"Lynch, no!" Captain Childs commanded.

Simon jerked to a halt just before the cyborg's outreached right arm. He uttered a sound like "hurk!" The noise of metal on metal, then metal on bone was unmistakable...and the tip of a sharp blade emerged from the engineer's back.

Simon went limp, and the sound of metal on metal as the blade was withdrawn reached them. The engineer crumpled to the deck, Lynch grinning as he retracted the last of the blade into his mechanical arm.

"That was not necessary!" Childs stated.

Lynch turned. "The lesson is learned. They'll cause us no further problems."

"That isn't the point," Childs said. "I am in charge here, Lynch. If I say we give quarter, we give quarter. Is that clear?"

"Yes ma'am," he replied smartly. Booth did not doubt the cyborg felt no remorse for his actions.

"Wat," Childs ordered. "Take the map to the bridge."

The big man looked to his captain. She nodded her head to him, and he was gone.

"Since you've nowhere else to go, you will be accompanying us," Lynch stated.

"Petty, Barnes...take our guests to the unoccupied barracks," Childs ordered. "When you get there, unbind them, and keep them under guard."

"Aye, Captain," said one of the pirates she had addressed.

"Don't try anything," Lynch stated. "Unless you want to join your friend."

Several days had passed. Captain Booth and his crew had not been treated harshly, though all were still feeling the pain of the loss of both their friend and their ship.

They were standing together before the forward observation portal, watching the floating city called Cy-Ondon grow larger as they neared. It was anchored just atop the clouds, at a point where they often rolled over and obscured the buildings. As such, the streets and steel, copper and glass remaining in the abandoned city was washed clean, gleaming greys and whites and browns.

Booth could not deny that the sight before him was beautiful.

Childs had sent one of her crew ahead to scout out the city in a biplane. The short range, delta-winged craft had soared out ahead of the far larger armored airship, carefully looking to find the aerodrome, or any functional dock for the *Warbird*.

The *Warbird*, Booth learned, possessed a pair of biplanes. Both were well armed, though neither could fly for more than a couple hours before running out of energy. While he and Tarik could pilot them, they could only carry one or two each, and would not be an option to make any kind of escape.

Childs and her first mate had included Booth and Tarik when they went over the map of the long-abandoned city. They determined the approximate location of the elevator to the surface, and as such had instructed the biplane pilot to find a place to dock near that area.

As disturbed as he was by both the loss of his airship and the murder of his friend, Booth couldn't deny he was still feeling excited to be exploring this place.

The *Warbird* was starting to descend. The biplane must have found a suitable dock.

"Captain," Lowen Andrew Basil, his cargo master, addressed him just above a whisper. "If they bring us with them...we might have a chance to overpower them." The former soldier was always on the lookout for an escape.

"Maybe," Tarik, standing near, murmured. "But they will be armed, and outnumber us."

"Stay alert," Booth ordered them quietly.

Lynch and Childs came in now. "Graves has found us a good dock. Less than a mile walk to the supposed elevator to the surface. You will all be equipped to come with us."

"Will we be coming back?" Dean Gwen Sarah, Booth's quartermaster, asked. The dark maroon of her short leather jacket seemed a mirror for her ire.

"That depends on you," Lynch replied. "Smart talk or attempt to escape, you stay below the cloud. If you ever get there in the first place."

"What if one of us does not care to go down there?" Russell Graham Thomas, Booth's medic, asked. His brown linen shirt was badly wrinkled, and his fingernails looked like he'd been chewing on them.

Lynch turned to him, grinning. "Then you will be killed and dropped into the cloud, so you will get there first. Would that be your preference?"

Lynch turned now to Childs. "Recommend we leave Graves and Watkins behind."

She shook her head. "I want Wat along."

"We only have one duster that is big enough for either him or I," Lynch commented off-handedly. "If you wish to bring him, then I will have to remain here."

She didn't look happy with that option. "Very well...Wat stays."

Lynch looked at Booth, and gestured "This way."

They were escorted to a room full of lockers. There the crew of the *Warbird* began to open the cabinets, pulling out waterproof coated dusters, hooded cowls and special breathing masks.

Booth felt a momentary foreboding. There were no stories of attempts to get below the clouds that ended well. People who tried were never heard from again, more often than not, and the few that had supposedly made it and returned were not credible, nor sane.

"We put this on when we reach the elevator," Childs ordered. The *Warbird* lurched slightly, and the sensation off the deck changed, as did the sound of the steam turbine engine. "Ah, we're docked."

They gathered at the external hatch. The dozen pirates were all well armed with a variety of knives, swords, pistols of varying sizes, and a couple rifles. Lynch made a show of arming the gun in his cybernetic arm.

"Wat, Graves, hold down the ship while we are gone," Childs ordered. "Whomever we leave to guard the elevator will check in every couple hours."

"Aye, Captain," replied Wat. Booth could not help but notice that it was Lynch whom Graves seemed to look to.

The hatch was opened, and soon they were making their way into the dock.

It was in excellent condition. There were no obvious signs of the abandonment of the space, but it looked and smelled of disuse. The pirates were also looking about.

"Kek, CL, bring the portable engine," ordered Captain Childs.

Together, the two pirates took hold of the portable simple expansion steam engine, which was on a wheeled cart. The unit was about four feet wide and three feet tall, with dials and knobs and gauges all over it, plus a trio of different types of connections. Atop it was a solar panel, which would provide a boost of electrical power to the unit, and an additional catalyst for heating the steam.

It occurred to Booth that in all likelihood the elevator would have no power. Of course, it was also possible that an elevator that would need to travel over two thousand feet to the surface, which had not been used in anywhere from six hundred to eight hundred years, might not work in the first place.

The motley crew found their way to the stairs, which would lead them down to the long abandoned city of Cy-Ondon. As they moved along, Booth observed his own crew. Gwen had a haughty glare in her eye, obviously displeased with their situation. Tarik was clearly observing everything around him. Graham was absently chewing on a fingernail, but also looking about curiously. Andrew was eyeing the pirate crew, probably attempting to discern who might be weakest among them.

Booth had the same thought. He was also convinced that it was moot. All of their captors looked to be hardened fighters, even Childs. And Lynch was just disturbing.

They emerged onto the abandoned street, washed eerily clean by centuries of cloud and water vapor. There was evidence of destruction among the buildings lining the street, signs of some kind of long ago fighting. Booth had seen the results of cannon fire and gunfire before, and it left obvious marks.

Childs and Lynch were consulting the map. The rest of the pirates were keeping a sharp eye on both his crew, and their surroundings.

"This way," said Lynch, pointing with his mechanical arm.

As they started down the road, Booth glanced up at the *Warbird* tethered to the dock. The warship was not all that large, relatively speaking, but had an impressive armored shell of polished titanium. He could see the hatches that held the recessed cannon batteries, and in the front the barrel of an unfamiliar weapon, in addition to four more forward cannons. At the rear, the propellers were within a box frame, which probably protected them from the fate of the propellers of the *Silver Huntress*.

Apart from some stains of rust along the body, the *Warbird* was an impressive looking ship. Additionally, from a distance, it did not look entirely like a warship. He wondered if that was by design, or if that was a modification on the part of the pirates.

Booth was brought back to the moment by a chuckle from Childs. "Impressed with my ship?"

"She's a beauty."

Childs glanced up towards the airship. "She's one tough old bird. When we found her, she was a rusted hulk, only barely flight worthy. Porter stumbled across her quite by accident when his first airship, the *Firebird*, was damaged, and hiding in the top of the cloud."

"So you used your old ship to repair the *Warbird*?"

"Porter, myself, and my old assistant worked for days to cobble together the old warship from what we had on the *Firebird*. But in the end, it was more than functional...and we deflated the balloon and dropped the *Firebird* below the clouds."

"You were with Porter a long time?" he asked.

"He was my captain for two years on the *Firebird*, and two more on the *Warbird*. When he died...the *Warbird* became mine, six months ago."

"How did he die?"

"It was a stupid accident," she remarked. "He and his first mate were awaiting the arrival of one of our biplanes. When it docked, somehow it shook things weird...and the catwalk they were on gave out from under them."

Booth looked towards the cyborg in the lead. "You're certain that was an accident?" he asked quietly.

Childs followed his gaze. "I am. I told him more than once I was uncertain about that particular set of gantries. There was a lot of rust, and they were not as stable as they should be. He was always headstrong...and paid for it."

"What in the clouded skies did you hit us with, anyhow?" Graham questioned, stepping towards them. "My teeth are still rattling, and it's been days."

"We found and salvaged an energy weapon. A lightning gun," Childs remarked. "It took everything I had, but I managed to get it functioning. Didn't you notice that most of the floors on the *Warbird* are rubberized?"

"That has to use an immense amount of power."

"We can fire it once every four days," Childs admitted. "We've never fired a full-powered shot, since it would probably overload the gun."

"So how did you wind up captain?" Booth asked.

Childs looked towards Lynch again. "It was a matter of authority and the whim of the remaining crew. Lynch made a claim, but I was chief engineer, and to all intents and purposes, second mate. As such, I assumed command. Lynch was aware that many of the crew were not comfortable following him, but I made him first mate to keep the peace."

Booth watched the crew as they walked along the street. "They seem to follow him just fine now, captain."

Childs made no response to that.

They continued on in silence. The streets of Cy-Ondon were nothing unusual. Before they were abandoned, there would have been bicycles and rickshaws and people all over them. The roads were pitted here and there, sometimes simply with age, other times with obvious destruction wrought by man.

It was eerily quiet, except for the sound of their passing, and the whistle of the shifting breeze at it passed through long abandoned buildings. As they made turns from time to time, Booth observed that the water vapor of the clouds had caused only slight erosion over the centuries.

At last, they reached a point where the road opened up into a half-shell structure with two wide doors, gilded in bronze and copper.

As they neared, Lynch and Childs both stepped up, examining the structure. Both began to pry apart panels, seeking the power and control circuits. They exposed gears and sprockets and wires and similar parts, checking to see if they could get the doors to open.

"I believe the car is up, and behind the doors," Childs stated.

"We need to get these doors to open, not pry them and cause damage," Lynch said.

"Bring me the engine, there is no power here."

Kek, a non-practicing Orcerician, and CL wheeled the engine up towards the elevator. Childs was examining the controls that had been exposed. She began to pull wires and connect the engine to the long abandoned elevator shaft.

Booth looked around to see if the pirates were distracted or paying too much attention to their captain – but they weren't. A trio of pirates, guns in hand, were keeping an eye on the crew of the *Silver Huntress*. Escape was not currently an option.

Childs was playing with the engine, and in a few moments she powered it on. At first nothing happened, but then lights inside the exposed control panel lit up.

Lynch pulled a lever...and with a groan, the pair of doors slid slowly open. The car had a metallic floor, and the walls were bronze and copper. The smell of long trapped air, metallic and cold, escaped.

Everyone looked on in silence.

"I don't think we should all descend in there," Childs remarked. "It would be best to make certain it can get us both there and back again."

"One of them should go," pointed Lynch.

Childs looked over the crew of the *Silver Huntress*. "Not alone. Lynch?"

The cyborg grunted and pointed at Gwen. "You come with me."

"No," Booth interrupted. "I'll go."

Lynch was about to say something when Childs stated, "Fine. Suit up, the both of you. Send the elevator back when you reach the bottom. If all goes well, the rest of us will join you."

Lynch stepped into the car of the elevator, buttoning up his duster. Booth looked once more to his crew, and joined the enormous man, pulling the hooded cowl on. He dropped the goggles down over his eyes, and put on his breathing mask and gloves.

"Good luck," Childs said.

"If I do not return – take care of my crew," Booth stated. His voice sounded unfamiliar through the breathing mask.

Lynch chuckled, reached out to the lever, and closed the doors. Then he looked to the other lever, and turned it.

There was a groan, followed by a series of screeches and pops. A few more moments of odd sounds, and the elevator car began to descend.

"Scared?" Lynch asked, his voice taking a metallic tinge through the breathing mask.

"No, should I be?" Booth chided him.

Lynch just chuckled ominously.

The elevator began to speed up, but not in an uncontrolled free-falling manner. There was a rattling sound as the car descended, and the hum of its motor. No words were spoken as Lynch kept his non-mechanical hand unnecessarily on the rotating lever.

Booth contemplated if he could knock out the cyborg somehow, but between his lack of a weapon, and the fairly large difference in size between then, he didn't believe this would be possible.

He felt his ears pop, and yawned behind his mask to correct

that. After five minutes, the elevator car began to shiver slightly, and seemed to reduce speed. Soon it was perceptible that they were slowing down. With a terrible grinding noise, the car came to a halt.

Booth looked to Lynch, who returned the lever to its original position.

Lynch gestured to the door. "Go ahead. Open it up."

Booth reached forward, and pulled the lever. He then switched on the lantern he carried and waited, a mix of excitement and tension.

For a moment it seemed that nothing would happen. But then, slowly, the doors opened.

It was, unsurprisingly, raining. Visibility through the rain, Booth guessed, was less than ten feet, though with a harder look you could see further through the droplets. But what he saw was a bit of a surprise.

Before the elevator was a cement platform. From the platform were a trio of roads, each made of a dark material Booth was unfamiliar with. Just past the platform, between the roads were trees and bushes covered in greenery.

"Apparently the flora has adapted to the poison," he said aloud.

"Trees," Lynch breathed, unable to hide his excitement.

Since the people of Amasheer had taken to life above the clouds, wood was among the most rare of commodities. In fact, the coin of the world was made of wood, special hardwoods maintained and guarded by the Maju-Orcericians. Wood was an incredible treasure. If they could harvest some of the trees, they would have a fortune on their hands. Let alone anything else they came across.

Lynch tapped the radio headset in his ear. "Captain? Elspeth? Yeah...signal is poor...we're down. See if you can retrieve the car."

Booth watched as the doors slowly closed. He heard the creaking and rattling as the car began its ascent back up the shaft. He glanced up, and was amazed at what he saw.

The elevator shaft was a long metallic tube that ran from the ground as far up as he could see. It was a fairly wide tube, gleaming green copper from centuries of rain. It seemed to stretch up forever, vanishing in the cloud.

Then Booth realized the most unusual thing about the world below the cloud. It was light. And that was because the bottom of the perpetual cloud glowed.

The light was dim, but constant, and clearly enough for the growth of the rich plant life around them. Booth noticed streaks of lightning across the glowing clouds above from time to time. It was beautiful, but eerie.

Lynch gave him a slight shove. "Stay where I can see you. Don't think about running."

Booth switched off the lantern, and looked around at his surroundings. Between the rain, the dim light, and the unfamiliarity, running seemed like a bad idea anyhow.

He couldn't smell the air through his breathing mask, nor was he feeling much of the rain between his goggles and hood. But his skin was crawling, and he had a sense of discomfort. He was standing on the surface of Amasheer, where no one but a very few had tread in over eight centuries. *Which is greater here*, he wondered, *the danger or the potential lost treasures?*

Lynch was walking around the platform, clearly trying to look down the roads, keeping his armed mechanical arm pointed towards Booth at all times.

After just over ten minutes of waiting, Booth was feeling completely soaked, even though the duster and hooded cowl were keeping his skin mostly dry. But the sound of the car faintly came to him, and then there was a terrible grinding noise as the elevator car arrived.

The door opened, and twelve figures emerged, dressed similarly in the rainproof dusters, hooded cowls, breathing masks and goggles. Eight had various weapons, which Booth knew to be the pirate crew.

"Who did you leave up top?" Lynch asked.

Booth was able now to identify Childs by her metallic, muffled voice through the breathing mask. "Kek and CL. They know enough about the engine to keep an eye on it and make sure it runs so we can get back up."

"Nothing apparent down this road," Lynch stated, pointing his good arm. "Ahead we have what looks like a city. Over there we have what appears to be something industrial."

Childs nodded her head. "The trees alone would be worth harvesting. But we didn't bring tools for that. Maybe another trip down. Let's see what they had going in this industrial space you've spotted, see if there is something we can take back up now."

"Agreed," Lynch said. He looked back to the elevator. "We leave someone here?"

"No," Childs said, looking around them. "Close the doors, and let's keep together."

"Dog," Lynch addressed the pirate closest to the elevator, still.

As the door was closed, Booth looked to his crew. Gwen was the shortest there, and Andrew was the largest after the cyborg. He could just make out the darkness of Tarik's cheeks under the hood, leaving the last unarmed person to be Graham.

"Lynch, you're with me in the middle, as well as Booth's Orcerician and Barnes," Childs ordered. "Dog, take Bishop, Salter, and Booth's big guy and bring up the rear. Booth, you and the rest of your people take the lead. Jack, Cork, Petty, just behind them, and shoot if they try to run."

Gwen and Graham stepped to Booth's left and right respectively, and as they began down the road the pirates followed.

"We're in deep, Captain," said Gwen as quietly as she could through the breathing mask.

Booth didn't say anything. He was fascinated by the greenery along either side of the road, as well as the odd material of the road itself. The surface was smooth and wet from the perpetual rain, but not slick beneath his feet. It was, curiously, in amazingly good repair, considering centuries of rain. The only sounds were the fabric of his cowl against his body as he moved, and the impact of the raindrops.

As he tried to calculate the immense value of all the wood around them, something to his right caught his eye, and Booth froze in his tracks.

"What is it?" Childs questioned.

Booth turned. "I could have sworn I just saw someone."

"You're seeing things," Lynch sneered. "Keep moving. We're the only living animals down here."

Saying nothing further, they continued on. But more than once Booth was certain he saw the shadows of other people out there, moving in the rain, between the trees. It was disturbing.

As they walked further away from the elevator, Booth could not help but feel his skin crawl, and sense they were being watched.

Graham hissed. "Damn!"

"What?" Booth asked.

"I'm sure I just saw someone out there," Graham stated softly.

"Glad I'm not the only one," Gwen remarked.

There was an unusual noise, like a wet slurping, along with the sound of skin slapping against skin from behind the group. Booth and the others turned immediately.

Lynch, Childs and the rest of the pirates had their weapons up. The quartet who had been bringing up the rear were not there anymore.

"What's this cack?" Lynch demanded angrily. He turned to Booth, pointing his mechanical arm. "What did you have your man do?"

"Seriously?" Booth responded. "Nothing. He was surrounded by three of your crew, all armed. What could he do?"

"Where are they?" the pirate called Barnes questioned.

"Dog? Salter? Bish?" Childs called into the rain.

Booth looked into the woods, but he saw nothing

Lynch went to the back of the group, and pushed at something with the toe of his boot on the ground. He bent down, and picked up something in the pincher of his mechanical hand. He held it up to examine it himself, before holding it out for the others to see.

A pair of goggles, the left lens cracked, just like those they were each wearing. If Booth didn't know better, he would have thought the cyborg looked uncomfortable.

"Well, if they're gone...they're gone," Lynch stated.

"Gone where?" the pirate called Barnes asked.

Lynch tossed the goggles away, and spread his arms wide.

"Where? Doesn't matter. Maybe they all chose to run off together."

"Perhaps we should double back, start to look for them," Childs mused.

"We're here now," Lynch remarked. "We should keep going."

"Captain Childs?" Tarik asked. "We've lost a man, too. Something is wrong with this. I don't think Andrew would have made any sort of deal with your men. We should look for them, then go back up to the cloud."

Childs shook her head. "No, Lynch is right. We go on. Let's not start jumping at shadows. We need to see what else is here."

She tapped the right side of her cowl, where she must have had a headset. "Kek? Kek? Can you hear me? If the elevator comes up before I contact you again, disable whomever steps off it, and send it back down. Copy? Very good." Childs tapped the headset again, and turned her attention to Booth and company. "Stay closer together, everyone...and let's go."

"Maybe it would be better to go back," Barnes, said, shifting his feet. "We don't belong down here. We should leave while we still live to tell the tale!"

"No," Childs stated. "We have come this far. The complex is just up ahead. We stick together, and see what is there. We might have the greatest score anyone has ever made!"

"We won't survive!" Barnes exclaimed. "We need to go before none of us make it back! What in the cloudy skies happened to them? How long until we suffer a similar fate?"

"Calm down, Mister Barnes," Childs ordered. "We close up our ranks, and we continue together."

"No!" Barnes cried. He began to run back the way they had come.

Captain Childs raised her pistol, and fired two shots. Two loud hiss-pop noises filled the air as the compressed gas expelled the bullets. Both connected, and Barnes dropped to the ground.

"No more of this!" Childs ordered, turning back to the others. "Close it up, and move!"

No one spoke as they continued towards the industrial buildings. They were grouped together, keeping about an arms length apart. Booth found that the sensation of being observed had lessened, but not gone.

As the facility in front of them became more distinct, the road began to descend. Soon a pool of water stood at the road's edge.

Booth waded in, Gwen and Graham remaining at his side. The water continued to rise, until it was just above Booth's knees.

The structure ahead was the crumbled remains of two or three square buildings. To one side of them stood a bunch of squat, round white buildings of some sort, which looked more solid. Among them were a number of tower structures, metal frames rusted red and orange and brown by centuries of exposure to rain and wind. But they were still whole, with broken pieces hanging oddly.

"We should head towards those," Childs said, pointing to the round structures. "They look to me like storage of some kind."

"After all this time, shouldn't they be in as bad shape as these?" questioned Graham, pointing to the tumbled remains.

"Hard to say," remarked Gwen. "The rain isn't entirely natural, after all. But you would still think eight centuries of erosion would leave more of a mark on the road as well."

Booth and the pair with him altered their course, and made their way through the water towards the cylindrical buildings.

As they got nearer, Booth observed that the buildings were quite a bit taller than they had seemed at the distance. There were stains of rust at various points along the metal, not visible against the white cylinders from the distance. Yet they were still far more whole than he would have thought possible after so much time.

Booth noticed a raised platform, and a pipe emerging from the side of the nearest structure, with a wheel at its side. "Over there," he said, pointing.

The group made their way to the waist high platform. Booth, Gwen and Graham climbed upon it, and stood before the large, wide metal spigot.

"Join them," Lynch said, giving Tarik a shove. Booth's Orcerician first mate ascended the platform now.

"Help me get this open," Booth ordered. Together they fought the long rusted valve, putting all the strength they could into it. Finally, it began to give, and turn.

At first nothing happened. But then a thick, sludgy black liquid started to seep out.

"Well?" Childs asked.

Booth turned. "Oil."

The pirates began to chuckle. Childs stepped closer to the platform. "Oil? Are you certain?"

"Yes," Booth said, placing a pair of gloved fingers below he trickle of black fluid, then showing that to the pirates. "It's definitely oil."

Oil was a very rare commodity indeed. The entire supply for the world above the clouds was the remains that had been brought from the world below, long ago. The very limited amount of oil the people of Amasheer knew was highly prized, and if used, was largely used in explosive devices.

Captain, Tarik's voice in Booth's head almost made him start. Only once or twice before had Tarik used the telepathic ability Orcericians were gifted with to communicate with his friend. *Don't react...but this platform is covered in rubber. I have an idea. Crouch down and stay away from the wall when I say so.*

Booth had an inkling about what his friend might do. But the actions of the pirates distracted him.

Lynch had Jack, Cork and Petty in a semi-circle around him. He raised his mechanical arm towards Childs.

"Well, Captain...I believe we have no further need of you... or them," Lynch said.

Childs faced him. "You're really going to mutiny? Now?"

You could almost hear the grin on Lynch's face as he spoke through the mask. "These men are mine, and Graves can handle Wat. We've found a fortune here, between the wood and oil. I think the time has come for a new leader of this crew."

Behind the pirates, movement caught his eye, and Booth noticed something even more disturbing. A half dozen figures had appeared. They stood silently, in colorless, hooded rubbery cloaks. Beneath those they appeared to be clothed with some kind of duster.

In the dim light, Booth could only just make out that they wore some sort of dark mask, with an air filter grill and round goggles of weathered brass. The way they had simply seemed to appear, and stood stone still, unnerved him.

"I always knew I couldn't trust you," continued Childs, showing no fear, not even dropping her weapon. She did not appear to notice the figures behind the pirates and Lynch. "You bastards are going to stay with him?"

None of them moved, except to raise their weapons towards Childs and the crew of the *Silver Huntress*.

"Greater share of the treasure for all," Lynch stated. "We are all going to be very rich men. And you are unnecessary."

Booth felt an odd tingling in the air, and knew what was coming. The cloaked figures made no move closer.

"Goodbye, Elspeth," Lynch said.

Now! cried Tarik's voice in Booth's head at that same moment.

Reacting instantly, Booth grabbed Childs and hauled her onto the platform.

A bolt of lightning dropped from the sky, touching the water right next to Lynch. He and the pirates all froze in place a moment, before an incredible boom and a blinding flash almost knocked Booth unconscious.

Booth was down on the platform, holding onto Childs, as the crash of thunder faded away. He turned to look out across the water.

The cyborg was frozen in place. He was completely stiff, and the glass of his goggles was blown out. He had been electrocuted in the lightning strike, and was unquestionably dead. The rest of the crew were nowhere to be seen, likely down, under the knee-high water. The cloaked figures were absent as well.

Booth took hold of Childs' pistol before she could act. He looked to his crew, and saw they were all there, alive, though Tarik was doubled over.

"Tarik!"

The Orcerician held up a hand. "It's...alright, captain," he gasped. "Just...gonna need...a moment."

Childs was rising up now. "You left me alive."

Booth did not point the pistol at her, but held it in a manner that she would know he was aware of how to use it. "I did. And I hope I don't regret that. Follow my lead, or I'll leave you down here." Childs nodded her head affirmatively in reply. He addressed his crew. "We need to get out of here. Now."

"Should we take any of this?" Gwen asked, gesturing around.

"If we could do so easily," Booth replied. "But I think we have already pressed our luck far enough. We are not alone down here. We need to get topside while we still can."

They dropped off the platform, moving past the creepy spectre of Lynch standing still as stone, fried to the place he had taken his last breath. Tarik seemed to have recovered as they moved through the knee-high water, back towards the elevator.

"I don't think anyone but us saw them, Captain," Tarik told Booth quietly as they waded through the water. Booth didn't care to respond.

No one commented when they passed where Barnes' body should have been. It was gone. They did start to walk faster, and reached the elevator without incident. They paused only a moment while Gwen tore a dead branch of wood off a tree. The elevator's car was still there.

"Elspeth, call your men up top," Booth ordered. "Let them know not to attack us, or you stay down here."

Childs nodded her head, then reached up to her ear. "Kek, do you read? The elevator about to come up is us, copy? Very good."

They stepped into the lift, closed the door to the surface, and began to ascend.

"Keep your gear on," Booth instructed to the others. "I am sure Kek and CL are both Lynch's. "

They were all silent for the remainder of the ride to the top of the clouds.

The elevator slowed, and stopped. The doors opened, and Booth stepped out first.

"What did you find?" asked Kek, nearest to them.

"Come here and see," said Booth, gesturing toward the interior of the car.

As Kek stepped near, Booth used the butt of the pistol to bash him on the back of his head. The Orcerician pirate dropped to the ground, unconscious.

"Hey!" CL cried, but Gwen slammed the branch into his face, knocking him down and out.

Booth took Kek's rifle, and also removed the pistol he had carried. He passed the rifle to Gwen and the pistol to Tarik as Graham disarmed CL. "We have to get back to the *Warbird*. I want to get out of here before they wake up, or anyone follows us up here."

No one commented as they began to walk away, removing the cowls, goggles, and waterproof dusters.

"There are still two on the ship," Gwen remarked.

"We'll deal with them when we get there," Booth replied.

"You needn't worry about Wat, he's loyal to me," Childs stated. "Graves is another story."

As Tarik removed his hood, Booth could not help but notice the new streak of grey that ran along the right side of his dreadlocks. He knew it was a choice his friend would have to live with.

Not another word was said as they made their way along the streets towards the dock where the *Warbird* floated.

They boarded the airship and began to look about cautiously for Wat and Graves.

As they rounded a corner, they found Wat, leaning against the bulkhead with his arms crossed. Graves was lying at his feet, eyes wide open, unquestionably dead.

"Watkins Hugh Martin was attacked," Wat said, referring to himself in the third person, as was his way. "That was unacceptable. Watkins Hugh Martin presumes the rest of the crew and Lynch are gone?"

"Yes, they are," Childs replied. She looked at Booth. "What happens now?"

"I have concerns about what found *us* down there. We may have found more than just a way to the surface. We need to shove off."

"What about Wat and I?" Childs questioned.

His own crew would also be awaiting his answer. "Wat, I

suspect, will be happy to join us if we continue to provide him room, board and pay. Am I right?"

Wat grinned. "Just so. Watkins Hugh Martin is yours, Captain."

"What about me?" she persisted

"You have two choices, Childs Elspeth Rachel," Booth stated. "We leave you here to find your own way. Or...you join us and become a member of my crew."

"Your crew?" she asked.

Booth gestured to the bulkheads. "You are, by all evidence, a genius engineer. You know this ship better than anyone else. And...I don't think you really wanted to be captain in the first place."

"What makes you think you can trust me?" Childs asked.

"Your love for this ship," Booth said. "More than you care about being captain. You will want to help us keep her in the skies. That I trust."

Childs put her hands on her hips, looking around at the bulkheads of the *Warbird*. She began to nod her head. "Yes, alright. I'll join your crew...Captain."

"Tarik, head for the bridge, take the helm, and get us out of here while we get this boat undocked," Booth ordered.

"She's going to need a new name," Tarik remarked.

"That she will," Booth agreed. "The *Warbird* has a terrible reputation. Any thoughts?"

"Considering how we managed to wind up here, captain," Gwen commented, "I think *Thunderbolt* would be apropos."

MJ Blehart has become quite enamored of the world of Steampunk. This story is only the beginning. For a closer, more detailed look at the society and technologies of the world of Amasheer, please visit www.vaporrogues.com. MJ is a writer, blogger, and sci-fi and fantasy geek extraordinaire. MJ is also an active member of the Society for Creative Anachronism, where you may have met him in the fencing lists or at a Pennsic War as Don Malcolm Bowman. For more information about the author, and examples of other works of his, please visit www.mjblehart.com

The Goddess Clause

A.D.R. FORTE

The boy's name was Rohnar, but he went by boy mostly. Except for when they called him *dhjal*, which meant son of a goat and was the very lowest form of insult, rivaled only by son of a sow. But he didn't pay much attention to the names unless there was a beating involved, and those he managed to avoid. Mostly.

Except for the days when the farmer he served drank a little too much or quarreled with his wife. Or the days the goats gnawed through their ropes and he had to go after them, spending all night in the colorless rocks and stinging nettles of the mountains beyond the farm until he could find and bring the errants home. Or the days it rained and the cold soaked into the bones of his feet and became agony.

But that was just life. Unfortunate occurrences were fated to all, as well as joy, said the priests. Some were born gold-clad lords. Some, like him, were born to obscurity and mud.

For a long time, he daydreamed that some priest or wandering magic user might find him, might reveal the history of a noble origin, a realm missing its rightful heir or perhaps a prophecy that demanded his skill and courage. He was ready to put down his crook and pick up sword or staff at a moment's notice. Such were the comforts of not knowing one's parentage.

But instead of priest or sorcerer he was given Nayla the gossip. She clucked her tongue and shook her head the moment she laid eyes on him.

"Come here, come here, boy. So this is Mella's boy. Poor Mella. Too beautiful to die so young, but there's no good to come of beauty. Put your chin up, boy. Strong chin, yes. Potential there, you know," she told the farmer's wife, wagging her greasy head. "Pity your father was a thief and your grandfather no better."

So much, then, for any hope of secret destiny. It made him angry. And then it made him determined.

When he'd earned out his service bond, he left the farm and found his way to the narrow, smelly, bustling streets of the coast city filled with the incessant noise of human and dog and seagull voices, the creak of wood and the sigh and whistle of wind.

He found a ship with ease. There were always plenty of those in need of strong arms and quick ears to understand orders barked over the slap of sail and rigging. He sailed away, never looking over his shoulder to study where he had been.

For in his case, the path behind had nothing to teach.

"Captain, Captain! Wake up, Captain!"

The unmistakable rasp and squeak that broke through his slumber belonged to his first mate. Not many in the world had such a voice, gods be thanked.

The man who'd once been a boy called Rohnar and various other things, who'd once tended goats and endured beatings, sat up and swung his legs off the ship bench, the smooth, controlled motion seemingly impossible for a man just risen from sleep. Like a lynx ready to pounce, they said when they talked of him.

Cilhala – The Sea Lynx.

That's what he'd named the ship after he cut off the head of the naval officer and taken her for his own sea-bride. Sleek and fast, with a set of the navy's newest, lightest guns that could fire with half the normal powder, she was more cobra than lynx. And her captain's reputation had grown from merely fearsome to formidable to the nature of those things whispered of by the kind of men who didn't admit to fear.

"I'm awake, Thay. What worries you, my friend?" He looked at the man before him, whose broken voice belied his thick arms and thicker neck. He'd first found Thay with the wrong end of a rope twined around that neck, from which he'd promptly delivered the first mate. At the time he hadn't been thinking of blood debts, but such things were handy to a man in his profession. Thay's loyalty over the years had in no small part aided the legend of the Sea Lynx.

He was glad too of Thay's excitable nature, of his unquenchable, enamored joy with existence. The captain of the *Cilhala* often found himself lacking in joy, and at such times it helped to have Thay around. Although that was not something he would say to anyone, even the first mate.

The captain must be the compass that guided the ship. Without it, they were adrift in fog and terrible things happened to men in such situations. They saw demons and fool's gold, and grasped after the phantoms with bloody, rebellious knives. Still, there were days... gods, there were days he missed the fucking goats. They, at least, never did more than get lost. They didn't plot, or rebel, or betray. The goats didn't care about the shade of his skin was or whether his father had been a drunk or that he broke some fat lord's law.

But Thay was talking, arms flying in every direction like a whore's skirt in a gale, and he had to pay attention.

"... a day's journey, no more. Maybe less at this wind. I tell you, Captain, true or not true never in my days have I seen such a thing through a 'glass."

He frowned, resisting the urge to rub his fingers across his forehead. There was a slight pain settling itself there behind his eyes. He'd slept even less than usual the night before, pacing the deck and staring across a velvety, warm sea that seemed to chatter as it rolled away in the wake of the ship. He'd felt answering restlessness dance along his shoulders and his spine, and taken it as a sign. He expected anything from a naval destroyer to a summer storm, but the day had dawned like a golden embrace and as peaceful as a priestess. And after a morning of nothing, he'd risked a nap, fallen into dreams of walking through golden green trees as silent, no, more silent than the farm had ever been.

Until Thay's voice summoned him.

"What are you babbling about, Thay? What have you seen? Or not seen?" Fuck it. He rubbed his forehead.

Thay stared at him, and then shook his head. "Have you not been listening, Captain?"

He didn't reply. In silence they crossed the deck and Thay pushed the 'glass into his hand.

"The rocks, Captain. Look."

It didn't even take a 'glass to see the shoreline in the distance. Jagged peaks the color of charcoal tore the clear blue, unfurled like a murderous ribbon against the horizon, seeming to move and shift as they watched. Now a strip of sand might obscure a dark angle, then a moment later the charcoal would swallow the gleam of sun on sand like a greedy animal catching prey.

"Black as night," came Thay's voice at his side, barely a rasp.

The Black Coast, said to be a land where the gods walked. No one had charted it, for it shifted like the waters from one moment to another.

More likely, he thought, because you couldn't chart what didn't exist.

For a breath he felt the restlessness of the night before like a shimmer in the air, a low hum just out of hearing, but he ignored it. Destiny was won with sword and sense, and nothing else. He lowered the 'glass and grinned at Thay.

"Shall we go ashore then?"

Thay put on his best manner of scolding, as he invariably did when perceiving a lack of sincerity in his commander.

"Captain, I'm not a man given to idle wonder..."

"Then there's nothing to stop us, is there?" Rohnar grinned wider as he watched consternation war with doubt in the other man's face.

"Before you, my friend, is indeed a wonder of the gods. The very bowels of the earth belched up and cooled at the fount of the sea, creating black monsters." He clapped the first mate on the shoulder and handed him the 'glass. "But, I fear, no magic in this, Thay."

In the space after his words the call of a seabird echoed across the wind. Was it affirmation or denial?

Rohnar shook the thought away. He was captain, and a man of knowledge and science. Or at least so they thought him.

He'd wrung what he could from odd books he gathered over the years. Stolen, or bought with the money that other men would have spent at the tavern or the brothel. A captain was expected to be different from other men in one way or another, and the Lynx's reputation lay as much in his ability to read as in the terror of his sword. No one living in the world knew or remembered that a ship's doctor had once, many a year before, taken pity on a goat-boy and taught him the mystery of letters and numbers.

He frowned. Thay's Black Coast had suddenly blurred, as if it noticed their attention and had decided to hide. The sky too had transformed itself, turning from strident blue to soft, coy, like a girl shedding a dress, and a gust of wind in his face brought Rohnar the sweet smell of rain.

With one accord, the two men moved, barking orders with the authority of practice. The noise of the ship, sail and rigging, booted feet across the deck, and the chaos of voices drowned out thoughts. For that, he was glad. He didn't like the direction his had taken.

Better to keep occupied, to keep moving. Having to think about wind and speed and the sharp teeth of those rocks would fill his mind. Keep memories at bay. But the rain didn't increase. And they sailed into a bay between the black arms of two giants in a steady, gentle drizzle of grey.

First went the scouting party, cutlasses at the ready, more from habit and discipline than any need, for the stretches of pale sand turning to dark rock lay empty in every direction as far as the eye could see. This place offered no terrain for concealment, no chance for surprise. Only rocks striped with runnels of clear water where they filled their canisters and containers and washed faces rough from weeks of salt-spray. Some wandered off in search of game. Some stretched skins between outcroppings and slept in the shade of the dark guardians.

He himself came ashore last, leaving the ship empty. And he wondered at this bending of his own rules even for a land so forsaken. The Lynx never took risks, never assumed the best. But, he told himself, they'd been at sea many a week and the bay was small. He'd post a guard before nightfall, if they even stayed so long. There looked to be nothing of use here but fresh water...

Sand crunched under his feet, but he hardly noticed it. Sound filled his ears as if he faced headlong into a wind, roaring and whistling. Obliterating the world around him with its ferocity. Then like a door slammed shut, the roar vanished, replaced by the sound of water and ordinary wind, men's voices and the cries of birds.

It would not do to show weakness, to stumble and draw attention to the beads of sweat trickling chill down his face as his heart pumped furious and panicked. He stood, arms akimbo, and surveyed the ebony faces of the cliffs as he tried to find the accustomed pace of his breath again. The drizzle had stopped, but clouds still hid the face of the sky, cool and still. And against the blanket of grey something high, high up at the very top of one saw-tooth summit flashed and sparkled like light caught on a mirror or a jewel. Then gone. In an instant. Like the noise.

And like his sanity, apparently.

He looked around for Thay or for his second mate to issue some order, some meaningless thing that would ground him in reality once again. To confirm, if nothing else, that he still had the power of speech.

He looked again. And his heart began to thud in the way it did when he faced a sword point aimed at his throat. Only worse. Far worse. He understood swords. What they could and couldn't do. He feared swords because man fears his own mortality, not for the nature of the weapons themselves.

But the empty beach that met his gaze— empty as if no man had ever set foot on it, the sand smooth and undisturbed by footprint or backside-print or the prow of the ship— held a threat he did not fathom, that he couldn't begin to comprehend. Nausea threatened, as it hadn't for many, many years. Not since the boy who would be the Lynx had become a man.

Because it was comforting, his hand went to the hilt of his sword. But there it stayed. For how did one wield a sword against a foe that snatched men out of existence and erased all trace of their passing? In fact, where did one even find such a foe to face it?

He waited, readying himself for what might come next. Death he could face, but something inside told him that was not to be his fate this day. He clenched his jaw and then his fingers. The sword might be useless but given the chance, he would have the comfort of knowing he'd met his doom with a fight.

Given the chance.

Soft, the wind brushed his face. Offering comfort, he imagined. And then shivered at the thought. Even the wind was more than wind, possessed of a mind of its own. Though it made no sense, he stared about him. He knew without knowing that to find the source of the wind would be to find the heart of this place, the soul behind the dark faces above. Instead, it was movement that caught his gaze. Real movement, of living, breathing beasts and not phantoms. There was no mistaking the spindly legs and sleek bodies that came hurtling across the rocks with the precision of arrows, bounding from outcrop to outcrop, skipping rivulets and cracks with effortless, comical grace. And without meaning to, he exhaled, felt his face relax into something that might be the beginnings of a smile.

The goats raced towards the beach, bleats pinging in bell-like staccato off the cliffs. As they caught sight of the human in their path, they veered, hooves flashing into a blur, tails pointed and ears flopping. They passed him barely a handsbreadth away, so close flying sand from a myriad of hooves whooshed against his boots, dusting the tops with a layer of greyish-white. Bleating voices familiar as those of his childhood. He might close his eyes and be transported in time to a country of dusty rocks and scrub-covered hills strewn with the odd pine. For a moment the smells of wood smoke and mud overshadowed the scent of brine, and the picture of thatched huts and tilled patches of dirt filled his inner eye.

He shook himself.

Once again he stood on an alien shore, alone and surrounded by the inexplicable. But there were the goats, a river of brown and black and eggshell white streaming off into the distance. Something brushed his leg, and a small, demanding bleat insisted on his attention. He looked down to see a bundle of downy black, a small black head topped with a patch of fuzzy white from which a pair of large, dark blue eyes peered up at him. Asking a silent question.

No, it wasn't a question. A diminutive, fearless black hoof landed squarely on his boot, refused to budge. It was an imperious, irresistible order, and this time the smile that had tried in vain for so long finally broke free.

The Lynx let go of the hilt of the sword that had killed a thousand men. He bent and scooped the warm, wobbly body into his arms as he had a thousand times before. The kid nestled down against his chest, at home as if it saw humans every day, and Rohnar scanned the cliff tops again, but nothing moved there except the wind in the scrawny trees just visible over the tops of the saw-teeth. The kid bleated, insistent, bumping the top of its head against his chin.

"All right, small one. I hear you."

He could see the tail end of the river just vanishing around the base of one giant, and he started after it at a trot. At a bump on his chin and an impatient bleat he quickened his pace, but as they left the beach the sand underfoot turned to powdery drifts. It sucked at his steps, sending him stumbling, panting as he raced to follow his quixotic guides to what destination he didn't dare imagine.

The sand gave way at last to rocky ground that sloped steadily upward, through hill faces cut by lean, twisted trees and uneven outcrops of rock, climbing up and up to the summit of the giant. The goats streamed across it, and he followed, urged on by the impatient bundle under his arm. Fiery pain burned down his legs and across his lower back. Keeping hold of the kid with one arm, he grasped at rocks and tree limbs to pull himself up when the trail sloped steepest, and after a while he left bloody handprints with every touch. Heat baked down through the clouds, a cloying, stifling hand pressing him down and back, making him fight for every step, every breath. But every time his steps faltered another bleat, another bump on his chin would send him stumbling on, gritting his teeth, cursing every goat ever born under the sun, but always up. And up. And up.

Blinding sweat dripped into his eyes and as he raised an arm to wipe them, his noisy burden wriggled, kicked him in the ribs, and jumped to the ground. He stopped and wiped his face, gasped air and coughed, and took stock of his bearings. The goats had disappeared but he heard them arguing amongst themselves and the rustle of grass under wind and hoof. Before him stretched a carpet of meadow dotted with pinks and purple thistles and the tiny blue flowers the country people called *gods-kiss*. Here, the wind ruffled strong and cool through his hair. He stood atop the giant.

There below, the *Cilhala* bobbed at anchor in the tiny bay, caught between the deserted beach and a pink and gold sunset under the clouds on the horizon. He took a few shambling steps forward and dropped to his knees, then his ass. A goat trotted by, nose down among the flowers, oblivious to his presence. With a sigh, he fell back into the soft grass. A green, sweet bed where he might happily sleep forever, he thought...

Cold light woke him. The nearly-full moon stared him in the face, and he realized he was thirsty. Deadly thirsty. As he thought it, he heard the unmistakable gurgle and trickle of water nearby. Slowly he pushed himself to one elbow and then two. That stream, bubbling up out of the rock near the cliff's edge hadn't been there before. Or had it? Honesty allowed, he didn't trust the state of his powers of observation before he'd fallen asleep. It might have existed, or not. That didn't stop him from drinking long and deep of the clear, cold water before he got to his feet.

He decided to stick to the cliff's edge. He might have been led here, but he had no mind to strike off into unknown country that couldn't be trusted to stay the same from one minute to the next. He could always trace his way back along the cliff and down. Or thinking so made him feel better, thus he would think it. He had little enough time to think it however, for no sooner had he gone a quarter of a mile than he saw something at the edge of the cliff.

Rather, he saw someone.

A woman. Painting.

He rubbed his eyes, just in case the light might have been to blame. But no. There she sat, palette in one hand, before her easel that somehow remained perfectly still in the night wind. In the moonlight her skin shone ivory and her hair lay unbound, a mass of tight pale curls down her back. The Northerners looked like that, skin leached of color and unnerving eyes the colors of sky and storm clouds. And their women ran wild, barefoot and unkempt and barbaric as the men. But just as the easel didn't fall or blow away, neither did she unnerve him.

She turned as he approached and smiled, and the moonlight caught a great, white jewel lying against her milky skin. Light on such a jewel, he thought, would sparkle from a great distance away. Except there had been no sun that afternoon.

"At last we meet, Cilhala." She didn't speak like a Northerner.

"At last?" he asked, and his voice croaked as if it hadn't been used in years.

She smiled again. "I have watched you a long time." She put the palette down and picked up a great book from her side. "Look."

He walked to where she sat, and she held up the book and opened it. The half-finished canvas on the easel showed a picture of a wind-tossed sea under a nearly-full moon. He looked away from it and took the book from her hands, if indeed it could be called a book. Canvas after canvas was bound together in place of pages.

And on each he found his own face.

He saw himself covered with the blood of his foes in the thick of battle. Locked in deadly struggle, teetering on the sword edge of death. Poring over books at a binder's marketplace stall or over ale in the smoky dark of a tavern. Standing alone at the prow of the *Cilhala* looking across a perfect blue sea. Each image gave him a memory, sharp with smell and sound and thoughts.

He closed it with a snap.

"Why?" he asked.

It was an impertinent question to ask for he knew now whom he faced. The Northerners called her Aegena, Lady of the Sea and the Moon. His own people gave her no name for their priests did not acknowledge her existence. But every sailor who braved the waves knew enough to offer a whisper of thanks for kind wind and tide to She who governed the waves.

"Forgive me, Lady," he amended. "But of what interest is the life of one such as I to you? I am not one of your disciples."

She laughed, a tinkling sound like the chime of the tiny silver bells dancing girls wore about their bellies and ankles. She took the book from his hands, set it aside and stood to face him.

"Are you not?" she asked. "Do I not heed your prayers every day for fair wind and full sail?"

"But..."

"You go by many names, Cilhala. Are you not the same man?"

"But my face does not change with my name," he countered, wondering at his own cheek even as he spoke.

She threw back her head as she laughed again, and he could see that her hair was not pale as he'd thought. It held a ruddy hue that promised softness. It made him want to touch it, to bury his fingers in it. He stopped the thought before it materialized. Madness enough to offer cheek to a goddess. He didn't need to make things worse with thoughts like that.

"There you have me, Cilhala. But you are a man and you and your mortal brethren cannot agree on the face I must wear. So, I wear many."

He rubbed the back of his neck. Sighed. "It is a terrible thing to undermine a man's faith and steal his crew all in one day, Lady." She only smiled, but her strange, pale eyes filled with light and the stone at her breast glowed with the moon's radiance.

"Your crew are safe." She pointed to a painting lying on the ground near the easel, and he squatted to look at it. He found a scene of the beach strewn with campfires and made out the swarthy frame of Thay silhouetted against orange flames that flickered and moved before his eyes. He heard Thay's raspy voice wondering if they should take the captain a slice of the boar roasting on a makeshift spit over the biggest fire.

"By rights, it should be one of us staying out on the ship to keep watch." Thay squinted at the dark bay where the *Cilhala* sat all but invisible. "I thought he'd have come ashore by now."

"You know the captain," answered another. "He has his moods. Rather be left alone. He'll be along when he has a mind."

"True."

The flames flickered again and he blinked, felt a cool hand on his cheek.

"They will wait for you," she said.

"How long must they wait?" he asked, fearing the answer.

"That is up to you." She stood and the wind caught the tendrils of her long, loose hair, sent it flying around her arms and face. "Come find me, Cilhala. I will wait for you too."

"Find you?"

The wind picked up, rustling the canvas at his feet,

threatening to send it flying.

"Why?" he demanded again, determined she should give him that much.

The wind nearly swallowed her voice. "Because too seldom do I see you smile, Cilhala. And I would have you smile."

He didn't have a chance to reply. The roar of wind and storm deafened him. The light of the moon blinded him.

"The moon is full in two days. I will expect you then. I will wait for you."

The words filled his mind, clear over the cacophony. Then all was silent again. He opened his eyes and took his hands that had been pressed over his face away. In the gentle moonlight, the black hide of the tiny kid glowed pale. But its imperious baa was just the same.

He shook his head and ran a hand through his hair. Got to his feet.

"I might have known. Very well then. Lead on, small one. And we will see what your mistress has in store for me."

They walked through the night. The meadow near the cliff gave way to a broad, unpaved road they followed until the sun rose dewy and humid into a washed-out blue sky. Other goats trotted beside them, bleating encouragement or perhaps gossip. Watching their antics took his mind off his exhaustion. Off the reason for their journey. He'd filled his waterskin at the spring the night before, but he didn't know the length of the goddess' path, and the sun didn't seem to care either way. It beat down without stopping, and he was just beginning to think he should worry when the path curved again and he heard the babble of running water.

They came upon the stream and the broken-down cart at the same time. The old man with the staff seated beside the cart looked up. It didn't take asking to know he was a magic user, even without the piles of oilskin-wrapped books loaded in the cart or the jewel set in the staff.

"Welcome, friend. Your coming is well timed."

This then was the first test.

He was angry, inside. Why should he follow the whims of a goddess? For her entertainment? What if he didn't follow her rules at all? What if he simply walked back to the cliff and leaped from it into air and nothing? And if she blocked the path back, his sword edge was still sharp. She couldn't get between him and his sword. The crew would eventually get tired of waiting and venture back to the ship, find him gone. They would sail away, and the legend of the Lynx would end in mystery. It would be fitting.

"But you will break her heart," the magic user said, as if he, Rohnar, had spoken aloud. And Rohnar found he longed to see her face again. Found he could not bear the thought of her laugh silenced, even for an instant of mortal time. Even if his pitiful mortal struggle and longing were to serve merely for her amusement.

So he rolled up his sleeves and unbuckled his sword belt, and spent the day fixing the broken wheel while the goats wandered around and got in the way. In the evening they ate yeasty bread with small, salted fish that the old man fried in an iron pot and drank bottled goat's milk from the stash in the cart. Then they stretched out under the trees and watched the stars fade into the sky.

"Have I passed?" he asked.

"Do you think you have?" the old man replied.

He closed his eyes. "I don't know. I know would have given my soul once to have met the likes of you. I dreamed of being a magic user's apprentice. Of having knowledge and power beyond reckoning."

"What would you have done with such knowledge?"

"I have no idea." He'd seen the lot of so-called magic users, soothsayers and charlatans entangled in politics, ridiculous in their fancy, flamboyant tunics and beholden to the will of fat lords. Real magic-users, if they existed, kept their existence to themselves. Traveled in silence like the grizzled old scholar beside him. He thought of the ship's doctor who'd taught him long ago, and the way his eyes always seemed to see through every word. Were magic users no more than ordinary men, leading ordinary lives but for the knowledge they carried?

A small nose at his elbow made him open his eyes. The kid fit itself under his raised arm, snuggled itself down against his side. He put his displaced arm under his head and looked at the leaves waving across the starry canopy overhead. He smiled at the idea of himself as the goat mage, wandering from farm to farm healing everything from foot rot to worms.

"Probably have found a charm to cure foot rot," he said.

"There are more books in that cart than you might read in a lifetime," said the old man. "You are welcome to them with my thanks."

"If I had a fine library I might accept your offer." The bitterness in his voice surprised him. "But a man in my profession can't carry more books than he can gunpowder and water." He closed his eyes and let the gentle snore of the kid lull him to sleep.

In the morning he parted ways with the magic user.

"Perhaps we may meet again," said the old man.

"Perhaps."

They shook hands and he watched the cart trundle off. Then he turned and followed his impatient guide who was already bleating and running in circles to indicate they should be off.

This time they followed the course of the stream, and it seemed they walked great, great distances though it could have been no more than a mile or two. The sun had barely crested the tops of the trees when they came upon the three maidens seated on the stream bank. All crying.

A confusion of sobs and fluttering veils greeted him, then a bristle of sword points from the escort of men at arms hovering near the three. He stopped and lifted his hands to show he meant no threat while his guide sidled puppy-like between his legs and stood still with warm flanks pressed reassuringly against his knees.

One of the three on the riverbank stood and pushed her way through the bristle, waving the swords away like flies.

She stood before Rohnar and lifted her veil. Of course she was lovely beyond words. But sorrow had reddened and swollen her pretty face and tears streaked the *kajal* around her eyes, drawing ugly black lines down her cheeks.

"Have you come to help us?" she said.

He thought about it a moment, and then nodded. No point in prolonging this nonsense. She too nodded, and turned to point at the stream. Here, it rushed frantic and violent between the banks as if fed by too many tears, foaming and roaring as it sped by. On the far bank a great house surrounded by a wall of stone overlooked the torrent.

"There," said the maiden. "There the ogre holds our father prisoner."

"And you wish me to kill the ogre and release your father."

She looked back at him and said nothing. He sighed.

"Very well." He looked at the river again. "I will help you."

The men at arms tied a rope to a tree and he tied the other end to his waist. He strung his boots about his neck, hoisted his sword and cutlass over his head, and stepped into the flood. The water tugged at him, getting under his footing and pounding him with a murderous fist. A silent voice whispered in his head. It urged him to give in, to stop struggling, let the water take him. He ground his teeth and thought of the old man's words again, thought of the maidens waiting on the bank, their faces marked by ebony claws of sorrow.

"What a weak-hearted fool I am," he grunted. But it crushed the voice's deadly whisper and he pushed on through the raging stream to the far bank and the ogre's house. There he scaled the wall of the back garden like a thief and found the ogre and his prisoner at prayer.

He contemplated them a moment from the shelter of a spreading tree at the top of the wall. The nobleman wore chains around his neck and feet and hands, and his face was drawn in the way of slaves who have lost all hope of freedom. Still, he was a lord. Concerned only with laws to swell his own coffers and damnation to any who might contest his greed. What was the use of freeing a man like that? Even if his daughters wept a river into flood.

But then, what was the use of anything? Might as well free this poor wretch as any.

With the arrogance of his kind, the ogre didn't expect attack in his own back yard. Certainly not while he was praying. But to the Lynx such delicacies didn't matter. He took advantage where advantage offered itself.

"Filthy little *dhjal*. How dare you challenge me?" the ogre bellowed, swinging a great iron club. "I'll feed you to my pigs!"

"Will you?" said the Lynx, and he turned and slid, brought his sword up beneath the ogre's arm, right into the armpit. The iron club went clattering and the ogre roared in anger. But the Lynx twisted away from the ogre's great grasping fist, took hold of the cutlass with both hands and plunged it deep into the small of the ogre's back. With the noise of a falling tree, the monster went down, and the Lynx picked up his bloodied sword and calmly, cleanly sliced off the head of his foe.

"Thank you," said the nobleman when his chains were removed. With his own hands he brought hot water steeped with fragrant leaves, and pristine cloths to wipe the blood from sword and cutlass and face. Cold, clean water to drink.

"Tell me your name, friend," he said. "For I owe you more than my life."

The Lynx looked at him and shrugged. "Some call me this and that. Once my name was Rohnar."

The nobleman smiled. "Well met then, Rohnar. I can see in your eyes you have no love for me, yet you have done me the greatest kindness one can do for another. You have restored to me both liberty and hope and I will not forget it. My daughters are beautiful. My lands more than one man can enjoy in fifteen lifetimes. Take my hand and any of my girls that you choose and I shall call you son and heir."

He looked at the nobleman's hand, worn with service to the ogre and thin with care, and he reached his own hand out before he could think too much about it.

"I take your hand gladly," he said. "And your daughters are fair beyond belief. But..." He hesitated. "They stir only my desire, and not my soul. And that is a bad basis for any marriage."

Despite his weakened state, the nobleman threw back his head and laughed long and richly. "Wisely said. And that makes me all the sorrier you will not take my offer. But my estates have no heart to break. Should you choose to claim them, your lands will be waiting for you, Rohnar. Our paths have crossed for a reason, and I will not be remiss in my side of this duty."

For a time then, Rohnar could say nothing and only stare. And had the nobleman not led them from the house and down to the stream that now ran quiet and merrily gurgling to itself, he might have sat staring longer still.

"Thank you" at last was all he could say, but the nobleman nodded and gripped his shoulder, and he knew it had been answer enough.

"Will you come with us and rest a while?" the eldest daughter asked. Joy colored her face now as she embraced her father and it felt a greater reward than land and wealth. But he shook his head.

"I have a journey I must complete." The sun had dipped once more groundwards, and he felt the prickle of urgency beneath his skin. The black kid stood quiet and docile, watching him. Offering no incentive for he no longer needed encouragement.

His heart led him now.

"At least let me give you a steed," said the nobleman, and one of the men led forward a beautiful gelding trapped in harness of the softest leather.

"Until we meet again," said the nobleman.

"Until then," he replied.

And he rode off, leaving nobles and goats and books and lands and ship all behind. Racing the sun so that he might find the moon.

It was late in the afternoon when he came upon the wood, and halted the horse at its border. Once more he felt as if he'd traversed many thousands of leagues, though he knew it impossible. But what was impossible for her?

He dropped to the ground and slipped loose the horse's halter, leaving the animal to find its way home if it would. Leaves of green and gold shone in the setting sun and waved softly in a gentle wind. Just as they had in his dream. Had it been but two days ago? It might have been lifetimes. He went forth with his heart in his mouth, and perhaps on his sleeve, and passed under the dappled canopy into the heart of the wood.

The light never grew less under the trees, and gold shafts of sunlight illumined his path until he gained the clearing. And found a white figure seated before an easel outside a tiny hut, paintbrush and palette in hand.

She rose and put her tools down as she saw him approach.

"You are early." But she smiled as she said it and all thought of what he himself meant to say fled from his mind.

"Yes. Here I am," he managed to blurt, as he stood before her. "And I have passed your tests."

Tinkling laughter swept over him like silk. "And have you won your heart's desire at last? Both a lord and a scholar now."

He felt his jaw clench. "Nay, lady. I have gained much through your kindness. But I have not won my heart's desire yet."

He took a step closer and reached up with both hands, knowing that his actions meant possibly death, possibly rather worse. But he hadn't fought the siren song of despair so long to give up now. Her own lessons had taught him that much. He pressed his palms to skin as pale as milk but soft as any woman's. As tremulous with sensation when he caressed the arch of her neck and brushed his fingers against the curls that shadowed it.

"Ah Cilhala. You have grown brave," she said, but her voice

came out a whisper, a timid hare about to take flight.

"Brave. Foolish. I cannot tell which."

"I should not. As a goddess," she said. But her lips were red as a bitten pomegranate, and gold light caught in the rosier gold of her hair. Circled the moon with fire.

"That is exactly why you should," he said. "Have you not taught me that even a goat boy can be a lord? Why should a goddess not..."

But the moon was full and he could think of words no more. He bent his head and pressed his lips to hers, and the sun fell down behind the trees, left the clearing bathed in the fiery silver light of the Lady who rules the seas.

Thay saw the figure walking up the beach first and sprang to his feet. But the words he'd been about to say died as the figure drew nearer and he caught sight of his captain's face. They said men who'd seen gods had that light in their eyes. Holy men who could walk across fiery coals or offer their arms to venomous serpents and suffer nothing at all. But silence had never been Thay's forte, even in the midst of awe.

"Captain?" he said. The captain turned and Thay looked into the eyes of the same man he'd known and fought with and bled with for many and many a year. He heaved a little sigh of relief. "The Most Revered be praised. We feared... we feared for you, sir."

The Captain reached up and gripped Thay's shoulder. "No need for that. I am returned and well. I..." For an instant the light flashed in his eyes again, so bright Thay blinked and had to look away. But then the moment passed. And his captain looked at the gathered, gaping crew and smiled.

"I am well. But..." He turned and glanced at the *Cilhala* across the bay. "I feel I'm of a mind to trade in my sea legs for something a bit more solid. Somewhere I can stand still and see the moon at night. The sea has given me all she can in this life." He looked at them all again.

"Wh... what do you mean, Captain?"

He smiled again, and clapped Thay's shoulder. "I've come into some good fortune, I'm afraid. Tell me, Thay, how do you feel about becoming a respectable man? I was thinking... I was thinking perhaps we could raise goats..."

ADR Forte is an author of short fiction. Her tales of romantic and erotic fantasy can be found in several anthology collections.

Anne Bonny's Child

Tera Fulbright

"'You'll be damned if ye give quarter, Mary!'"

The child sitting at the edge of my four-poster bed flinched and turned to look at me.

"What did you say, Grandmother?" My granddaughter curled her feet up beside her. Picking at the faded yellow lace coverlet, she looked at me, her eyes widened in surprise.

"You'll be dammed if ye give quarter! Those were the first words the ghost of Blackbeard ever said to me." I leaned back against my pillows, closing my eyes, remembering.

"The ghost of Blackbeard?"

"Yes, Anne. Long before your time, or even your mother's time, I used to sail the seas. And the ship I sailed upon was haunted by Blackbeard himself."

My granddaughter, a blue-eyed girl with curly blonde hair, was named after my mother. The child suddenly stopped her plucking and looked at me with the disbelief that only a 12 year old can display.

"You see, child, when I turned 16, your great-great grandfather he told me that he had arranged my marriage to some old man and so, like my mother; I ran away and joined a ship."

I kept a low profile for the first several years aboard ship, binding my breasts and cutting my hair. I swabbed the deck and loaded the cargo like any other sailor. It was not until fate intervened and the crew named me captain did Blackbeard first appear to me.

How did I, a woman, become captain, you wonder? It was a quiet day at sea when another pirate nearly captured the sloop I served upon. Some upstart scallywag thought that by attacking our ship, the *Morningstar*, he could add our crew to his. The battle aboard the ships had been fierce and deadly. As I looked around, a smoky haze drifted across the ship. I could see many of my fellow shipmates lay unmoving or moaning in agony as they clutched at bleeding wounds. I had shot or stabbed my own share of men and sustained wounds of my own. Blood dripped across my face from a painful gash across my forehead. Loose pistols, rapiers and spent bullets covered the wooden deck. As I watched, a pirate shot my captain at point blank range. When I saw the captain fall, his sword flying out of his hand to skid across the deck and land at my feet, I feared ending up back at the farm, married with screaming children. A whisper of a breeze brought the crisp, salty scent of the sea to me.

Wiping the blood away from my eyes, I reached down and picked up the sword. Shouting, yelling, screaming at the top of my lungs, I charged into the fray and attacked the bastard that shot our captain with both my dagger and the captain's bloody rapier. As I continued to exhort my fellow shipmates to fight, the tide of battle soon turned; it was our ship that forced the other to surrender. When the young pirate captain called for quarter, I heard Blackbeard's voice for the first time.

"*You'll be damned if you give quarter, Mary.*" I looked around for the voice but heard nothing. I followed the ghostly advice that day and threw the young popinjay overboard but accepted the surrender of his crew, adding them to our own.

The Ghost appeared to me that night after the men acclaimed me Captain of the *Rocinante*. Many said it was the sight of me fighting, the scarlet blood of my enemies covering me that encouraged them to continue the battle. Calling me Mary Scarlett, the pirates felt sure that I could lead them in battle and on to great rewards.

As I stood at the bow of the ship looking over what was now my crew, the Ghost appeared; a vision of terror, half-seen, half-unseen. I recognized him immediately. Growing up outside of Wilmington, where everyone knew of Blackbeard, he was easy to recognize. Hells, half the women in the red quarter claimed to have slept with him at the height of his power. Though I suspect that was more wishful thinking than truth, given that even I knew Maynard had killed Blackbeard in 1718, 22 years ago. The ghost still looked like legends painted the man – dark wild eyes with black braids in his beard and hair. Slow burning hemp reflected the setting sun and wisps of smoke surrounded his face adding to his ethereal appearance.

"Ye'll need more guns, if ye want to evade the hunters."

To this day, I am not certain why he chose me...unless the rumors were true and his ship, now my ship, was originally called the *Adventure*... the ship Blackbeard died upon. When I became captain, we re-named the ship the *Rocinante*, after the horse in the famous Spanish tale. I figured there was nothing wrong with naming a pirate ship captained by a 19-year-old girl after a story about a crazy man who tilted at windmills. Dreams were worth following. And I added more guns.

"*You'll be damned if ye give quarter!*" roared Blackbeard's Ghost at me, from his regular perch beside the ship's wheel. For three years, the Ghost had exhorted no quarter and for three years, I had rarely listened. A reputation I had gained but it was not nearly as bloodthirsty as his own was.

"*I know, I know. Shut up!*" I thought at the ghost. Aloud I said, "Fine, throw down your weapons and prepare to be boarded!"

The merchant ship I faced surrendered quickly and my men brought the captain before me. A typical merchant, the captain was dressed in fine calico and carried a well-made sword, which I noted showed no signs of wear. It didn't appear as if he had ever drawn the sword in battle.

Following in Blackbeard's steps, I tried to present an imposing presence. I was taller than most women, a legacy of Rackham, I suspected. Dressed in men's clothes, in the colors of black and blood scarlet, my swords and pistols by my side, I had been told that I appeared both beautiful and deadly. I wore my black hair in long braids beneath a wide brimmed hat with, again, scarlet trim.

"Kill him! The useless fop! Kill him!" urged the wild-eyed ghost.

I tried to keep my frustration out of my voice as I spoke to the merchant captain, "What ye be carrying?"

"Spices and silks from India," said the frightened man. His eyes darted this way and that as he grumbled the reply.

"Ah, good," I smiled. "Have your men move the cargo to my ship." I turned to my quartermaster, Wulf. "Have our men stow it below. We'll leave for Savannah immediately to sell it."

The merchant captain looked at me. "How is it you command this ship?" he asked. "You're nothing but a woman. Women don't belong at sea."

I laughed. "My mother did! And by all accounts did better than some of the men!"

"Now that was a woman I wish I'd met," Blackbeard said. *"I'd have liked to shown her what a real man was like. Not that coward Rackham."*

"Shut up." I thought at the ghost.

"Bah, I don't believe it. What whore birthed you?" asked the merchant.

My black eyes flashed as I drew my sword and placed its point at his heart. "Not a whore, ye bastard, but Anne Bonny. Mary Scarlett be my name, and I suggest you remember it."

The merchant gulped noisily and gave a short bow, not willing to argue with the point of my sword.

As Wulf escorted him back to his ship, I called out, "Oh, and add that worthless dog's sword to the pile."

After the cargo had been loaded, my crew threw off the boarding lines tying the ships together. As we raised our sails into the wind and turned the boat away, the merchant captain yelled after us, "You'd best enjoy it while ye can, girl. Captain Maynard saw an end to Blackbeard and he'll see an end to the rest of you pirates too!" A rumble of thunder echoed his words. As our ship sailed away, a rain began to fall, splashing against the wooden deck.

"*Damn the man,*" grumbled the ghost of Blackbeard. I glanced up at the ghost from my spot on the deck. His swarthy face was dark with anger.

The lights of Savannah were a welcome sight as our ship sailed into the port late evening several weeks later. A gentle bump against the dock and my crew leapt to the boards to tie her up. A short conversation with the night watchman and a bit of passing of gold, and I and my men stepped on to the cobblestone roads of Savannah to spend a little money. Tomorrow would be soon enough to find a regular buyer for the spices of the merchant.

We headed toward our favorite spot, a rough & tumble tavern called the Crossed Daggers. Entering the tavern, I smiled to see the odd placement of the tables. On one wall, a heavy wooden bar took up the entire side. Immediately opposite the door, a fire burned merrily behind several large comfortable chairs and a small table set with a chessboard. The remaining tables and chairs were crowded one beside the other against the third wall. It left a wide-open space in the middle of the room.

I glanced around and saw that as usual city workers filled many of the tables. As we made our way to the bar, two of the men stood up and walked to the middle of the room. Silence fell for a second, as the two men shook hands and then the room exploded in shouts and yells as the two men charged at each other, each trying to bring the other to the ground. My fellow pirates were quick to join in the yelling and cheering and betting. I shook my head and waved down the barman. After ordering drinks, I took a seat at the bar and turned back to watch the fighters. It didn't take long before several of my pirates were trying their hands against the city workers. Unfortunately, it also didn't take long for me to see that something had changed since our last visit. It seemed that my pirates were winning a bit too much and quickly turning the mood of the bar. As I tried to signal Wulf that we needed to leave, one of my sailors won his fight very quickly and the mood of the crowd turned angry. An all-out brawl soon followed. As I dodged and wound my way through the combatants, pushing, shoving and knocking heads in order to reach my quartermaster, I found myself carried out of the tavern by the press of the crowd.

Though my sailors were talented fighters, the sheer mass of the brawl soon spread the fight out into the street. Once out of the bar, the melee quickly moved from fists and heads to daggers and rapiers. I found myself surrounded by a young group of boys who grinned at the sight of me.

"Hey, look boys, we got ourselves another Pinkbeard!"

"Pinkbeard?" I raised an eyebrow.

The tough facing me tossed his sword from one hand to the other and grinned. "Yeah, a Pinkbeard is a woman who thinks she's a pirate. One is known for plundering the Carolinas." The speaker was a young man, perhaps in his twenties. He was clearly a regular in the bar fights. His unkempt hair was an indeterminate color of brown or black that hung across his face, nearly hiding a pair of scars that ran across one cheek.

"Was," corrected one of the other young men.

"Ah, right. Was. Just like you'll be," Twoscar said as he lunged at me. Expecting the attack, I quickly stepped aside and pushed the boy into one of his companions who had been trying to sneak up behind me. The two tangled together and fell to the ground, leaving me a moment to face the remaining fighter. He hesitated for a moment and I took advantage to close and with a quick twist of my new sword disarmed him. Glancing around, he quickly turned tail and ran. Scoffing, I glanced around seeing the rest of my pirates continuing to defend themselves.

"To me, boys!" I shouted.

"Only if you're still alive, wench," said a voice behind me.

I turned to face the speaker. Twoscar had untangled himself and walked up behind me. As his companion stood back, he grinned and sprang toward me. Unlike his first compatriot, he did not hesitate. He charged at me with a pair of daggers in each hand. I met his attacks with my own, clashing rapier to dagger as fast as he attacked. He managed to slide one dagger into the guard of the rapier and bound the weapons. As I struggled to disengage, Twoscar swiped at me with the other dagger. I leaped back and lost the grip on the sword. Even as I struggled to regain my balance and pull my dagger from behind my back, the remaining boy stuck out a foot and tripped me to the ground.

As Twoscar approached, having picked up my rapier in his hand, I heard Blackbeard's voice.

"Get up, girl and fight. Wipe these cowardly puppies from the earth."

"How?" I thought to myself. *"He holds my rapier and I can't get to my dagger."*

"Have I not taught you better than that girl? Look around you...on the ship there are belaying pins, marlinspikes, rope. Is there nothing near you?"

One part of me heard Twoscar as he rambled on about what he would do to me as I looked around for a weapon. Carefully, I collected a bit of rock and dust from the cobblestone street. When Twoscar knelt before me, I threw it in his face. As he reared back and roared in anger, I rolled to my side, pulled my dagger and rose to one knee, placing my dagger beside a rather sensitive part of his anatomy.

"Are you sure you want to finish this, boy?" I said.

"I do believe that you be bit outnumbered," said Wulf as the rest of my crew ran to stand behind me. Having dispatched or run off the other tavern brawlers, my crew looked as rough and ready to fight as ever.

The boy looked around, wiping the grime his eyes. "Damn pirates, think you own the world," he spat as he backed away.

"Give it time," said his companion as he backed away with him. "It won't be long before Maynard wipes them all from the seas." With those parting words, the two remaining combatants fled.

"Bloody hell, he took my new rapier." I grumbled as I looked around at the damage from the bar and surrounding street. "Time to return to the ship, men."

That was the second mention of Maynard recently. I was beginning to think that perhaps our own days as pirates were numbered. I was not normally a suspicious person but between Blackbeard himself haunting me and two references to his killer within the same month, I was beginning to feel as if something was conspiring against us.

I sent the men grumbling back to the ship, and though I knew it meant getting less money, went to wake my contact to sell the spices. Wulf and I walked through the town toward the home of my contact. George was a merchant of questionable values and regular buyer who did not ask where my cargo came from. Reaching the home, Wulf banged on the door loud enough to wake the neighbors.

"Mary, what the blazes?" George asked, as he peeked around his door, still dressed in his nightshirt.

"My apologies, George." I said. "But I think our stay in Savannah will be shorter than normal this trip. I'd like you to come out to the boat for the cargo tonight."

"Tonight? Mary..."

"Tonight, George." My tone brooked no argument.

George sighed, "Well, what do you have Mary?"

"Spices and silks from India," I replied, knowing that such a valuable cargo would draw even George out the comfort of his bed.

"Fine," he said grumpily. "Let me dress and wake my bearers. I'll meet you outside in a minute."

A few minutes later, George, leading several slaves, walked around the corner of his home. One slave carried a small chest; several others carried large heavy cudgels or daggers with which to guard the gold.

As we walked along the willow-lined streets of Savannah, I noticed that George kept shooting sidelong glances as me each time we passed under one of the lamplights.

"What is it, George?"

He took a deep breath. "Please understand that I mean no offense, Mary."

"What is it?"

"We've known each other for quite a while. I mean, you've been coming to me to sell goods for several years. And I know that you are clearly a woman of moral upbringing...how is that you turned pirate?"

"Hmmph," I said. "Fair enough question. I suppose." I took off my hat and ran a hand through my hair. "I suppose it was probably a combination of things."

"Yes?" said George.

"I ran away to avoid an arranged marriage and...well, my mother was a pirate."

"Your mother was a pirate?" George raised his eyebrows in surprise. "Who?"

"Anne Bonny."

"Huh." George said. "Seems like a dangerous life for a girl."

I shrugged. "It's been interesting to say the least."

George looked thoughtful as we made our way through the city.

When we reached the port, George and I climbed up the *Rocinante* and then back down into the hold to view the cargo.

I walked him over to where the merchant's cargo lay stacked against a wall. Bolts of bright colorful silks lay crisscrossed across each other. Streaks of gold, orange and red glimmered in the light from the lanterns.

George walked over the silks and ran his hands across the bolts. "Not bad," he said. "The silk is fine quality." He pulled some of the silk out and held it to the light, looking at both sides. "A little thin but I could probably make something out of it."

I smiled, knowing that each criticism George made was designed to lower the value he was willing to give me. Nevertheless, I also knew how much he would get from the silks and spices so I kept silent.

He walked over to the spices. Lifting the lid and looking into the small jars of blue, green, and purple, he glanced at me. "Which spices?"

I sauntered over to stand beside him, lifting the lid of one; the pungent aroma of curry filled the room. The second was the soft yellow of saffron and the third held the deep green-brown of cumin. George carefully placed a finger in the curry jar, scooping a little; he brought it to his nose and took a deep sniff, coughing slightly as a result. Then placing a small amount on the tip of his tongue, he rolled it around his mouth. "Fairly strong," he said. "It would take a specific buyer to purchase the curry at this strength." He repeated his actions with the saffron and cumin but finding little to criticize about those spices, George sighed and turned back to me.

"I don't know, Mary," he said. "The silks are a little thin and the spices a bit strong. It's going to take me some time to find buyers for each of these."

I tilted my head and placed a hand on George's arm. Smiling my softest smile, I replied, "I understand, George, but if you would like me to continue to supply you with fine quality items, I have to pay my men. Surely, you can see that."

George nodded and sighed. "Ah, Mary, you will bankrupt me yet. Let's go up."

As we reached the deck, he named a price that was outrageously low.

"George!" I said in my most indignant voice. "That price is not even worth the blood I shed." I turned my back to look out across the sea. "If that's the best you can do, I'll have to consider taking my cargo to St. Augustine."

"Now, Mary, don't do that." George said. "Perhaps I can do a bit better." As I had expected, George was still not terribly pleased to be negotiating in the middle of the night and as a result bargained significantly harder than he would have in the morning. However, since I was not sure I wanted to risk another night in port not knowing if the city authorities would investigate the brawl, I let him get the better of the deal. After concluding the sale, I took the small chest of gold and silver coins from the slave and handed it to Wulf to distribute the shares amongst the men.

After leaving orders to set back out to sea with the morning tide, I returned to my cabin for a short night's rest. Rubbing my wrist from where the boy had twisted it when he disarmed me, I looked out the window at the night sky. Dark grey clouds began to cross the sky.

Lying down on the bunk, I closed my eyes. I was surprised that Blackbeard's Ghost had nothing to say to me. Perhaps the boy's reference to his killer unsettled the ghost as well. As I drifted off to sleep, I heard the soft patter of rain against the deck.

The next several weeks passed with less success then I would have preferred. Though the sight of my flag was enough to scare a few ships into turning over their cargo, none of it was of great value and the men were beginning to get restless. I decided to head back north in the hopes of targeting the ports at Charles Town and Wilmington, perhaps sailing even as far north as Baltimore.

As we got closer to the former haunts of Blackbeard, the ghost seemed to get restless. He would manifest at the wheel most evenings. And while no one else saw him, he began to tell me more stories of his time as a pirate. When we reached Charles Town, he told of me of the blockade to get medicine for his men.

"Aye, that was a challenge." The ghost said. *"Half my men were down with the clap and I needed medicine badly. I sent some men into town to get the medicine with a deadline of two days. However, two days passed and my men hadn't returned. The prisoners begged me to wait. At the end of the third day, I was furious that the town had not responded.*

I gave the order to hang one of the prisoners but even as the rope was being strung, a rowboat came across the bay carrying my men and the medicine. Keeping my promise, I sent the prisoners back. Though upon finding out my men had gotten drunk and that was why they didn't return on time, I should have used the rope on them instead."

"Why did you get the medicine?" I asked. "I can't imagine most pirates cared?"

"Ah, girl, that's where you are wrong. My men chose me to lead them. It was my job to provide for them, either in gold or goods."

He admitted to wishing he had managed to get some gold out of the mayor before sending him back to his town. I could not help but admire the fact that, for whatever his sins, Blackbeard did take care of his men. Even grounding them in the Beaufort Inlet was a way to save a few from hanging though I suspected his crew of pirates did not see it that way. I know mine would not. Pirates are a rare group, I thought to myself. Some deadly cutthroats, others drunks and lechers. But I suspected there were few pirates that would have blockaded a town for medicine rather than just throwing the men overboard or leaving them at the last port to fend for themselves.

Outside Wilmington, we captured two ships in quick succession, sending them back into the port after divesting them of their cargo of cotton and grain. Without a cargo the men could claim as their own and knowing that I did not have long before they reached a point of challenging my leadership, I decided to head north to Norfolk in the hopes of getting past the Navy ships there and into Baltimore to sell the cotton. If we could, the gold would go far to regaining the loyalty of my men.

We sailed up the edge of the outer banks of Carolina. The orange and gold of the farms blended into a quilt of autumn colors. From my vantage point on the bow, I could see the port of Wilmington and shuddered. Thankful that I had escaped the fate planned for me by my grandfather. Though the command of the ship was not easy, and I risked death with each fight, I was free and that freedom was worth all the risk.

A few miles outside of Norfolk, two ships flying Navy colors began to follow us. I had our colors lowered and we tried to outrun them, staying close to the shoals. But the wind didn't cooperate and as the sun began to set on the Atlantic Ocean, we found ourselves bracketed by the two ships. As the ships sailed closer, a rain began to fall.

"Heave too, and prepare to be boarded!" shouted a voice from across the water.

"By what right?" shouted back Wulf.

"By order of the Royal Navy."

"And who commands?"

"I do," came a second voice. "Captain Robert Maynard."

At this voice, a low and angry wail came across the ship. Blackbeard appeared in his spot at the wheel. The other pirates all turned and looked at each other at the sound.

"*No Quarter!*" cried Blackbeard. And for the first time, my crew heard him and the shout was taken up.

"No Quarter!"

"No Quarter!"

"Death to the Navy!"

"No Quarter!"

An answering shout came from across the bow.

"So be it! No Quarter to pirates!" Thunder rolled and lightning flashed as the words were spoken.

"Hoist my colors, men!" I shouted as I drew my sword and prepared to face the Royal Navy. The black flag with the crossed swords of Jack Rackham and a single teardrop in blood red waved in the wind.

"Fire the cannon!" I ordered and a barrage of cannon shot from one side of my ship forcing holes into one of the Navy ships and sending splinters of wood to splash in the water. The echo of the cannon repeated in the thundering sky.

"Use some grape shot on their sails, boys!" I yelled. Another round of cannon fired from the two ships, sending bodies flying across the deck. Rain began to fall harder, peppering the ships and fighters with sharp pellets of water. The waves beneath the ship began rise and fall.

The Royal Navy sailors threw grappling hooks across both sides of the *Rocinante* and nearly split the ship in two as they both tried to pull it closer. The wooden boards on the ship groaned with such volume that the only image that came to my mind was that of a giant serpent squeezing the hull, tearing it apart. The crew rushed to one side and hacked at the ropes with boarding axes freeing us from one ship, yet allowing the other to pull alongside us. Naval sailors in dark blue and white leaped and tumbled over the rails, pistols pointed and sabers ready. The smell of black powder and sweat soon mixed with the acrid smell of blood as the battle was enjoined on both sides. Lightning lit the sky and sent ghostly shadows flickering across the faces of all.

"*Kill them! Kill them all! Damn Navy!*" I heard the apparition of Blackbeard shout. His own ghostly sword and pistol waving wildly. His black eyes glowed an evil red in the smoke. His cries echoed in the air.

I found myself facing a sailor with a pistol and saber. He fired his pistol but missed me and moved to attack me with his saber. My own saber met his with a ringing clang, sliding my sword up his; I dodged under him to aim an attack at his back. He moved quicker than expected to block it. Pushing me off, he tried again to swipe at my side but I moved my own blade to meet his. We backed away and each looked for an opening. Suddenly, the sailor cried out in pain as a pistol shot came through his leg.

"*Kill him now, Mary!*" shouted the ghost.

The sailor reached down reflexively, leaving himself open for my killing blow.

As I withdrew my saber from his body and looked around,

a tall, dark haired man wearing a long coat and tricorn approached. I recognized the captain's uniform and turned to face him myself.

"Mary Scarlett, I presume?" he said as he approached.

Wiping the rain from my face, I nodded. My heart beat furiously as I realized I faced the man that killed Blackbeard. The man who had sworn to end piracy in the Atlantic.

"You could surrender, you know," he said conversationally as he approached me. He ignored the rain dripping from his hat onto his face. "You'd still hang...but perhaps some of your men would only serve time." He charged at me with his sword. I raised my own to block it. He grabbed my wrist with his offhand and pushed down on me.

"I'll not surrender to the likes of you!" I shouted as I twisted away, pushing his sword off mine and followed quickly with a swipe at his stomach. He leaped back out of the way.

"*That's the way, girl! Have at him!*" shouted Blackbeard. "*Show the old man what it means to be a pirate!*"

I tried to block the sounds of the battle from my ears and concentrate on the man facing me, holding his sword easily in his right hand. He seemed unaffected by the shouts and screams of dying men that lay across my ship.

He smiled and brought his sword up and across toward my chest. I blocked it and again slid the swords against each other to come up and under him. Turning, I tried to attack his unprotected back, but his sword came back to meet mine in a move that belied his age but showed clearly his experience and training.

We traded blows back and forth until it seemed that time stopped and we were the only two left fighting on the ship. Rain fell in sheets across the deck; the wind whipped the sails, snapping them sharply. Lightning flashed as thunder rolled across the sky.

Then time did stop, as I slipped on the deck wet with blood and rain and fell to the floor. As I lay sprawled across the wood, Maynard rushed forward and brought his sword up for the killing blow. Though I tried to position my own saber to block him, I knew it was too late.

Suddenly, a scream of rage and vengeance echoed across the ship as Blackbeard flew across the *Rocinante*, his long black beard and hair streaming behind him in the wind. The battle stopped as everyone turned toward the source of the sound.

Even I was astonished as Blackbeard appeared before Maynard. His merciless eyes glowed in the dark night. *"Ye may have ended me but you'll not have this pirate, ye cowardly puppy!"* he shouted as he pushed his old enemy across the side of the ship and down into the water.

As Maynard's men scrambled to get their captain out of the freezing water, I took advantage of the confusion to climb to my feet. Seeing the stunned looks on the other sailors, I shouted. "At the ropes men, 'tis time we give these Navy scallywags the slip." I grabbed an axe and began to hack at the ropes tying our ships together, all the while shouting at my men to push the rest of the Navy sailors into the water to join their captain. After clearing our deck, we sailed away as fast as our ship could take us.

"Mary, what the blazes was that?" Wulf asked, coming to stand beside me as I watched Blackbeard taunting the floundering Maynard in the cold Atlantic Ocean.

"Blackbeard." I replied.

"I could see that," he said, a hint of anger in voice. "I meant... what the *hell* was he doing here?"

I shook the rain from my hair and turned to face him. I raised my voice so the crew could hear me over the storm. "Blackbeard has haunted this ship and me for the last three years. Why me? Why us? I don't know. What I do know is that it has been with his advice and suggestions did I pick my battles. Why he chose now to appear?" I shrugged my shoulders and turned back to the ocean.

"Ey, what day is it, captain?" shouted up Nikalus, a grizzled old veteran of the seas.

I looked at Wulf.

He thought for a moment, scratching his chin. "It be the 22 of November, I believe."

"Aye, there's your answer, cap'n."

"Oh?"

The old man nodded. "Aye, 25 years ago today did Maynard kill Blackbeard. And if the stories be true, and this do be the *Adventure*, why 'tis understandable that today would be the day Blackbeard would reappear to face his old enemy."

The other sailors began to nod and murmur acceptance. As they began the tedious process of cleaning the ship, Wulf looked at me.

"To Baltimore."

"My own pirate history ended then, as I and my crew sailed into Baltimore Port, sold our cargo and the ship and chose to make honest livings till the end of our days..." I leaned back into the pillows and closed my eyes.

"Really, Grandmother? You did all that?" the child asked.

"Aye, child. She did. But now it's time for her to join me sailing aboard a new ship." Blackbeard reappeared before me and held out his hand. I could see a ghostly ship flying my colors through the wall behind him.

I reached out to take the Ghost's hand and he pulled me to my feet.

"Don't look back, girl," he said.

But I couldn't resist and glanced back. I watched as tears fell from my granddaughter's eyes as she shut the unseeing ones of my own.

"I warned ya, girl. 'Tis always hard to say good-bye to one's own self."

I sighed. "Ah, but I said good-bye to my own self many years ago when I left the sea. Now, I'm just coming home." I turned back to Blackbeard; walked out of my room and stepped onto the ghostly ship.

Tera Fulbright has been a fan of the SF genre since first reading C. S. Lewis's *The Chronicles of Narnia* in the 4th grade. Her experiences and interests range from costuming and stage combat to running conventions to writing.

Her first short story, "History in the Making" was published in the anthology *Rum and Runestones* in 2010. Her second story, "Faith" was published in Michael Ventrella's *Tales of Fortannis: A Bard's Eye View* (June 2011).

In her non-writing life, Tera works as the Employee Relations Coordinator for Unifi Manufacturing, Inc. And in what, admittedly limited, spare time she has, she enjoys miniature painting, playing D&D, reading and spending time with her husband and daughter at their home in Greensboro, NC.

Maskèd Panama

Erin M. Hartshorn

Captain Richards leaned back in his chair and stared at his visitor. Osborne's brocade coat glistened with metallic thread, but the cuffs shone with worn spots; no doubt he wrote his own letters and some for the treasury as well. "Morgan has been commissioned by His Majesty; I would think the Crown could ask the good captain for this bit of treasure."

Thomas Osborne, commissioner of the state treasury for His Majesty King Charles II, grimaced and made shushing motions with his hand. "Morgan has taken advantage of a small hole in the commission. Although it is true that he must divide everything that he takes at sea with the Crown, that is not true of battles on land."

"I see." Richards steepled his fingers on his chest. "And the trinket His Majesty fancies was taken in such a raid." He tilted his head to the side. "Why come to me? The ports of Jamaica surely have hands a-plenty who would be happy to get a bit of Morgan's treasure for themselves in exchange for one item."

Osborne rested his elbows on the table and leaned forward over them. "You have a reputation for the daring. The French ambassador has assured me that you can do the impossible, although he won't be any more specific than that."

He'd dealt with the French ambassador? Richards filed that bit of information away. He would have to watch for a profitable time jaunt in that direction.

Shih Hwei pushed open the cabin door, and Osborne paused to watch her enter. She carried a lacquered tray with three dainty cups and a steaming tea pot. Today's red silk dress swept the tops of her shoes, hiding the trousers she wore beneath its snug fit.

Richards exchanged a smile with Hwei. "Impossible? Daring? How intriguing."

Osborne delayed answering.

Richards accepted a cup of tea from Hwei and inhaled the delicate fragrance of jasmine. He sipped before looking back at his visitor. "Has anyone else been telling tales on me?"

Osborne frowned. "I'd expected to speak to you in confidence, not in front of a wo—anyone else."

Hwei spoke in Cantonese. "That is the same from your time to mine and beyond from what you have told me."

Her time was a mere 120 years in the future, not as far as Richards had been in either direction in the time stream, but a pivotal point in his life just the same. Shih Hwei was the sister of Shih Yang, better known as Zheng Yisao, the wife of Zheng and a pirate queen in her own right.

Somehow, most of his work came down to dealing with pirates, but that might be because he preferred to work on the open seas.

The Pacific Ocean, however, was more moody than the Atlantic, and instead of the time he'd intended, he arrived in a broken ship in 1800, prey for the pirates plying the coastal waters of Qing China. Hwei had helped him to escape, and in return, he brought her with him to his own time. After four years of working together, they were partners in every sense, and Richards was not about to see her slighted by their visitor.

He set down his cup and stood. Osborne's hesitation about Hwei was unsurprising, but if he wanted Richards' help, he'd do things Richards' way. "I'm sorry we will not be able to assist His Majesty. My choice of confidantes is not your concern."

Osborne brushed at his coat sleeve. He didn't stand. "His Majesty is disinclined to make this public knowledge. The item in question is quite valuable."

"Shih Hwei is not His Majesty's public, nor is her honesty open to question. Good day."

"I just don't want—" Osborne squared his shoulders. "Very well. A mask reputed to have healing properties was last heard of in Panama; we believe Morgan acquired it in a recent raid on that city. The Jesuit priests insist it is just a ceremonial mask. His Majesty would like to test its powers himself."

Certainly he would; anyone might want magical healing as a prize. Richards himself, however, wouldn't keep it, not if he agreed to the job. If he said he would turn it over to King Charles, he would do so. Experimenting first might be an option; his left knee bothered him whenever a storm blew up—a concern for his time jaunts. Magic ran in his blood, in every member of his family on both sides for more generations than he could count, but Richards was the first to tame time. He simply needed the energy of a storm to do so, and this mask might make that easier on him.

Richards said, "Morgan and Modyford are to face criminal charges for their actions in Panama. Won't their plunder be forfeit?"

"They are on their way back to England even now." Osborne did not ask the source of Richards' knowledge. Presumably, the French ambassador had already told him Richards knew more than most. "However, the mask was not found with their treasure. We need someone who can discover the hiding place Morgan used."

Richards eased back into his chair. "What payment is His Majesty offering for such a rare find?"

"He can be most generous; there might even be a knighthood in it for you."

Picking up his cup, Richards realized it was empty. He held it toward Hwei, who refilled it without comment.

"A knighthood doesn't pay any bills. I'd like something more solid—enough money to outfit the ship for the journey up front, and five times as much when we return." When Osborne didn't blink, Richards added, "Also the jade lion figurine that His Majesty recently received from the Chinese emperor."

"I can't... His Majesty... That is not mine to speak for."

"That's the price. His Majesty is free to find someone willing to do the work for less." Richards waved at the door behind Osborne. "You know where to find me."

Osborne emptied his tea cup, made a face, and stood. "I had heard you were a reasonable man."

Richards said nothing. Hwei stood, minced toward the door, and opened it. Their visitor glowered at them but left.

"Your king will not agree to give up the lion." She came back and sank into her chair. "That was an outrageous request."

"Certainly it was." Richards grinned. "I need to know how much His Majesty wants this mask. I expect him to offer me more up front and some lesser trinket when we surrender the mask to him."

Hwei poured a cup of tea for herself and sipped. "Do you have a trinket in mind?"

"No." He picked up his cup and drained it. "I need to think about how to do this. Or, rather, when."

After Hwei finished her tea, she cleared away the tea service, and Richards rummaged through his map drawer. Soon maps blanketed the table, hand-written notations and curling yellowed edges overlapping crisp pages that would not be printed for another hundred years. Pence served as markers for Panama City and Morgan's home port in Jamaica. Richards rubbed his chin before jotting dates down with a quill.

Morgan had landed his pinnaces off Santa Catalina Island in mid-December and taken possession of the castle of Chagres before the end of the month. The pirates had paddled canoes up the Chagres River and crossed overland from there to take Panama City on January 18. Richards drummed his fingers on the maps. He'd need to anchor elsewhere and cross entirely on foot, a more time-consuming option. A knock on the door interrupted his calculations.

One of the crew stood at the door. "Beg pardon, sir, but that fellow is back to talk to you again."

"Is he indeed? Do show him in."

Sooner than he'd expected—Richards grinned. The king was eager. Hwei rolled the maps and laid them on Richards' bed. She lifted her dress, sat down cross-legged beside the parchments, and rested her hands on her knees. No doubt their visitor would be appalled by her flagrant display of trousers. Richards closed his log book and pushed it off to the left. He looked up with polite interest when the door opened.

"Captain."

Richards nodded at Osborne. "Do come in. Has His Majesty considered my terms?"

Osborne didn't pass the doorway. His gaze barely flicked toward Hwei. "His Majesty says he cannot give you the lion because a deputation from that yellow country—beg pardon—will be visiting him next month."

"I see," Richards picked up his quill and reached for his log book. "Thank you for letting me know."

"If you could consider taking late delivery of the lion?" He took a step forward. "After the ambassador has departed, perhaps? He may even be gone before you have returned from the New World."

Richards ignored Hwei's in-drawn breath behind him. He hadn't expected the king to bend this much. Of course, payment delayed might never come.

"Perhaps His Majesty would prefer to offer some other trinket in exchange for my services?" Richards parried.

Osborne stepped inside and closed the door. "His Majesty thought you a man of reason." He reached into his pocket. "He bade me give you this as earnest of his good faith, along with twice the gold you requested."

Richards put his hand out to receive the watch. The casing was inset with gold and silver; sapphires sparkled in a circle around a central ruby. He pressed the spring to open the watch. The watch face itself was unornamented, although its single hand was chased with a spiral of gold wire. The back of the casing was engraved "To HM, good fortune always. JD."

He laid the watch on the table before him, minimizing motion that might betray his excitement. However, the king's man had probably not opened it, and certainly had no idea it had been a gift from John Dee, the most talented wizard of the previous century. His Majesty had given him a prize worth far more than the jade lion, if Richards could decipher its magic.

"This will suffice. Give the coin to the quartermaster; as soon as he declares the ship and sailors fit, we sail."

Osborne's relief was palpable. He bowed twice, backed up, bumped into the door, felt behind him for the handle and opened it, then continued backing until he was out of sight. Richards walked around the table to close the door.

Hwei's brows were lowered, and she tapped a single long nail on the roll of maps. "Truly, Richards—for a pocket watch?"

He winked. "One should never ignore the gift of a king, especially if he does not recognize his own largesse. This watch's maker tamed magic in ways my family has never dreamed of."

Two weeks out of port, the lookout spotted clouds on the horizon, moving fast. Richards' left knee pulsed in time with the gusts. A big storm, then. Richards gave orders to tack across the storm's path. "Be prepared to drop the sails when I give the order, boys."

The rigging hummed with wind, and the sails pulled taut against their hitches. Richards stood on the deck, watching anxiously. The energy from the wind would make time transition easier, but he didn't want the *Virtue* damaged in the process.

Hwei came to stand by him. "Nervous?"

"I spent two years in your era the last time I guessed wrong."

"Was that so very bad?" Her voice was quiet.

Richards glanced at her without answering. No, it had not been bad. Was her presence here not evidence of his feelings? Hwei's bangs whipped in the salt wind, but her queue hung solid on her back. The parts of her compass were tucked into her belt. Her arms stretched forward, welcoming the wind.

However, the wind and sails told only part of the story. He leaned into the railing; his shoulders relaxed as pressure eased off his left leg. Energy pulsed within the ship, but the sea dampened the flow. Richards tried to push more energy into the wood, to little avail. The response was sluggish.

Lightning arced above the mainmast with a roar. The storm was on them.

"Drop the mainsail!"

The sailors furled the sail, and the ship slowed. The hair on Richards' arms stood on end. His scalp tingled, and he grinned with relief.

Richards pulled the energy to him, then pushed it below, filling the hull and everything within until he felt the entire ship resonate. He pushed the ship sideways into time.

They sailed on a blue jade sea. Richards sagged against the rail.

"Rough transition?" Hwei murmured. The previous tension might never have been—too late now to tell her he had no regrets.

"No more than usual."

She placed her iron spoon on the metal plate of the compass and watched until it steadied. "We've crossed most of the ocean. And from our shadows, we're south of where we were."

"Good." He pushed himself upright. "I'm going to rest for a bit. Wake me when the stars are out; if Fortune favored me, we won't need any more transitions."

His men waved and smiled at him as he headed back to his cabin. The sailors who couldn't adjust to the idea of magic and passing through time had been paid well and encouraged to seek work elsewhere. Those who'd stayed—well, leaving an English spring for a tropical paradise was one of the benefits of crewing the *Virtue*.

Despite his words to Hwei, Richards couldn't sleep. His knee burned. He lay on his bed to ease the throbbing and examined the pocket watch. The second hand swept around the face, its spiral wire glinting with the motion. If he could unriddle its workings...

Hwei shook him awake. He still clutched the watch; he tucked it into his vest pocket and stood, brushing at his clothes. His astrolabe rested in a drawer with other instruments. The navigator had one, but Richards preferred to verify the time shifts himself.

A glance at the mid-November constellations gave him the time of year even before he pulled out the astrolabe, which confirmed that the *Virtue* had shifted back a year and a half, to 1670. Richards rubbed his hands together. He had a month's head start over Morgan—more, since Richards wouldn't be laying siege to the castle of Chagres. He just needed to ensure it was time enough.

The next day, they sailed within sight of land. Richards, Hwei, and the navigator conferred to determine their position and the best place to make landfall. That evening, they anchored in a cove. No major towns lay within a day's walk, but there was a nearby village where they might hire guides. Richards had hired his men as sailors; he didn't expect them to be competent in the jungle.

Before leaving the ship, Richards gave his standard speech to the crew. "If we're not back within three months, sail without us. Anchor off the Bermuda Isles; return to England in a year or so." Hwei—now wearing a shorter tunic more suitable for jungle travel—went with him for the negotiations, as did the quartermaster with a chest of trade goods. Two of the sailors, Archer and Clarkson, rowed them ashore.

Richards's bastardized Spanish was sufficient to reach an agreement. He bowed and extended his arms, draped with ceremonial cloth, to the leader of the village. The leader grinned and said something in his own tongue. Bits of green leaf sprayed toward the cloth, but Richards held it steady.

One of the younger men spat, barely missing Richards's feet. His words were angry but unintelligible.

Hwei moved up behind Richards. Her voice didn't carry far. "He's saying something about the Spanish. He doesn't want us here."

"He's not alone." Several others were jerking their heads

and muttering. The chief glared at them before turning back to Morgan and taking the cloth.

Richards let his shoulders sag. The other half of the payment—Spanish pots—would be payable when they returned. The quartermaster took the dinghy back to the *Virtue*; the others set out with a pair of the less recalcitrant natives.

Hwei picked up their guides' language with little difficulty over the first week. With understanding on both sides, warnings about caimans and mudslides were heeded the first time, and travel became quicker.

The guides eyed the party skeptically until they reached the first rope bridge across a chasm, a knotted creation any sailor would approve if the ropes hadn't been decades old. Hwei crossed before the guides finished their warning. Richards and his sailors followed suit, with the glowering guides trailing behind. The bridge frayed further with each crossing, breaking under the second guide, and Archer scrambled down the remains, caught the guide under his arms, and clambered back up.

Hwei cocked her head to listen to the guides then nodded at Archer. "They like you, say it's clear you're not Spanish."

"I could've done the same thing," Clarkson muttered.

"As could any on the ship," Richards said. "Let's move."

He caught Hwei's arm to hold her back while the guides and sailors moved ahead. "They don't like the Spanish?"

She glanced at the guides then turned to face him. "Would you, in their place?"

"That will make Morgan's journey easier. I hadn't counted on that." He brushed dust off his hands. "Should make life interesting."

Richards's party hiked into Panama City. only days before Christmas, later than he'd hoped but still in advance of Morgan. Hwei accompanied their guides to the market while Richards and the sailors sought a tavern. Spanish wines suffered on the journey across the sea, but one of the native products, made from a fermented corn, intrigued Richards. He resolved to drink a single cup.

He was still sitting at the table, cup in front of him, when

Hwei arrived, guides in tow. "How many have you had?"

"Not sure." He peered up at her disappointed face. Was she unhappy with him? "Too many."

She hooked her arm around one of his and tugged upward. Richards didn't move. She pursed her lips. "We should find a room for the night."

"Already taken care of." Richards waved at the door. "Gentleman who runs this place offered a room for the night if I could keep down this swill."

The guides hauled him to his feet, and Richards was dimly aware of Hwei arguing with the bartender. Then he was lying on a louse-infested pallet, certain that his head would roll off if he moved. He closed his eyes.

Morning light streamed through a window, and Richards squinted against its sharpness. Hwei, kneeling by the room's door, snorted. "Chew on this." She passed him some willow bark.

He almost spat it out. "That was rather idiotic of me. However, I did learn where to find the mask."

"Good. I've sent the others out to the market for fresh fruit. After you've eaten, we can get to work."

Preparing took longer than that. A mango moistened his mouth, which helped a little. Richards cleaned himself up, and his headache settled into a dull throb. Then he studied the sketch Hwei had made of the city, with neighborhoods and central avenues marked in ink.

Richards put his finger on one of the poorer neighborhoods. "The church here keeps the mask."

He outlined his plan.

Once everyone understood the scheme, the group broke up, traveling separately to the church. Richards went in first, an English dandy bent on examining the Popish curiosities. The mask wasn't apparent near the altar or at any of the side shrines. While he stood before a statue of an indistinct saint, its paint long since flaked off, Hwei entered, lit a candle before a statue of Mary, and knelt. She hardly looked native; Richards hoped it wouldn't matter. Archer entered, grabbed her arm, and yanked her to her feet.

"You filthy harlot! How dare you show your face in here? You'd be better off praying to the Magdalene."

She pulled back, but he held tight and continued to harangue her. Clarkson slammed the church door open and stalked over to them. His fist smashed Archer into the rows of candles.

Archer jumped up, swinging. Candles toppled behind him, and Hwei darted between the two men.

Soon all three of them were shouting and shoving each other. Clarkson fell into the statue of the Virgin, and he steadied it. While he was occupied, Archer grabbed Hwei and dragged her toward the door of the church.

"What is going on?" A priest in simple brown robes stood in the doorway. About time there was an official reaction.

Hwei and the two sailors explained simultaneously with large gestures.

"One at a time." The priest spotted Richards. "You, there. Did you see what happened?"

"I'm sorry, Father. I was trying to identify this carving, and I don't know how the altercation started."

The priest crossed his arms. "Very well. You three—out. This is no behavior for a church."

They returned to babbling.

"Silence!" He opened his arms in an abrupt gesture. "Out. We will discuss this next door, in my study. You will not defile the Lord's House further."

"But—" Hwei said.

"I can call the guards."

Hwei and the sailors filed meekly out of the church. The priest stared at Richards.

"I'm sorry I cannot be more help, Father," Richards said, "but I will clean up for you."

Richards crossed to the statue of Mary. He knelt and began picking up candles. The priest watched him for a moment before swiveling to follow the others from the church. Straightening the benches and candles didn't take long, although Richards didn't know where to dispose of the wax that had spilled on the dirt floor. He settled for scraping it into a pile off to one side.

The church had a dearth of hiding places—the altar stood bare, and the shrines had only statues and candles. That left the tabernacle or the confessional. However holy the priest might deem the mask, he would not keep it with his Lord's Body and Blood.

Richards glanced around, but no one else had entered the church. He opened the priest's side of the confessional, slid in, and closed the door. The mask lay in a niche below the priest's seat. Richards grinned and slipped it inside his shirt.

The stroll back to the tavern was uneventful. Richards ordered a sherry while he waited for the others to return; he'd had enough of the local brew but didn't trust the water. To occupy himself, he flipped open the pocket watch and stared at the inscription. There had to be a clue about how to use it. Hwei entered by herself, asked the bartender for a sherry as well, and sat across from Richards.

"That was interesting," she said.

"Where are the men?"

"A brothel." She shrugged. "They get lonely."

Trust her to think of that. Her sister Yang would start out as a prostitute; he didn't know whether Hwei would. He'd never asked.

However, he didn't want the men dawdling in the town. "I want to leave in the morning. We should be well away before Morgan gets anywhere near."

"I'm certain they will be ready." She rested her hand on his. "We'll have to amuse ourselves tonight."

They hadn't been alone since the ship, and even there, she had doubted his commitment to her. He would show her yet again that she was the only one for him. He drained his glass and followed her back to the room.

The next morning, Richard rolled over and stretched, noting the angle of the sun through the window. He hadn't intended to sleep so long, but they'd had a late night. Hwei still slept, her head pillowed on her bare arm, black tendrils that had escaped from her queue curling over her cheek. She didn't often let herself appear so vulnerable. He pushed the curl back, leaned over, and kissed her cheek. Let her rest while he dressed.

He had his shirt buttoned before he realized the mask was gone.

It wasn't with Hwei's clothes, or in any of the sacks, or hidden in a corner. She had not moved it for safekeeping, then. Richards shook her awake, little noting that the wool blanket slid down when she sat up.

"The mask's gone."

Her brow furrowed, and she glanced toward the table in the far corner. "You set it down when I unbuttoned—"

"And now it's gone." Richards threw Hwei's clothes at her. They had to move quickly to find it again, and he didn't care if he appeared brusque.

She pulled her dress from where it had landed on her head and donned it, all the while talking. "Whoever took it entered while we were asleep, then. No matter how occupied we were, we would have seen him. He took a huge chance."

"His risk paid off. How are we to find him and the mask?"

To a certain degree, it didn't matter how long they took to find the mask, even years. Richards could still take them back to the spring of 1672, with yet another success to add to his legend. However, Richards did not want to wait years.

He tugged his cuffs straight and strode to the door. He hesitated before opening it, but Hwei had already drawn her trousers up and fastened the lacings. Now to learn who had access to their room during the night.

The sailors and guides waited in the main room, an untouched platter of tortillas and stew before them. Richards didn't comment on Archer's black eye, or on Clarkson's fat lip and cut cheek. He noted with amusement that the sailors gave Hwei a wide berth. He'd ask her—later—whether she was responsible for some of their injuries.

Richards propped one foot on the bench next to Archer and leaned forward to look at each man in turn. "What time did you return last night?" Hwei translated for the guides.

Archer and Clarkson glanced at each other, then back at the table. Clarkson muttered, "Sun was up. Not too long ago."

Richards glared at them. Clarkson likely told the truth. "Fine. Get to the room, get some rest. Eat when your bellies let you. Tomorrow, I'm going to work you ragged."

"But I thought we were leaving?" Archer asked.

"Change of plans." Richards pinched the bridge of his nose. "Go nurse your hangovers. I'll explain later."

They pushed back from the table and left without another word, leaving Richards and Hwei with the guides, who had yet to say anything. Richards slumped onto the bench. "Ask them again, would you?"

Hwei said something, sounding like a macaw and a caiman carrying on a conversation. The guides stared at the table. One stuffed a tortilla in his mouth. Hwei spoke again, her voice rising enough to draw looks from around the room. A few of the other patrons left.

Their guides said nothing. Richards reached for one's sleeve, but the man spun and spat in Richards's face. As Richards wiped the spittle away, he heard benches scraping back. When he looked up, the guides were disappearing out the door with Hwei right behind them.

He caught up to her just outside; the guides had vanished into a mass of native workers. Groaning, he grabbed her arm and pulled her back into the tavern.

"I guess we know who took it."

"Or if not, they know who did." Hwei stared at the door. "I should have followed them."

"It wouldn't have done any good." He ladled some of the stew into a small wooden bowl. "I figure I'll be heading back to the church this afternoon, alone this time."

"Why would they go back there? If they wanted the mask, wouldn't they take it to their village?" Hwei asked.

"Perhaps. I'd feel rather stupid, however, if we got all the way back to the coast and the mask wasn't there. We start with the church, and expand out into the city from there."

It couldn't be that easy, of course. There was no sign of the mask in the confessional, and the priest entered the church as Richards slipped back out of the closeted space. Richards grinned, as full of bonhomie as he'd ever been in a tavern.

"I've always wondered what it looked like in there."

"I've had quite the rash of people in there. I'm thinking of installing a lock." The priest didn't smile.

"Shocking." Richards pulled out a small purse of money. "You must let me contribute, since I have offended."

The priest accepted the purse without a word, and Richards left the church. He would not be welcome there again, he was certain.

For a week, Hwei watched the market for their guides. Archer and Clarkson alternated keeping an eye on trails into the jungle and wandering the brothels and taverns (with a limited supply of money, Richards made sure), their eyes and ears open for news of the mask or anything out of the ordinary. Richards spent his time fretting and pacing. He did his best not to snap at the others when they returned with no news, but Hwei's emotional distance told him that his anxiety was showing.

After the first week, Hwei said, "This is doing no good. They have probably left with the mask already. We should head back to their village."

"Not until you find someone who saw them leave the city." Richards rubbed his chin, now covered in a fine beard. "The village will still be there later. The city won't be."

"All the more reason to leave *now*, before we die as well." She placed her hand on his shoulder. "We can find it again, take another trip."

He shrugged her off. "It's still here, and I'm not leaving. Morgan won't arrive until next month; by his accounts, the castle fell yesterday. You're welcome to go if you wish."

Not that he wanted her to, but she had to understand that gaining the mask was the most important thing right now — taking it, while they knew where it was, before it vanished in the fire and sacking of Panama City after Morgan arrived. Yes, they could make another time trip, and his control improved with every jaunt, but if they didn't know where and when to find it in the future, that was meaningless. (The past was out of the question, or it would not have been in the church for him to find, of that much he was certain.) He'd undertaken a commission, and he would uphold his reputation by fulfilling it.

She did not go, but instead moved on from the markets to the residential areas, rising early to see the workers leaving their homes in the morning. Her exchanges with him grew more curt. Richards barely noticed when she stopped speaking to him; he was too busy trying to make friends with Spanish soldiers and sailors, people who would watch for troublemakers. Archer and Clarkson started doing odd jobs for the tavern owner and some of his friends in exchange for continued room and board. Richards was failing.

Their break didn't come until the Feast of the Epiphany. Richards had grown so weary he almost missed the guides in the throng of natives who paraded past the tavern behind priests and acolytes. He drained his cup of local beer, grabbed Archer from behind the bar—leaving Clarkson to bring Hwei when she returned from her latest outing, wherever it might be—and set out after the parade.

Clarkson and Hwei caught up with them outside the cathedral. They watched in silence as a priest marked letters above the door. "Caspar, Melchior, Balthasar," Clarkson murmured. Richards gave him a sidelong glance but made no comment. It was none of his business what his men believed, as long as they did their jobs, and even the High Church had Epiphany celebrations, if not popish ones.

Archer followed the crowd inside, while the others moved to flank the entrances. Two hours later, Clarkson's whistle signaled from the far side of the cathedral, and Richards moved to join him.

"Archer waved me off," Clarkson said. "But he had them."

Hwei said, "I will wait back at the room."

"We all will." Richards didn't want to lose track of anyone now; his objective was to get that mask and get out of town before Morgan arrived, and the faster the better. "Archer knows where to find us."

Richards and Clarkson stopped in the main room at the tavern, although Hwei continued into the sleeping room.

Clarkson nodded after her. "What you going to do about her?"

Richards shrugged. He wasn't sure he could do anything *about* her. Losing Hwei wasn't something he wanted to worry about, let alone talk about, especially with one of his men. He just had to believe her actions were because he'd pushed them all too hard, and time would mend her anger toward him. Time—right. He stared at the door, willing Archer to walk through.

They didn't have to wait long. Archer started talking before he'd reached their table. "They're holed up with cousins out the west side. Distant cousins, I think—I've seen the cousins hanging about on the edges of town, probably watching to see if we've given up yet so our guides could leave the city safely."

That sounded reasonable; Richards had been certain the mask was still here in Panama.

"Let's go," Richards said.

"What about Hwei?" Archer looked toward the back.

Richards was halfway to the door. She wanted time without him? He'd give it to her. "We'll go without her."

Archer and Clarkson caught up with him in the street, both frowning but not commenting. Archer led the way through the city. Many people were celebrating the feast. Richards nodded at the soldiers and citizens without smiling, wishing he could warn them of what was coming, what Morgan would do.

When Richards and his men were still three houses away from their quarry, their erstwhile guides saw them and ran. One yelled and pointed back toward the house, but the other grabbed his arm and pulled. Clarkson took off after them, while Richards followed Archer to the house itself. The guide would not be so agitated if they had the mask on them; presumably, they had it hidden until they felt it safe to leave.

The natives inside the house jumped up when Richards and Archer entered. Richards ignored them, tossing pots and blankets aside in his search for the mask. He found it in a corner and lifted it reverently.

The natives jumped at him, but Archer knocked one down. The other swung a pot at him, but Clarkson, entering behind the native, struck the back of his neck. Richards brushed past them. He had what he had come for; his reputation would remain intact.

When they arrived back at the tavern, Richards went to their room to begin packing. Morgan would arrive in the city in a dozen days, and even now his men marched toward it. Richards needed to avoid the encounter — they all did, for even if they were Englishmen, Morgan was certain to examine their belongings for anything of value.

Hwei greeted Richards' activity with a single raised eyebrow. "You have it again, then?"

"I do."

"Don't lose it this time."

Before he could point out that she had been as much to blame as he had, she had left the room. Still, it was the most words she had spoken to him in a week. Perhaps now, without the mask's retrieval weighing so heavily on his mind, he might make his peace with her.

They left the next day in the pouring rain.

The smells of the city washed off them: the humanity, the stale alcohol, the cook smoke. The world filled with flowers and rotting vegetation. A parrot flitted across in front of them, and Archer paused to pick up a fallen red feather. Richards limped behind, his knee setting the pace for the party.

The rainy season had intensified; even if their guides had been with them, the trek back would have taken longer than the trip inland had. Without their guides? Richards comforted himself that at least the *Virtue* shouldn't sail without them; it was only January.

Still Hwei spoke to him only when necessary.

Rain washed out the path before them, and twice the party missed being caught in a mudslide. The third time, they were not so fortunate; they spent half a day digging Clarkson's trapped legs free of the mud.

The jungle wore on Richards. Moss grew in patches on his mud-stained clothing. It would be good to get back to sea, with the far horizon before him and no dangers he couldn't see coming. Now, for example, he heard motion off in the trees, but couldn't see the cause. He waved to the others to stop.

Not an animal—the sounds spread too far; there were too many. Men, then. Richards nodded at the nearby trees. Archer and Clarkson shinned up without a word. Hwei moved farther from the path and climbed a vine-laden tree, using the lines to guide her. Richards listened a moment longer before selecting his own perch, near Hwei but not in the same tree.

The men came closer. Richards stared down at the path, urging them into sight. Their voices carried, though, and he didn't need to see them to know that Morgan's men approached on their march to Panama City. Richards raised his hand to caution the others to silence. The men cut across the path, heading northwest, passing a few at a time.

"I want to catch me some of those toucan-birds," one said. "They sell pretty damn good back in Port Royal."

Another man laughed at him. "Yah? How you going to carry them?"

The first man shoved him and glanced upward. "Still, I'd like to find some."

Richards froze as the man's gaze swept past. There was no reaction. Richards released his breath as the men continued on. He couldn't count on being so lucky a second time, discolored clothing or no. Perhaps a small time jaunt? No, the others were too far away, in separate trees. Without something binding them together, as a boat did its crew and passengers, he could not carry them with him, and even if he could bring himself to abandon his men, he would not leave Hwei behind.

He braced himself in a crotch of the tree and watched the passersby while fiddling with the pocket watch. No one else looked up. Richards pulled the stem out to wind the watch. The internal tension wouldn't permit him to wind it backward, so that wasn't the secret. Pity.

Late the next day, even the stragglers had gone by. Richards slid to the ground and waited for the others to join him, catching Hwei just before she touched down. She nodded her thanks at him, and he held her a moment longer before directing the others to seek shelter for the night.

"Boughs are not comfortable berths, even for sailors." Richards flexed his knee a couple of times to stretch it. "We'll need to get used to being on the ground again before we move on."

That night, Hwei curled against him in the dark, and he knew they were moving back to where they had been. Would that be enough, though, or would something on their next journey divide them again? Time he could understand, but people were hard.

The sole bright spot of the journey was that Richards had time to play with the mask. Huddled under a tree during a downpour, he slipped the mask on. It prickled, not unlike his ship during a time shift. He concentrated on his aches, and the pain in his knee faded. Richards would have danced a hornpipe if the path hadn't been six inches of mud.

They skirted the village to get back to the cove. Richards had no desire to account for the missing men, and he considered the balance of the village's payment forfeit for the treachery of their guides. Hwei did not argue with him.

Once on the beach, they signaled the ship. The quartermaster rowed out to retrieve them. He raised his eyebrows when Richards hopped into the dinghy. "I take it the trip was a success, sir?"

"Indeed." Richards leaned back, luxuriating in the touch of sun that had broken through the omnipresent clouds. "I want to get underway before Morgan puts back out to sea."

The quartermaster nodded, and both Archer and Clarkson bent over the oars to help. On the ship, the sailors climbed rigging, tightening ropes and unfurling sails. They may have been taking their ease while Richards was away, but his crew worked hard when necessary. He nodded to them and moved to his cabin, intent on a fresh suit of clothes.

Hwei met him there with a steaming basin of water. As they laved the caked mud from their bodies, Richards said, "Thank you."

"I would have used the water anyway."

"Not for the water." He hesitated, but he had been long

enough saying this. "Thank you for being there for me, for not leaving, even when I have treated you poorly. I cannot imagine life without you again."

She continued to wash her arms. With a small smile, she said, "That's a start."

Despite the rains of the season, none of the storms intersecting their path across the Atlantic provided enough energy for a time shift. Richards fretted. He could arrive before Osborne contacted him and simply wait two years to fulfill the commission, but too much might happen in the meantime. Besides, he didn't want to run into himself; it seemed... awkward.

Three weeks away from England, he thought of the pocket watch once again.

He sat at the table in his quarters and turned the watch over in his hands. He stared at the sapphires — lightning blue. Did they hold the same energy? Could it be that simple? The ship rolled beneath him, wood solid and anchored to the present. He brushed his fingers along the case of the watch, and the ship hummed with energy. His eyes closed, and the ship slid into time again.

Two days later, the *Virtue* slipped into a berth on the Thames. Richards sent Clarkson to fetch Osborne, and the quartermaster showed him to Richards' cabin when he arrived. Hwei sat cross-legged on the bed once more. Their differences were not resolved, but they had time. More, she knew he cared.

Richards waited beside his table. A silk scarf covered the mask where it lay before him.

"I hadn't expected to see you so soon. Morgan and Modyford haven't arrived for their trial yet. Did you have a change of heart?" Osborne asked.

"Not at all," Richards said.

Hwei stood and whipped the scarf from the mask, which she presented to Osborne.

Richards grinned. "The impossible, remember?"

Erin M. Hartshorn is a desert rat (native Nevadan) transplanted to a humid climate. Her ideal home has bookcases in every room. She is a moderator at Forward Motion for Writers, an online writers community. Her fiction has appeared both on-line and in print in various places, placed in the PARSEC short story contest, earned honorable mentions in the Writers of the Future contest, and been short-listed for the UPC Award. When she's not writing, she enjoys various handicrafts, though she prefers spending time with her family. She blogs online at erinmhartshorn.com/blog and can be found on Twitter @ ErinMHartshorn.

Pinkbeard

DANNY BIRT

Editor's Note: This story occurs directly after those chronicled in Rum and Runestones. If you haven't read "Booty Haul" yet, do so now. Ye be warned!

What looked like two worms made of ocean water were busy gnawing away at a part of an island. Carl the Reefer, a.k.a. Coral Reef, Wizard of the Eastern Caribbean, sat in a little rowboat egging the water on until the two worms met on the opposite side of the beach bungalow and formed one body of water.

"Gotcha!" Carl exulted when he finally felt the island separate into two distinct parts, island and islet. With a gleeful cackle, Carl jumped out of his rowboat, splashed ashore, and planted his staff like a flagpole firmly in the sand while announcing, "I hereby reclaim and proclaim this island as *mine*."

As soon as he felt control over the island return to him, he tugged his staff up, turned toward the moat he had made and cut off the water flow, thereby returning the islet to being no more than a small part of his island. There was a momentary struggle for control, but the island subsumed the islet into itself.

A flabbergasted squawk emanated from the bungalow that the moat had momentarily surrounded: music to Carl's ears. He waited with patient anticipation, being almost certain of what the bungalow's squatting inhabitant would do next.

His patience was affirmed and rewarded a moment later by a parrot's frantic flight out the bungalow's front door toward the ocean...

...which was rudely interrupted in mid-flight when the parrot bonked its head on no visible obstruction. The parrot's wings folded and it dropped like it had been bludgeoned by a hunting falcon. It splashed down in the surf near the beach, and the bedraggled bird clambered its way up onto the sand, there to collapse in a wet mound of misery.

Carl sauntered over to it. When his shadow fell across the fallen bird, it opened its eyes and looked up.

"Raak?" the parrot said.

Carl crossed his arms. "Give it up, Roland. I know you're still in that body."

The parrot looked around. He looked back at Carl, and cocked his head. "Raak?"

"A normal parrot would have passed through my barrier," Carl noted.

"Polly want a cracker?"

"As a matter of fact, I do have some crackers." Carl fished around in a pocket and produced a wax paper package. "Since you're just a parrot, you won't mind my telling you that they're to go with my lunch today: *parrot soup*."

The parrot lurched away from the wizard, but Carl brought his staff down on the cowardly bird's tail feathers. It tried to flap away, then it hesitantly tugged at its trapped feathers, and finally heaved a little sigh of resignation.

"Fine, you win. Again." Roland waited for a moment, then tugged at his tail feathers. "Ahem?"

Carl considered keeping his staff right where it was out of spite, and finally decided that was *exactly* what he was going to do. This parrot had it coming to him, and a lot more besides.

Roland stopped tugging at his tail feathers a moment later, and looked fearfully at Carl. "You were just kidding about that whole soup thing... right?"

"That depends."

The parrot cringed. "On?"

"On what other damage you've done to my island since you stole it."

"Damage? What damage? Everything's ship-shape! I even made some improvements!"

"Oh, really? And would those 'improvements' include letting the vegetation wilt? How about allowing *trash* to accumulate on my beaches?" Carl kicked a bottle that had lodged in the sand near the parrot as a perfect example of what he meant. The bottle sailed down the beach, and its cork fell out. Pink smoke billowed out of it.

Roland and Carl glared at one another, each making obvious who they thought was at fault for whatever was about to happen.

The cloud took on the form of what might charitably be called a body. It spoke. "Wizard of the Eastern Caribbean?"

Remembering the last time that he was addressed by his full formal title and what had come of it, Carl shuddered. "If I admit that I am, what happens?"

"Hearken unto my missive, O wizard: My mistress, Lady Hildegaard B. Smythe, Pinkbeard, Captain of the Dread Pirate Ship Bob, Scourge of Lake Norman, entreats you to come to her immediate aid as per the Round Table Rule in the Code of the Brotherhood of Merlyn. Do you agree to my mistress' missive?"

Carl's brow wrinkled. He had to agree to help whoever this woman was or else he might be thrown out of the Brotherhood – as well he should be, for one who did not honor the Code was no Brother – but he had never seen her name on the Brotherhood's roster. And her name would have stood out: not only was it an unusual name, women were not allowed to be Brothers. Women joined the Sisterhood of Medea, or one of the lesser sorceress's sororities. (Carl had once gone on a blind date to a 'Sumptuous Saturday Soiree' put on by such a sorority when he was still an apprentice. His date happened to have a lisp. It was a memorable night.)

"I will keep the Code," Carl said. "What aid does your mistress request?"

The cloud's wispy arm detached from the rest of the cloud and became defined enough that it was obvious a finger was pointing at the bottle lying on the sand. "Gather my vessel into thy hands, and take care ye hold it most firmly."

"*Raak!* Hold his vessel! Hold his vessel!"

Carl bent down and grabbed the parrot in a not-quite-stranglehold, then walked over to the bottle and picked it up with the hand that held his staff. As soon as he did, the world turned pink and cloudy. He had a sensation of movement. He could not feel the sand under his feet.

What just happened? Carl wondered. *Did that pink thing just eat me? Am I being abducted? How do I fight smoke?*

The wizard did some quick thinking, and decided to let go of the bottle. The smoke dissipated... and Carl found himself plummeting toward the ocean in sight of the unmistakable pristine white beaches of Florida.

"AAAaaaaaa!" Carl screamed.

"Raaaaaaaaak!" Roland joined him in duet, flapping his wings. "Leggoleggoleggo!"

Carl had his eye on the bottle that was falling just ahead of him. He folded his arms and parrot to his chest and dove after the bottle. His fingers finally wrapped around it, and the pink smoke overtook his world again.

Eyes wide, perspiring, and panting, Carl made the firm decision that wherever he was going was better than trying that again.

Time passed, though Carl could not know how much. Right about the moment Carl started wondering whether breathing pink smoke into his lungs was bad for him, the object of his contemplation sucked itself away into the bottle he was still holding, and Carl found he stood on the deck of a ship that appeared to be landlocked.

Disorientation and panic set in before Carl could get a hold of himself. He simply wasn't prepared for this. He had just gotten home after a long, arduous, and more than slightly ridiculous journey, and before he could so much as step foot in his bungalow, he was whisked off to... where?

He rushed to the rail of the ship to get a better look around. He had been wrong: the ship was not landlocked. It floated in water, just not very much of it. There were some treetops sticking out of the water at the edges of the miniature lake – which was puzzling, since it was late summer and the water level of any lake should be going down. It was then that Carl caught sight of what appeared to be a beaver dam the size of which made him scared to ever meet the beaver.

"May I have my genie back, wizard?"

Carl spun, putting his staff and the parrot between him and...

He was not entirely sure what to make of the person who had addressed him. Said person had a neatly trimmed beard – a *pink* beard – but also had a voluptuous chest that vehemently belied manliness. The woman wore a large amount of gold jewelry, so much so that his ears distinctly heard the word 'bling' as the sun struck it. Her head was adorned by a poofy hat decorated with purple ocelot fur; her feet, ankles, calves, knees, and thighs were encased in leather stiletto-heeled boot scabbards; and in between the hat and boots was scanty clothing and scads of weapons.

And yet, he could feel the orderliness of her magical self, and he suddenly knew that he was addressing a member of the Brotherhood of Merlin — the person who had called for his help.

The woman had held up her hands and backed up a step, as had the majority of her crew who happened to be on deck. "Whoa, no need to sick your familiar on me, Coral."

Carl looked at the parrot he held, then placed the bird on his shoulder. "Him? Oh, no, he's—" Suddenly Carl had second thoughts about trying to explain Roland "—not my familiar. I was in the process of making lunch when I received your message."

"...bite yer ear off..."

She peered closer at the bird as she took back the genie-in-a-bottle.

"His stomach gurgles," Carl explained hastily. "He's more of a dodo than a parrot – he regularly bites off more than he can chew."

"Still, it's a beautiful bird," the woman said. "Norwegian Blue, isn't it? Beautiful plumage. I used to have one myself, when I was a little girl." She shook her head. "Where are my manners? I am Hildegaard B. Smith, and I thank you for coming here to assist me, Coral Reef."

"You're welcome. Call me Carl," Carl said graciously. "If I may ask, where *is* 'here?'"

"Lake Norman."

Carl's head cocked. The parrot's head mirrored it in perfect pantomime. "Where?"

"It's in the Carolinas, fed by the upper part of the Catawba River."

"But the upper Catawba isn't-"

"-deep enough to pass a vessel this size. I know."

"So how-"

"-did we get here?" Hildegaard smiled. "Believe it or not, in a fashion similar to how you arrived. I was sailing from Bermuda back to my family's stronghold, and just before we came in sight of land we sailed through a fog bank... right into the middle of the Carolinas."

"The Bermudas are treacherous," Carl noted. "You're lucky to be alive, if a bit landlocked."

"We weren't quite this lucky at first," Hildegaard disagreed. "When we came out of the fog, we were on a river that wasn't large enough to even keep the *Bob* bobbing. We had to build that dam over there from the materials at hand just to keep her from drying out. Of course, solving that problem only led to more problems," she sighed.

"With a dam in the way, you couldn't go downriver?"

"Actually, that was my initial plan: break the dam and surf the resulting wave all the way to the ocean. Only, when I sent scouts down the river, I found there were towns along the way, so..." She shrugged in resignation.

Carl nodded. The Brotherhood of Merlin stood staunchly

against magical malfeasance both in their ranks and outside them. Destroying all the towns along the Catawba just to move her ship to its rightful place would go against their code.

"What problems were you talking about, then?" he asked.

"Apparently the waters of Lake Norman are covering what used to be a native tribe's preferred hunting grounds. They've been growing feistier in their attempts to be rid of us lately."

"Why don't they just pull the dam apart?"

"They can't stand up to our cannon and musket fire, that's why. Not that they haven't tried a few times over the last month or two."

"My goodness, how long have you been here?"

"Probably a half a year. It feels longer."

"*Raak*! Feels longer! Feels longer!"

Hildegaard snorted. "You could say that again, parrot."

Carl snatched Roland off his shoulder and stared at him sternly. "*Don't.*" He stuffed the bird in a small draw-string satchel he kept at his waist, and drew the string tight so that only Roland's head was still visible.

One of the crew just above him in the rigging laughed. "Do ye often carry a parrot around in your pocket, mate?"

"*Raak*! Or are you just happy to see me?"

A bemused noise came from another crewmember who sat on a barrel at the rail, petting his own parrot. "It's a lively one he's got there, eh, Captain?"

"Indeed," Pinkbeard said. "Carl, meet my first mate, Good Dick."

Carl's eyebrows shot up and he blinked. Roland was shaking with helpless paroxysms of silent, disbelieving laughter.

"Richard Alligood at your service," the man denoted with wounded dignity. He hopped off the barrel and coming forward to shake Carl's hand. "Call me Rich."

"*Raak*! Good Dick! Good Dick!" Roland belatedly managed to gasp.

Rich looked at the parrot, then looked at his own bird. "The poor little blighter sounds like he has unmet needs, doesn't he, Amore?"

The gold-earringed bird on Rich's shoulder fixed eyes on Roland and whistled.

Roland's laughter suddenly died as if shot through the heart. Wild-eyed, Roland looked up at Carl. "Please don't."

"Oh, gosh, yes," Carl answered Rich. "I'm not sure he's *ever* known the pleasure of another bird's flesh."

Roland shook his head a tiny bit. "I'm begging you, man to man!"

"Well as it just so happens, Amore here hasn't seen another parrot since before we arrived on Lake Norman," Rich said. "She's been eyeing the hummingbirds of late, she's so desperate. Why don't we let these two have a room to themselves for a night?"

"Carl, I'll do anything!"

"Sounds good to me: maybe he'll keep his mouth shut after this." Carl handed Roland over, and the first mate walked down through the hatch with both birds.

"But to get back to your problem, Hildegaard, I take it that you summoned me because you already have a plan of how to get yourself and your crew out of this mess, and all you need is an extra set of hands, magically speaking?"

"Close – what I need is a little more strength," she replied. "My plan is to loft the *Bob* up into the airstream and use the winds to sail us back to the ocean."

Carl gave a near-silent whistle. That would require a *lot* of strength, actually, leaving little to nothing for forward impetus, depending on how powerful Hildegaard turned out to be. He looked up at the masts, and frowned. "Are your sails reinforced in some way I can't see?"

"No. Why?"

"I've been up in the airstream – just last week, actually – and in my opinion it's probably strong enough to tear your sails to shreds or maybe even break the mast. We'll have to stay close to the Earth."

"But the wind won't be powerful enough near ground level: I won't be able to hold the ship up for that long, even with your help."

The two fell silent as they tried to think a way around their predicament.

Suddenly, Carl snapped his fingers. "Of course!"

"What?" Hildegaard asked.

Her question made Carl realize the reception his plan would probably receive. He shut his mouth for a moment so he could consider how best to explain it, and he finally decided the less, the better. "I'm going to need the longest piece of rope you have."

"Done."

"A fearless messenger your genie can transport back to the Caribbean."

"I know just the woman."

"A nice assortment of fruits and vegetables."

Hildegaard gave him a puzzled look, but still said, "The cook will have them to you whenever you need them."

"Actually, the messenger will be taking them as a goodwill gift."

"As you say. What else?"

He shook his head. "That's it."

Hildegaard's look turned sharper at the apparent lack of need of any magical assistance, but she did not want to question Carl as if she did not trust him. Instead, all she asked was, "Who is my messenger going to be messaging? I don't want to come out of this with any more debts than the one I owe you."

"If any debt is incurred, it shall be mine to pay," Carl assured her. "My message is to be delivered to Siegfried, a crewmember of the *Topsy-Turvy*."

"And why do we need him?"

"He's... an avigation specialist."

"Avigation? You mean, *navigation*?"

"No. ...You'll understand everything when he arrives."

"The dam's on fire!"

Carl was out of his hammock and up on the deck faster than a marine could load a musket. He joined the majority of the crew at the rail watching a large blaze brighten the edge of the lake. As he watched, a few more fire arrows arced through the night sky from the tree line. He could hear the whoops and hollers of the natives as they celebrated their victory.

"Damn," Hildegaard said. "Oh, well. I suppose we should be thankful they didn't think of this earlier."

"Will it hold?" Carl asked.

"Not all of it's made of wood," Hildegaard said. "There was a lot of mud that went into the dam construction, and of course there's all that dammed water on the other side. But for the water to get to the fire, it would have to burst through the dam."

"Okay, how *long* will it hold?"

"It's going to gradually weaken, but not completely collapse. I can make it last longer if I hold it together with a structural spell."

"No, don't tire yourself out; we'll need your strength to loft the ship. ...Oh, no: what about all those towns downriver?"

"That's actually the good news," she said. "The fire will eat away the smaller twigs and branches, but it won't be able to affect the main tree trunks. The river level downstream will rise for a few days as the lake drains, but it will be like it's going through a sieve, not all at once. And since it's late summer, the river probably won't even get above its spring watermark."

Carl nodded. "You know, this might actually turn out quite well for all involved."

"Yeah. So long as the lake doesn't shrink enough for the natives' bows to come into range of the *Bob* before your friend Siegfried gets here."

"I thought you said they were afraid of your cannons."

"On the open water, yes. But there are still trees under the surface, and as the lake water recedes they'll provide plenty of cover close-in... whereas *we* will be sitting ducks."

Carl gulped. "Perhaps the most prudent course of action would be for us to loft the *Bob* a bit early, then?"

Hildegaard winked. "You read my mind. Crow's nest!"

A sailor looked down from his perch. "Aye, Captain?"

"Keep an eye on the range-to-shore. If we're coming anywhere close to bow-and-arrow range, sing out."

"Aye, Captain."

"I'm going to make sure everything's battened down for the voyage," Hildegaard muttered to Carl. "Make ready however you need to, then meet me back up on deck."

Carl wistfully looked at the shoreline, wishing he could get over there and summon his imp-servant Sasisu to help out with this predicament, but the number of arrows flying through the air made a visit ashore inadvisable, and the fiery little demon could not be summoned atop water. *Oh, well.*

Instead, Carl decided to get some rest. He moved toward the hatch, only to be stopped by the first mate.

"Thank ye, wizard," Rich said as he handed Roland back to Carl. "Amore's looking pretty satisfied with herself; your boy did a good job!"

Faintly, Carl said he was welcome, and went down the ladder. Only then did he bring Roland to eye level. Despairing and disgusted at what he saw, he said, "Oh, Roland, I didn't think you would *actually*—!"

"I couldn't help it!" Roland burst out. "This body I'm in just took over, and I was along for the ride! Literally," he added with a shudder.

Carl could not think of a single thing he could say which could make the situation any more palatable, so he put the bird back on his shoulder – not without some inherent revulsion – and returned to his hammock to rest up for the coming endurance trial.

From up on deck came a lullaby in the form of a sea chantey that was familiar to Carl from his time sailing on the *Topsy-Turvy*, until he started paying attention to the lyrics.

Chorus:

What do you do with a woman named Fortune,
what do you do with a woman named Fortune,
what do you do with a woman named Fortune,
early in the morning?
Way, hey, and up she rises,
way, hey, and up she rises,

way, hey, and up she rises
early in the morning.

Verses:

Sprinkle her linens with petals of roses.
Then you serve her breakfast in bed
Breakfast should consist of chocolates.
Watch her wash it down with a bottle of liquor.
Rub her feet before she rises.
But never, EVER wake her early!

Coral had little trouble figuring out for whom 'Woman Named Fortune' was a codename. He was left wondering if the weapons which Captain Pinkbeard wore about herself were for more than mere show.

Winks remained too nimble for Carl to catch, so when the call of "Natives ahoy!" came from above deck, he was already composed and ready to go.

Roland flapped his way from the perch at the end of the hammock to the wizard's shoulder.

"You might want to stay down here, just in case there are arrows in the air," Carl said.

"No, I want to stay with you," Roland replied.

Carl's head backed away from the parrot as far as it could go. "Why the sudden wish for a bonding experience?"

The parrot shrugged his wings. "I just don't want to be alone down here, that's all."

His eyes rolled, but Carl said nothing more. As soon as he came on deck the Captain yelled out, "Hoist the flag, maties!"

Making his way to the bridge, Carl looked up to see a black flag with a skeleton's hand on it present a reversed two-fingered "V" to the world. As if the hidden natives understood what the piratical symbol meant, a shower of arrows launched their way toward the ship. None made it to the deck, but some thunked ominously into the siding below.

"Are you ready, Carl?" Hildegaard asked.

Carl looked around the lake and in the skies, then nodded and closed his eyes to concentrate. He reached out and used his staff as a magical lever to help him push the ship up out of the water. He knew he could not have done this without the help of Hildegaard, because for the first three seconds he was pushing on his own and while the ship became more buoyant, the hull did not clear the water.

From below he could hear the cries of the natives as the ship sailed up over their heads toward the clouds. He grinned. Soon they would have their hunting grounds back, the *Bob* would be back on the ocean, and everyone would be happy.

Thunder rolled. Carl's grin vanished.

"Carl!" Roland whispered. "The clouds are turning black awful fast. It must be the natives' shamans doing it – they're gonna zap us in mid-air!"

For a moment, Carl opened his eyes to look at the clouds. Indeed, from what had been peaceful white puffy clouds had suddenly come what looked like angry, wooly black sheep getting ready to ram the ship. But through the clouds he saw the individual he had been looking for all morning.

"Siegfried!" he called out.

The crew called out in fear. It was too much for them to handle all at once: natives attacking, their ship flying, lightning-heads building, and now it appeared that a dragon was about to roast them alive in mid-air.

But the dragon did not do any roasting. Instead, he flew under the ship, snatched the length of rope that was dangling from the *Bob's* prow, and began to tug them eastward.

"Attaboy, Siegfried," Carl yelled. He had his eyes closed again to concentrate.

A moment later, he heard Hildegaard mutter, "Avigation specialist?"

Not wanting to waste his breath, Carl replied, "Are you saying I lied?"

There was no reply.

For a tenuous minute there was a race between the dragon's

speed and the shamans' abilities, but in the end Siegfried was able to tow the *Bob* fast enough that they left the threatening clouds behind them before they could build up enough power to do damage. For the moment, they were safe.

But as the day wore on, the ship started to feel heavier and heavier. Carl knew it was only that he was tiring, but the illusion still remained. He blearily wondered if they had been following the Catawba well enough that they could set down for a rest in a deeper part of the river, but he was not entirely sure he had it in him to do delicate enough work to set the ship down in a specific spot – it needed to be the ocean or nothing.

"Ocean ho!" called Rich from the prow, the crow's nest having been deemed too dangerous to be manned in such high winds. "And may I never have reason to say that again in my entire life!"

Carl felt Hildegaard gently decreasing the strength with which she held up the ship, allowing it to settle down toward the ocean, and Siegfried tugging the ship down, too. He began to relax his hold, and groaned aloud in delight at the lessening of pressure. Suddenly, the ship started to drop like a stone when Hildegaard let go completely.

He opened his eyes just in time to see the captain hop over the prow of the ship. His already-pounding heart skipped a beat, but a moment later he was relieved to see Hildegaard hanging from one of her blades and zip-lining her way down the rope to Siegfried. Even from here he could hear her yelling at him, though he could not make out much more than his name.

Straining mightily, Carl kept the ship from simply falling in place. He was tugged off his feet when Siegfried gave one more massive flap of his wings and let go of the rope. The *Bob* made a hissing sound as it contacted the ocean and slowed its velocity via the friction of the hull against the water. A flock of seagulls took off in belated panic, minus a few stunned members floating near the hull of the ship.

Siegfried turned around and delivered Hildegaard back to the ship. Rich caught her as she fell from the dragon's claws. They tumbled to the deck. Laughing in delight, Hildegaard gave her first mate an impromptu, fuzzy kiss before standing. After she turned her back, Rich surreptitiously yet frantically scrubbed at his face.

"Thank you, Siegfried!" Carl called out.

The dragon tipped his wings then flapped his way back south, too big to set down on the deck, too tired to hover and chat.

With Siegfried gone, Carl stomped up to Hildegaard. "What's the big idea, leaving me to carry the whole ship on my own? I'd be surprised if I haven't burst a blood vessel!"

"Your dragon was going to land us on top of a coral reef," Hildegaard replied. "I haven't brought the *Bob* this far just have him wrecked!"

"Oh." Carl calmed down, and with the reduction in adrenaline came a reduction in ability to stay on his own two feet: he unceremoniously fell over onto a large coil of rope, taking Roland with him almost the whole way.

"*Raak*! Watch it, jerk!"

"Oh, shut up, Roland," Carl snapped irritably.

"You almost crushed me, you son of a bi-"

"*Roland*?!"

The parrot froze where he perched atop the rope coil, and put on a look of dumb innocence before he looked at Hildegaard. "Raak?"

"It *is* you," she murmured. "I'd recognize that 'who, little ol' innocent me?' look even on a parrot's face."

"Polly wanna cracker?"

Hildegaard lunged at him, but Roland took off toward the shore.

"Get your feathered behind back here, little twerp!" When the bird did not comply, Hildegaard rubbed one of her rings, whispered something so soft Carl could not hear, and threw her grasping hand toward the rapidly departing parrot. Roland was snatched out of mid-air and returned to Hildegaard's hand so fast that he left a trail of feathers mid-air.

"Give me one reason not to squeeze," Hildegaard growled.

Her first mate spoke up. "Didn't you want him to remove his curse from you, Captain?"

Carl gasped. "You cursed someone? That's malfeasance!"

"Not a literal curse – *this*." Hildegaard pointed at her face. "Come on, Carl, you don't think I was born with a pink beard, did you? Roland Junior here thought—"

"*Junior*? He isn't Roland the Magnificent?"

"Daddy was the Magnificent. Technically Junior inherited the title along with the family's estates because he's male and I'm not. But I sailed all the way to England to have my status in the Brotherhood of Merlin formally acknowledged, and when I got back I was fully intending to press my claim to the family estates – which is probably the reason why he sent that fog to abduct me and my crew into the middle of the Carolinas. Isn't it, Roly-Poly?"

"Shut up!" Roland whined.

"Did I miss something there?" Carl asked.

Smirking, Hildegaard explained, "Roly here had quite an appetite on him when he was younger. He got so fat I used to call him 'Roly-Poly.'" Her eyes widened in delight. "Omigod, I just realized: Roly-Poly's a Roly-Polly!" She burst into laughter.

Roland glowered back at her. "Gee, you're a barrel of monkeys, *Bartholomew*."

"Bartholomew?" Carl was feeling decidedly behind the times.

Hildegaard rolled her eyes. "Daddy was the traditional sort. He'd had his heart set on having a boy, so he had my name all picked out before I was born. When I came out a girl mom added my first name: I became Hildegaard Bartholomew Smythe. Daddy was a little disappointed at first, but once he finally got his son he'd wanted, he ended up wanting to put it back where it came from."

"I can understand the sentiment." Carl also had another riddle solved for him: he remembered that there was an H. Bartholomew Smythe in the rolls of the Brotherhood of Merlin.

"Now how the heck did you become a parrot?" Hildegaard asked Roland.

"The Black Island Buccaneers had a certain quarrel with me," he answered her. "They attacked when I was still tired from casting that teleportation spell on your ship, so I had to trade minds with my parrot right before they shot me."

"With *my* parrot, you mean?" Hildegaard shouted. "That's it – you're a dead bird!" She started to squeeze harder.

"I'm pregnant!"

It took a fraction of a second for the meaning of those words to register with Hildegaard. When they did, she dropped the parrot on the deck and backed up, hands spread wide and a look of horrified belief on her face.

"Oh... my... *God*," she enunciated. "He's probably telling the truth; my parrot was female. And he—*she*—just mated with Good Dick's parrot!"

Rich looked at his bird in surprise. "Good thing I gave you a unisex name, Amore."

Carl was feeling a little lightheaded, too. "Well, look on the bright side: with Polly here no longer being the man of the house – in more ways than one – your claim on your estates can't be contested on grounds of gender."

"True," Hildegaard mused, staring at the parrot. "And I always wanted a sister. But am I about to have intelligent parrot-nieces and parrot-nephews, too, or just more pets?" She sighed in real aggravation. "This is why you don't screw around with magic you don't understand, Roland. You never listened to Daddy, and now look what you've gotten yourself into."

Hildegaard suddenly became aware of the combined gaze of Carl, Rich, and the majority of her crew. Her manner formalized, and she stood to make an address. "Coral Reef, it appears I am in your debt many times over today: saving my ship, saving my life and my crew's lives, and reuniting me with my... sibling. Though it is but poor compensation, I offer you this token of repayment, along with my word that if you need me any day in the future, you have but to ask and I will be yours to command."

Carl's eyes widened as Hildegaard held out the bottle which held her family's genie. Given that the number of genies in the world was finite since nobody had been able to uncover how the ancient Egyptian wizards had created or found them, the gift was priceless. Of course, given Carl's preexisting imp servant's tendency toward jealousy, this genie might turn out to be a bit of a curse, too. Still, it was too great a gift to turn down.

"I thank you, Hildegaard B. Smythe," Carl said. "I shall return to my dwelling now, content in knowing that Roland is safe in your hands, and the world is finally safe from *him*."

As Carl popped the cork on the bottle and the smoke enveloped him to take him back to his island, he heard a tiny bit of conversation that provided him with a smile all the way home:

"Roland, after you bear this clutch of eggs, I'm getting you neutered."

"*RAAAAK!*"

Danny has been a contributing author to several sci-fi, fantasy, and professional magazines, anthologies, and journals. He is also an editor for small-press publisher Cyberwizard Productions. His fantasy series *The Laurian Pentology* is being published through Ancient Tomes Press, starting with *Ending an Ending*. His first children's/YA novel "*Between a Roc and a Hard Place*" has won The National Parenting Center's 2010 Seal of Approval, Creative Child Magazine's 2010 Seal of Excellence, and was named one of Dr. Toy's Best Picks of 2010. In addition to literary publication, Danny composes classical and filk music, such as his nonstop hour-long piano solo "Piano Petrissage," and the ever-peculiar album "Warped Children's Songs." Danny's humorous music has been featured on radio and internet programs such as The Dr. Demento Show and The Funny Music Project.

William Did

ERIK AMUNDSEN

William did think last of his boots — shiny silver buckles, shiny black leather — not to wonder which of his captors would come to inherit them once the business was done, but to imagine how they must look over the empty space below the gallows in the instant between the fall of the door and the passage of the man halfway through.

William Kidd, as he sailed down between the planks, he saw a moment of light and tumbled to the ground, hands and feet unbound, the hanging rope broken about his neck. Again. And he stood and he laughed, tearing off the noose and sackcloth black bag over his head. He resurrected himself from the gallows, in full view of no one, narrowed his eyes and peered around. William laughed at the joke it must be, the second time they'd failed to hang him out on the docks in Wapping. Now they flee the scene? Surely, he thought, he must be so much more the fearsome pirate than even East India had painted him.

It was dark out on the dock, the execution dock where they had twice tried and failed to hang the man whom history and song would name the most infamous pirate of them all. William did stretch his neck to one side and the other, listening for the satisfying pops and snaps within. He looked out over the Thames for a moment, half opened his mouth for a toothy, vulpine grin, and seeing no constable to replace the irons on him, no redcoat soldier sighting down his musket and no magistrate thundering with wrath snuck from God's sweetie jar, made to take his leave with a shrug, and a second helping of that grin.

When William did turn himself about, he spied standing at the foot of the dock a man with an unmistakable face, for William did see that face in a shaving glass every morning since first he could shave. This man was younger, though, for his beard and brow were full black and his eyes were twinkling with arrogant and angry yellow light, as if reflecting some secret fire far away. Smartly dressed he was, in red and black, with an amber scarf tied at his neck and a watch on a golden chain. William did not quail at the sight of the man, nor the realization that there were a scattering of black, burnt-off feathers in that hair or that his eyes (huge in the pupil, narrow in the golden iris) were those of a crow, but walked forth to greet him. The man closed the distance between them in a series of stiff legged strides, like a crane; for all of their resemblance to one another when the other was still, it vanished when he moved. William did not like the look of the man; it seemed to him that the other was every inch the pirate William Kidd was not.

"Forgive me, sir," William said. "But have we met? You seem quite familiar."

"We have," the other replied, his voice gravely, raw, as if from breathing smoke. "But I do not think you recognized me on those previous occasions."

William Kidd was not a fool, nor was he dense, and he strongly suspected the other's identity. If such was the case, and his suspicions proved correct, it would disappoint him gravely to learn the truth, and the possibility threw into doubt all the things he'd learned on the narrow benches of his youth.

"I'm afraid you have me at a disadvantage, sir."

"Had I but a penny for every time I've heard a man say that," replied the other.

"Have we been introduced?"

"Not specifically. I have any number of names, but for now, I will use the name Captain William Kidd," the other said. "As in 'God's laws I did forbid, and most wickedly I did' and all of that."

"What a coincidence," William said, letting just a touch of droll disgust out on his breath. "William Kidd is also my name."

"Not anymore," said the other. "The duly designated authorities of the Crown of Britain and the East India Company have impounded that name and ceded it unto me, on my instructions, for considerations in kind over which you needn't concern yourself."

"You're a captain, then," William said, switching the tack of the conversation. "Might I be so bold to inquire the name of your ship?"

"Hell is the name of my ship." The other swept out his hand and William saw his shadow pass over the man, rimmed in crimson light.

William did turn around as beckoned and saw the ship, dark red in the hull and red of sail, strung with hundreds of red and yellow paper lanterns as if for a party; thin little sounds streamed from those lanterns, a faraway chorus of whining and weeping, buzzing along the wires that held them. On the decks, a fell crew pulled lines and sang blasphemous songs to the time of an unseen lash. The *Hell* was as smartly rigged and run as any ship William had ever seen; that he could tell from the dock. He also noted that the river had widened; he could no longer see Bermondsey or Rotherhithe on the far shore, and the sky had grown dark and steely, with striations of black smoke twining through the low clouds. Massive fish with heads like barracuda, bone colored scales and white blind eyes swam around her as she sat anchored, and the gangplank lowered to admit them.

"So I am to take it that Satan is another name to which you would answer, and that it is my soul you've come to collect?" William asked, and for the first time, felt the fear. It rose, but he rose atop it; the devil could break him, he knew, but William did resolve to hold out until the very last moment.

"If the shoe fits," said the other, which drew William's gaze to his feet, which had become the black iron cloven hooves of traditional description in the intervening moments. "You have murdered and are therefore technically mine, but I have something more valuable of you than your meager, bitter old soul."

"Are your mountebank's theatrics meant to be a feature of my torment?"

"Ha! If that displeases you, more's the better; such is my nature and my way."

"All men can supersede their natures."

"I cannot," said the devil. "And you did not, which leads me to the nature of your predicament. I am in my rights to claim your soul; God will not have you, any more than he has any of your accursed race, but as I said before, you have given me something more valuable still than yet another soul."

"Which is?" William asked.

"Your name, and your deeds, the ones you never did, three ships of France, three ships of Spain. To those who yet live, you are a pirate, and the worst of a horrid lot. Your name and your infamy will inspire men to sin and violence for years to come. Those ripples of violence and hate will set off more and wider sin for generations, long after your infamy is forgotten as the source. Your infamy itself, however, that will not be forgotten."

William thought on this for a moment. Beyond the reputations of his widowed wife and his daughters, he found he did not much care for what the world might suffer under the pall of the story of the infamous and bloodthirsty Captain Kidd. William did turn to the other and give him his vulpine grin.

"Is that knowledge meant to be a portion of my torment? For it does not torment me at all to know."

"Which is precisely why I told you," said the other. "When I torment you, you shall know torment."

For all the other's asininity and shabby huckster theatrics, William believed what he said.

"Why, then," William asked, "would you choose to tell me?"

"That's an interesting question. Let me say that you feel yourself falsely accused and a victim of injustice. Even here, at the gates of hell, you hold in your secret heart that you deserve not this fate, but let me tell you, this fate is well deserved. Your soul is every bit as black as the song I wrote for you claims it is."

"I am no pirate, sir. I held a letter of marque to hunt pirates. I took a ship under foreign flag according to the law. If my soul has blackened in this venture, it is from betrayal, lack of support, and not seldom did I speculate your own intervention."

"My, but you sound awfully familiar," said the Other. "Your words have a certain similarity to those spoken last by William Moore, before you struck him dead."

William did have some time to reflect on this matter, as he always suspected his judgment might come down to this, and he had, in the solitude of his cell, composed a rebuttal or two, but the language he had used was what one might speak before the Lord, and it did not seem appropriate to bother since the Lord had not so much as seen fit to judge William Himself. William did notice that in heaven as on earth, he was sentenced before the hearing had ever begun, and that tore the words he dropped away from his mind like the wind with so many strips of paper.

"Moore was a mutineer," William said. "I struck him in anger, but I did not mean for that blow to be mortal."

"And such was the second thing said Cain unto my Adversary after the part about being his brother's keeper. Time hasn't been kind to its freshness. As for William Moore, yes, a mutineer; and for that, he received his just reward. As I'm sure you apprehend, I've a bit of affinity for that kind. Also, to return to matters of salience, for pirates."

"I am no pirate."

"The judgment of men is that you were a pirate, William Kidd, and a shabby one at that. No choice you make in the hour of your death is going to reverse that, any more than your actions now can reverse the judgment of heaven. The options left to you are to resent, be sullen and suffer, or to embrace the judgment and use it as the prisoner uses his shackles to garrote the guard."

"I don't see how death is meant to improve my reputation, make me feared when I was not in life. A shabby, luckless, unwitting pirate is not something to inspire the terror you seem set on making of me."

"But you could be quite inspiring, if you let me inspire you. You could be such a pirate, if you chose. In life you found yourself a victim of circumstances, ones you assured yourself were beyond your control. For all your assurances, all your nights praying that they were true into the dark that is the only thing that ever listened; you know in your heart that you had the means to change your situation. You had the ways and means to your ends in mind, but you shied away from them."

"My parents taught me well to shun the gates of hell," William said distantly, but when he looked inside his heart, and found the other was speaking truth, or something very close to truth.

"And look where you ended."

"So then, what is it that you want?" William asked, and the other knew he had won by the softness of William's voice.

"What every good captain wants, ere he retires," said the other. "To be commodore. That ship is a fine ship, but the coming age will require more ships to house all the crew and fare I intend to gain. In that case I need captains to sail for me, and not flinch from the orders I give, men such as the man you could be, once you allow yourself the latitude to act as your nature demands."

"I could refuse," William said.

"But you won't," the other replied.

"Enlighten me," William said.

"It would be my delight. You came here, to this execution dock, to the very River Styx, pushed and dragged every step by liars, false witnesses, mutineers and fools. You have sailed the seven seas, you have seen that these breeds of man come in no short supply, and tonight, they sleep in comfortable beds, eat capon, drink wine, take comfort in their families, and you, who are no liar, fool, nor false witness are damned for them. What I offer is a rare opportunity; you can have naught but torment, or you can have the chance to torment those who brought you here."

"It's an attractive offer," William said.

"As you consider, and consider quickly, I've spent longer on your case than I'd intended – I invite you to add the fact that, for the first time since your creation, you are not being watched, nor will your answer bring greater censure from those you used to hope to please."

William looked out at the ship again, the dark red sails against the black and grey sky, the lanterns that glowed with the celebratory light of hellfire, listened to the creak of the timbers, smelled pitch.

"Right," William said. "Let us have a look at my ship."

The other laughed and ushered him onto the gangplank. William did walk up, onto the deck, and the plank was raised. For a moment, all was silent, and the sails hung slack. Then a wind caught and filled them, and from the billowing, bloody cloth flickered a lick of fire, then two or three, and suddenly the sails caught and burst into flame. The ship of *Hell* caught at the mast, the riggings burned, the deck lit up, and the hull blazed.

Captain Kidd called his orders with a voice that howled from the abyss, and his ship broke like a Child ballad, and sank into the silent black water.

As he sailed.

Erik Amundsen: Always Chaotic Evil.

The Vengeance Garden

LAUREL ANNE HILL

The heat of anger flushed through Michaela Cordova as she looked down from her cliff. Pirates! All were scum on Satan's pond. She turned away from the two-masted pirate ship anchored in the cove below, the corvette's rigging hanging like corrupted flesh on bones. Tonight, her magic would avenge Mama, Papa and Santiago, murdered by these cutthroats the year before last. Not a single soul aboard deserved mercy.

A low whistle arose like a sudden wind. Concha's signal? Why would her servant disobey instructions to remain in their adobe dwelling? She glanced around.

The being who called himself El Diablo leaned against a twisted pine, whistled again and waved in her direction. His thick lips bore the grin of a fox beside a chicken roost. This time, neither sulfur fumes nor puffs of scarlet smoke heralded his arrival. He had first appeared to her last autumn when she had cast her vengeance spell. How long had he been watching her tonight?

"Sand in the hourglass runs low," El Diablo said. "Do you have a request to make of me, or not?" He tightened his woolen cloak around his stocky frame. Wind blowing in from the ocean swept across the cliff and lifted his dark, shoulder-length locks. "As I have told you, the initial favor comes without obligation."

"I am sure it does," Michaela said.

The powers of Hell always had a way of making a second request necessary, or so her mother used to claim. But Michaela did not need El Diablo's assistance to obtain revenge. The earth-spirit magic she had already set in motion would serve her well enough, even if she had not spoken all the incantations in proper order. Besides, this devil had neither horns nor cloven hooves. A lesser henchman of Satan, no doubt. Why would she sell her soul for a mere underling's help?

"You truly believe your spell of vengeance shall protect you without my assistance?" El Diablo laughed. "Bewitching those pirates to return here and relieving them of their lives—before they slowly relieve you of yours—are two different pots of beans." He folded his arms against his chest. The black goatee on his chin glistened in the moonlight. "Yield your will to me and I shall safeguard your life, honor and future motherhood."

"Yield to you?" Michaela tightened her grip on the handle of her lantern. "I would rather perish." How heavy those words rested upon her tongue.

Well, why not accept death and rejoin the family she had lost? Her beloved second cousin—the only man who had ever stirred her heart—would soon be trapped in an arranged marriage to someone else. An ache spread across her stomach. Only vengeance against a shipload of cutthroats gave her life purpose anymore. Her reason for living would die tonight with the pirate ship's ruthless crew. Besides, the pirates had burned down most of Hacienda Vista a year-and-a-half ago. She might as well make her new home in Heaven.

"Then perish you shall." El Diablo sauntered over to her. The tips of his thick fingers tilted her chin upward, his breath rancid as spoiled butter. "A little at a time."

El Diablo faded to gray threads of mist and disappeared. Michaela clamped her lips together and purged air through her nostrils. Leave it to a devil to issue threats and instill uncertainty. She again gazed out into the night toward Alta

California's coastal waters, south of the Monterey Presidio and north of Mission Santa Barbara. She must attain vengeance without sacrificing her salvation and eternal joy. This meant no suicide, no cowardice and no deals with devils.

Michaela maneuvered across uneven ground and away from the cliff's edge. Her bare feet clenched loose soil. When the pirates found her tonight, she could not expect saints to intercede on her behalf. She already had the gift of magic to assist her. Heaven would answer her pitiful prayers last, if ever.

But it was time to make haste back to her little house. The pirates would have noticed her lantern by now, as she had planned, for she had remained clear of nearby cypress trees and pines. She must send Concha to the safety of the oak grove before enticing the murderers to their doom.

Ahead, moonlight illuminated Michaela's tangled garden of squash and creeping vines. She hurried through the plot of dark green squash grown for food. Next came the squash vines she and Concha had planted last autumn under a full moon. These vines had a special purpose. Her pace slowed.

"Oh, moon of gold," she said. "Call forth the seeds of blood." Or had Mama told her to call the seeds of blood forth? She had never dared to write down Mama's spells, for fear Papa would find out she knew them. Now, once again, the exact order of words eluded her.

"Call the seeds of blood forth," Michaela said. One petition or the other would be correct.

Something tugged at Michaela's foot. She halted and looked down. A vine curled around her ankle. Did the enchanted plant wish to impart a vision, the way it had last month? A nearby pale yellow squash, the length of her arm, gleamed in the moonlight. Months past Twelfth Night, this ripe squash and a hundred others still remained unspoiled. Michaela's imperfect chants under the full moon on the eve of All Saints Day had managed to seal the vengeance spell. But then, Mama had always said the inherited gift of power was more important than the words.

Now the enchanted leaves caressed both of Michaela's ankles. Ah, yes, murky visions formed within her mind.

Ragged sailors gathered on the deck of the anchored corvette. Cutthroats lowered longboats into the cove's quiet waters. Oar tips dipped below a kelp-covered surface. She could even hear the creaking of the pirate ship's wooden hull in seawater.

How could the plants know all this and reach into her mind? No matter. They knew and made sure she did, too. The strength of the spell she had cast was strong.

Another vision—near the ship's helm stood a slender youth with dark hair and large green eyes, like haunted emeralds. Mist shrouded many of his facial features. Such a strong resemblance he bore to her beloved second cousin, who now lived near Mission San Diego de Acala. Foul vision! Her gentle cousin never would become a pirate, dishonor his family in any manner. El Diablo must have come back here, projecting lies to disturb her.

The invisible devil belted out a hardy guffaw from somewhere nearby. Yes, he mocked her with deceitful images. A shudder passed across Michaela's shoulders. The vine released one of her ankles and stroked her instep. The false vision of the pirate youth faded.

Oh, to see her cousin once more in this life, to be the recipient of his loving smile. But she would not sell her soul for El Diablo's protection. Cousin would marry this summer and she would die by tomorrow. Right now, Michaela must concentrate on present action and ensure Concha's safety.

"Please release me," Michaela said to the vine. The greenery loosened its grip.

"One shall remain," the wind said.

Such a feminine voice—those words must have come from earth spirits. She ran toward her dwelling. The wind had referred to Concha or one of the pirates, perhaps. But her spell had called for only the guilty pirates to return to this cove, thus, the magic would spare none of the swashbucklers. Concha, then, would be the lone survivor at Hacienda Vista tonight.

As for the fate of the pirates, Mama never had mentioned how squash, even enchanted ones, could harm anyone. Perhaps earth-spirit magic would transform the squash into fierce dragoons—a cavalry to champion Michaela's cause.

Or the squash might become grizzly bears and claw the men apart. Either way, the magic would not require her to witness such horrors. She already had seen more than her share. Perhaps a chasm in the land would open and simply engulf the swashbuckling scum.

Vengeance is mine, sayeth the Lord. Those were words the Catholic padre at Mission San Carlos Borromeo de Carmelo used to recite. The ball of Michaela's foot landed upon a flat stone, the grave marker in memory of Mama, Papa, little Santiago and two servant women. The pirates had severed Mama's head from her body, then split Michaela's two-year-old brother in half.

Vengeance belonged to more than the Lord.

Michaela opened the door of her home. Home? Only two years ago this wretched one-room adobe with cracked walls and a dirt floor had been the sleeping quarters for a dozen servants. Now only she, this hovel and Concha—an Indian born at the nearest mission—remained. Concha stood in the middle of the room. The light from flickering candles framed her round face and wide, dark eyes.

"Is it they?" Concha said, her voice small and timid.

"*Si,*" Michaela said. "Yes. All is as your vision claimed." How thoughtful Concha's ancestors were to bring her useful information. Michaela, more Spaniard than Indian, received many of her visions through less reliable means.

Michaela set down her lantern and removed her wool cloak. The chill of the room cut through her muslin nightdress. She shivered. Something moved over there in the corner. Did faint odors of smoke and sulfur drift through the air? She searched the room's shadows. No El Diablo.

His unanticipated appearances continued to fuel her imagination and fear. Would her inner strength and resolve hold tonight if pirates attacked and tortured her before they perished? She must not plead to El Diablo for mercy the saints would not provide. If only Mama had taught her a spell to protect her life and Concha's.

Moonlight shone through the window. By now, the pirates must be wading in the sheltered cove, guiding their rowboats through the rocky shallows. Men with foul breaths—like El Diablo's—and large, rough hands. El Diablo had said she would die a little at a time unless she requested his help. Michaela fingered the silver crucifix around her neck.

"Are you ready?" Michaela crossed her arms against her chest and tightened her fists. So cold now. Her rough, uneven fingernails dug into her palms.

"*Sí*," Concha said. Her womanly shape was noticeable under her night clothes as she walked toward Michaela. Childhood had passed for her, too. Soon, Concha would turn nineteen, but, of course, Michaela would not.

Michaela grasped Concha's hand as though she were her sister. How could Michaela have once grabbed a willow switch and lashed Concha for disobedience? Had Concha forgiven her? People did not always reveal their true feelings.

"You must go to the oak grove now," Michaela said. "If I die tonight, you know where Papa's gold doubloons lay buried."

"I." Concha lowered her eyelids and pinched together her full lips. "I stay with you."

"No," Michaela said. They had discussed this before. "Your life waits to be lived."

"You think I am like a child," Concha said, her eyes now open wide. "A child to be sent away to safety." She shook her head from side-to-side several times. "Those pirates, they killed people I loved, too."

"There is no need for both of us to suffer and die," Michaela said. Plus, El Diablo could trick Concha into begging for his help. "Must I order you to leave?"

"Order me?" Concha straightened and tightened her fists. "The time for orders, it has passed. If your mama had ordered us to plant squash under the full moon, if she had woven a protective spell for Hacienda Vista, then five innocent people would not lay buried in our garden."

Michaela's cheeks warmed and the crown of her head tingled. Papa never would have permitted the planting of a bewitched garden. Concha knew that. Of course, her beloved cousin would not have allowed such a garden, either, although he probably did not know earth magic existed. To Cousin, all magic spells were Satan's handiwork.

"If I cannot order," Michaela said, "may I plead?"

"We sowed the ground together," Concha said, "watered the vines together. You spoke the words but my heart repeated them."

Michaela pressed her hands over her mouth and nose. The responsibility for tonight—for Concha—rested upon her. To make matters worse, the fearful emerald eyes of the youth in her false vision glowed in the darkness of her thoughts. What if an innocent man had joined the pirates and feared to attempt an escape?

No, the pirates would have killed anyone they did not trust. Besides, only the murderers of her family would have embarked upon the voyage to this cove. Still, Michaela had been unsure of Mama's exact instructions for incantations. An innocent man among the crew might be possible.

"If the saints find error with what I have done," Michaela said, "the mark must be upon my soul alone."

"Saints and the Devil," Concha said. "I'm sure they exist somewhere yet neither have come to me. But my ancestors have. When the pirates arrived here two years ago, my vision told me to take you up the hill to the oak grove and crawl into that tree snag. Tonight, spirits told me to stay with you."

"You do not understand," Michaela said. "I never wrote down the magic words Mama told me." She should have admitted this to Concha before. "What if I accidentally drew an innocent man back here with the guilty ones?"

"If any of them are innocent," Concha said, "an owl will hoot seven times."

Hooting would do no good if the squash already had turned into grizzly bears. Michaela's temples throbbed, as though all her blood tried to rush to her brain at once. Why had she not perceived Concha's strong feelings before?

Tragic, the way Michaela's mystical gift had arrived as a legacy. If she had possessed power when Mama were still alive, all of this might never have happened.

Michaela and Concha stood side-by-side amidst the tangle of enchanted squash vines. Only a few minutes had passed since she and Concha had argued inside their dwelling. The night wind, colder than before, raised tiny bumps on Michaela's skin.

Above the moan of rushing air and the lapping of seawater, Michaela's imagination could hear pirates' boots tromping through wet sand. Soon the scum wearing those boots would climb the narrow path up the cliff beside the cove. They would not expect to discover two beautiful young *señoritas* dressed only in white nightgowns. Macho lust would triumph over caution. The pirates would come to the vengeance garden and die.

Wind whipped the skirt and long sleeves of their bed clothes, and tossed about Concha's waist-length black hair. Good Christian women should not dress in such a suggestive manner beyond the privacy of their homes. But now, Michaela had to obey the bewitched squash rather than the teachings of her parents and the padres. She needed to obey her own heart, too, and try to protect Concha as best she could.

"The cliff moves." Concha pointed beyond the squash field toward the cove.

Cliffs could not move except to fall into the sea. Michaela shifted position and focused her eyes upon the darkness. A cloud had passed over the moon. Her tallow lantern showed little more than nearby squash and vines. Then dim light from the emerging moon revealed shadows against the velvet night. Something rose out there, far beyond the garden. Something near the cliff's edge grew taller. A ball of light appeared and quivered in the air—a lantern. The pirates must have crested the rise above the beach.

"Who goes there?" A gruff voice scratched at the air.

"Women of God," Michaela shouted. A half-truth, perhaps, these days. Something tickled her ankle. A vine's tendril. Her heartbeat quickened.

She glanced toward Concha. The servant's skin glimmered in lantern light. On the ground, the squash shimmered like citron stones catching rays of morning sun.

A vine curled around Michaela's lower calf. How tight the growth pressed, like a rope used for cattle. A vine had not the strength to hold her fast yet this one did. She could no longer move her tethered leg.

She reached down and tugged on the vine. The thin rope of greenery would neither move nor tear. The vines were supposed to trap the pirates, not her. Now the pirates would capture her for sure. Michaela's fate was sealed.

Michaela knew she must calm herself, control her fear. She would meet this challenge bravely, and live long enough to see the squash turn into soldiers or bears. Or witness the earth opening and swallowing the murderers.

The moon radiated a growing brightness. The pirate cluster advanced, like an amorphous sea monster with many heads, legs and arms. Most of the monster's chests wore striped or white shirts. Calf-length pantaloons or slit cowhide breeches covered the legs. Feet stuffed into leather boots pounded the rocky terrain. Whoops and hollers merged with catcalls and whistles. The wind carried the stink of unwashed men.

"The whore of good fortune," a male voice called, "she tips her arse in our direction."

"Can ye still tell the difference" another said, "between one hole in her arse and the other?"

"You no could tell a maidenhead from dung if you kissed the Holy Virgin's."

Michaela pushed away their blasphemies against heaven and women, lest her mind accidentally repeat them. She tried to lift her foot—to step away from the vines—but they would not release her. There was no turning back now.

"Oh, earth spirits who walk beside my family," she said, clutching her lantern. "Hear these words. Moon of gold, call forth seeds of blood. Or the seeds of blood forth. Avenge Mama, Papa and little Santiago." She glanced toward Concha. "And avenge Concha and those she loved. And me."

It was done. She had not spoken everything the best way. Too late, now. What would be, would be.

Then a single flash of lightning—like the blink of a fiery eye—darted across the sky. Distant thunder rumbled. The sea monster of men plodded through the squash, smashing the fruit underfoot.

No cavalry or bears arose from the soil or the mutilated squash. No angry spirits attacked the onslaught of blasphemous men. Had Michaela waited too long to say the magic words? What if she had said the words so wrong they could not work? Maybe she just needed to speak louder.

"I demand vengeance! Bring forth seeds of blood."

The pirates were only a dozen cart lengths away from her and closing in fast. Beards bristled on their faces, their breaths rotten from spoiled teeth and grog. Dear God, the magic words did not halt them.

Another figure appeared, in front of the others, his back turned toward Michaela. So tall, he was. The pirates' heads only reached the height of his shoulders. The man's curly hair brushed against his shoulders—shoulders covered with a woolen cloak. Michaela knew that woolen cloak, that curly, shoulder-length hair. The man was El Diablo.

"Stand back, you scoundrels," El Diablo shouted at the men. He stretched out his arms toward the murderers. Moonlight glinted on metal. He grasped two long knives, one in each hand. "Your hour, she has come."

The front of the pirate monster collapsed on several sets of knees. Those behind the leading edge stumbled over the fallen and plummeted to the ground. Men shouted. Lightning flashed, brightening El Diablo's form. A gust of wind spread his dark locks as though his hair might transform into wings. There was little more distance between the mass of men and Michaela than between a matador and lunging bull at a fiesta. And still the vines held her legs fast.

A pirate with a crazed glare broke away from the monster. He leaped toward Michaela. Was her strength sufficient to push him away? Her every muscle braced.

El Diablo locked his hands onto the attacking pirate's waist. He jerked the cutthroat backwards, lifted him high, then pivoted. The pirate sailed through the air and crashed into the throng of his fallen crewmates. Another flash of lightning arrived.

Thunder answered and something on the ground moved, something more than pirates. Michaela lifted her lantern. The squash, even the broken pieces, rocked against the earth. The fruit of the full moon edged toward the fallen cutthroats. And the vines—the squash vines curled upward like snakes preparing to strike. The vines became slithering ropes, no longer tethered by their roots. They lashed forward and wrapped themselves around the clump of human scum. A third flash of lightning filled the heavens. Squash crawled over men.

Fallen pirates screamed. Blood spewed as though from fountains. El Diablo stepped away from the writhing mass of pirates, plants and gore.

Michaela snapped shut her eyes, the warm, sticky spray clinging to her face, her lips, her entire body.

"Mercy," a man yelled, "I beg ye."

"I change me ways," another cried.

"May the devil frig the devil," a gruff voice added.

Shouts, pleas, vile language and screams blended, pounding into Michaela's ears. Some dared to call for mercy. They had not listened when Mama and Papa had done the same. Michaela opened her eyes. She must witness the death of those who had ripped her family from her.

A leg here, an arm there. Blood and battered flesh littered the once peaceful garden. The stench of blood and excrement caused Michaela's stomach to twist and sour. This was not the simple, clean, satisfying retribution she had imagined, one where El Diablo opened a hole in the earth and threw the men into it, one where all that need be known was the wrongdoers' fate to burn in Hell's eternal fire. Her dream of vengeance had transformed into the reality of blood, horror, fury and desperation.

And she remained alive, tethered by the vines. She was a captive to the magic she had wrought. Was Concha safe? Had any of the men been innocent? She listened for an owl hooting. The air carried only the groans of the dying.

Michaela opened her eyes to moonlight. She had not intended to sleep but must have. She lay on damp ground. Perhaps a little rain had fallen. The lightning storm had passed.

"Concha," Michaela called. She had to be here somewhere.

El Diablo stood beside a heap of limp bodies and dismembered limbs. He raised his lantern. The lamp burned as bright as morning sun. Slit breeches clothed some figures on the ground. Others wore torn shirts and pantaloons. The pirates' skins were gray and cracked like parched earth in summer. So dry, the night wind should have crumbled and dispersed their remains.

The blood of murderers soaked her clothes. Her hair hung in clotted tangles. Little blood coated the victims. No remnants of smashed squash lay anywhere. The disparity made no sense.

A soft sobbing—Michaela turned her head toward the sound. Yes, Concha was alive. Blessed Mother of God. The Indian sat upon a patch of earth beyond El Diablo and the dead, gray pirates, her face clutched in her bloody hands. A pile of intact yellow squash rested nearby.

"It is finished," Michaela said.

She needed to comfort her friend. The vines uncurled from her legs. But why shouldn't they? Her ordeal was over, although demon memories born this night might forever haunt her dreams. Michaela stood and picked up her lantern.

Now vines twisted around Concha's legs and held fast. El Diablo sneered and lifted an unbroken yellow squash above Concha's captive form.

"Oh, moon of gold," he said, "call forth seeds for blood."

"What are you doing?" Michaela yelled.

"Using the correct words." He laughed. "Which you failed to accomplish."

The wrong words? She had used the wrong words to destroy the pirates? Yet that mattered little now. This devil meant to destroy Concha—dear innocent Concha—the same way magic had claimed the pirates' lives. How dared he do that?

"Let her be!" Michaela said.

The man spewed out a bellow of laughter and turned his bearded face toward Michaela. Oh, blessed saints. She had requested a favor from one of Satan's henchmen.

"Two pleas have flowed from between your lips," he said. His eyes glowed crimson, then the color of yellow bile. "First you cried out for vengeance. I assumed you must have invoked me. And now this. You owe me a debt of fearsome magnitude."

Dear Mother of God. She was condemned.

"But, but I asked the earth magic for vengeance," she said. "Not you—"

"I am the source of your magic," he said.

"You are lying," Michaela said. Mama never would have dealt with Satan's kind.

"Take my soul instead of hers," Concha begged. The Indian's hands pulled at the vines around her legs. The ropelike growth did not yield. "She only asked for help because of me."

"Your soul?" El Diablo said. A thin veil of smoke rose around him. "What think you? Satan exists through me? I am a forefather who begat Michaela's forefathers. I first called the family magic from the wells of earth." He bellowed louder. "Devilry lives mainly within the living. Well, during most hours of night and day."

This El Diablo was Michaela's ancestor? Certainly not an Indian ancestor. And how could Satan not exist? The many teachings she had learned could not be wrong. Her stomach muscles tightened. And then there was the matter of a fearsome debt.

"What do you demand of me?" Michaela said.

El Diablo strode over to Michaela, his eyes as red and refractive as a rat's in lantern light after sunset.

"Continue our family line," El Diablo said. He thumped the squash he held and grinned down at her. "You will wed the man of my choosing. The remaining man aboard the ship should do fine."

"Marriage to a pirate?" Michaela might as well burn in Hell's fire—well, if Hell was a real place. She set down her lantern, straightened her body to its full height and put her hands on her hips. "You cannot make me do such a—"

El Diablo hurled the squash he held at Michaela. The fruit of the vine, now scarlet, hit her shoulder and burst. A crimson shower—surely the pirate's blood—erupted from the fruit and flowed down her arm. The foul fluid spayed her already blood-covered nightdress, coated nearby vines and seeped into cracks in the earth.

"Seeds for blood. Blood for seeds." El Diablo's laughter echoed in Michaela's ears.

The broken pieces of squash rocked upon the earth and edged toward her. They would kill her as they had the pirates, turn her flesh dry and gray. This was not a manner of death she had envisioned.

A piece of squash, seeds transformed into teeth, sprang upward and bit Michaela's arm. She screamed. A force, like a strong wind, pushed her down upon her knees. She deserved a better fate than this.

"Please," she said, "I beg mercy of you—"

"Aha," El Diablo said, "a third request. Marry the young man, you shall. You used to think rather well of him, at least before I convinced him to join a certain crew of disreputable sea-scum in San Diego. Let's see, that was nearly two months ago."

"I used to—"

"Michaela?" a man's uneven voice said from behind her.

Something about the cadence of his voice triggered a memory. A cool hand rested upon her shoulder, a touch she had felt years before. Michaela sucked in a short breath. Was she dreaming? Dared she turn around?

An owl hooted in the distance, the bird's calls run together. Too fast to count. Oh, for the owl's hoots to total seven, the number of innocence.

Michaela gathered courage, rose and faced her beloved second cousin. Seawater dripped from his dark hair, flannel undershirt and knee breeches. He shivered, must have swum from the pirate's corvette to the beach. How wide his green eyes appeared. Perhaps he had arrived while the squash attacked her.

"I sailed here," Cousin said, "praying to rescue you, to wed you against my father's wishes. And now I find you half-dressed and pleading for mercy—not to the Holy Virgin, but Satan himself."

"But I swear, he is not—"

"Demon witch!" Her cousin stepped backward, his wrists crossed in front of his shadowy face. "I have forsaken a pious bride for this unholy union. Oh, heaven have mercy upon my soul."

The fearful, haunted look Michaela had seen in tonight's vision filled his emerald eyes. How could he look upon her this way? Moisture slipped from her tear ducts and clouded her eyes. Blessed saints, give her strength to endure.

El Diablo grasped Michaela's wrist and Cousin's arm, forcing their hands to join. Ceremonial words poured from between El Diablo's crimson lips. His irises glowed brilliant orange.

"I pledge thee my troth." Cousin hissed. He jerked his hand free from Michaela's and spat upon the ground.

"I pledge, too," Michaela whispered.

She had given no mercy. In return, little mercy would be received. Unless...

Yield your will to me, El Diablo had said to her.

Michaela's soul chilled, as though snowmelt coursed through her veins.

KOMENAR Publishing released *Heroes Arise*, Laurel Anne Hill's award-winning novel, in 2007. Her shorter works of fiction and nonfiction have appeared in a variety of publications, including the anthologies *Tales of Fortannis: A Bard's Eye View* (Double Dragon Publishing) and *Rum and Runestones* (Dragon Moon Press). The fans of HorrorAddicts.net voted Laurel "Most Wicked 2011" for her steampunk/horror short-story podcast, "Flight of Destiny."

Laurel gives creative writing workshops for adults and young adults, and has served as a writing contest judge. She also "geeks for good" by moderating the Minds Clearing Land Mines WordPress blog, a site dedicated to providing information about current land mine clearance technology. Laurel is a member of California Writers Club, Broad Universe, Wicked Women Writers and Women Writing the West. Visit her website and podcast athttp://www.laurelannehill.com.

Blood of the Hydra

CHRIS A. JACKSON AND ANNE L. McMILLEN-JACKSON

The young lieutenant wiped his sword clean on the hem of his uniform jacket as he gazed at the captain's tri-corner hat bobbing on the waves beside the ship. Farther astern floated the captain's body, face down in a halo of blood. Crimson swirled as gray fins eddied the water, and the body shuddered and jerked as the denizens of the deep fed. The halo grew as the body shrank, until finally there was nothing left. The lieutenant sheathed his cutlass, stripped off his uniform jacket and threw it into the sea.

A raucous cheer erupted, and the lieutenant turned toward the crew. Many hung over the bulwarks, spitting into the blood-stained water and gesturing curses. Others hung back, eyes down, quiet, nervously putting lines in order and adjusting the sails. These were the ones who hadn't joined the mutiny wholeheartedly, who had complained of their wretched treatment, but hadn't raised arms to fight against the captain and the eleven bloody-handed officers who remained loyal to him. Oddly enough, these men didn't worry him; like sheep, they would follow without question or complaint. The others, however... Another cry went up from the frenzied crew, but this time they called for rum. As one, they surged toward the companionway to the aft cabins and the captain's private stores, eager to reap the benefits of their murderous deeds.

"Halt!" The lieutenant blocked the companionway, drawing his sword. *This is the moment,* he thought as he returned the glares of the crew, *to triumph...or suffer the captain's fate.* "We can celebrate later. Right now we need to haul down the imperial flag, break out the paint and disguise our appearance. Then—"

"Right now I need a drink," bellowed Old Rob, shouldering his way forward through his crewmates. He squinted at the lieutenant through his one good eye—the other having been put out by the captain for some offense years ago—and flexed his meaty fists. Hauling sails was hard work, and despite the meager rations they had been living on, these sailors were sinewy and strong. "An' ain't no one gonna stand in me way!" He pressed forward, encouraged by catcalls from his mates.

With one slash, the lieutenant opened the brazen sailor's throat. Blood sprayed, but before any could react, even before the body hit the deck, the lieutenant sprinted up the steps to the quarterdeck. He cast a defiant stare over the crew before pointing down to the body spilling its blood onto the deck.

"That is what will happen to all of us," he cried, "if we are caught. Do you understand what we have done here? We have killed imperial officers—killed the captain!—and seized an imperial warship! The emperor won't care that the bastard had men flogged or hanged for minor offenses, because discipline on a warship is the captain's prerogative." He pointed aloft to where the imperial flag fluttered. "We were to rendezvous with the fleet tomorrow. How easy do you think it will be for them to find and capture us if we're all drunken sots?"

The crew hung back, cold reality dousing their blood lust. *Loyalty,* the lieutenant thought. *Power stems from loyalty.* What the captain didn't understand was that you can't beat loyalty into a man; the stick is useless without the carrot. So he offered them a carrot. Swinging his sword, he slashed at the mizzen mast, parting the flag halyard. Slowly, the imperial flag floated down, catching briefly on the quarterdeck rail before falling into the water.

"We are free men now!" shouted the lieutenant. "Pirates! The emperor has no hold on us. Together, we will find a new home—build a new nation!—one based on loyalty to one another. We will reap riches beyond our wildest dreams! Follow me, and I will set a course true to our principles. What say you?"

The crew shouted out an overwhelming cheer. Even the most hesitant were caught up in the enthusiasm, waving their arms and slapping one another on the back.

"Then let's be at it!" the lieutenant called out. "Ethan, there; you're my new first mate, and Rogers will back you up as bosun. I'm going below to plot our new course, and when I come out again, I don't want to recognize this ship. Everyone to work!"

"Aye aye, Lieutenant Strongwind!" the crew called as they rushed to their tasks.

"Captain!" he corrected them as he pointed his sword toward the bloody deck. "Call me Captain Bloodwind."

Captain Bloodwind cast a steely eye around the tavern. It was dark and dirty and altogether an unsavory place situated along a lonely stretch of shore where their thinly disguised warship would be ignored. But his men needed a diversion, and Bloodwind needed time to think. In the month since their mutiny, they had only managed to eke out a meager subsistence, scavenging the unarmed fishing fleet while avoiding finer prey. Attacking a richly laden merchant fleet with their military escorts was a sure way to be recognized and captured. He needed a safe haven, a more suitable ship, and better luck...much better luck.

Aboard his ship, the new captain had heard the whispered conversations that ceased as he neared, felt the belligerent stares of the crew as yet another day passed without their vision reaching fruition. He had taken to bolting his cabin door and sleeping with his sword by his side. If he was to save his command—and his life—he needed a successful raid, and he needed it soon.

The scent of roses wafted over him, sweetly superseding the stink of stale rum and unwashed men. Turning his head, he found a woman seated beside him. Dark hair flowed over white shoulders and framed a lovely face that would not have looked out of place beneath a royal crown. Her blood-red lips curved up in a sly smile, and though her eyes were hidden in shadow, they occasionally caught the flickering lamp light and seemed to glow red.

"Captain Bloodwind." Her voice was low and husky, and he felt his body respond. The rum-warmth in his stomach crept down to his loins, but suspicion banked the blaze of lust. He considered for a moment that his crew might have engaged her to kill him, then dismissed the notion; they had neither the brains nor the gold to hire a woman such as this. Besides, attracting women had always been easy for him; he smiled when he considered the many women he had sweet-talked onto their backs.

"You know my name," he said as he straightened and leaned close, inhaling her alluring scent even as he caressed the hilt of the dagger at his waist.

"Your reputation precedes you," she said as she laid a long slender hand on his forearm. "I like a man with a sense of danger, willing to risk everything to gain what he...desires."

"And what do you think I desire?" he asked, the cold ball of suspicion in his gut undiminished.

She raised her hand to his face and caressed his cheek, then ran her fingers down his neck, scratching him gently with her long nails. The stroke sent shivers down his spine, and his body surged with the power in her delicate touch.

"You desire me," she replied. "And I desire you."

"I have no money," he said.

She smiled. "I have no interest in money."

She slowly rose to her feet, white bosom barely tucked into the bodice of her close-fitting dress, slender waist, and the swell of hips passing close before his eyes. It was only with a great force of will that he refrained from seizing her and having his way with her right there on the table top; force of will and the fear that his crew might slip a dagger between his ribs while he was preoccupied. She turned away and took a step, then looked back at him.

"First room at the top of the stairs," she said, "in five minutes." Then she walked away.

All eyes watched as she crossed the room and ascended the stairs, none more intently than those of Captain Bloodwind. The exaggerated sway of her hips reminded him of the undulations of a sea snake as it swam languidly across placid water. Sea snakes were beautiful but deadly; so, too, he felt, was this woman, and the sense of danger excited him even more. He gulped down the rest of his rum, carelessly tossed a coin on the table, and strode toward the stairs.

Bloodwind flung himself back on the bed and closed his eyes, breathing raggedly. The woman's desires had been as deep as his own, and they had both selfishly taken from the other as much pleasure as they could. Now they parted, their bodies slick with sweat and pleasantly exhausted.

The woman propped herself up on her elbow and stared at him. She reached one fingertip to his chest and ran it through the bloody scratches left by her fingernails, then raised the finger to her mouth. Her tongue darted out to lick the blood, and she closed her eyes and smiled a sly smile.

"You and I, Captain Bloodwind, are two of a kind," she said. "We see what we want, and we take it. What we want most of all is power, and I believe that we can help each other achieve our goals...together."

Bloodwind snorted. A woman sleeps with you, and she automatically thinks she's indispensable. Well, a night's passion was one thing, but a woman such as this had no business aboard a pirate ship. He sat up and turned away.

"Don't mock me!" she said, her tone as sharp as the fingernails she dug into his arm. "You will fail as a pirate and end up murdered by your own crew if you don't take a rich haul soon."

At his incredulous stare, she merely laughed. "Don't look so surprised; I know many things. For example, you are son to a wealthy father who doled out gold and favors sparingly as a show of his power, who pushed you into the navy against your will, and against whom you have always rebelled." Then she whispered harshly, as if afraid that malicious ears might be listening, "Have you never heard of sorcery?"

"What are you?" he asked; he had never told anyone of his background, of his wretched father who had been pleased at nothing his son achieved. The chill hand of danger gripped his heart, and he reached for the dagger he had placed beside the bed. "A seer?"

She laughed. The coarse sound was abrasive to his ear and disconcerting, coming as it did from such a beautiful mouth, a mouth he had enjoyed so thoroughly only moments before. Then she smiled at him again and loosened her grip, spreading her arms wide and shaking her head so that her ebon waves of hair brushed softly over her breasts. He could bury his dagger in her heart in an instant, but curiosity stayed his hand

"I am far more than a seer, my captain," she said. "I am a sorceress. My muse is the ocean. I can calm the seas or raise the waves. I can summon fog, shift the tides, and keep the mer at bay. I can even see far across the ocean to where the rich merchant ships run, unattended by the empire. I can provide you with a secure lair from which you can raid and plunder to your heart's content. What say you?"

Bloodwind lay back and pondered her pronouncement. She certainly had been able to see into his thoughts, pull out those black memories. Could she actually do what she said? His heart beat a little faster at the thought of all he could achieve with such power behind him, but still he hesitated, suspicious.

"Why?" he finally asked.

"Because," she said as she ran a finger along his jaw, "I have the needs of a woman, of course. But for my magic I need...more."

"More?"

"My magic requires a blood sacrifice; sometimes a little, sometimes a lot. You saw what information I could pull from your mind with just a tiny taste. Consider what I could do with even more. Bring back captives from the ships you take, and my power will grow. There will be no equal to Bloodwind's fleet if the two of us unite." She mounted him as she spoke. Her words were as enticing as her body, and he couldn't tell which provoked the explosive rush that overwhelmed him. He dropped the dagger and grabbed her tight as she posed the question once more. "What say you?"

"I say yes."

Bloodwind eyed the sorceress as she stood next to him on the quarterdeck, her hands clutching the rail, her body curving forward as if she could make them go faster. Her hair whipped about her face like a wild tangle of serpents, making her resemble her multi-headed namesake: Hydra. Her name was a source of consternation among the superstitious crew, and he often saw them wiggling their fingers in gestures of warding. Curious; usually a beautiful woman aboard would attract sailors like flies to honey, but the men all kept their distance. It was just as well, because he had no intention of sharing her. Possessively, his arm encircled her waist. She smiled up and him, then pointed into the distance, along the archipelago of the Shattered Isles.

"There!"

"Plume Isle?" he asked. "It's a volcano; too dangerous to anchor there. Ships avoid it."

"Exactly!" she answered. "What better place to hide? The emperor's fleet would never consider searching there. But there really is no danger; the volcano is dormant. It's not smoke you see, but merely steam and ash. I know. I lived there many years."

Bloodwind stared at her incredulously. "Why?"

"It harbors a great source of power—magical power," she

whispered in an awe-struck voice as she stared at the island. "It was there that I was birthed into my powers, and there that I am strongest."

They were silent as the ship raced ever closer, the white sails billowed by the brisk wind. As the waters shallowed, their hue shifted from deep blue to green to turquoise. Waves broke on the great brown ring of coral that surrounded the island, but with Hydra's direction, they steered the ship safely through a break in the reef, into the calm of the lagoon. A long white beach lined with palm trees stretched along the shore to the south, while directly ahead was a massive wall of tall mangroves.

Bloodwind could discern no place to conceal the ship, and he grew irritated as he eyed the waning sunlight. Hydra laughed softly and patted his forearm.

"I speak the truth," she said. "We will find shelter here. At morning's first light, I'll show you the way."

His order to "Drop anchor!" was immediately followed by Hydra's hiss.

"'Ware the coral!" she warned. "Until my powers are renewed, we are at the mercy of the mer, and they do not tolerate harm to their home."

"Drop anchor in sand," Bloodwind amended. The sky had turned scarlet and the breeze cool.

"Nearly home," he heard his sorceress whisper into the growing darkness. "Nearly home."

The launch splashed into the water just as a crimson sun cleared the horizon the following morning. Bloodwind and Hydra stood in the prow, and she directed their course toward the mangroves. Though he doubted they would find a channel through the trees wide or deep enough for the launch, much less the ship, he ordered his men to comply, and they rowed in silence. They passed the aerial roots of the great trees, outstretched like bony fingers ready to grasp them, turned beyond, and... The sailors all gasped, and Hydra smiled. Before them lay a broad channel, the water white-blue over the shallow sand at the edges, darker blue at the deeper center. The entrance had been completely concealed from offshore, detectable only from close in and at the correct angle. The winding course through the mangroves opened onto a natural bay, deep and encircled by a black-sand shore, and backed by steep cliffs.

"A sunken caldera," Hydra explained. "Twin to the volcano that now shrouds the island."

Bloodwind's heart skipped a beat and his mind raced. The bay was large enough to moor a small fleet of ships. A quay could be built out from the beach, and a small yard for ship repairs. An acrid scent drifted toward him from the flats to the west; tar pits, perfect for coating rigging and caulking hulls. A natural cave in the cliff face overlooked the harbor, and would make a fine home with a little work, and the narrow waterfall tumbling down the opposite cliff would provide abundant fresh water. It was a pirate's paradise, and it was all his.

"Put ashore!" he ordered. As the boat ground up onto the sand, he leapt lightly onto the beach, then turned and grasped Hydra's slender waist, lifting her high and placing her down above the waterline.

"Ethan, return to the ship and launch the rest of the boats. First thing: sound out the channel depths and bring the ship in. I don't want any passing ships to see her anchored in the lagoon. Second: scout out the area for food. Take all you find to the cook and tell him to prepare a feast; we celebrate tonight! But no one," he warned as he glared at the men who had dared to cheer, "touches the rum until I say so. We don't know yet if natives inhabit the island, or if fishermen use the harbor as a refuge. Secrecy is our first concern, and we can never let down our guard."

Hydra tugged at his hand, but he resisted until he had watched his men pull strongly on their oars on a course back through the mangrove channel. Only then did he follow her across the beach toward the cave. She scrambled up the hillside, amazingly agile despite the hindrance of her long skirt, grasping rocks and hanging foliage until she reached the cave mouth. He was breathing hard when he joined her there, but she looked as fresh as when they had started.

"Back here!" she called as she darted between several boulders at the rear of the cave. A wide crack gaped darkly in the floor, and she lowered herself down into it. Bloodwind hesitated, then followed. Her advise so far had been flawless, and if this was where she needed to go, then so be it.

Light filtered down from the crack behind him. Ahead, beams of light shot in through gaps and holes where the stone had been worn away by water. The illumination was just enough for him to catch glimpses of Hydra quickly clambering down the loose rocks below. Finally at the bottom, he picked his way carefully across the stone-scattered floor. As his eyes adjusted to the dimness, he saw bones shining pale among the rocks; undoubtedly small animals had fallen through the eroded holes above to die in the gloom of the cavern. He shuddered as he considered such an obscure death. He'd expected the cavern air to be dank, and its warmth was disconcerting until he remembered that the island was volcanic. It smelled of low tide, as well as something unidentifiable and unpleasant. All around he heard the steady drip-drip of water falling into the cavern from the holes and crevices in the ceiling and walls.

Bloodwind found Hydra leaning over a short, thick pillar of stone. The top was deeply hollowed out and filled with water. She swirled the water with one long, pale finger, and whispered to herself. The pool glowed a faint red. Hydra hissed.

"I need blood, Captain. My power requires it."

For the first time since joining with the sorceress, Bloodwind felt uneasy. Previously, as part of their bed games, he had allowed her to taste of his blood, amused by the observations she was able to summon. But now... He glanced about the cavern, at the bones, then back at Hydra. Her attention was focused on the pool, her face eerily illumed by the reddish glow. He thought suddenly of a witch peering into a bubbling cauldron, but shook off the macabre image.

"We have several goats aboard; you may have one of them."

She flashed him a red-tinted glare, then looked back to the pool. "I require human blood."

"You can't have it," he said. His temper flared as she reached a fingernail out toward his chest, and he caught her wrist in an iron grip. "I said, you can't have it."

She surprised him with her laughter.

"Ships pass by the Shattered Isles daily, but it's a large ocean, my captain. If you expect me to find prey for you, I'll need human blood. Or are all our efforts, and all this," she swung an arm around to indicate the island, "for naught?"

Bloodwind considered for a moment. She was right. The island made an ideal hideout, but it would be like trying to find a needle in the haystack to locate passing ships by chance. The men would be restless soon, once they were settled here, and he couldn't expect to last long as their leader if he didn't deliver the goods.

"All right, Hydra," he said as he turned to leave the cavern, "you'll get your blood, but not right now. Tonight."

The crescent moon shone like a keen blade above the darkness of the mangroves, silvering a path across the still waters of the bay.

"Men!" Bloodwind shouted above the songs as the men feasted and danced around the bonfire they had built. "Men, we have found our home. Blood Bay, we'll call it. From here we'll raid and plunder and grow rich!" He waited until the drunken cheers subsided before continuing.

"I am your leader, but every single man here is essential to ensure our prosperity. We are as brothers...no, more than brothers! As you are loyal to me, I am loyal to you. So let us make an oath and mingle our blood, and ask the sea goddess Odea for a fat prize to take! I will start."

Bloodwind glanced into the shadows where Hydra sat by herself, only her eyes visible as they reflected the red flames of the bonfire. Laying a silver bowl in front of him, he pulled his dagger from its sheath and held it aloft.

"By blood, by wind, by water and wave, loyal as one, or a watery grave."

With that pronouncement, he slashed his forearm and let the blood drip into the bowl. After a long moment, he wrapped his arm in a cloth and nodded to Ethan. The first mate came forward and repeated the oath, then slashed his own arm and bled into the bowl. One by one, the sailors gave their blood oaths. By the time the last man had pledged, the bowl was nearly full.

"Now celebrate and dream of our good fortunes to come with another cask of rum!" Bloodwind called out. As the men rushed for the drink, he surreptitiously picked up the bowl and slipped into the darkness. Hydra joined him and they hurried down the beach toward the cavern.

Hydra dipped her fingertips into the bowl of blood, then swirled them in the pool of water atop the boulder, all the while murmuring softly. Several times she dipped her fingers into the blood, then back into the pool. Once she licked her blood-coated fingers, shuddered and closed her eyes for a long moment before placing them in the water once again. Intently, she peered into the water.

"There is a ship, my captain," she said, her tone triumphant.

"Where?" he asked as his heart beat faster. Could this really work? Could she locate ships for him to raid? He had gambled everything for this. If she failed...he failed. "What kind of ship?"

"It's a merchant ship, sleek and fast to pass quickly along the trading routes. She'll make a fine corsair."

"But where?" he asked again between gritted teeth.

"It is heading north along the Shattered Isles," she said. "It will pass by Plume Isle the day after tomorrow. It travels alone."

"And it's probably filled with spices and jewels from the southern kingdoms." He grinned broadly and whooped with pleasure. Turning Hydra around and grabbing her by the waist, he lifted her up to him and kissed her. It seemed at first that she resisted, but soon she was returning his passion. And there in the cavern, atop the rough boulders, they consummated their pact of mutual ambition.

The ship was indeed a beauty. She flew lightly over the waves despite her deep cargo holds, and her wheel turned with the touch of a finger. Bloodwind relished the feel of the wind in his face as they raced back toward Blood Bay, reveling in his conquest. But it wasn't only the capture of the ship that pleased him. His esteem had trebled in the eyes of his men. Certainly they had grumbled when he ordered them to repaint the warship in military colors, hangover or no, but he had shown them the wisdom of his plan. When he led them directly to the merchant ship, they were surprised. When the merchant ship's captain immediately furled sail to converse with what he thought was an imperial warship, they were stunned. With few injuries and no fatalities on their side, they overwhelmed the crew and took the vessel. Bloodwind had slain the merchant captain to prevent an uprising, and imprisoned the rest of the crew in the hold for delivery to Hydra, the fulfillment of his vow.

"What'll we name 'er, Captain?" Cut Leg asked as he limped by the wheel on his way to shorten sail on the aft mast.

"She's got a mighty fine sharp bow to slice through the waves," Bloodwind answered. "I think I'll call her *Guillotine*. She'll be our new flagship. We don't dare try this trick again; the imperial fleet would be down here in no time if there are rumors of a warship chasing down merchants. No, we'll dismantle the old lady and use the lumber for buildings ashore."

Hells, he thought, *they're carrying enough gold to go out and buy another ship. But that's not something I'll tell the men...*

Back ashore, he left Ethan to inventory the merchant ship cargo. Grabbing a scowling merchant sailor with bound hands, he strode toward the cave. While they were gone, the men he had left ashore had laid a ladder up the slope, widened the crack and installed a ladder down into the cavern for easier access.

"Hydra!" Bloodwind called down the hole. "I have your first

prize! Down you go," he said to the prisoner. When the man balked, the point of the captain's sword changed his mind, and he climbed awkwardly down the ladder. Bloodwind had just stepped onto the first rung when a bloodcurdling scream rose from the depths.

"Hydra!" he called as he hurtled down the ladder. His sorceress had proved her worth to him in so many ways, and he would not allow a belligerent captive to harm her. But by the time he had descended, the screaming had stopped. Hydra stood nearby, the sailor prone at her feet. They were both covered in blood.

"Are you all right?" he asked as he grasped her shoulders and looked her over.

"I'm fine," she smiled as she wiped the blood from her face with her sleeve. "I'm afraid it's been a while since I conducted a sacrifice, and I made a mess. Don't worry, I'll clean it up. I'm sure you're busy with the rest of your plunder. I'll come up and meet you later."

Bloodwind looked at her with misgivings, but the sailor was dead and she was unharmed, so there was nothing for him to do here. He turned to the ladder.

"My captain!" Hydra's voice was low and sultry as she stepped to his side. "Thank you." She reached up and kissed him hard, then turned and disappeared into the gloom of the cavern.

Bloodwind climbed the ladder and strode toward the ships. The first thing he did when he reached his cabin was take a big swallow of rum to rid his mouth of the taste of blood.

Captain Bloodwind looked proudly over his growing empire. Below him, three corsairs floated at anchor in Blood Bay, their lanterns gleaming in the twilight. They'd taken a dozen merchants in as many months, but only suitable ships were kept for pirating; the others were sunk or dismantled for materials. A shantytown of shacks crowded the shore, housing sailors and others who helped keep the community running:

cooks, fishermen, and leisure women. The sound of sea chanteys rose through the air. Smiling, he turned back in to his home. The residence was still incomplete, but the capture of a skilled mason had significantly improved its lines. When done, it would be a castle carved into the wall of the caldera itself, complete with balconies and luxurious rooms.

Hydra lounged on the soft bed, stretching her long, slender limbs out to him as an invitation. She seemed even more beautiful than she had the day they met a year ago. He laughed as he fell onto the silk sheets beside her. They kissed long and hard, and made love with unsuppressed passion. They didn't see much of each other lately; he was busy with his raids, and she spent nearly all her time practicing her magics. Prisoner after prisoner climbed down into the cavern; he never saw any of them again.

"Have you any rich prizes for me to pursue?" he asked as he stroked her hair.

"Don't I always?" she replied. "A convoy will be passing later in the week, and one over-laden ship is falling behind. You can be the wolf, picking off the straggler from the herd."

He kissed her again, and they drifted off to asleep.

A storm hit during the evening, waking the captain. Bloodwind lay with his arms behind his head, musing on his good luck and ever-improving circumstances. Good luck that had started when he met Hydra. He turned and contemplated her sleeping countenance. A flash of lightening illuminated the room, and an appalling vision flashed before his eyes: Hydra as a decrepit old woman, then an indescribable horror of tentacles and teeth. As quickly as the lightening was gone, so was the vision. Hydra opened her eyes and smiled at him, beautiful as ever, rolled over and went back to sleep. Bloodwind, shaken to the core, rolled in the other direction and spent the rest of the night with his face buried in his pillow, not daring to cast his eyes in his lover's direction.

Bloodwind had captured numerous women during his raids; those who chose to live ended up in the pirate community—some as leisure women or cooks, some as pirates—for none could leave the island alive for fear of giving away their location. But this woman was blond, blue-eyed, and absolutely beautiful, and the captain couldn't keep his eyes—or hands—off of her. She seemed willing enough, even eager, which was not surprising, considering her situation. Regardless, it sated his ego to hear her complimentary platitudes, and even if her words were vacuous, her body was heavenly.

"Would you like to accompany me to my quarters?" he asked her though, truth be told, she was going there whether she wanted to or no. But she complied with a giggle, hanging onto his arm as they made their way up the stone stairs. As he drew the dress off of her shoulders, he thought of Hydra with a brief spasm of guilt. She spent nearly all of her time in the cavern now, and he didn't expect her for another day or two; when she was tracking a target, she worked day and night. Besides, her charms had waned since his vision of a month ago. He knew it was ridiculous, that he had been having a bad dream, but it still affected his attraction to her. Luckily, she hadn't seemed to notice. He turned his attention back to his eager new captive.

Later that afternoon, a knock on the door woke him. It was Ethan, back from his own raid, ready to report on his success. The blond slept, so he left her lying on the white sheets and followed Ethan down to inventory their haul.

Finally done with the business end of pirating, Bloodwind returned to his rooms with a bottle of wine and two glasses. He'd been thinking of the blond and her slender body, so different from Hydra's voluptuous curves, and was eager to pick up where they had left off.

I'll have to have a room made for her, he thought, *where she can stay and I can visit her. I suppose I should ask her name. She really is luscious, and what man doesn't like variety?* He smiled seductively as he pushed open the door... and stopped dead.

Hydra lay across the bed, one hand behind the blonde's head, the other on her belly. A quick and pleasant thought shot through Bloodwind's mind; *Ah, Hydra's tastes match my own. Perhaps we shall both enjoy our new captive!*

Then he saw the blood...

Hydra's head whipped around as the bottle and wine glasses shattered on the floor. His nightmare resurfaced: black tentacles fringing a maw of sharp black teeth. He blinked, and Hydra was herself again, black hair swaying as she moved, a necklace of shark teeth around her throat. But blood smeared her mouth... and she swallowed. Bloodwind felt hot bile in his throat and clutched the bedpost. He had killed many men, but this... this was grotesque beyond any death he had ever seen, let alone delivered.

He grabbed Hydra by the shoulders and threw her off of the bed, but it was too late. The blonde's throat had been torn out. Blood flowed from the ragged flesh, but there was no sign of life. The horror he felt flared into anger.

"What have you done?" he roared as he rounded on Hydra. To his surprise, she laughed as she stood up and faced him. She had fallen among the broken glass, and shards of crystal protruded from the flesh of her hands. One by one she picked them out, but instead of blood, a black ichor oozed from the wounds.

"You said the captives were mine," she reminded him. "I grow powerful, and my magics require that I feed. So when I found this one in our bed, I fed." She licked her lips with a red tongue.

"This is not *our* bed!" he yelled hoarsely as he snatched up his sword and advanced on her. "You're an abomination, not fit to live. And you won't..."

"Then I suppose you're ready to give up your life as a pirate, or at least a successful one," she said as she stood her ground, undaunted by the blade inches from her chest. She swept her arm around. "Who gave you this? Do you think you'll find another to provide you with details of ships and routes, to speed your ships along while hindering your prey or pursuers? You won't. We made a deal. Besides," her voice softened and she pushed the sword aside and raised a blood-stained hand to stroke his cheek, "we're so good together."

Repulsed, he batted her hand aside. For an instant her eyes flared red, then they went black...black and lifeless.

"Get out!" he ordered her, his voice harsh and low. "Go down to your cavern and stay there until I send for you. You will not approach me, you will not enter my rooms, and you will not feed on anyone except those I send to you. Get out now!"

Hydra laughed again and, as she laughed...she changed. Her hair became gray and scraggly, her face wrinkled, and her back hunched. Instead of a generous bosom, shrunken breasts hung loosely beneath her bodice. And her voice...the dulcet tones degenerated into a rasping croak, and still she laughed. She laughed as she grabbed the ankle of the dead woman on the bed, and she laughed as she dragged the corpse down the stair.

Bloodwind collapsed onto the bed, face slick with sweat and legs weak with dismay. He gazed around his richly furnished room, out the balcony to the bay and his fleet, across the forested hills of his island. He had worked so hard to get here; how could he give it all up?

"What have I done?" he whispered.

You made a deal with a devil, answered his conscience. *But it was a good one.*

Slowly Captain Bloodwind got to his feet and rang the bell that sat on the mahogany table by his bedside. He ignored the gasps of the servants who responded, ordering them to clean up the mess. In his dressing room, he donned his finest garments and strapped his sheathed sword onto his hip. Looking in the mirror, he forced the despair from his eyes, replaced it with cold calculation. Then he made his way down to the cavern to plan his next raid.

Chris A. Jackson and Anne L. McMillen-Jackson met in graduate school, in a state that arguably produces the best Mexican food and the worst politicians in the U.S. They fell in love playing fantasy RPGs together, and tested their love by living on a thirty-two foot sailboat while co-writing a fantasy trilogy. On the theory that if you can find a person you can do this with, and not kill each other, you have found your life mate, they were married. That was nearly twenty-five years ago, and they have been writing, sailing, and not killing each other ever since. Chris has written several award-winning fantasy novels, including the highly-acclaimed *Scimitar Seas* novels. Anne contributed greatly to this series, and is the reason there are four books in what was planned to have been trilogy. "Blood of the Hydra" is a prequel to the *Scimitar Seas* novels.

Currently, the couple are sailing and writing full time, working their way through the Caribbean and their next literary project. Anne also writes freelance articles about their cruising adventures for sailing and travel magazines, and has numerous scientific publications to boot. You can cruise along with them at sailmrmac. blogspot.com, and immerse yourself in Chris' fantasy world at jaxbooks.com, where you can download free audiobooks, excerpts of all his novels, and keep current with his writing and review blog.

The Sorrow Sea

ROBERT E. WATERS

Captain Victorio "Tomorrow's Wind" Nantan knelt beside
the body of the young woman. Not a spot of skin remained
on her frail bones, and only the tattered scraps of a blue
uniform lying nearby indicated that she had once been an
ensign. Young, inexperienced, and perhaps thinking a billet
on a Union freighter would provide a few years of calm and
uneventful service before joining a real warship.

So much for that, Victorio thought, as he placed his hand
on her cold forehead, closed his eyes, and spoke a silent prayer
to help aid her soul into the hereafter.

He moved to the next body; a young man, a bo'sun perhaps,
his flesh equally desecrated. His lips had been cut away,
revealing swollen gums and a ghoulish clown grin of broken
teeth. Victorio had to turn away lest he become sick at the
sight of it. All around him, the crew of the *Genoese* lay equally
still and dead. Not a man, woman, or child alive. The massacre
had been swift and brutal.

"The Gulo?"

The sharp voice behind Victorio startled him. He had
quite forgotten that Shines Like the Sun was video-logging
everything for Admiral Cho.

The captain stood. "Perhaps, but I doubt it. The Gulo would have breached the hull. They would have crippled the ship, swarmed it, taken what they wanted, then scuttled what remained. Whoever did this docked and gained access through deception, deceit. The Gulo would not have wasted so much time."

"But the bodies, sir. They've been skinned."

Victorio nodded. The savagery of the attack was, indeed, Gulo in its nature. He shuddered. Even after fifteen Stellar years, the name of that wolverine-like race gave him chills. The Federated Union had been at war with the Gulo forever, it seemed. They were feral, savage fighters, their technology on par with humans. They were a formidable foe.

But this was different; this attack, this massacre, was something else, perpetrated by... who? By what? He did not know for sure, but he had his suspicions. The skinning was precise and carefully administered with deft hands, with patience. The Gulo would have simply ripped them to shreds.

"Captain!" Blue Bird called from across the bridge. "Come look at this."

He stepped over bodies and went to her side. His second-in-command knelt beside a young boy. His hair had been removed, a clean and efficient scalping, a *bitsa-ha-digihz*, that Victorio had seen many times as a young Apache boy on Earth during the Rebellion of 2235. Blue Bird's face grew pale and her hand quivered as she held up the knife which had obviously done the deed.

Victorio grabbed the blade quickly, turning it over in his hand, his heart fluttering. It was a crude weapon. The handle was cured buckskin wrapped tightly over deer bone and smeared with red clay. The blade was a piece of grey chert chipped to razor perfection. This was not a Union-issued knife.

"It's him, isn't it?"

Blue Bird's question cut like the hewed stone in his hand. As much as he wanted to say no, he could not deny the truth that lay in bloody heaps around him.

Victorio gritted his teeth then tucked the blade into his belt. "Yes," he said. "It's him."

Mangus Coloradas flipped a knife effortlessly from hand to hand, then jabbed it into the stale air before him. A sharp, clean thrust. A killing thrust. It was a skill he had perfected in prison with a test blade fashioned from shop scraps. He'd gotten a good beating when the guards had found it beneath his bedroll, but it was worth it now. The knowledge acquired from that tiny weapon had paid off ten-fold, now that he was light years away from that dank cell. He'd fashioned two other blades since then: the one in his hand now and the one he had foolishly left near the White Eyes boy who had tried to open his belly with a Muck carbine. Or had it been so foolish? In his dreams, the great lord of the People, Yusn Life-Giver, had shown him the face of the one who would come for him. A pilot. A captain. A Devil Dancer. The one who had conspired to steal his command so many years ago.

And they call me a pirate!

He flipped the knife over again, caught the tip between thumb and index, then hurled it into the neck of the target ten meters away. The feeble wood and foam of the mannequin burst into a cloud of dust and splinters as the stone blade bit deep. "That's what I'm going to do to you, *Captain* Victory!"

The comm signal on his armband flashed green. "Red Sleeves," said a scruffy voice. "We are approaching the *Loch Ness*."

He always smiled at his true name, his Apache name. He was, indeed, the resurrection of that great warrior that had brought pride and dignity to The People. He was proud of the name and the status.

But to his enemies, he was Coloradas, a pirate, a butcher.

"Keep us steady and a thousand kilometers down on her port-side," he said, wiping sweat from his face as he exited the training cube. "And keep those asteroids between us. We can't be seen until we're close."

"Aye, sir!"

The Union did not consider him and his Red Paint People a threat to a full destroyer, especially the *Loch Ness*, which had fought honorably against the Gulo so many times. That's why they had sent it into the Sorrow Sea to root him out, to get him back on the "reservation" as it were. But this vast field of asteroids and dust in the Carina Nebula held incalculable places to hide and to wait out anything White Eyes might send in. The supply lines that ran along the edge of the Keyhole Nebula, a smaller and much darker expanse within the Carina, was a font of goods and materiel that could sustain an entire fleet forever... as long as the freighters moved. The Union could not afford to shut down this supply line; the human colonies beyond the keyhole were under Gulo pressure (or so White Eyes claimed). So send in the *Loch Ness* and whip those pirates!

But White Eyes will get an education, he thought to himself as he stopped in front of a door panel, *and that right soon.*

He tapped the security panel, and the blast door on the main cargo bay opened to wild activity. His crew was scrambling to tiny fighters strapped into this honeycomb of a ship. His ship. The *Ahagahe*. It was the size of a small freighter, but in truth, it was an old abandoned drill platform modified to serve as a small carrier. The length of its hull was a cylinder which had originally housed an ion beam used to carve through hundreds of meters of solid iron ore. The cannon was gone, replaced by rows of lockers that, when opened to space, scattered fighters like glass. The Union did not know that he had such a ship, and he was going to make damn sure they never did.

"Strap in, you wild coyotes!" he screamed over the hum of the chaos. Someone handed him an oxygen mask. He took it and placed it over his face, strapped it around his head, and breathed deeply.

"You should activate your boots as well, sir," said a small man to his right. "The launch bay will depressurize in thirty."

Coloradas sighed. Little Dog was always yapping at his heels, always telling him his business. The runt had a gift for stating the obvious. "Look to your own deportment, Little

Dog. I know my ship better than you."

"Yes, sir. But this is the *Loch Ness* we're up against. A warship. We've never taken one on before, and I'm just making sure everything goes—"

"I know my enemy, boy." Indeed he did. Rocket and torpedo tubes fore and aft; broadside point-defense; retractable cupolas along its spine. Everything it needed to render a pirate fleet inoperable. *Everything*, Coloradas thought, *but the Sorrow Sea*. The *Loch Ness* had sailed into his battleground. Its crew did not understand where it was, did not understand the lay of the land. The Sorrow Sea would provide, he knew, as Yusn Life-Giver had shown him in his dreams. *The Sorrow Sea provides*.

Little Dog offered the captain an *izze-kloth*, a cord of powerful medicine affixed with war charms, which Coloradas laid across his chest and snapped into place. He then took his tiny bag of pollen and his war club and tied them to his belt. All of these things a warrior took into battle, to protect himself from evil spirits if such a bloody end was near. But he was not afraid; neither the Union nor an aged destroyer could move him to fear. If the end would come today, so be it. Mangus Coloradas would happily die a warrior.

He dipped his fingers into a cup of red paint that Little Dog held up, then ran them across his skull. With these lines he would meet the enemy, and they would know who he was. "Is my fighter ready?" he asked as he punched a button on his belt and felt his boots tighten against the hard floor.

Little Dog nodded. "Aye, captain. Refitted and ready."

The bay walls opened and Coloradas felt the rush of decompression. He stopped for a moment, however, to enjoy the view. The Sorrow Sea opened to him, like the petals of the desert flowers he remembered as a child. An unending ocean of rocks floating effortless in the void, grabbing bits of light from the nebula around her, and casting them back ten-fold. He smiled. She was brilliant, beautiful. Beautiful and deadly.

He stepped up to his fighter, climbed in and lowered the cockpit hood. He could feel the hum of her small engine as it warmed his legs. He strapped in tightly and activated his dashboard which lit up white, red, and green. Somewhere beyond the myriad green dots lay the *Loch Ness*.

"All steady now, you Mimbres, you Red Paint People!" Coloradas said into the comm connecting him to every fighter. He gunned the engine and tapped a touch-pad four times. "Roll the cylinder!"

Not all his crew of one hundred and fifty-nine were Mimbres Apaches, but many were. And many were from other tribes which had fled Earth to find a better life among the stars. But White Eyes always had a way of making their lives miserable, even light years from Earth. The war with the Gulo was such an aggravation. An unnecessary, useless war which went on and on, far longer than it needed to, ending the lives of (at least) a billion Union citizens, many of them of Native American descent. He had tried to warn them, had tried to bring a peaceful end to the war years ago. And what had it gotten him? Pain. Sorrow. Exile. But he would show them, and make White Eyes and their native traitors pay.

They will pay.

The cylinder began to roll by the thrusters of the fighter craft, and its impetus moved the mining platform forward. Cries filled the comm as his men whipped themselves into a frenzy. This was the first time the entire fleet was mobilized, but such a target required a war party, not just a raiding group.

Through the Sorrow Sea the cylinder rolled, the fighters turning it over and over like a Ferris wheel, spinning the mighty cylinder round and round as it gained speed through the fine star dust and pebbles that lay quiet and unfettered in its path. In a way, Coloradas was sorry to disrupt such a beautiful field of rock. But the sea would fix itself anew in time, providing again and again the protection he and his men needed. And a field of larger asteroids lay ahead, and they did indeed need those mighty rocks.

"Disembark!" he yelled, and one by one, lockers released and out streamed corkscrews of fighters aided by the motion of the cylinder.. Like finely-tipped arrows from bows, they streamed outward as the cylinder fell away and took its hiding place among the stellar winds.

"Okay, boys!" Coloradas said. "Set sites on those rocks. Fifty up, fifty down. Raven Pattern. Land and set grapples!"

They did as commanded, half the fleet breaking away and pulling themselves up and behind a line of asteroids many times larger than themselves. Coloradas picked his rock and moved to it, bringing his fighter down gently on its backside, then locking it down tightly. He waited until the white dots on his monitor clamped themselves fully to other asteroids, then said, "Now is the time, my friends, where we put White Eyes in his place. He has come to make his war upon us, and we will show him the error of his ways. We will drown him in the Sorrow Sea." More joyous cries he heard across the comm. His men were ready. Coloradas breathed deeply, then said, "Strike the engines!"

And so a hundred fighters strong-gunned their engines, and the asteroids they were on began to roll, and roll, and roll, like bowling balls down slick lanes. Beyond the wall of rock, already the *Loch Ness* was trying to keel left to meet this unexpected threat. In his mind, Coloradas could hear the mighty ship answer with point defense, but it would do no good. He was *di-yin*, and he had seen the end in his dreams. "Release!"

The fighters unclamped themselves from their rocks and burst upward and out of harm's way. *Let the Sorrow Sea do its worst*, he said to himself as he burst from behind the line of whirling asteroids and refreshed his targeting reticule. *And then, like brave Mimbres all, we will finish the job.*

"Ahagahe!" Coloradas roared, turned his fighter toward the destroyer, and opened fire.

Victorio watched the video display as the asteroids smashed into the *Loch Ness*, breaking its spine and crushing its bridge. Its point-defense and shields had thwarted some of the attack, but not enough, as he could see its gunnery teams frantically tap monitors to launch hopeless volleys of rockets and torpedoes. And then a horrible cry, like mothers wailing their sorrow over fallen sons, as the pirates swarmed the battered hull like mosquitoes, pricking here and there, ripping the ship apart. Over the crackling audio of the destroyer's compromised comm net, he could hear the word *Ahagahe* shouted again and again.

Admiral Cho turned off the screen and fell into his chair. He rubbed his eyes and said, "What does the word mean, captain?"

Victorio cleared his throat. "It's a battle cry, sir. A challenge."

"Who is he challenging?"

Me. "The captain of the *Loch Ness*, sir. The Union in general, I suppose."

"You know this man?"

Victorio nodded. "Aye, sir."

"Tell me about him."

Admiral Cho was a relatively new admiral, having come up to Barracuda Task Force after the Gulo had massacred its admiral and crew and most of its subordinate ships. It had been the worst Union defeat in the entire war, and the young Cho had been brought in to cobble together what remained. Victorio was surprised that the admiral did not know Mangus Coloradas. But then, perhaps he did, and he simply wanted to measure Victorio's answer. He might be young, but Admiral Cho was as cagey as Coyote.

"Mangus Coloradas used to be my captain, sir, and dare I say, a good friend. He was older than me, but our families shared the same village on Earth until shortly after the Rebellion. They left, and I did not see him again until I joined the Devil Dancers. He had served as their captain for five years before I came along. Two years later, he made me his second in command, where I remained until his court martial."

"Ah, yes, the Paladin Conspiracy." Admiral Cho's dark face wrinkled in disbelief. "I find it hard to believe that this *butcher* was involved in that pacifist movement."

"Coloradas was not always a violent man, Admiral. There was a time when he was quite gentle, despite his skills as a fighter pilot. In many ways, he made the Devil Dancers what we are today. He believes that he is the reincarnation of Mangus Coloradas, the great Apache chief. He has the stature and bearing, for sure, and the temperament at least before his incarceration. But, like his namesake, he's been betrayed again and again. It is clear that he has not forgotten what White Eyes – as he would call the Union – did to his family and to his career."

"And what do you think, Captain? Did the Union betray him?"

Victorio measured his answer. The memory of the Paladin trial was strong in his mind still, as if it had happened just a week ago. "I did what I had to do, sir, to protect the integrity of the Devil Dancers and for the fleet as a whole."

The Devil Dancers were the finest fighter squadron in the fleet. Its kill ratio and its number of aces rivaled that of whole flights. Comprised mostly of Apache warriors, it was named after the *Ganh* Mountain Spirits that Yusn Life-Giver had sent to earth to teach the People how to live a good and virtuous life. The term "devil dancer" was one given to them by a White Eyes who had mistaken their ceremonial dancing as erratic, out of control, evil. Though he did not particularly like the name, it was an effective one in the Union's struggle against the Gulo. A devil garnered respect, even from its enemies.

"There is one other thing you should know about Coloradas, Admiral," he said, clearing his mind of painful memories. "He is *di-yin*."

"*Di-yin*?"

"He's a shaman. One of great stature. And he has ghost power. He believes that he can touch the dead and subsume their spirit. That is why he is being so brutal in his attacks on our ships. He is collecting the spirits of those he kills violently because he believes that their unsettled spirits give him strength."

Admiral Cho rose to his feet. "How do you know this, Captain?"

I've seen it in my dreams. "I... just know, sir. I know."

"And you believe this foolishness?"

Yes. "No, sir. But he does, and that makes him unpredictable, dangerous."

"I don't need a lecture on ancient Apache mythology, Captain, to know that." Admiral Cho stepped from behind his desk and faced Victorio. He was short, but Victorio did not bow his head to show any disrespect. He could see the lines of stress and anger on the little man's brow. "Let me bring the matter back to reality for you, Victorio. Mangus Coloradas and his Red Paint People, as you call them, have captured and/or destroyed twenty Union cargo ships. He has stolen a million tons of weaponry and supplies along the Keyhole transit line. He has massacred at least a dozen crews." He pointed to the blank video screen. "And he has just scuttled a destroyer. The *Loch Ness*! All attempts to end his terror have failed. He's holed up somewhere in the Sorrow Sea, and we can't get him out. The matter is desperate. Do you understand?"

Victorio nodded. He knew all too well. He waited to see if the admiral would say anything further, but he just stood there silently, staring up with those strong, green eyes that could intimidate even the most stalwart naval officer. *We're all in this together...*

"Yes, sir. What can I do to help?"

The admiral let a smile cross his thin lips. He returned to his chair. He scooped up a small tablet and punched out a noisy code. "Effective immediately, you, your squadron, and the *Justice* are hereby assigned to Barracuda Task Force for special duty." He finished tapping out the transfer order, then laid the tablet on the desk. He looked up. "Captain Nantan, you are hereby ordered to take your Devil Dancers into the Sorrow Sea... and kill that sick son of a bitch."

Victorio's heart leapt into his throat.

In his dream, Coloradas danced like a devil. Like he used to in better days, when he was a young captain full of hope and honor, fighting against the common enemy. He moved in the rhythmic patterns as ordained by the mountain spirits of his people. On his body he wore the dress of the *Ganh*: buckskin kilt and brightly colored headdress with feathers attached to wave about majestically as he and his kin moved around the bonfire. Attached to a hood which hid his face were u-shaped arms lined with sharp teeth that pushed into the night sky to connect mortal flesh to the cosmos. He danced for the well-being of the People; he danced for Yusn Life-Giver; he danced for victory; he danced for himself.

Out of the dried bushes leapt the clown, its bare chest and stomach smeared with white and red clay. It flailed around wildly, its face a twist of silly expressions that brought laughter from the young children watching nearby. The clown was a thing of mirth, one who entertained the crowd and lightened the mood of such a serious ritual. As the crowd laughed and pelted the clown with tiny pebbles, he moved forward. *It will not steal the show*, he said to himself as he doubled his efforts to win back their attention.

So they danced and danced, he and the clown, each pushing the other, desperate to win the crowd's cheers. The clown tripped him, and he grew angry. He stood up to protest and felt a warm, sick feeling in his stomach. The dance stopped and he faced the clown, whose contortions now smoothed to reveal its true face.

You! He whispered. He looked down and saw a blade of stone sticking out of his belly and warm blood trickling down his breechcloth.

The clown laughed and said, *I see you...Can you see me?*

The comm signal on his armband buzzed and blinked to life. Coloradas sat upright on his bunk and wiped sweat from his brow. He clicked the comm. "What is it?"

Bright Star's voice was anxious. "Freighter sighting, sir. Three cargo ships. In good shape."

He sniffed and cleared his throat. "Any escorts?"

"A few light squads. Nothing of concern."

He was surprised by that. After destroying the *Loch Ness*, he would have expected a better showing. *Are they stupid*, he wondered, *or do they not fear me?* He could not decide which was worse. Either way, it was humiliating. He gnashed his teeth. "Rouse the crew. All of them."

"Are you sure, sir?"

"What do you mean, Star?"

She hesitated, then said, "It's just that, we suffered a lot of casualties against the *Loch Ness*. And many are exhausted. I think it best to just let this one—"

"If the Union sees fit to continually try me, Star, by sending in near-defenseless cargo vessels, then so be it. We will keep the pressure on until they fear and respect us. We will attack, in force, and leave none alive. Is that understood?"

A pause. Then, "Yes, sir."

Coloradas shut off the comm and stood. A sudden rush of heat and dizziness washed over his face. He sat down and placed his hand on his stomach. He gasped as he pulled his hand away and looked at it.

It was covered in blood.

Victorio sat cross-legged on his meditation quilt while Blue Bird ran thick lines of red-and-white clay across his face, neck, and chest. He opened his eyes and saw the worry in hers. "What do you fear, kind heart?" he asked.

Blue Bird was a warrior, as true and strong as any Devil Dancer. She was fearless and uncompromising in the seat of her *Radiant*-class fighter. He had promoted her to second in command. He loved her. It was forbidden, of course, for captains and their officers to express such feelings, but he could not help it. She was beautiful, powerful, and he wanted nothing more than to steal away with her to some quiet planet and make "a thousand babies," as she would say. But not today. The war with the Gulo still raged, and now this matter with Coloradas had arisen. He would do his duty as ordered. He would do it... even if it killed him.

"I fear the agitation of troubled dreams," she said, "that cannot be tempered by awaking." Her eyes watered as she bit back the growing trepidation in her voice. "I fear the Sorrow Sea. I fear Coloradas. I fear the *di-yin*."

He took her hand and stood. He put out his arms and she helped him into his blue shirt and buckskin vest. He buckled his belt and took his *izze-kloth* and war club, his holstered pistol, and bag of pollen. He accepted his helmet but did not put it on. Instead he rested it on his hip, took Blue Bird's arm in his, and whispered, "These things I fear too, sweet. But they cannot burden our minds now. We must keep these feelings hidden away, until such a time as we can think upon them clearly. Out there, he waits. We have danced to Yusn for strength, for honor, for courage. He will keep us safe. We are Devil Dancers. We are mountain spirits. And if today is the day I die..."

Blue Bird put her finger to his mouth. "Shh! Do not speak anymore." A tear fell down her face, but she took his helmet and placed it on his head, leaned into it, and kissed him firmly on his face-plate. "I want to keep your smiling face in my memory. Just go... and be safe."

She let him go. Victorio turned and walked to his fighter. It waited patiently, its engine humming as it pulled on the chains that held it to the floor of the cargo bay. He turned once more to her, saluted, then climbed in.

Blue Bird pulled a lever on the floor and the chains fell away. His fighter was free, and he guided it slowly to the bay door. It opened, and the light of the Sorrow Sea flooded in. He leaned his head back and the fighter fell back as well, until it was through the door. He waved goodbye, but already Blue Bird and the rest of the Devil Dancers were mere specks in his vision. The bay door closed and he was alone.

He tapped a dashboard panel, his engine went dead, and he floated away silently into the brilliant cold dust of the Sorrow Sea. He closed his eyes.

Let the dance begin.

Coloradas and his pirates corkscrewed off the *Ahagahe* in long, roping lines. They spun out in wave after wave of fighter craft, armed and determined. Around them lay such a quiet and serene stretch of space; it seemed almost blasphemous to disrupt the beautiful tranquility of the Sorrow Sea. Yet despite Star's and Little Dog's constant yapping to sit this one out, he gave the order. He wrapped his wound tightly and did not let them know of it. They might have mutinied right then and there had they discovered the blood on his stomach. Nothing, not even a little scratch, would stop him. But it wasn't such a little scratch, was it? It was something more, something... What? The images from his dream flooded back into his mind. He tried blocking them out, but he could not wipe away the face below the clown mask. But where *was* he? Where was Victorio? Ahead of them, three cargo ships awaited, flanked by a tiny and insignificant escort that would quickly fall at the first volley of rockets.

Where are you, Victorio? I can't see you.

"Sir, there is a line of asteroids ahead three hundred kilometers. Shall we make for them?"

"No," Coloradas answered Little Dog's question sharply. "Not this time. Today, we go straight in."

"But, sir —"

"Enough talk! We go in, and that's an order. Triple lines and rotating packages. Leave no ordnance unfired. We will make them bleed today!"

"Yes, sir."

Coloradas cut the link. There would be no more communication, no more talk. Today, he would sweep the Sorrow Sea of any trace of White Eyes. Today would be his greatest victory yet.

Coloradas closed his eyes, gunned his fighter forward, and tried to discern the face in the fog of his mind.

Victorio floated quietly through a vast field of rock and dust, the automatic thrust of his passive alignment coils the only thing keeping his fighter from being destroyed by the tumbling debris. He was cold, frigid in fact, but he would not bring his engines on-line until the right moment.

And when will that moment come? he wondered. The Red Paint People had already begun their attack against the Union freighters; three empty and old freighters. Empty, save for three squadrons of the Union's finest... plus the Devil Dancers. One of the freighters had already been destroyed and their hidden squadron decimated; another listed badly to its port side. Victorio listened to the chaotic radio chatter over his comm link; listened but did not respond, for he would not give away his position. He wanted badly to be among them, with Blue Bird and Shines Like the Sun and all the others. But he would grit his teeth and wait, wait for the one that had not shown himself yet.

"Where are you?" Victorio whispered in the dark of his cockpit. "Where are you?"

I'm right here...

The words flowed through Victorio's mind like water, and before he could gun his engines, something nicked his fuselage and he went spiraling round and round. The thick dust of the Sorrow Sea collided across his wings and threw him dangerously close to an asteroid. He blinked furiously, cocked his head, and lit his engine. The *Radiant* sprang to life and flew upwards, catching the wind of the nearby sun and disappearing in a flash of heat and energy.

But his pursuer was relentless. Rockets raced along his side, and Victorio had to twist between two massive rocks to keep from being incinerated. Another rocket sprang off his side, the *Radiant's* point shield turning it away. The rocket hit an asteroid, exploded and knocked him starboard. Victorio worked his dash frantically.

He cursed himself. Blue Bird had warned him. *I fear the di-yin,* she had said. He had listened to her warning, but he had been too confident in his abilities to reject the shaman's mind spirits. His old captain was stronger than he had imagined. *I'm such a fool. I should have been more cautious. I should not have let him in my mind.*

"And there I will stay, old friend." Coloradas spoke over the comm. "It's good to see you again."

Victorio grunted. "You should have stayed in the brig, Coloradas. That old *Zoot* won't last long in this rock field."

Coloradas laughed. "We shall see."

In truth, the *Zoot* was fast and agile, the perfect fighter in an asteroid field and a good pirate craft. Yet it lacked power and stamina. It worked best in packs. It had to strike first, expel its munitions and then dog its opponent with laser fire. But laser fire did not work well in the Sorrow Sea. So why such an antiquated ship?

Victorio banked left and spun through another line of asteroids. He purposely knocked apart smaller rock clusters with his wings. He would suffer damage, but the swirl of dust left in his wake was enough to blind even the most sophisticated sensors. He turned and turned, leaving Coloradas and his tiny *Zoot* choking.

It worked. Whatever rockets the *Zoot* had left tried to penetrate the swirling stardust, but the radiated heat ignited them all. Victorio smiled, turned his fighter right and barrel-rolled through a maze of boulders the size of tiny houses. He rolled his finger up a line of pads on his dash, then tapped the last one.

Thirty rockets burst from his wings.

He watched as the tiny specks on his radar closed in on their target. They closed and closed as Coloradas zigged and zagged through the heavy dust, spinning and spinning his *Zoot* with a fury that Victorio found quite impressive. His old captain had not lost a bit of his flying skills. Still the best pilot in the Union. *What a waste to see it blown to cinders*, he thought as he watched and waited for the end.

But it did not come. As they closed, each rocket in turn suddenly changed course and impacted against a meteor cluster. Ten, then twenty, then thirty. Every one. All of them. *How in the hell did*—Of course: the *Zoot* had an old, outmoded homing signature, and *Radiant* rockets were tuned to different, more modern frequencies.

Coloradas laughed over the comm. "An old, yet effective, trick."

"Goddamn you, Coloradas," Victorio said. "Stop playing

games. Face me and fight like a man. Fight like a true Mimbres."

Coloradas laughed again. "When a pirate, act like a pirate. My world is different than yours, Victorio. I live by the rules of the Sorrow Sea, and she loves a good chase." Coloradas pulled up beside him; Victorio could almost see him through the bright haze. "But you're right," he said. "I grow tired of this dance. Follow me, and let's go fight like old times."

Victorio followed Coloradas out of the sea and into a small patch of hollow space. Was this a trap? Perhaps. He would find out soon enough.

As they burst out of the sea, a large, long cylinder emerged in his vision. A mighty ship, almost as long as a Union frigate, but it lacked any sizable amount of point-defense. It was beautiful in a way. It caught the light of the sea and shone it back bright and vibrant. Almost blinding. Yet, peering into the glow, Victorio felt at peace. This was clearly the vessel he had seen in his dreams. This was...

"Yes, the *Ahagahe*," Coloradas said over the comm. "My ship. Isn't she wonderful?"

Victorio nodded, then stopped himself quickly. He was being manipulated again. The *di-yin* was getting into his mind, affecting his perspective. He blinked quickly and edged his fighter down to keep pace with the *Zoot*. "She is. But stop the tour, Coloradas. If you've led me into an ambush, then spring the trap. I grow tired of your babbling."

"No one is here, Victorio," he said. "My people are fighting and dying against yours. We are alone. This is our fight."

"Then let's have it."

They flew around the *Ahagahe* twice, then panels on the starboard side opened and out rolled a circular and domed platform. It slid into space and detached itself from the ship and floated gently in place. On either side, thrusters equalized its mass and kept it from tipping. Coloradas dropped his *Zoot* until it hovered just above the top of the dome. Then the dome irised open. He centered his craft over the opening, then slipped through the gap and disappeared inside.

"Come," he said calmly. "I welcome you."

Victorio reluctantly followed, bringing his *Radiant* down and squeezing through the opening. His wings barely fit through, but he dropped in and watched as the dome shut behind him.

Below was a paradise.

Not paradise exactly, but nearly so. A jungle, with carefully planted trees and vines of lush, green palm-sized leaves. Through the cockpit window he could see a waterfall and a small stream circling the splendor. He almost didn't want to touch down, for fear of disrupting the delicate balance of flora that blanketed the floor. But he followed Coloradas down until they set their fighters beside each other. Victorio killed his engines. He let them come to a complete stop, then depressurized the cockpit. He waited for a moment, then opened the canopy. He removed his helmet, unlocked his belt, and stood up. Clear, fresh air filled his lungs. He breathed deeply. It had been a long time.

He climbed out onto a wing. He stopped to enjoy the scent of lilac and rosewood, but then held his breath when he saw Coloradas standing on the ground, tall, still, and commanding, holding a stone knife in one hand, a war club in the other. Victorio dropped his helmet, reached into his boot and drew out the stone knife that he had found at the *Genoese* massacre. Then he unclipped his war club from his belt and dropped to the ground. He ripped his shirt open to show the long red-and-white streaks running down his chest. Coloradas did the same.

Victorio moved cautiously toward his old captain. He stopped and raised his weapons.

"*I am the lightning flashing and streaking,*" Coloradas said as he bowed to his opponent.

Victorio knew the phrase well and replied with a phrase from the same song that Yusn Life-Giver had given the *Ganh* mountain spirits long, long ago. He bowed and said, "*And my song shall encircle these dancers.*"

And they danced.

"I trusted you. You betrayed me."

"You betrayed yourself," Victorio said, watching carefully Coloradas move as they jockeyed for position inside the battle platform, daggers and clubs held tightly. "And more importantly, you betrayed the Devil Dancers. You and your conspirators willfully disobeyed orders, or implemented such orders so slowly as to affect the same result. Millions died because of your inaction."

Coloradas nodded. "And billions would be alive today had you listened. This war with the Gulo is destroying the Union. They are no longer a threat."

"That is a lie! They attack us at every turn."

"Only to defend what little space they have left. The war has been over for a long time, Victorio, and you know this. You have had the same dreams as I, old friend. The Gulo have been removed from every segment of Union space. Now it's just genocide." He jabbed with his blade. "They fight simply to stay alive, to keep White Eyes from taking more. In your own life, you have *seen* what White Eyes is capable of. You've seen it in your own family."

Victorio pushed away the painful memories. "We are all in this together, *old* friend. Why do you persist in these terrible attacks? Why do you massacre innocent people?"

Coloradas huffed. "You're forgetting your history, Victorio. My Mimbres and I do this to make White Eyes see the futility of his actions. To make him see how terrible war really is. To make him pay such a high price as to force him to stop this terrible, terrible thing which he has put in motion. And it's obvious that I've had an impact, for they've sent Captain *Victory* into the Sorrow Sea to kill me."

Victorio shook his head. "I've been sent here to bring you to justice."

"No. You've been sent here to die!"

Coloradas lunged forward. He brought his war club down hard, and Victorio stepped to the side. The club grazed his shoulder. He gritted his teeth and kept his eyes from closing against the pain. *I will not show pain to this man*, he said to himself and did not care if the *di-yin* heard it. *No pain.*

He brought his own war club up and swung it towards Coloradas's neck, but the big man was faster, more agile than he had anticipated. Coloradas ducked, rolled and came up slashing with his knife. He caught Victorio across his chest and opened a line of blood that mixed with sweat and clay across his stomach. Victorio swung upward and caught the knife square with his own and dislodged it. The stone blade flew through the air and Victorio jabbed forward and drove his blade into Coloradas's stomach. But he only ripped through a thick bandage that covered another wound.

Victorio's eyes beamed. It had worked; his own try at dream manipulation had worked, and Coloradas had awakened with a slash at his stomach. Wonderful. The *di-yin* was not so tough after all.

Coloradas roared in anger. He knocked Victorio's arm aside and tried to land a fist against his throat, but Victorio caught it and turned the wrist. Coloradas screamed and tried to pull away, but Victorio lifted a boot and drove it into his opponent's stomach, knocking him back and into the stream. Coloradas disappeared beneath the water.

Finish him! His own words in his mind were sound. But no. That would not be the honorable thing to do, to drown your opponent while he flailed around to get his balance. No. Victorio watched as Coloradas reached out of the water and grabbed the bank. He turned, looked for and found Coloradas's knife, grabbed it, tucked it away into his belt, then fled into the thick foliage.

You want a chase, old friend? Victorio shouted the words in his mind. *Then come and find me.*

He ran and ran, down a thin footpath. He remembered racing his brother, Naiche, up mountain passes as a young boy, each trying to reach the top with a mouthful of water. Those were pleasant memories now, and he always kept them close. This chase was not so pleasant, but he felt good on solid ground, with brown soil beneath his feet. This was not the tough, dry, unforgiving land of his childhood, but it would do.

He rounded a corner and took an arm in the throat.

He hit the path hard, his neck in agonizing pain. He gasped for air. The wind had been knocked from his lungs. He clutched his chest and curled up tightly. A boot landed on his side, then again and again. He tried pushing away his assailant, but Coloradas stood above him, stolid and unmoving, smiling his nasty grin. The big man pulled his leg back and kicked again. Blood seeped from Victorio's mouth.

"I've been planning this for a long time, Victorio," Coloradas said, circling around like a crazed dog. "A long, long time. And now it's over."

Victorio tried to move, tried to reach out and strike a leg, but he could not breathe. His ribs exploded in pain with every movement. He stayed cuddled up, and managed to squeak out, "You... are... *bini-e-dine!*"

Coloradas laughed and ripped away Victorio's war club and knife. He tossed the club into the stream but held the knife tightly in his hand. "No, sir. I have a mind, and a strong one. And I am right." He knelt down beside Victorio. "With your death, with your scalp upon my wall, all the Union will mourn the loss of their *precious* Captain Victory. And then a discussion will begin. 'Is this war worth it?' someone will ask, and then another, and another, until the voice of opposition is so overwhelming as to be unstoppable. And then I'll have won. I'll have won."

Coloradas raised his empty hand and placed it upon Victorio's face. "And now accept these ghosts, brother. Accept them and take them with you into the underworld."

A rush of lives filled Victorio, from the young ensign on the *Genoese* to an old gunner on the *Loch Ness*. The spirit of every man, woman, and child that Coloradas had killed spilled into his mind. He felt their pain, their fear, their anger as their own lives ended at the hands of this madman that knelt at his side. And he was mad. Whatever honor and dignity Magnus Coloradas had held was washed away with each drop of blood from these souls. And yet, beyond their own deaths, Victorio could see the Gulo, could see each engagement with that fierce enemy that these dead had experienced: hundreds, thousands, millions of Gulo perishing under a relentless campaign that had seen the Union sweep into Gulo space and annihilate world after world. The man at his side was indeed insane. But was he right?

With shaking hand, Victorio reached behind his back and pulled the knife from his belt. He gripped it tightly, turned the blade outward, and then with all his strength, plunged it into Coloradas's neck.

The power of the strike shocked Red Sleeves, and he pulled his hand away. The voices in Victorio's mind stopped and that gave him strength. He pushed again, driving the knife deeper. Coloradas fell back and tried to pull the knife away, but Victorio's new-found power was too great. He flailed a few more times, slapped meekly at Victorio's face, but could not dislodge the blade. Blood flowed down his chest and stomach and pooled on the ground. Victorio rose up and fell onto his old captain, now pushing the blade deeper with both hands.

"You were once a great, great man, Coloradas," he said, watching the life drain from the big man's face. "I loved you. I would have done anything for you. But your lightning is out, and it will streak no more. Goodbye, and may Yusn Life-Giver forgive you."

He pushed the blade up to the hilt, turned it quickly, and watched Mangus Coloradas die.

Victorio limped out of the woods and saw Blue Bird. He shook his head, impressed by the speed of her arrival. She had been monitoring his movements from her fighter, with strict orders not to intervene unless directed to do so. She never listened.

He grinned and reached for her. She came to his side and took his hands. Tears streaked her face. "You are alive," she said. "Thank Yusn, you are alive."

He nodded weakly and tossed the bloody blade to the

ground. He accepted her help and leaned into her soft body. "It's good to see you again, kind heart. The squad?"

She shook her head. "The Devil Dancers are fine."

"The Red Paint People?"

"Killed and scattered."

A weight fell from his shoulders. It was over. The pirate scourge had been broken, its members routed.

"Is the *di-yin* dead?" Blue Bird asked.

Victorio nodded. "Yes. He will dance no more, but let's not talk about it right now, sweet. Please get me to my fighter."

She did and Victorio pulled himself up and into the cockpit. He strapped in, although the blinking pain of his broken ribs fought against him. Yet despite the pain, he felt good. For the first time in a long time, he felt at peace. He did not want to kill his old captain, but he had done so, and he did not feel bad about it. Still...

He tapped his dash and thumbed up the comm unit. He waited until the frequency found a lone beacon in space. He accepted the link and heard Admiral Cho's voice. "Report, Captain Victorio. Is he dead?"

He cleared his throat and talked through the pain. "Yes, admiral. Your pirate is dead."

"Praise the Union. And his crew?"

Victorio told him everything. When he was done, the Admiral said, "Very well, Captain. The Union thanks you. I thank you. Please report back to the *Justice* for a full debriefing."

"Yes, admiral," Victorio said, as his hand moved to light the engines. "One more thing, sir, and I want this on the record. I have followed your orders and I have done my duty for the Union and its people, and I proudly stand by my actions. But know one thing: this is the last time I will chase down and kill pirates for you. This is the last time the Devil Dancers will be your executioners."

Before the admiral could respond, Victorio killed the link. He then closed his cockpit, lit his engines, and looked at Blue Bird through his window. He smiled. Perhaps her idea of running away and having babies wasn't such a bad idea after all.

He lifted up and guided his fighter through the opening of the battle platform. He waited for Blue Bird, and then together, they sailed into the Sorrow Sea.

Since 1994, Robert E. Waters has worked in the computer and board gaming industry as technical writer, editor, designer, and producer. A member of the Science Fiction and Fantasy Writers of America, his first professional fiction sale came in 2003 with the story "The Assassin's Retirement Party," Weird Tales, Issue #332. Since then he has sold stories to Nth Degree, Nth Zine, Black Library Publishing (Games Workshop), Dark Quest Books, Padwolf Publishing, Mundania Press, Marietta Publishing, Rogue Blades Entertainment, and now Dragon Moon Press. His two most recent stories ("The Game of War" and "The Heirloom") were published in the *Grantville Gazette*, Baen Books' online magazine dedicated to stories set in their best-selling 1632/*Ring of Fire* Alternate History series. Between the years of 1998 – 2006, he also served as an assistant editor to *Weird Tales*. Robert currently lives in Baltimore, Maryland, with his wife Beth, their son Jason, and their cat Buzz.

By Silent Spell Caught

(A Tale of the Last Celdraig)

DANIELLE ACKLEY-MCPHAIL

*Editor's note: This is the sequel to In the Runes,
which appeared in Rum and Runestones.*

The last of the dragons climbed through the mists of memory toward wakefulness.

She was Camirel, daughter of the Celdraig...daughter of the Last Mother. Transformed in the belly of the earth, she was no longer Man alone, but Dragon also. That sounded grand, but at the moment she was naked, spent, and from the feel of it, possibly injured. It was an effort to focus her thoughts, to separate nightmare from dream from memory. Sleep had taken her—exhaustion really—but now instinct demanded she wake.

The spell that veiled her must have faded.

Camirel felt exposed. She worried about herself, but even more about the pouch secured about her waist, its contents more precious than her virtue. Though she had barely enough energy built back up to clothe herself with a thought, she made the effort anyway. Her temples pounded as she bent her will on donning the simple cotton robe she usually called forth by magic when transitioning from dragon to human form. And none too soon....

As the soft, warm folds wrapped around her chilled flesh, hiding her body and the pouch from view, someone entered the cabin.

Unable to move, Cami listened to the heavy thud of footsteps crossing the floor. Wisps of memory came a bit clear, borne upon the briny air, jostled by the shifting of the deck beneath her. She was aboard the *Devil's Get*. Its captain, the pirate Tulo, had something that didn't belong to him. She'd come to take it back. At the moment she couldn't say if she'd succeeded. Or who approached her now. She tried to ready a defense only to awaken a piercing pain in the space behind her eyes. She lay there, praying to remain unnoticed, for there was no hope of protecting herself.

She prayed in vain.

Whoever it was stopped beside her; someone large and singularly disinclined to go away. A hard toe prodded her roughly until Cami slowly opened her eyes and let her head roll back. She could do nothing more. Not even groan with the effort. She lay there drained and battered, her shoulder throbbing.

In the moment it took to open her eyes, she assessed her surroundings. She lay in darkness barely lightened by the twilight slipping past the broken windows of the captain's cabin. The sounds of the sea came to her ears: waves lapping against the outer hull, the splash of something breaking the skin of the water, airborne nocterns taunting the vessel, which now that she was conscious Camirel noted dipped and bobbed more than a ship at dock ought. The damaged window brought with it another memory: the captain falling dead at the hand of Camirel's nemesis, Malizia, just before the waterwitch escaped, breaking out through the glass. Even now the stench of Captain Tulo's voided body was growing ripe.

Then the memory deepened...Malizia had slaughtered *all* of the crew.

Yet standing above Camirel was a deepening of the darkness, outlined in a half-familiar form. Before she could clear the fog from her thoughts, the shadow stooped and something more chilling than the metal it was made of clicked around her neck. Feebly, her hands rose to touch it and discovered a collar with no seam or hinge, sealed about her throat with pure magic.

The sickly pale glow of that connecting spell illuminated her captor, revealing a smooth, bald head marred on the right side by a three-inch gap to bare skull and a face mostly masked in dried blood. The man's nose was misshapen and his lower lip split near diagonal: Cragg, former first mate to the sack of meat poisoning the air...the only other who knew the secret of the runestones. He had aided Tulo in using them to steal spells from unwitting runecasters. But the stones were more than uncut gems; they were the cache Camirel had come to snatch away, safe now in the pouch she wore beneath her robe. They were not gems at all, but dragon young. Emberlings. She had vowed to see every one of them returned to their earthfire nests. Here was a man with a vested interest in stopping her. Silently, she stared up at him, trying to read his expression, but the light from the spell rapidly faded, leaving Camirel with no clue of his temper.

Until he spoke.

"Don't bother wishin' for death, *witch*. I don't have a bit of mercy in me." He swiftly stood. Then the heel of his booted foot came down upon her left forearm. The thud ended in a sharp crack.

Camirel discovered she could not voice a scream. She could not make any sound. She curled around her injured arm, taut with new-minted agony, pulse beating frantically a scale's thickness away from the edge of the razor-sharp control collar. That collar was kept from parting her skin only by a rune easily spoken away by her captor at any time should it catch his whim. Morrow's corpse had worn such a collar... sunk deep into the flesh of his neck by the time she made his spirit's acquaintance.

Morrow! More mist lifted from Camirel's brain. Morrow was the unhoused soul of Captain Tulo's last—and final— victim. Cami had come to count him a friend. She longed to reach down to see if she still retained the emberling he was bound to, among those she had come to steal way, but she dare, not beneath Cragg's harsh gaze.

"You'll not catch me again with your 'casting," the surviving pirate muttered as he moved toward the captain's remains. With little care and no ceremony, the pirate stripped the corpse of all valuables and dumped it overboard through the broken window. He then left the cabin with his loot, not bothering to close the door. Cami soon heard the distant splash of Malizia's other victims being consigned to the sea.

Cami stared at the wreckage of the window and then toward the unbarred door.

Clearly, Cragg saw her as no physical threat even as he assumed silencing her would hobble her magic.

He was wrong. She was no weak-powered runecaster, needing to speak or write her runes. Even with her personal energy nigh spent, magic for her was but a thought and the tapping of a ready power source.

Despite her weariness, despite her pain, she reached out her senses and drew upon the earthfire, called it to her, and ordered her thoughts. The earthfire answered, but did not come, *could* not come to her summons. In that moment, Cami sensed the depth of her ill-fated luck: they were no longer secure at dock, but afloat at sea, surrounded by water, the antithesis of her fire. Anywhere but on open water she could call on the mage energy generated by all life. Here she was too far from the earth and the fire at its core. Here, without personal energy to draw on, she was crippled, like any other mortal. If she were in dragon form it would not matter how much water surrounded her.

Of course, if she were in dragon form, she wouldn't have been captured.

Her head fell back in a silent wail, the last of her energy spent.

M'lady...Camirel...by the First Mother, girl, speak to me!
There was a desperate edge to the voice whispering direct into her mind. She was tempted not to answer, to retreat back

into oblivion. But compassion and duty united to prevent her from such a selfish act. She half opened her eyes and looked about her. It was still night and darkness filled the room, but for a few patches of moonlight.

Camirel... the voice repeated.

As Cami came more awake, her annoyance gave way to deep-seated relief. The voice was Morrow, and through the touch of his thoughts she sensed that he and the emberlings were safe in the pouch she wore beneath her robe. His fate and that of the emberlings weighed upon her.

She did not move. She could not speak. But there was no such governor on her thoughts.

What know you, my friend?

Morrow's relief was palpable. *Once they saw what was done, and how, the constables fled the ship and cut it loose,* he told her. *Apparently trusting the tide to take care of the matter, rather than risk getting tangled with what wrought such slaughter. They knew nothing of yourself or Malizia. They certainly knew nothing of the runestones, or they would not have acted with such haste. None came aboard any further than the main deck before debarking with all swiftness.*

Interesting, and something she had not considered when she'd planned to wait out the authorities. *What of the pirates?*

They are dead, but for Cragg. Though why he isn't, is a wonder.

Camirel agreed. She had gotten a good look at that gash up close. If he didn't attend to Malizia's handiwork, neglect would not be long in finishing the deed.

Cami wondered what Cragg intended. Other than the collar, he had not bound her, nor had he stripped her of her belongings. Her clothes were intact and the pouch of emberlings still safe beneath them. Of course, it would take a mage stronger than she was to even sense the pouch and its contents were there, let along separate the two. Not many could claim such power.

That woke in her a chilling thought: *He thinks it was me. He thinks I was the witch that maimed him and slaughtered the captain and crew.*

Oh, Great Mother! Alarm welled up and Cami was frantic for a way free of her predicament. Her breath raced and her throat locked tight as every muscle tensed. There was no telling what vengeance the sailor planned or when he would strike. She'd already had a taste of his cruelty. She forced the panic down, walled it off in a back portion of her brain and refused it any attention. It would not serve her now. She needed to rebuild her resources and figure out a plan. But first she must get herself together.

What is wrong? Morrow asked.

My arm, she murmured back. *I must tend to it or we have no hope of getting free.*

She sensed uneasiness in Morrow's thoughts. Some hesitation. But when he did not speak again, she discounted it and went about the goal she'd set for herself.

Moving with a care for her broken arm, Camirel sat up and scanned the cabin, looking for something to bind up her injury. Nothing lay nearby and none of the captain's effects visible in the moonlight were even remotely suited. Cursing the need, she drew herself to her feet, her good arm gripping one of the cabin's bracings. Iced drops of sweat beaded her brow by the time she was upright and her teeth gritted against the pain. The collar alone kept her from the humiliation of whimpering. As much as she was able, she followed the wall, carefully skirting the bed and the heavy cedar chest bolted to the deck beside it, her good arm steadying her as she made her way around the room, searching until she came back to the point where she'd started with nothing to show for the effort but a bit of fruit, some travel bread of higher quality than hard tack, and the dregs of a bottle of wine. She set all that aside for later. For now, her stomach roiled with each step; between the pain of her arm and the lingering stench it was a wonder she had not already heaved. Likely she would have, if not for the fresh air coming in off the open sea.

The thought brought her head rearing up, her eyes locked upon the broken window with its long, straight lengths of pane no longer needed for their given task. If her startled laugh had had voice there would have been a touch of the hysterical about it. Camirel abandoned the wall and made straight for the window, only to stumble as the ship lurched over a swell. She came down on her bad arm until bone grated against bone. The loose splinters and jagged ends cut into her flesh until she feared they would break through the skin. The roiling in her gut immediately turned to retching, though precious little came up. For a time, she blacked out. Resurfacing through a cascade of pain, unsure of how long she'd been unconscious, she found herself in a puddle of sick that was little more than bile, the pain flashing colored jags across her vision.

Ah! she cried out in the silence of her thoughts as tears streamed down her cheeks. Her features contorted with the agony.

Camirel! Morrow answered her cry, his tone a mix of concern and frustration.

Give me a minute. Even her mental voice sounded faint.

No, Camirel, he insisted. *Listen to me. The stones...* and here the hesitation crept back in, *...the ruby-colored runesto...emberlings, they are marked with a spell for healing.*

For a moment she knew pure hope despite the dire situation. And yet, Morrow had hesitated. She had to wonder why. *Morrow...what happens to the stones once the magic has been spent?*

Silence.

Morrow? Pain made her tone harsh.

I don't know...until you told me they were emberlings, it didn't matter. I didn't even know what they really were. She could not dispute that. No one beside herself knew that runestones were actually dragon young torn from the earth before their time. Their magical nature was what made it possible for Tulo to capture spells upon them.

Every curse she'd ever heard streamed through Camirel's mind. Injured she stood little chance of getting *any* of the emberlings to safety, but she was sworn to care for and protect them all. In her battle with Malizia, one of the emberlings had been destroyed. Cami still felt the cry of that lost soul. Dare she risk that using the imprinted rune would do harm to the one it was bound to? Dare she not? Was she to lose them all, or perhaps just one? The pain was unbearable; the uncertainty even worse.

What... she had to force the thought. *What is the trigger?*

He gave her the word.

It sat heavy in her mind. Morrow did not push her as she huddled in a pool of moonlight halfway to the window, considering the unsavory option he'd offered. As she pondered, the square of moonlight traveled across the floor, leaving her again in darkness. The sounds of bodies being fed to the sea were long faded and the smells of sick were lessened, if not gone, thanks to the breeze. And still, though hours passed, Cami made no move to use the trigger word or even bind her arm by more mundane means. She could sense Morrow patiently waiting. In a way she wished he'd push her, that she would not feel the blame so heavily should her fears be proved out. But no...it would not matter. The responsibility and any corresponding guilt were and always would be her own.

Camirel thought the trigger word.

One minute, then two passed and she wondered had she gotten something wrong. Hard to imagine, mind to mind, but she was pain-dazed and exhausted. She considered 'uttering' it again, only her arm began to tingle and then all she could think to do was scream until her mind rang with a silent cry as unseen forces pulled muscle and bone taut and straight, and the fire of the 'casting fused the very cells back into place. Cold ache was replaced by the lingering heat of that momentary burn. Camirel's knuckles popped when her hand involuntarily flexed with the healing. Even the last vestiges of pain in her shoulder were no more.

Bind it.

Cami jerked at the unexpected order, making no move to obey.

Bind it, now! Morrow snapped at her again. *Or do you wish Cragg to know you have the means to work magic?*

First Mother help her if the pirate learned that! What a price he could command for a controlled runecaster!

She nodded sharply in agreement. Moving with much surer steps toward the casement, Camirel noted that the collar began to vibrate uncomfortably the closer she approached the opening. She growled soundlessly and her stomach clenched as she realized what that meant for her, and why she'd not been secured. Stopping two feet from theoretical freedom, she stretched out her arms and broke off two lengths of damaged pane roughly equal to her forearm. As she did so, her mouth opened wide and her breath was trapped in her chest as she felt the sting of several layers of skin about her neck parting beneath the collar's edge. Hastily she jerked herself back and thought all manner of dire thoughts at the one responsible. She grimaced and reflected, *It's important to know one's boundaries.*

Morrow's response was a rude sound deep in her mind. Cami almost laughed.

By touch and faint moonlight, she carefully examined her prize, working away a splinter or two before deeming the wood serviceable for her needs. Setting them down she then turned her attention toward the bindings she would need. Her gaze lingered on the captain's bed. Tulo struck her as the type that had commanded creature comforts. She was not wrong in this. Tugging the heavy down covering from the bed to the floor, with satisfaction she considered the costly silk sheets beneath. Cragg could get a nice bit of gold for them, if he weren't inclined to enjoy them himself....

With no small amount of glee, she squandered a bit of regained energy to briefly transform her fingers to dragon talons, the better to shred the sheets, not caring if the sound of tearing cloth traveled. Now for the binding.... It was awkward, but she managed to sandwich her arm between the splints and wrap it tight with strips of silk until no flesh showed, employing her right hand, teeth, and both knees to get the deed accomplished. With a final strip of silk she made a sling to support her arm, a reminder really, that it was not to be used. As for pain; there was no need to feign discomfort once she was done. Healed her arm might be, but not without lingering effect.

With that thought came a reminder of what she had risked.

Taking a deep breath she turned her senses to the pouch of emberlings, tried to feel if the life had gone out of any one of them. But it was as if her mage senses were encased in cloudy ice. Or perhaps it was that she could not tell with the emberlings jumbled together so closely; if so, she did not dare to draw them out to inspect them one by one. No telling when the pirate would return.

Can you sense him, Morrow?

The spirit grew a little distant as he focused elsewhere, searching for Cragg. *Enough to tell he's below, but not what he's doing.*

Weary and aching and no small amount heartsick, Cami turned and considered the door. There was a runelock on it. When she'd first entered the chamber (what seemed another lifetime ago), she'd had to shield herself and wait for Tulo to show so she could follow him past the safeguard. She had had no choice, not knowing the trigger word. She rued the fact that she herself had prevented the door from closing then, thinking she might need a quick escape. If she had let it close behind her, she might have saved herself a broken arm.

Then again...maybe not.

Does Cragg know the trigger for the runelock?

Tulo didn't trust anyone and he didn't share power, Morrow answered. *Safe to say, I think, that the answer is no.*

Dare she trust Morrow was right? Truth was, it didn't matter. Cami was so spent she trembled all over and her eyes now showed her the world in only black and white and shades of grey. Again bracing herself against the wall, she made her way to the door and closed it firmly, but softly. Her heart did not slow its pace until her mage senses confirmed the rune engaged. Once it did, she nearly slumped to the ground as the tension went out of her; only by sheer will did she manage to keep her feet. At the least she would have warning should Cragg return for her while she slept. That would have to be enough for now.

You must eat, Morrow said, jarring her from the haze she'd settled into.

I don't think I can, she answered. **I'm too tired.**

Sleep alone will not restore you, m'lady.

Camirel, she reminded him, as if his use of her name now that she'd granted it was more vital to her than food.

He growled and she could feel the weight of his regard, no matter he had no physical form. She sighed, or thought to anyway, and knew that he was right. Standing propped against the wall, she ate a quarter portion of what she had found earlier and limited herself to two swigs of the harsh wine. The rest she tucked inside the chest for later.

With her last moments of consciousness, she tugged the bedcovering from where she'd dropped it earlier and made a nest for herself between the cedar chest and the wall. She was asleep practically before she crawled inside.

Her sleep was disturbed by the sound of chopping.

Thunk. Crack! Thunk. Crack! Echoed in her dreams as the ax head entered and was torn from solid wood.

Camirel huddled deep beneath the down and tried to ignore the sound, annoyed that one of the Brothers would do the chore at such an impolite hour. True, the Order that had taken her in and offered her sanctuary at Mabet after her parents' death was an industrious one, but they were generally more considerate of those not required to rise so early. She shifted and tried to draw the blankets closer against the chill when an aching twinge in her arm served the last clue to her memory. *Thunk! Crack!* The cabin door split with the sound of finality, just as Cami shook off sleep. She stared defiantly at the pirate as the splintered remnants fell away.

So much for the runelock....

Cragg stalked through the wreckage to stand over her, ax still half hefted in his right hand. At some time in the night he'd stitched closed his scalp wound with thick, raw silk thread. Except for the bruising, his face was stark white in comparison. His eyes blazed. Something about the intent look he gave her made her uneasy. "Move, *witch*," he snapped at her. "Before we lose the tide." She wanted to snap back. Just as well she couldn't as the impulse was hardly wise. As she scrambled to her feet, he grabbed her unbound arm the moment she was in reach and propelled her toward the door, following fast on her heels.

The morning light near blinded her as she stumbled out on to the deck. The air was chilled and the waves choppy, making it hard for her to find her legs so shortly drawn from sleep. She stopped, blinking and swaying as she looked around her, only to be pushed toward where the longboat waited to be lowered. The craft was packed with a few casks and sacks, the contents of which she couldn't identify, but on the deck of the ship was a more substantial pile of sturdy, well-sealed containers, all lashed together with thick, stout rope, and anchored to a buoy.

Morrow, what's going on?* she asked the spirit, who'd spent more time aboard a pirate ship than she.

That's his lagan,* he answered. *Loot he wants to salvage but can't take with him. He's going to sink it with the ship and that buoy will help him find the stuff when he comes back for it.**

Now that Morrow mentioned it, she could smell guncotton on the air. She looked over her shoulder at the ship and nearly jumped back. Cragg stood practically on top of her, a burning brand in his hand and a sack strapped across his back. "Get in the longboat," he ordered.

It wasn't like she could argue, but she also wasn't above a bit of revenge. Gathering the tiniest bit of her restored mage energy she thought a rune of unbinding, ensuring the buoy was no longer tethered to the treasure.

"Ah! I thought so!" The grin on Cragg's face was like a cannon round passing through Camirel's gut. "You aren't the only one what has the Sense, *witch*. Who is it you figure made that little trinket you're wearin'? Certainly wasn't that ass, Tulo, or his slave 'casters." His gaze took on a leer. "I felt whatever you wrought in the night. More fool you, not usin' it to try and get free. Now I know enough to keep you in my sight, at least for the short while it matters. Try one thing false and you can consider the trigger spoken. I value my skin more than any profit you may bring." He paused then and looked her up and down in frank assessment. "I thank you in particular, though...you just trebled the price I'll settle on you and those stones you think you're hidin' once we hit shore."

Unable to yell or curse or scream at him to her satisfaction, Camirel spat upon him, her face surely twisted with the rage and desperation she felt inside. Cragg only laughed and cuffed her hard until she stumbled against the bulwark, just catching herself before she tumbled over the rail. "Get in the boat!" he roared after her. With little choice otherwise, she scrambled to obey, pressing herself as far back as the goods would allow as she watched him climb aboard, tossing the brand to the far side of the ship as he left the deck. Camirel barely had time to wrap herself around the lashings holding the cargo in place when she noticed Cragg draw a machete from the bilge of the boat and with a quick slash, severed the winch line holding the longboat aloft.

It hurt screaming with no sound. It was as if her body strained all the harder to be heard and she paid the price for its failure. Cragg just laughed all the way.

As the longboat splashed down into the sea, taking on a good bit of water in the process, he tossed her a bilge bucket.

"You might as well do away with those bandages and get to work. By the way you're wrapped around that rope, it's fair clear now what you spent yourself on in the night."

Camirel had never used her magic to do harm. The very thought was anathema to her, as it would have been to all Celdraig. Just as well. Her expression must have given her away as she remotely considered doing so now.

"Shall I say it," Cragg murmured, leaning close, his thick, callused finger running just below the collar ringing her neck. Her scored skin stung at his touch. "One word and I'll finish what you've just barely started here." His finger came away with dried flecks of her blood speckling the tip. Cami schooled her expression to remain neutral and slowly shook her head.

"Start bailing, then," Cragg said. "I don't fancy soaking my feet all the way to landfall."

Presuming her complete compliance with his order, Cragg applied himself to the oars with haste, long, deep pulls sending them flying across the mostly calm water as fast as his well-muscled arms could manage. They were barely far enough away when the ship blew. Concussion waves swamped the longboat, sinking their draft a little deeper.

At a hard glance from her captor Cami bent more energetically to her task.

With care, but less than half a thought on the process, she dumped each bucket over the edge. With the rest she barraged Morrow with questions. *Did you know this? Did you know the man was a 'caster?*

Morrow's mental tone was both rueful and wry. *When I was graced with my collar they'd knocked me cold first with the runestone from Tulo's dagger. There were no others come after me until yourself.*

The spirit fell silent and Camirel was distracted by her own thoughts.

The dagger...she'd forgotten the dagger! Set into the pommel was one of her emberlings. Cragg had pocketed it with the rest of Tulo's belongings before he'd tossed the body to the sea. She had to get it if she could.

She took a quick moment to assess the water level in the bottom of the boat. Without a thimble she wasn't likely to bail out much more, the level being below the rim of her current bucket. She set it aside and scurried to the far side of the boat, propping herself against the cargo and looking out at the churning sea.

Tension knotted her gut at what she saw. The waves cause by the sinking ship should have exhausted by now. With no obvious weather darkening the sky, the choppy look of the wake was unnerving. In the distance, she thought she caught the occasional wisp of vapor rising from the water.... Such spoke of power beneath the waves. But what the source? Dare she hope...? There were places where the ocean floor rose to meet the waves, rather than the other way around. If they passed above one of those fault-lines, and the underwater volcanoes such generally caused, she would have a chance at tapping into the earthfire.

Reeling out a bit of personal energy, Cami probed beneath the water, only to find herself frustrated. She could not tell. It was like her senses were hobbled.

The rogue never gave me reason, that I can recall, to believe he was a runecaster. Morrow finally spoke again, his tone reflective. *I have delved as deep as I am able into memory and there is none that I can hold up to say 'I should have known.'*

The sudden resumption of the previous conversation startled Camirel from her efforts. It took her a moment to focus on what he said.

Of course, the collar dampens the mage sense, which you may have noticed, and I was never much around him when I wasn't working runes myself. But I think it is telling that Cragg was the only one of the crew who knew the secret of the runestones and was involved in their creation.

Another silent sigh rose from Cami. *Can you tell me anything about the collar?*

Not much. I was not strong enough to fight it, or even test it. Mine allowed me speech and movement, only holding over me the dire threat that came with disobedience. I did not have the boundaries set upon me that you do. But perhaps that is because the villains had time to prepare for my ambush, but not for yours? Thus he had to bind you in more ways to make up for other weakness in the runes?

Her teeth clenched behind her smooth expression. This was all supposition. She needed to know more.

What if you look closer at this one? Perhaps you can tell what I cannot.

She felt a gentle probing from Morrow.

It does feel different, but I cannot say how as I did not know the composition of my own.

The frustration ran deep and it was her turn to fall silent. It wasn't Morrow's fault, but that scarcely mattered given her current mood. She had not taken up her charge from the Last Mother to fail so utterly. With less than a handful of emberlings interred there was not even the hope her efforts might be enough were she to fall now to this foe.

Morrow, she said, after long moments of thought. *Do you know what it is made of?*

Again the probing.

Steel, he finally answered. *Nothing more than steel. I can see the runes upon it as I never could with mortal eyes and they do nothing more than hold the edge from your skin or, be the trigger word spoken or set boundaries breached, draw the elements of the metal closer to one another, sinking the blade into your flesh.*

Pleasant thought, that. Camirel figured she could have done without confirmation of those particulars, no matter that she'd already known.

Morrow went on, *A separate rune keeps you silent, most likely because he knew nothing of your skill. There is another to keep you from sketching runes, but as you don't need to, it has not hindered you.*

She barely 'heard' him, her mind locked on the matter of the steel. Only...it did her no good *now*, but what if she had a chance to transform? Common steel, even magicked, was no proof against dragon scales, not with earthfire strengthening them beyond the hardness of diamonds. Runespelled or not, the steel would shatter the moment she drew the 'fire and took on the form.

Again, it did her no good now...

...but let her be right about the approaching source of earthfire, and Cragg would soon piss himself in the face of the Dragon in her.

She let the prospect smolder as she watched the surface of the sea for more signs of sub-aquatic venting. There was a feel about the air that gave her hope, a subtle vibration against her skin that had nothing to do with fear or runes or rage.

Finally, she spied that for which she searched: a massive plume of steam rising from the surface of the water, as like the wisps she noted earlier as a whale was to a new-spawned fish. She lurched to her feet and turned toward the glorious earthfire rising from below.

Behind her she heard Cragg curse as she off-balanced the boat. She sensed him falter and jerk, but did not let her attention waver from her goal. Camirel locked her eyes on the vapors. Ahead lurked an underwater volcano; the purest source of earthfire to be had upon the sea. A few more strokes, just a few more, and she could begin to draw upon its energy.

As they drifted closer Cami began to gather the trailing wisps to her.

"What the hell are you doing?" She felt Cragg finally lunge for her.

Camirel grimaced, unable to retort. With her left hand, she gripped the rope binding the cargo to steady herself against the lurching of the boat; with the other, she yanked one of her splints out of its binding, leaving splinters of wood in her flesh, but gaining what she could in the way of a projectile. Closing her eyes, she resumed drawing the earthfire from the superheated, ambient air. It wasn't quite enough to change, but it was more than sufficient to send the hardened wood spearing toward the pirate. As a weapon, it had no hope of even scratching Cragg's skin, but as a distraction...just enough! He batted the projectile away. The motion unbalanced him a vital moment as he regained his center.

And then...they were there.

Though he no longer stroked the oars, their momentum brought the longboat over the slope of the volcano's cone. Camirel's back arched and she gasped without sound as 'fire suddenly flooded the empty spaces within her that had been aching for its burn. She barely heard Cragg's startled cry as the power filled her up to the limit of her human form, and then she drew more.

Her skin throbbed and her head thrashed. For a moment she was overwhelmed by the sensations, like sleep-numbed limbs that pulsed with the return of blood flow, only hotter. Somewhere distant in her thoughts Morrow whispered, talked her down, reminded her of her goal, her purpose beyond that glorious moment of restoration. He warned her as Cragg uttered the rune holding the collar from her flesh. A growl rumbled from her throat, deepening in pitch as it went on. Newly grounded and steeped in power, Camirel guided it with her mind, thought 'Dragon' and put on that skin, that shape. As always, her clothing disappeared and the pouch holding the emberlings sank magically beneath her dragon hide, protected and secure. The tightening steel, however, shattered against her scales as she rose on the surging plume of ash and gas brought to the surface by her draw upon the volcano's power.

Freed, she bellowed her challenge to the world.

She barely heard the frightened cry rise from the longboat below.

Camirel spread the dual sets of sail-like wings that had replaced her human arms and bugled a triumphant call no spell could silence. The frilled vanes that graced her elegant head fanned about her and she briefly hovered there in full glory, tail thrashing and underbelly reflecting the blues and greens of the sea. Arching her now-sinuous neck, she gazed at the man crouching in her shadow.

Pivoting with ease on a wingtip, she swooped down and grasped Cragg carefully in her claws, bearing him up until he trailed beneath her. She then arrowed toward an island she'd sighted in the distance; an island seemingly untouched by humankind, but surely capable of sustaining one lone man.

She was not unmoved by his frantic thrashing. A glance down revealed his attempts to sketch runes upon the wind, only she flew too swiftly for him to complete them, leaving a trail of disjointed magic in her wake. She took some satisfaction in absorbing the lingering energy, which Cragg was surely able to sense, given his bellowed rage.

"Don't bother wishing for death, *sir...*" she said, human words coming without difficulty from her dragon's muzzle. "I am sure you will suffer much more having to live with my mercy." And with those words, she dropped him none too gently upon the hot sands of the deserted beach.

Are you sure it is wise to leave him breathing?* Morrow cautioned.

Camirel sighed, and then snarled in frustration. *No, not at all. However, I am not such as he; I have no choice. But first, I claim what is mine.*

She reached out with razor talons and tore open the sack secured across the pirate's back. Out tumbled valuables looted from the ship, Tulo's belongings among them. With a triumphant roar, Camirel snatched up the sheathed dagger bearing the emberling pommel and soared away across the sky, heading for the volcano, whose maw led straight to the belly of the First Mother.

And the last of dragonkind returned her hard-won emberlings to their nests. All but the one to which Morrow was bound.

Award-winning author Danielle Ackley-McPhail has worked both sides of the publishing industry for over sixteen years. Currently, she is a project editor and promotions manager for Dark Quest Books.

Her published works include four urban fantasy novels, *Yesterday's Dreams*, *Tomorrow's Memories*, the upcoming *Today's Promise*, and *The Halfling's Court: A Bad-Ass Faerie Tale*. She is also the author of the non-fiction writers guide, *The Literary Handyman* and is the senior editor of the *Bad-Ass Faeries* anthology series. Her work is included in numerous other anthologies and collections, including *Rum and Runestones*, *Dark Furies*, *Breach the Hull*, *So It Begins*, *By Other Means*, *No Man's Land*, *Space Pirates*, *Space Horrors*, *Barbarians at the Jumpgate*, and *New Blood*.

She is a member of The Garden State Horror Writers, the New Jersey Authors Network, and Broad Universe, a writer's organization focusing on promoting the works of women authors in the speculative genres.

Danielle lives somewhere in New Jersey with husband and fellow writer, Mike McPhail, mother-in-law Teresa, and three extremely spoiled cats. She can be found on LiveJournal (damcphail, badassfaeries, darkquestbooks, lit_handyman), Facebook (Danielle Ackley-McPhail), and Twitter (DMcPhail).

To learn more about her work visit: visitsidhenadaire. com, literaryhandyman.com, or badassfaeries.com.

Facing the Wind

BERNIE MOJZES

It was an ill wind that blew them here, a *westerly* wind, screaming and howling as it tore at the sails and gnawed at the masts and railings, driving the *Grey Perl* so far east that the shadows of mountains on the horizon occluded the stars.

Captain Deadbeef stared out after the westerly through infrared binoculars as the last of its demons—both flaming yellow and deep purple varieties—swooped and dove and shrieked at imaginary victims. An angelic ballet danced to a hellish chorus. He called to his first mate, who had run aft to assist with the wounded.

"How many did we lose, Ms. Canbrach?"

"Unknown, sir. Still doing triage."

Dilsson called out from the crow's-nest. "Metzger's gone, sir, blown overboard. And..." He hesitated. "Jamie's dead."

"Where?" Deadbeef's jaw tightened as he scanned the deck. "Up here."

Dilsson stood within the crow's-nest's padlocked cage, pointing up into the dark of the night sky. Jamie's body hung above him, impaled on the mast and disemboweled by the wind's cruel claws, cooling to a blood red through the binoculars' lenses.

"Right. All hands on deck for a head count. Get the wounded back to Ms. Canbrach and Doc, and gather the dead for burial." Deadbeef wiped liquid salt from his eyes. Blood, almost entirely. He kicked the dead thing at his feet, stomping on the dry, withered claw that had raked across his face in the midst of the storm. The claw crumbled to dust under his heel. He grabbed the rest of the thing and heaved it overboard.

Fucking westerlies.

Fucking Jamie. He'd been ordered to stay below deck.

"I'm coming up, Dilsson. Let's get the boy down with a little bit of respect, you hear?"

It was blood in his eyes. That's all.

It was not the worst they'd suffered in the fifteen-odd years since Canbrach's press gang had dragged Doc Fitzwater from Wesley Medical's parking garage. Not the worst, but it was close, and more gruesome than most. There were two dead in the storm: Jamie on the mast, and Mad Jim Hollander, who had cut down a half dozen demons before his machete lodged in the rail, and he was beaten to the deck and eviscerated. Metzger had gone overboard, presumed dead...if he was lucky. Of the dozen wounded, Tam had suffered the most grievously – her skin ripped entirely from her flesh – and Doc Fitzwater used some of their precious heroin to ease her passing.

"A bullet's faster," Canbrach said. "And cheaper."

Doc spat, wasting valuable fluids to make her point. No denying Melissa Canbrach was a vital part of the crew and had saved all their asses, individually and collectively, more times than she cared to count. But the first mate was as heartless as they came.

Lying on the bloody deck, Tam sighed into the drug and let it take her. Her breathing slowed.

Doc Fitzwater made her rounds, stitching lacerations and tending to burns, and when she returned, Tam was dead, lipless mouth hanging open, revealing the severed root of her tongue. Doc laid her handkerchief over the empty lidless sockets and wondered if, wherever they were, Tam's eyes had glazed over at her death.

More likely sucked dry and discarded, by now.

Doc shuddered.

A heavy hand settled on her shoulder. "Go on, get some rest." The captain's voice. "Only a couple hours till sun up, and tomorrow's going to be a long day."

After the funeral, Doc processed the dead and readied them for internment. Captain Deadbeef stood at her side and watched the condenser drip.

"Maybe it was a blessing," he said. "The storm."

"How so?" *That's Jamie lying there, for fuck's sake.*

"How long had it been since we last saw anyone out there? Anyone alive, that is. Two months? More? We're almost out of water. Another few days..." He shrugged. "There's a settlement near the base of the mountains. A live settlement. I saw the heat signature last night, after the storm passed on."

Doc frowned. "A raid?" She hated raids. Taking on another ship was one thing—they were fighting pirates, then, evil bastards who preyed on the helpless, and those battles helped her forget the unpleasant truth: she was a pirate, too. They all were.

Deadbeef shrugged again. "If that's what it comes to." He caught a drop of Jamie's water on a fingertip and brought it to his lips. "Probably."

Doc turned away, looked out the porthole so she wouldn't have to see the cabin boy's shriveling corpse or the mask of the captain's face, immobile and affectless. More mannequin than man. *PTSD*, she thought. *Shell shock. Don't judge.*

Outside, the crew struggled to dig three graves in the rocky soil that lay under the ever-present dust that sucked at their thighs.

"It's just.... There's so few of us left."

"You got a better plan?" Deadbeef slammed his hands against the table in sudden anger. The condenser rained.

"Hurry up so we can get these husks in the ground. Longer we wait the more time they have to mount a defense. If any of them survived the storm, that is."

The dust swirled around the unmarked graves, erasing them as quickly as it erased the crew's footprints. As quickly as it had erased everything.

With a shout, the crew tugged at gritty ropes. The sails unfurled, and the *Grey Perl* began to move. Soil and rock cracked and crumbled under the ship's prow as they ground their way across the Great American Desert, a deep furrow ripped into the Earth and spat out into long ridges, a static wake to mark their passing. For Doc, that trail ran from what had once been Wichita, Kansas, meandering across the lifeless heartland to the eastern mountains. If you could find it under the dust.

Where the *Grey Perl* and Captain Deadbeef had come from before, she didn't know. Nobody talked about the past, just as nobody talked about the future.

Doc thought back to her geography lessons. The captain had said they were probably in Ohio, which made these what? Blue Ridge? Adirondacks? Catskills? She'd always hated maps. Didn't much matter; those books were dust, devoured by the same creatures that had literally flattened America, tearing hunks out of buildings and hills until all that remained was an endless, sifting sea.

The demons bound to the hull screamed as they tore through what was left of one of the ridges of dense rock that striated the softer, ubiquitous shale. The settlement rumbled into view. Canbrach cursed, and Doc Fitzwater laughed, earning herself a stern glare. Captain Deadbeef just nodded, acceptance without expression. There would be no lightning raid; the settlement was protected with a wind-break.

The wind-break danced in the breeze like abandoned Christmas decorations, glittering like diamonds and silver across tinsel-draped nylon lines that stretched for miles, suspended from an ad-hoc framework of telephone poles and street lamps arrayed in an enormous semicircle around the settlement. The bodies of demons, drawn like moths to the glittering trap, lay in heaps in front of the wind-break, not yet returned to dust.

Almost as if of its own volition, the ship turned toward the closest section of the wind-break.

The *Grey Perl* could not penetrate that wall, not without killing the demons that served them and wrecking against a reef of their own making. The demons cackled and laughed, lemmings racing to meet death. Captain Deadbeef adjusted their course to compensate.

Beyond the wind-break were buildings, some still standing as high as two stories, improvised roofing appended to truncated structures, and mile after mile of fields that waved green and golden in a benign breeze.

It had been a long time since any of them had seen fresh food. Since they had seen anything this *alive*. Years, maybe.

"We'll swing around from the south," Canbrach said. "Maybe we can't take them by surprise, but if we hit them hard enough..." When Deadbeef didn't respond, she called the order herself. The crew hastened to adjust the sails, and the *Grey Perl* began the long, wide arc around the wind-break.

"This isn't right," Doc said. "We can't do this."

Canbrach turned on her. "Don't give me that self-righteous bullshit. I didn't see you complaining when you ate your breakfast. I didn't see you whining when you got your ration of water. And *you know where that came from*. There's no space for right and wrong anymore. There's just living another day, or not. So shut the fuck up."

"But..."

Canbrach drove a black-gloved finger into her solar plexus. Hard. "*Don't fucking judge me.*" Each word punctuated with a jab. "I do what needs to be done. No more, no less. Now get the fuck out of my way."

"Captain..."

Deadbeef glanced at her, a shift of the eyes, no more, then back at the rolling fields.

"Ms. Canbrach, you have the helm. I'll be in my cabin."

Doc watched with a rising sense of dread as Canbrach coordinated the assault. The first mate worked with ruthless efficiency, assessing the settlement's defenses and plotting a course that would allow the pirates to strike the settlement's strongest points—the three massive guns that stood guard North, South and West of the town, each capable of firing shells that would break the *Grey Perl* apart. Destroy those right off, identify and eliminate the leadership, and resistance would crumble.

Hit them so hard they'd be too stunned to respond.

All they needed to do was get around the wind-break. Canbrach's demon-enhanced missiles had greater range than the town's artillery, and Doc knew she wouldn't hesitate to use them. No matter the collateral damage. Taking out all three guns would erase half the town, but would leave most of the food—and, more importantly, the water tanks—unscathed.

They gave the wind-break a wide berth as they tacked south and east. As they rounded the southernmost pole, Canbrach adjusted course, bringing the *Grey Perl* around in a sweeping arc that would end with her right in the middle of town.

"Elkins! Barkowski! Prepare to fire! Carrigan, you'll be up in about five." She adjusted course, bringing them into range.

Ahead of them, one of the big guns fired a warning shot. The shell threw a plume of flame and dust into air, less than a mile ahead of them. The crater was deep enough to lose a tank in. Nothing to worry about; the *Grey Perl* could just dig its way out.

"Stop!" For a second Doc thought that maybe she had shouted the words, given voice to the screaming in her head. But she hadn't. It was the captain.

"All hands stand down!" Deadbeef strode out onto the command deck. "Bring us up next to that crater and lay anchor."

Canbrach's eyes when she faced him were feral. "What are you doing? Are you insane?"

"The world's insane," he said. "Has been for going on two decades. Park the damned ship next to the crater to show we're not afraid of them. I'm going in to negotiate."

"Parlay," Doc said.

Deadbeef laughed. "Yeah. Parlay. D'arr! Where's me damned eyepatch?"

"That's suicide," Canbrach snapped.

"Then you'll be captain. Congrats on your imminent promotion. But while I'm still breathing, you take orders from me, and so does everyone else." Deadbeef turned to address the crew. "Y'hear that? If Ms. Canbrach does anything to accelerate her career, each and every one of you is to put a bullet in her."

Canbrach scowled. "If I'd wanted to be captain, I already would be. Who needs the fucking responsibility?"

"That, Ms. Canbrach, is why you're still alive, and why I'm the one walking into the lion's den."

The dirt bike was aptly named. Even with the Plexiglas shielding that all but encompassed them, protecting both the riders and—more importantly—the engine, dust and grit flew up around it and the sidecar. It stained their goggles and clogged the scarves that they wore in layers across their faces. Deadbeef drove carefully, concerned about the possibility of pitching headlong into ditches or craters hidden in the sea of dust.

Doc helped the captain lift the bike over the dust-wall, a low ridge of broken shale that kept rose high enough above the dust line to keep the sea of dust from sifting into and burying the cornfields. Free of the choking ashes of a dead world, they were able to shake out their scarves and breathe.

Before they started out again and the sound of the bike's engine made speech impractical, Doc tugged at Deadbeef's sleeve.

"Why'd you bring me?"

"You actually care about what happens to these people. They'll see that in your eyes and be more likely to trust us."

"Really? You've got a lot of faith in my eyes."

"Well, there's another reason. Ms. Canbrach likes you."

"Canbrach hates everyone."

Deadbeef snorted. "Very true. But she likes *you*. Why do you think she gets so mad when you disagree with her? Me she'll argue with, because I'm her boss. Everyone else she ignores. Not worth her consideration. Except for you. You heard her: '*Don't judge me.*' I've never seen her give a rat's ass about what anyone else has ever thought about her, and I've known her since before the dust."

"She's abusive because she loves me? I think that's the most disturbing thing anyone's ever said to me. I've got pretty good gaydar, and I didn't get that kind of vibe from her at all."

"Wasn't what I was talking about. I don't think she thinks in those terms at all. I've never known her to take anyone to her bed, male or female or even mechanical. She once told me that my relationship with Jamie was, how'd she put it? 'An irresponsible and inefficient expenditure of energy and fluids.'" Deadbeef paused, though he kept all expression out of his face. "Doesn't matter, forget I said anything."

Jamie's name hung like a cloud of bile between them, and Deadbeef kicked the bike to life just as Doc opened her mouth to speak, and steered them down one of the irrigation ditches that led toward the center of town.

The town smelled like life. Which is to say, it stank of garbage and shit, of muddy livestock and unwashed people, of rotting vegetation and fertilizer. It was, Doc thought, glorious.

Almost glorious enough to ignore the shotguns, assault rifles and machetes leveled at them as they rolled into town. The townspeople encircled them as they slowed and stopped. Deadbeef popped the goggles off his eyes and swung himself off the bike, dusted off his coat. Flashed a smile so bright that

Doc's heart ached.

"Mornin'."

One of the townspeople spoke over the barrel of his rifle. "You're a long way from home. You might want to turn around and head back now, before the next storm comes through."

Deadbeef helped Doc out of the sidecar. "'Fraid I can't do that. Home don't exist anymore, and we're running low on supplies. So I'm here to negotiate."

"Parlay," said Doc.

"That, too."

"There's nothing to parlay," the man said. "We've got your ship in our sights. One signal and you'll be sailing home on a heap of tinder."

"If we were afraid of your little guns, we'd have taken you out already. You can't hit us. But we can erase you. And I've got a bug-fuck crazy first mate with her finger on the button of a couple specially enhanced hellfire missiles. Same kind of enhancement that lets us sail a ship across a desert. Got it?"

People glanced at each other, at the man who had spoken, and at a woman who held a flag at her side. She shook her head, almost imperceptible, and began to raise the flag to signal the town's gunners. Everyone tensed.

"Oh God, please," Doc said, the horror palpable in her voice. Canbrach would see the signal; she wouldn't wait for the town's defenses to fire first. "Not again."

The woman hesitated, staring at Doc. A muscle in her jaw twitched. She lowered the flag. "What do you want?"

Deadbeef hooked his thumbs under his belt, and smiled. "What does anyone want? We want to live."

Even with the upholstery worn thin and torn and the padding puffing out, the old office chair was far more comfortable than the *Grey Perl's* spartan furnishings. Doc leaned back, relishing the forgotten joys of ergonomic design and ice cold water, even as she pressed the cool glass against her throbbing thumb. She was unclear on why the townspeople had insisted on cutting them before they'd consent to speak in private.

"Can't be too careful," said the man who'd first confronted them, as the woman with the flag dragged a paring knife across Deadbeef's thumb. It bled, and she repeated the process with Doc.

She seemed satisfied with the results. "They're okay," she said. Then she cut her own thumb and held the blood up for Deadbeef and Doc to see. "I'm not a skinwalker, either. In case you were wondering. Name's Kat. That's Richard."

Kat and Richard were co-mayors of what remained of Dover, and city hall was a back room in what had once been a bar. A generator puttered in the back of the building, feeding power to run the air conditioner and the refrigerator.

And so she and Deadbeef sat across the table from Richard and Kat, sipping cold, fresh water and salivating over crisp slices of precious apple. As collegial as things seemed, Doc was painfully aware that the townspeople still kept guard, waiting just outside the door with weapons at hand, and the big guns were still targeting the *Grey Perl*.

Captain Deadbeef seemed oblivious, almost jolly. Only long years of serving under him gave Doc the insight to see that all this was as much a mask as he'd worn earlier, at Jamie's desiccation.

Kat and Richard seemed as nervous and worried as Doc, and grew more so as Deadbeef laid out his proposal.

"I didn't start out a pirate," he said. "Well, actually, I did. But it wasn't to prey on people like you. When the world turned to shit, there were folks who used the opportunity to create their own little empires, sending their goons to round up slaves, killing anyone who wouldn't submit to keep the others in line. We were the good guys, back then. I took my name from an old programmer's joke. DEADBEEF is hexadecimal, and it indicates a fatal memory error. I figured those folks had forgotten we were all human, and we were all in it together." Deadbeef held up his glass and considered the condensation beading up on the surface. "That was a long time ago. Everyone's gone, now. The good guys, the bad guys.

They're all dust. And none of us is innocent anymore."

"We haven't seen any signs of life for months now," Doc added. "It's all dead out there. And then there's this... this oasis."

"We want to live here," Deadbeef said. "We'll pull our weight. We'll farm. We'll help defend the place. We've got a good stock of antibiotics and other meds."

Kat studied the wood grain of the table top. "We used to trade with a town a bit north of here—it used to be Akron, back when names meant anything. A storm took them out about six months back, ate under the wind-break, we think, though there's some other rumors. There were seventy-three survivors. We figured we could take thirty, and still feed everyone through the winter."

"We did it by lottery," Richard continued. "They were friends, some of them. Toughest thing we ever had to do, sending them out in the desert. Forty-three people."

"I see." Deadbeef drained his glass and set it down in a slow, deliberate motion. He rose to his feet, just as slowly and deliberately. "It seems, my friends, that we have arrived at an impasse. Now, who wants to volunteer the first solution?"

Tension weighed oppressive on the silence. And then Doc spoke.

Ms. Canbrach was not pleased.

"What the fuck do you mean, teach them? So they can blow us out the water... out of the dirt or whatever *fuck*. You know we're inevitably coming back here. It's the only place that's left alive. And you want to give them the weapons they'd need to destroy us. And for what?"

Doc sighed. She'd expected this. "For a hold full of food and water, and for intelligence."

"Intelligence? We're in *Ohio*. Forget it. I'm not going to teach them how to bind demons."

"No, you're not." Deadbeef studied his log book, checking the status of their supplies. "I need someone who'll do it right. Doc, can you brief Barkowski? I've got a shopping list to compile."

Tensions never really eased. The pirates had become too used to taking, and the townspeople too used to people who wanted only to take. But Kat proved a capable study, and if the other two students lagged, both Barkowski and Doc were certain that Kat could finish their tutelage. The key was getting done and setting sail before Canbrach did something stupid. Or—more likely—provoked the townspeople into doing something stupid.

Once when Captain Deadbeef returned early to the ship after successfully negotiating for a goodly amount of duck-cloth, he overheard Canbrach and Barkowski arguing.

"That's tantamount to mutiny," Barkowski said.

"It's not mutiny if I'm not trying to take over the ship," Canbrach argued. "It's just... he's not thinking straight. Not since Jamie died. He's gone soft. He just needs a friendly push to make the right decisions."

Deadbeef nudged the cabin door open with his foot. It creaked on its hinges. He leaned against the doorframe. "And what decision is that?"

Barkowski paled. Canbrach's eyes flashed.

"That Kat woman. She's a water witch. Barkowski's seen it."

Deadbeef shrugged. "So?"

"So we should take her."

Deadbeef raised an eyebrow.

"If we had her, we wouldn't need this damned town. We could make our own." When the captain didn't respond, she continued, "You've bought us a couple months, maybe three. And then what? Then we die of thirst, choking on the dust. Or we come back here and raid the town anyway."

Deadbeef fished a toothpick out of his pocket, dug at something between his teeth.

"*She's an asset.* You owe it to the crew to use her. You owe it to *me!*"

"To you? You have an overly high opinion of yourself. You're confined to quarters until I say otherwise. You talk to nobody. If I hear that you've disobeyed, do not doubt that I'll take whatever steps are necessary. Barkowski, spread the news."

Deadbeef swept out of the cabin with a theatrical flare that would have earned him applause back when he was doing improv in San Francisco.

Back in town, Deadbeef captured Doc's arm and dragged her around until they found Kat, and then steered the two women into a secluded spot.

"We need to talk," he said.

"We've provided you with everything you've asked for." Kat looked around to see if anyone might be witnessing the exchange, anyone that might be able to intervene if she needed, or run for help.

"I know. But life just got complicated. You've met my first mate?"

"Melissa? Yes. I don't think she likes me."

"Ms. Canbrach doesn't like anyone. But she *wants* you. She says you're a water witch, and an asset we'd be foolish to let waste her talents here. She says I have an obligation to my ship and my crew, and she's not wrong." He held up a finger. "Let me finish. I'm officially offering you a position on my crew, if you want it."

"I..."

Deadbeef touched a finger to her lips. "Don't give me your answer now. Think about it, tell me when our business in this town is done, and I'll respect your decision."

"I see."

"I hope so. Keep in mind that the longer we spend here, the more likely Ms. Canbrach is to convince the crew that I've grown soft and sentimental in my old age. So the faster you learn what you need and give us what we need, the better. In the meantime, you might want to keep an escort with you."

Kat nodded. "I'll do that."

"Good. Don't talk to anyone about this. These are the sorts of rumors that end in bloodshed."

"Why am I here?" Doc asked.

"You're here so that you can see and understand what's at stake. Like I said before, Ms. Canbrach likes you. Yours is the only voice she respects enough to hear, sometimes."

Kat studied the two carefully. She turned to Doc.

"When he says he'll respect my decision, is he telling the truth?"

"Yes."

"So if, a week or two from now when our agreement is fulfilled, he'll just let me stay here if that's what I choose?"

Doc glanced at Deadbeef, whose mask revealed nothing. It was enough to tell Doc everything she needed to know. "I couldn't say. He'll respect your decision, but that doesn't mean circumstances will allow him to accommodate it."

"And right now?"

"Circumstances allow him to accommodate it."

"And I can trust him?"

"You can trust what has been said right now."

Kat nodded, rubbed a thumb against her lower lip. "You know, there used to be a lot of settlements around here. We had contact with most of them either through radio communications or using smoke signals. Yeah, primitive, but it worked. Anyway, things were sort of okay for a while; we got by, I mean. But about five years back the storms intensified, and one by one the settlements disappeared. Sometimes we found survivors. Mostly not, and most of those who survived were in such bad shape that they never made it to another town. If I leave, all these people are dead."

"I know," said Deadbeef.

"This was all hills, back when I was a kid. Demons ate them. Ripped them apart. But the mountains stopped them. Don't know what it is, maybe something in the rock, or they're just too high to get over. Could be that things are different on the other side. I don't know. Nobody we ever sent came back.

Some entire towns picked up and headed over the mountains. No idea what happened to them. But here's the truth of it— everything else is dead. If you leave here, you'll end up coming back. Unless you try to cross the mountains."

Deadbeef snorted. "Sail a pirate ship over the mountains? I should change my name to Hannibal."

A figure stepped from the shadows. Richard. Doc wondered how long he'd been listening.

"Old I70's your best bet," he said. "I'll get you a map."

Deadbeef nodded, seeming unsurprised at Richard's sudden appearance. A useful trick, Doc thought, always seeing more than you let on.

Kat and Richard exchanged glances. "And we'll get the last of the supplies to your ship by noon tomorrow," Kat said.

Deadbeef clapped her on the shoulder. "I knew I could count on you." He turned to Doc. "Now, about the troublesome Ms. Canbrach.... Do we still have that box of Zolpidem samples?"

Captain Deadbeef stood on the quarterdeck, watching the horizon beyond the *Grey Perl's* prow. As comforting it had been safe behind a wind-break, it was nice to be out on the open dust, with an honest wind filling the sails and the rumble of pulverizing rock filling the air. The breeze caught his long coat and whipped it in a suitably dramatic fashion. Jamie would have approved.

Canbrach fumed and paced. "I can't believe you left behind a perfectly good water witch."

"Don't need her," Deadbeef said. "We're Eden bound."

Canbrach hissed through her nose. "We were *in* Eden. Now we're back in hell. How the fuck do you expect to climb a mountain?"

"Ah, that's right, you slept through those meetings." Deadbeef winked at Doc. "Don't worry, it's all taken care of. Besides, aren't you still confined to quarters?"

"You can't be serious."

"Relax, Ms. Canbrach. It's a beautiful day, and there's nothing that needs killing."

"Have you looked in a fucking mirror recently?" Canbrach slammed the heel of her palm against the rail. "It's not too late to go back. We could come in at night, hit them before they know we're there...."

Doc put a hand on Canbrach's shoulder, felt her stiffen and flinch quicker than Doc could undo the gesture. "Melissa? It's done. The decision's made, and there's nothing to do but go forward."

"There's food, and water, and..."

Captain Deadbeef spoke with his back to them. "Behind us is death. Withered corpses. Shattered dreams. Ahead of us..." His voice stuck. "Ahead of us is something else. *Drive my dead thoughts...*" He paused. "*Like withered leaves to quicken a new birth.*"

Canbrach stared at the captain's back. "What?"

"Ashes and sparks, my love, ashes and sparks."

Doc took Ms. Canbrach's elbow and guided her from the quarterdeck. "He's not talking to us," she said. "Let's leave him be."

Interstate 70, when they found it, was wide enough to accommodate the *Grey Perl*, and then some. It hung suspended a few feet above the desert's highest reaches, the jagged edge just out of reach of the wind's snapping jaws, rising into the mountains like the ghost of a forgotten past. Beyond the dust, the dry air coming off the desert had still killed everything. Skeletal pines and firs lined the highway, stretching as far as the eye could see. Abandoned structures and vehicles dotted the landscape. The arid wind preserved everything in its most desiccated state.

Canbrach ordered the sails unfurled and everyone unnecessary to the rear of the ship. The *Grey Perl* ran before the wind, and with the demons howling bloody murder, crashed through the macadam ridge. The crew cheered, and Deadbeef allowed himself a small smile. Canbrach indulged in no such luxury.

The wind pushed them about half a mile up the road before the incline defeated them. The demons bound to the hull shrieked and wailed, but the wind faltered, and the ship started to slide backward toward the sea of dust.

"Now what?" Canbrach spat. "We get out and push?"

"Something like that," Deadbeef said. He called out orders. The anchor thumped to the ground, and the ship came to a halt. The side hold door opened to form a ramp, and deep within the ship a machine rumbled to life.

Canbrach watched in shock as the thing rolled out and down to the broken asphalt. "They gave you one of their tractors?"

"And you always said I'd have been easy prey in a boardroom."

"What's the catch?"

"I told them we'd send news back about what we found, if we could. And if we found Eden, we'd ferry them."

"So you're going back?"

Deadbeef laughed. "Would you?"

It was slow going. Most of the crew walked ahead of the tractor, which crawled at a snail's pace, straining at the chains binding it to the ship and spewing dirty black smoke. A skeleton crew kept the sails trimmed and provided as much additional momentum as the wind would offer. Where the wind blew strong and the terrain leveled out or began to decline, the crew leapt on board and rested their legs. But on particularly steep inclines, they heaved on ropes together, adding their strength to the tractor's pull.

The demons feasted on the tarry surface, savoring the fresh asphalt and reducing it to pebbles and dust in their wake.

They traveled this way for a week, following the highway signs toward Wheeling through the dead landscape, despairing at the continued infiltration of the dust sea in the valleys and riverbeds below.

And then, midday on the eighth day, they followed the road around a particularly steep summit, and into the green.

It sprawled, endless, before them. Emerald mountains as far as the eye could see. A river that glittered silver on deep blue, tracing its way through the mountains to a long lake suspended above a massive dam.

And soldiers. A veritable sea of soldiers.

They spread out across the road, bearing guns and swords or machetes. Three tanks sat directly in the *Grey Perl's* path, long guns aimed at the ship's prow.

The tractor stopped dead. The *Grey Perl* ground onward, the tanks' guns tracking it, until Captain Deadbeef ordered anchors weighed.

"I'm not sure what I expected," he said, pulling a white handkerchief from his coat pocket, "but this isn't it."

As the soldiers ran to surround the ship, he waved the handkerchief in the air and called to the crew to stand down.

"It seems we're saved," Canbrach said, fingering her pistol.

Down on the ground, one of the soldiers began screaming orders at them. Everybody out where they could be seen. Hands on their heads. A grappling hook fell to the deck, then caught on the rail.

"So it seems, Ms. Canbrach. So it seems. Tell Barkowski to stay out of sight and be ready for Operation Strangelove, then get back here and stick by my side."

Canbrach's eyes glittered. "Aye, Captain."

Mutually assured destruction. Canbrach had designed Operation Strangelove as a weapon of last resort, and as a bargaining tool. The threat of it had saved them twice before when facing overwhelming odds, but of course they had never been forced to execute it.

The signal would come from Canbrach – the unbinding of

the demons of the hull. Deep in the ship, Barkowski sat with the entire stock of the ship's armaments arrayed in front of him. Launching them all would rip the ship apart. But it would also inflict unimaginable damage to their enemies.

Canbrach was particularly proud of the rockets with the demon-cluster warheads. Captain Deadbeef hoped he never lived to see them used.

"Back to your stations," he growled, "and cut free any grapples. Ms. Canbrach and I are going in to discuss their surrender."

Deadbeef and Canbrach clambered down a rope ladder. Doc waited until they reached the bottom and strode purposefully toward the tanks, and toward what looked to be the soldiers' command center. Then she followed discretely.

A hard-eyed man in a neatly pressed uniform met them in front of the tank. Subordinates flanked him, weapons held at ready.

Deadbeef crossed his arms and stared at the man.

The man adjusted his hat and stuck a hand out. "First Lieutenant Cal Gardner. What brings you here, Mr..."

Deadbeef ignored the hand. "Captain. Which I believe means I outrank you."

Gardner scowled and retrieved his hand. "Captain, then."

"Captain Deadbeef, of the good ship *Grey Perl*. And you, sir, are standing in my way. You and your little tanks, too."

"Look, you're new here, you don't know the rules. Well, here they are. You do what I say. Your people get off that... that thing of yours and we take you to processing. They figure out where to send you, and we go back to guarding the borders against demons. Starting with that ship."

"I've got a crew of thirty-nine souls who want nothing but to be done with that desert forever. But I can't allow you to damage my ship."

"Thirty-nine, huh? Crazy. It's been almost a year since anyone's come out of the desert this way, and now forty in two days." Gardner shook his head. "Sorry. It's not a choice. We can't let even one demon get through. You've seen what they can do."

Canbrach watched Deadbeef, waiting for the faintest signal.

"Aye, that I have, more than you could ever imagine. Still, I've had the *Grey Perl* ever since she was barely a dinghy, saved her from a fate as a mini golf prop and raised her up to be the finest ship to sail the Sea of Dust. She's seen me through weather like you've never seen, and I'll not let...."

Doc, standing behind the others, swore suddenly. "Fuck. That's Tam."

"What?" Deadbeef's casual facade dropped.

Doc pointed at a woman standing by the Lieutenant's tent.

"I don't understand," Canbrach said.

Gardner glanced back and forth between them and frowned. "You know her? She didn't give us any idea that she wasn't alone."

Deadbeef ignored them all. He stepped around the Lieutenant and his men and walked toward the woman who looked like Tam.

"Tam? Tamara Hewitt?"

She blinked Tam's eyes at him. "Who are you?" Tam's voice, from Tam's lips.

Deadbeef pulled his pistol and shot her in the face. Dust puffed out from the ruptured skin. Her demonic shriek was punctuated by gunfire, and Deadbeef pitched forward.

Doc ran to his aid, praying that the soldiers in their confusion didn't shoot her, too.

Screaming, the skinwalker in Tam's flesh rushed toward Gardner, demon claws extending from Tam's fingers, demon fangs extruding from the tattered remains of Tam's face. Realizing their error, the soldiers turned their guns on the demon. The bullets tore at the flesh amidst puffs of smoke but did nothing to slow it down. Bullets could never cut the wind. Gardner's entourage scrambled to either side, fumbling for their blades. Too late; the thing in Tam's skin tossed their bleeding bodies aside like dead leaves in a tornado.

Gardner stood his ground and brandished his machete. Canbrach drew her cutlass as she stepped up beside him. With calm efficiency they dispatched the creature. It fell in three pieces at their feet.

Tam's skin sloughed off it and pooled at their feet. Gardner stared at it.

"We let it through. God, we almost took that thing in."

"Guess that's what they meant by 'skinwalkers,'" Canbrach said. "Fuckers stole Tam's skin right off her body, 'bout a month back in the middle of a storm. We had to put her down." She stepped over the puddled flesh and approached Doc, who knelt at Deadbeef's side.

"Doc." Canbrach stooped to check Deadbeef's pulse. She stepped back and chewed her lip, glancing between the *Grey Perl* and body. It was long seconds before she made her decision. "Captain Fitzwater, ma'am," she said. "How do you want to play this? It's your call."

It was a skeleton crew that manned *Deadbeef's Pride* as she tacked against the wind. Rock and dust broke against the prow, rising in a long zigzagged wake in their path. Behind them, the mountains slowly shrank into the distance.

Captain Fitzwater stood by the tiller, watching the horizon for the telltale green and gold of harvest time.

"Damned fool decision, if you ask me," Canbrach said. "He'd be proud of you."

"He gave his word, Ms. Canbrach." The Captain brought Deadbeef's looking glass to her eye, and smiled, wondering how long Dilsson had been napping up in the crow's-nest. She called the orders to adjust course.

"Time we made good on that."

Bernie Mojzes is the author of *The Evil Gazebo*, and is also responsible for a passle of short stories that have appeared in various anthologies and magazines, including *Daily Science Fiction*, *Dead Souls*, *Crossed Genres* and the *Bad-Ass Faeries* Series. In his copious free time, he co-edits "The Journal of Unlikely Entomology." Although he has on occasion been accused of committing Public Acts of Music and Philosophy, no charges were ever filed. To register a complaint, please visit www.kappamaki.com. A rather more sordid prequel to this sordid tale, "On Arid Seas," appears in *Like a Treasure Found*, an anthology of pirate-themed erotica from Circlet Press. If, you know, you like that sort of thing.

Running from the Storm

KATHRYN SCANNELL

Morien watched death bear down on them across glassy smooth seas under a cloudless blue sky. Death today was a massive, five-masted war junk. She flew no flag, but that was hardly surprising. Pirates rarely bothered. There was no question that she was a pirate – she was a Tengri design, and there was no legitimate trade with the Empire in these waters.

She was twice the size of *Demonfang*. They were outclassed, and not even managing to run away effectively. *Demonfang's* sails hung limp in the still air. Their pursuer's sails were filled with a convenient, suspiciously local breeze. His weather sense told him it wasn't natural wind, so they must have a strong wizard driving air elementals to keep their sails filled.

"We need a wind now, little Elf-toy." A deep voice growled threateningly from behind him.

Morien wasn't startled. He'd sensed Fong Kuo coming. "Unless you have the ear of a god, we're not going to get it. I work weather. I can't make it out of nothing." He gestured at the calm, empty sky without bothering to turn around to face the First Mate. He'd already seen more of him than he wanted.

"I don't think you've tried hard enough. The captain is busy. He won't be happy if I interrupt him to yank your leash. Want to change that answer?" A hand the size of an ordinary man's head grabbed Morien's shoulder, spinning him around to face the angry First Mate.

Fong Kuo was a mountain of a man, standing nearly eight feet tall, and half that across the shoulders. He towered over even the Tengri on board, who rarely ran to more than seven feet tall. Popular rumor said that his mother had been a soldier-wizard from Ch'in province, at least mostly human, who had lain with a demon by choice. Exactly what sort of demon was a source of endless speculation.

Certainly no one would mistake Fong Kuo for human. His facial features were vaguely Ch'in, but there was a faint greenish tint to his skin, and if one looked closely, parts of it were scaled. The scales were particularly obvious on his hairless skull. His ears were pointed, but much longer and thinner than the points on the ears of an Elf or a Tengri. To magical senses he reeked of demon, but Morien had never seen him perform any magic. He simply was magic – unreasonably tough, fast and strong. That suggested that his demon parent had been one of the less intelligent types.

It was unusual that someone who wasn't a wizard would rise as high as First Mate on a Tengri or Elven ship. Morien suspected Fong had done it simply by being too mean to argue with.

Morien shrugged, looking Fong in the eye. "I can't stop you if you're fool enough to interrupt him. It won't change anything. You know damned well that his spell was thorough. If there was anything I could see to do here, I'd be doing it. I don't have a choice." The bindings Captain Zothar had woven using Morien's True Name were extensive, enforcing obedience to the captain's will, driving Morien to protect *Demonfang* when he'd rather have seen them all at the bottom of the sea, and preventing him from committing suicide or attacking any of the crew.

Fong stared at him for a long moment, then shoved him away. "Chiu Jung take your soul! I guess you're telling the truth. We're dead then. "

"Very dead." Morien laughed wildly. "If the gods are kind, I'll manage to keep myself alive long enough to see you spitted on someone's sword."

"That won't be the end. I've got arrangements in Hell to come back, and so, my little toy, do you," Fong laughed cruelly. "Getting yourself killed won't get you out from under the captain's thumb."

Morien almost flinched away from that thought, but he managed not to let it show on his face. He knew the folly of letting these people see any weakness. "Mayhap. I'll take my pleasures where I can find them. "

"You'll pay for that later, one way or another," Fong growled, and strode off down the deck shouting orders to some of the sailors.

Morien looked back at the oncoming ship. He didn't think he'd outlive the captain or the First Mate. He wasn't much of a battle wizard. While he argued with Fong, their pursuer had come closer. He could see people on her deck readying ballistas and bows. Like *Demonfang's* crew, they were a motley mix of Tengri, humans, demons, and hybrids of all of the above. They'd be in ballista range in moments.

He took cover behind a deck rampart. Closing his eyes, he directed his inner vision down into the water around the *Demonfang*. The battle there had already begun. Their mer-folk allies were locked in combat with those from the other ship. Already there was blood in the water, and soon both sides would be fighting off scavengers as well as each other. Anyone who fell into the water now would be dead in moments.

To his inner sight the other ship was a blaze of power, its shields and wards shifting like fire. He couldn't guess at any details. With time, he might have tried to penetrate and see behind the wards, but he wouldn't have wagered much on his success. He suspected that the wizards aboard the other ship were both more numerous and at least some of them were stronger than he was.

His examination was interrupted by the hiss of an arrow passing above his head, followed by a solid thunk as it embedded itself in the deck behind him. His armor and magical defenses should bounce any that came too close, but it was a warning of more serious attacks to come. He slid his sword from its scabbard and waited. Aerial assault by flying wizards or demons would follow the barrage of arrows and ballistas. They would take care not to do more than superficial damage to the ship – building ships which could survive the dangers of Avalon's seas involved a lot of magical reinforcement. They were far too valuable to simply sink unless you were desperate.

As if on cue, a squad of winged demons, cloaked by magic until the last possible moment, dropped out of the sky. The deck around him was a chaos of slashing blades and dodging fighters within seconds. His world narrowed down to keeping himself alive. Time lost meaning in the chaos. He knew he'd killed people, but they were a blur. Even if the captain himself had been fighting next to him, Morien probably wouldn't have noticed.

Eventually weariness took its toll. Demon claws raked his sword arm. Distracted by the pain, he failed to block a sword blow. A fiercer pain in his gut made the arm fade into insignificance. Looking down, he saw a grinning Tengri drawing out the sword that had just impaled him, and felt something warm running down his legs. The world faded to a small bright spot, and then winked out.

Morien woke slowly. The world felt very flat. Opening his eyes, he saw he was lying in a ship's bunk. The rope safety net designed to keep a sleeper from falling out in rough weather was in place across the opening. Through it, he saw someone had left a bottle and a plate with bread and jerky on the cabin's small table. He was ravenously hungry. Something clinked as he reached to unhook the webbing, and he felt a drag on his wrist. When his hand came into his field of view, he wasn't surprised to see he was wearing a set of manacles.

Mechanically he unhooked the safety net and swung out of the bunk, taking stock of his situation as he did. He was naked, there were shackles on his ankles as well as his wrists, and a collar on his neck. He tried reflexively to sense what kind of magic was around, and failed. He felt nothing.

Gods, he wasn't thinking clearly. He should have recognized the dead, flat feeling of something suppressing his magic. It might be the shackles, but the collar seemed more likely. It was a familiar feeling – the captain of the *Demonfang* had been fond of it as a disciplinary technique. Take someone's magic away, and he was helpless against everything around him, including the rest of the crew, who would be happy to take advantage.

Still running on reflex, he shuffled over to the little table, and fell on the food like a starving wolf. He'd finished most of it before he began to think clearly. He was on a ship. This was probably a junior officer's cabin, judging by the size and furnishings.

He'd expected to wake up in Hell. *Demonfang's* captain had like to remind him that even death wasn't an escape – the captain had made a contract with a lord of Hell to have Morien's soul trapped there in a demon body. He wasn't sure he believed what he'd heard about Hell from the crew of *Demonfang*, but he didn't think they'd have ships there, so this probably wasn't Hell. Some of what they'd told him had probably been lies, intended to frighten the naïve Elf, but they'd all agreed that the process or resurrection there involved months of recuperation, learning to make the new body work properly. He was tired and hungry, but otherwise normal. Someone must have healed him after the battle, rather than killing him.

There was only one reason for someone to do that – this ship wanted his weather talent too. He shuddered, but kept eating. They'd want his Name, and would probably be willing to torture him to get it. At least this time there was no one he cared about to hold over him. Could he just give it to them? He considered the possibility. Nothing seemed to be preventing him. Maybe Captain Zothar hadn't thought of including that in the binding. It wasn't a very likely situation.

There was no reason to resist. He knew they'd get it eventually, and he had no loyalty to the crew of *Demonfang* beyond what the binding on him enforced. He'd been on that damned ship for nearly a year, and in that time he'd come to hate every last one of them. In fact, if this ship's captain wanted to torture the crew, he'd offer to help. That was a good measure of how far he'd fallen. Gods, if he'd only died in that first attack. But it was too late now. There was no going back, and no escape, even by dying, as long as the arrangements in Hell held.

A small sound drew his attention to the cabin door. It opened, framing a tall, elegant Tengri woman, wearing a scarlet coat and brilliant turquoise blue breeches. Her lustrous blue-black hair was arranged in ornate braids, laid close along her scalp. She was an inch or perhaps two shorter than he was – Elves tended to be taller than Tengri, and men were usually taller than women.

He promptly dropped to his knees, not meeting her eyes. Being naked and in chains didn't leave much doubt about his status here.

She shut the door and settled herself in the only chair. "Look at me."

He lifted his gaze obediently, waiting for further instructions. He'd learned early in his time aboard *Demonfang* that being disobedient got him nowhere useful.

"You're not in the brig with what remains of your contemptible crew because I'm curious. *Demonfang* is a pirate ship. There's a sizable reward for her officers, and lesser ones for the crew. Together with what the boat will bring at home those make this trip well worth while. But you are a mystery. What is an Elf doing as crew on a Tengri raider?"

"That's easily enough explained, my lady." Morien looked away. "Captain Zothar has my Name." He didn't need to say more than that. Like all Tengri, she would be a wizard, and would know the implications – that when another wizard had your True Name, he could use it to bypass all your defenses, and make you do anything he desired. Knowledge of his Name was the ultimate power over a wizard, and a kind of slavery from which there was no escape.

"Well, there'll be no bounty to claim for you then, since you weren't there voluntarily. We'll turn you over to the Elven ambassador, and hope perhaps there's some reward for helping distressed citizens. We won't see anything for the captain either. He managed to get himself killed. At least we got the rest of his officers." She looked Morien up and down. He felt as though he were being measured. "You're the weather mage, aren't you? That's why they went to the trouble of getting your Name instead of just killing you."

"Aye."

"You're valuable to your own people too then. Perhaps we will get a decent reward for you. Can I count on you to behave reasonably if we give you the freedom of the ship?"

"Yes, Captain." She hadn't introduced herself, but with these kinds of questions, she could hardly be anyone but the captain.

"Excellent." She left, closing the door behind her. He was surprised not to hear it lock. Why was she toying with him, talking about sending him back to the Sun Kingdom? She surely wanted a weather mage as badly as Captain Zothar had. Why hadn't she just demanded his Name?

Days turned into weeks as the *Shining Warrior* and *Demonfang*, with a prize crew aboard, made their way toward the Empire. As the captain had promised, Morien had the run of the ship. They unchained him, and let him keep the cabin where he'd woken up. Someone even fetched his meager possessions from aboard *Demonfang*. He might have been comfortable, except for the collar suppressing his magic. He couldn't blame them for leaving that on – he could give his parole with the best intentions in the world, and be unable to keep it if there was still someone out there who could use his

Name against him. Without his magic, the harm he could do if that happened was limited.

The crew treated him well enough. To his surprise, no one tried to take advantage of his defenselessness. Some were even friendly. He relaxed enough to be bored, and then to feel uneasy that he wasn't working. It wasn't right to be on board a ship and not pulling your weight. There were a limited number of places a man with no magic at all could be useful though. When he asked for work, he found himself in the galley, helping the cook. It didn't take magic to chop vegetables. It wasn't bad work, if a bit unglamorous, and after a couple of days he and the cook had become friends, as much as he was likely to become friends with anyone working crew on a Tengri pirate ship.

Demonfang's crew would have been quick to take advantage of anyone who couldn't defend themselves. The fact that no one on this crew did so spoke volumes about this captain. A captain tended to find crew who matched them, and *Demonfang's* had been a first class asshole who enjoyed hurting people. So had most of his crew. This one had a different character.

He was sitting in the galley, peeling telku roots for the evening dinner when one of the deckhands stuck his head in. "Batten down for heavy weather. We've got a storm coming over the horizon the like of which I've never seen." The man hurried away to secure things elsewhere, having delivered his message.

Morien tried reflexively to feel the storm, but with the collar on, there was nothing. He sighed and went back to peeling the vegetables. When he realized he'd tried to reach out for the storm half a dozen times without thinking about it, he gave up and put the paring knife down. "Gorliss, I'm going on deck for a minute to see what we're really dealing with here. I've got a pretty good eye for storms, even without my magic."

"Good idea. I'd hate to put dinner on hold because someone was over-reacting," Gorliss agreed. "Come back and give me a second opinion, and then we can either go on with dinner or tie things down thoroughly."

Gorliss was stowing things anyway, not waiting for him to return. Gorliss was taking the man's warning seriously.

Morien made his way on deck, dodging out of the way of crew who were rushing past on their own duties. He smelled the storm in the air before he'd actually cleared the hatchway. That wasn't good.

He paused to survey the sky after he stepped out of the way of the hatch. The storm loomed over the horizon, coming toward them across the sea like a great, moving black wall. Lightning played within the clouds. He'd never been this close to a storm this size, except on land, in a snug harbor.

Far ahead on the horizon, he could see another set of sails, showing full canvas. Running from them, or from the storm? The answer was probably both. Nothing normally in these waters would see this ship or *Demonfang* and expect friends.

Shining Warrior's crew were furling sails. The point where there was any hope of outrunning the storm was past, and they were preparing to try to ride it out. They'd probably been trying to run ahead of it, but even with a wizard pushing, there was only so fast a boat could move. The storm was surely faster. He wished he could feel what was happening. He tried futilely to reach past the effects of the collar. This storm was too big. Experience told him that, even without magic. They were dead unless they came up with something better.

Could he do anything to help if he had his magic? He wasn't sure. He'd never tried to work his will on a monster storm like this. Before the pirates took him, he'd have seen something this size long before it was visible on the horizon, and told his captain to shift their course away from it, rather than try to alter the storm itself. If you changed a big weather system, you might be just handing off your problem to someone else.

Captain Zothar hadn't cared about ethics. He'd wanted storms shifted to soften up his targets, and compelled by Zothar's magic, Morien had done it. Even with that experience, Morien wasn't sure he could do much to this one. It might not quite be a hurricane, but it looked damn close. Still, he had to try. He headed off to find the captain.

She wasn't on deck, so he went below. Eventually he persuaded one of the mates that he had a good reason to talk to the captain right now. Everyone knew he was a weather mage, or would be if his magic wasn't being suppressed. They were willing to believe he might know things about the storm that they didn't see.

"What?!" The captain snapped at him when he was ushered into her cabin. She had charts spread out on her desk, with a large scrying bowl of black shakudo metal in the middle. A puddle of something oily filled the bottom, but he saw nothing in it but reflected ceiling.

"Captain, I've seen a lot of storms. Even without my magic, I know them. This one is too big for us to ride out. Unless there's something special about this ship, or you have some trick up your sleeve, we're not going to make it." He tried to sound calmer than he felt. He had begun to hope he might get out of the clutches of *Demonfang's* captain. If he died now and was reborn in Hell, he'd be right back where he'd been before. They had to live through this.

"Very likely. Wasting my time right now is good way to insure it. Get out." She turned her attention back to the bowl.

Fear made a knot in his stomach, but he held his ground. "Captain, I'm a weather mage. Maybe I can work the storm enough for us live through this. I can't guarantee it, but let me try. What have you got to lose?"

"Out of the question. We don't know who that bastard Zothar might have shared your Name with. He could have friends out there just waiting for a chance to make use of it to get his ship and his crew back. They could make you turn on us in a heartbeat."

"Take what precautions you like. Just let me try to save us." Outside the wind shrieked. He was nearly shouting to be heard above it.

"There's no way I can put defenses up that would counter a spell based on your Name without having your Name myself. It wouldn't work." Her voice was softer, sounding more sad than angry now.

Her words hit him like a blow. He couldn't deny her logic. There was an obvious solution. She could protect him if she had his Name to weave into the defenses she gave him. Why wasn't she asking for it?

The storm was almost on them. The ship shuddered as the wind buffeted it. They were going to die here. All he had to do was let her have his Name, and he might have a chance to save them. It wasn't as if he had much to lose – gods alone knew how many people already had it. He'd never be truly free again. But if he lived to get back to the Kingdom of the Sun, maybe at least they could break the arrangement with Hell somehow, and he could die properly.

He took a deep, shuddering breath. "Then you need to have my Name too." It was hard to say the words. Giving someone your Name was either an act of ultimate trust, or submitting to something very like rape. He'd done that once already. He dreaded letting it happen again.

The captain stared at him. "I can't ask that."

"It's our only chance." He hadn't expected to have to argue. "Come, take it and let me get on with trying to save us."

She stared at him for a long moment. He felt as if he'd been weighed and measured. "You really mean that." He could hear the amazement in her voice. "You're one Hell of a brave man. Sit down." She gestured at her bunk. "I'll try to be gentle."

He sank down gratefully. His legs were shaky. In fact, all of him was shaking. He was terrified of doing this.

He felt her enter his mind, in spite of the collar that still deadened his magical senses. He gritted his teeth and tried not to fight her presence.

She waited as he fought down his panic. Her touch on his mind was gentle. It might have been pleasant if he hadn't known what they were here to do. After a moment he got himself under control.

This way. He guided her deeper into his mind, opening the path to his inner sanctum, the safe mental space where he worked his magic. Awareness of his body dropped away as he entered that space.

His inner landscape was a ship, of course. The sea was his life. His ship had been sadly affected by the past year. Once it had been clean and polished. Now it was scarred and ill cared for. His inner defenses were gone. A sound made him look behind him. There on the deck was a small dragon, the kind the Tengri liked to depict in their art. He stared, too startled to react. Next instant it was gone, replaced by Shining Warrior's captain. Her clothes were more somber, mostly black, and she wore a sword. He half remembered a comment by one of the pirates about black meaning something, but he was too frightened of what he was about to do to focus on the memory.

Come. He led her below. In times past he would have sought out the cabin that was his own, but not now. This wasn't his place anymore, just as he wasn't his own man. He led her past the empty crew quarters, down to the lowest hold. There, huddled in a corner, chained to the deck, he saw himself.

It wasn't really another him, of course. It was the way he visualized his Name. A Name wasn't something you could write down in a book. It was much more complicated than just a series of letters. Here, inside his deepest sanctum, he was handing himself over to this relative stranger. His name-self curled into an even tighter ball. Morien sank down onto the deck, shaking.

Gods damn him. Anger radiated from her.

He cringed at her feet, giving way to his terror. *Please. Don't hurt me. I'm trying to cooperate.*

I'm sorry. She knelt beside him, stroking his shoulders. *I'm not angry with you. You don't need to be frightened.*

Why are you angry then?

I'm angry that I have to put you through this to save my ship. She reached around to embrace him.

He shivered in her arms. Every nerve felt raw. He wouldn't have cared about actual, physical sex. He'd learned to play the Tengri sex games, and that no longer touched him. But this wasn't really sex – sex was just a metaphor for what was happening to his soul. This was far more intimate than sex, and he was terrified of doing it again. Zothar had reveled in the power that taking Morien's Name gave him. It had been horrible, and those wounds hadn't healed. He didn't think they'd ever heal.

Morien shuddered. He had to do this. It would only be worse if he fought it. He forced himself to open his last barriers, submitting to her. She held him, stroking his back gently. He could feel her trying to reassure him, but he was too close to losing his self control completely to really appreciate it.

She drew back, letting go of him. Things had shifted. This inner reality wasn't entirely bound by the laws of physics. He was within his name-self now, as he normally was when he worked serious magic, kneeling on the deck. The collar was cold and hard around his neck, and the heavy chain leading from it to the ring on the deck was a constant tug on it. The captain knelt facing him. She reached out, taking his face between her hands. Her grip was gentle, but implacable.

Morien had no power to pull away as she put her mouth on his for a fierce, possessive kiss, claiming him. His heart beat wildly in terror, but he'd already let her in too far to resist. He was helpless. Her power wrapped around him, through him. Finally she broke the kiss and let him go. There were tears running down his face. When had that started?

We're almost finished, my brave one. He felt the tenderness in her voice. Why should she feel that way?

With a finger, she traced a complex sigil on the skin above his heart. It didn't hurt, but he could feel the energy flowing through it. When she finished there was a brilliant flare of light, and he felt something unexpectedly warm and pleasant wrap around him.

What-? Morien looked down, startled. Where she had made the sigil, a small but detailed tattoo had appeared, a sinuous oriental dragon curled about a sword.

I have to mark you as mine, but I won't use a collar. I don't like them. This has to go. She took Zothar's heavy collar in both hands, and snapped it in two pieces.

He felt something release as she broke the collar. He couldn't see it, but he guessed it was a final remnant of the bindings *Demonfang's* captain had placed on him, using his Name. He felt lighter, as if he was no longer carrying a burden he hadn't really noticed before.

That's better. I wish I had time to do more clean-up here, but that will have to wait for a real healer. All we have time for today is to give you some protection. She drew more sigils in the air.

He imagined the power following her finger. He could almost see it, in spite of the block on his magic. A clicking noise drew his attention to a dark corner of the hold behind her. Something moved in the shadows. He cringed back, as the source of that movement emerged into the light.

Yesss? There was a hissing quality to the voice. It suited its owner perfectly. It was a dragon the size of a small horse, wingless like all the Tengri dragons, and a deep indigo blue in color. Its eyes blazed with golden light. It was definitely studying him.

This is Morien. He is mine. You will guard him. The captain addressed the dragon. Turning to Morien, she continued, *Po Lung will defend you if anyone else tries to use your Name against you. You need not fear his presence. Now we must return to the outer world. Time passes.*

Without waiting for a reply, she caught his hand, pulling his outer self away from his Name-self, and headed up out of the hold. Looking back once, he saw the dragon curled about his Name-self, who looked very uncertain about the whole idea. The dragon looked about to go to sleep.

His body was chilled, hungry and shaking with reaction to the emotional wringer he'd just been through. He had slumped back onto the captain's bed at an odd angle, and there was a cramp in his side. Wincing he straightened himself out and sat up.

"Rest there. I'm sending to the galley for a snack for us." She turned away to the door. He heard murmured words to someone in the hall.

"Someone should tell Gorliss I'm not going to get back there to help him." His voice was shaky.

"They'll take care of it." She shut the door and turned back to him. "We don't have a lot of time here. Hold still and I'll get that collar off."

His magic returned with an overwhelming rush as soon as she unlocked the collar. He swayed, very glad he was still sitting on the bed. The storm was even stronger than he'd imagined. Its energy swirled around him, spinning dizzily. There was no time to re-organize his personal defenses. He'd just have to trust in whatever the captain had done for him.

He reached out, feeling for the extent of the storm. It was a monster, its fringes hundreds of miles away. They were already well within it, and the heart was bearing down on them like an oncoming dragon. Lightning laced the clouds, heavy rain fell around them, and he could sense pockets of hail. There was no way to push this monster away from them; no time, even if he were strong enough to do so, which he very much doubted. Their best chance would be to try to steer for the least dangerous areas, and ride it out. He might be able to mitigate the worst of the forces of the storm in their immediate vicinity.

He moved his viewpoint up, watching the storm from above, where he could see its structure. Spread out below he saw *Shining Warrior*, *Demonfang*, and nearly on the horizon, a third ship. Seen through his magical perceptions, the other ship was clearly Elven. Could he find them a safe course too? He dared not split his efforts too much. The best he could do was show them the structure of the storm, and hope they had someone who could put the information to good use in steering a course.

He reached out for the Elven ship. There – he found a receptive mind. *Look. I have the structure of the storm to show you!*

Who are you? suspicion tinged the response. *There's nothing in the area but damned Tengri pirates.*

He didn't want to talk to these people, to have to explain where he was, and why he was doing what he was doing, never mind what he'd done over the past year. He ignored the questions. *No time. Here's the storm. Put it to good use and save yourselves, if you can. I have my hands full.* He shoved a mental image of the storm's structure at the man, and hoped he was skilled enough to make use of it.

Wait! Who are you? Where are you? He felt the other mage shouting at him, but he broke the connection and refused to let the other man reform it. He had to think of saving his own ship. And *Demonfang*, he added belatedly. He would have liked to see her sink without a trace, but the prize crew on board her probably didn't deserve that. Wait, why was he worried? They were just more pirates. They didn't matter. He pushed the question aside to focus on the immediate problem.

Turning his attention back to his immediate surroundings, he found that food had arrived. He grabbed a sticky sweet cake. After a few mouthfuls, he paused. "I'm going to feed you course changes. There's not a lot I can do to a storm this size, now that we're in it. The best I can do is give you insight to steer by to avoid the worst of it. We've got high winds, torrential rain, and bands of hail to contend with. "

"Guidance will help. That's what I was trying to do with the scrying bowl." The captain gulped down more of the high-calorie rations. "I'll keep a link open to you. Just focus on the storm. I'll be listening."

"Aye, Captain. You should know there's a third ship out there, north-northeast about twenty miles. Elven." Morien felt her touch on his mind, as she established the connection.

"Good to know." The captain rose and headed out the door.

Morien settled onto the bed, finding the storm webbing and strapping himself down securely. This was going to be a rough ride, and he couldn't afford to have his work disrupted by being dumped on his head if the ship heeled over hard. Secure, he flung his awareness out into the storm again.

He lost all sense of his body as he rode the storm, swirling with its currents. The captain's presence in his mind followed the pattern as he saw it. He was dimly aware of her passing orders and course corrections to someone else – it didn't matter who. The results were clear as the ship slipped aside to avoid bands of hail, and sudden downdrafts. Within the storm there was no sense of time – there was only now. Getting this wrapped up in a storm was dangerous, especially if you were working alone. You could forget to pay enough attention to your body to keep it safe, could even forget to come back to it. Storms were powerful, seductive things. Right now worrying about that was a luxury. The captain would get him back when it was time.

Riding the storm, he watched the ships bob about in it. The third one was drifting closer, making for the safest parts of the storm too. They obviously didn't have a weather mage, and couldn't see how things were shifting as time passed, but they had made some sense of what he showed them. They might still be all right. He hoped so.

Just as he began to think they were going to make it, a sudden wind gust changed the circulation in part of the storm. He could feel the air rotate, then tip slowly and inevitably from horizontal to vertical. Soon, unless he did something about it, a waterspout would form. He reached out and found a gust of wind he could manipulate, sending it along parallel to the ocean surface, slicing the bottom out from under the forming waterspout. The spinning air collapsed, and Morien gave a sigh of relief.

It was short-lived. Another spout was forming not far off. They seemed to be everywhere. No sooner had he dismantled one than another formed. There were too many. He stopped one about to strike the Elven vessel, only to see another sweep across her deck, shearing off one of her masts. Exhaustion threatened to overwhelm him. He stamped out one that was about to sweep across *Demonfang's* bow, then scrambled to deal with one that menaced *Shining Warrior*. His vision was growing hazy, but he dared not stop. Being struck by a waterspout was something they would not likely survive. Grimly he fought on.

With a roar he felt in his bones a monster water spout bore down on them. This wasn't one of the little ones he'd been shutting down. Cutting it off at its base wouldn't work. It was being powered by a cold downdraft from the storm above.

That would have to be disrupted. He looked around. It was a desperate idea, but it might work. Lightning leaped through the storm clouds around them. He seized a bolt, wrestling it into the path he needed it to follow.

The power blazed in his hands. Searing pain told him he was trying to handle too much, but there were no other options. His personal need to live through the storm no longer mattered. All he saw was the need to keep the ship safe. In this extremity, it was his ship. No matter that he hadn't come aboard voluntarily. He was committed.

With his last strength, he rammed the lightning down the throat of the giant waterspout, using it to heat the cold air that was keeping the spout going. There was a crack of thunder audible above the roar of the waterspout. The entire spout was lit from within by the lightning. His inner vision went dark. The last thing he saw was the waterspout collapsing into a wave of spray, so close to *Shining Warrior* that it crested over the gunwales.

"Morien, wake up! The captain needs you."

"Wha-" he mumbled groggily. He tried to raise a hand to push the annoying person away, but the storm webbing still pulled across him stopped him. He was sprawled on the bed where he'd been working the storm. Wait. What had happened to the storm? They must have made it – he felt like he'd worked all day loading cargo, and he was starved. You surely wouldn't feel that way if you were dead, or even in Hell getting a new body. The ship felt quiet under him, not still pitching in the storm. He reached out to locate the storm, but he couldn't feel a thing. Of course. Taking the magic-suppressing collar off had been temporary. He sighed and reached out to unhook the webbing so he could sit up.

The person shaking him was a Tengri he'd seen running errands for the captain. Beyond him on the table Morien could see a tray of food. He staggered to his feet and lurched over to it, ignoring the man. He'd done more magic on that storm than in the rest of his life put together, and he needed food now.

Once he'd started putting food in his mouth, he turned to the man who'd woken him. "What does the captain need?"

"I don't know. We're in hailing distance of that Elven ship we saw before the storm hit, and she sent me to fetch you."

Morien closed his eyes for a moment in pain. He should have known. These were pirates, after all. They would take the Elven ship, and he'd have to watch more of his own people die. Maybe he shouldn't have helped the Elven ship make it through the storm. Sinking would have been cleaner. Still he had no real choices here. "I'm coming."

He followed the man on deck. The storm had passed, and the sun was shining. Not far away he saw the Elven ship. Her main mast was snapped off about six feet above the deck. They were effectively dead in the water. He made his way slowly to the command deck where the Captain waited.

"I need your help here, Morien. I know you overextended yourself with the storm. You needed a lot of healing afterward. But I think you're the only chance I have to keep these people from doing something stupid. They're sitting ducks there, but they look like they're planning to fight anyway."

"Why shouldn't they? We all know that pirates don't take prisoners, except for lucky people like me who have special talents." Morien didn't bother to try to hide the bitter note in his voice. He was too tired to care about consequences.

"I don't want their damned ship – I have all the prisoners I can deal with already, and there's no bounty for bringing them back to the Imperial City." She rounded on him in frustration. "I could just sail off and leave them to their own devices, but I have spare materials. I thought I'd offer to sell them what they need to make repairs at the usual rates, but first we have to get them to talk to us."

Morien didn't believe she wasn't planning on taking the Elven ship. It made no sense, but he realized it didn't matter. She had his Name now. She could make him do whatever she wanted. Best not to push back and make her use it. "What do you need from me?"

"Get them to talk to us. Advise the people I send to negotiate on what's customary here." She turned to the mate, who hailed the other ship. After a brief exchange, they agreed to let a small party come over to parley.

Flying over the ocean was terrifying. He'd done it many times, often with someone else doing the flying for the group, but he'd always known that if something went wrong, he could catch himself. Doing it when he had no access to his magic was awful. Thankfully it took only a few moments, and then he and the Second Mate were landing on the deck of the Elven vessel. They were immediately surrounded by Elves with drawn crossbows.

"What kind of trick is this? You promised us an Elf to negotiate with. I can tell that one is a prisoner – you haven't even tried to hide the magic suppressor on him," one of the Elves surrounding them snarled angrily.

"Wait! It's not a trick." Morien stepped forward. "I'm Morien of the *Sun Herald*. I am here to negotiate."

"The *Sun Herald* was lost with all hands," the other Elf snapped. "You're either a prisoner, a turncoat who's cooperating with them, or both. Why should we talk to you?"

"Maybe because you'd like to live to see port again?" Morien was exhausted, and not in the best of temper. "As for the collar, it's a wise precaution. When the *Demonfang* overran *Sun Herald*, they took me alive, and their captain got my Name. I don't know how many people out there may have it now. At least this way if they use it against me I can't do too much damage." He watched the suspicion and contempt on the faces of the Elves surrounding them turn to horrified pity. He thought he preferred suspicion and contempt.

"Gods, I'm sorry." The man lowered his crossbow. "I'm Captain Ailil Fairwind. Welcome aboard the *Golden Gull*. Does this captain truly not mean to take us? That's a Tengri ship. What else would they be doing in these waters except being pirates?"

What else, indeed, Morien wondered. He couldn't think of a good explanation, but it was beginning to seem that perhaps it was something else. "She says not. She seems to be hunting pirates for the Imperial bounty on them. They've treated me all right so far. You probably don't have a lot to lose by taking her at her word."

"No, I suppose not. Maybe that treaty King Aran signed with the Empire about the pirates is doing some good after all. I didn't really think it would." The Elven captain shrugged. "Come down to the cabin, and we'll talk. We have a lot of repairs we need to make, and if she's truly willing to sell us materials, it will be a life-saver."

Suspicion hung heavy in the air, but they got down to the nuts and bolts of materials and prices. Most of the dickering was between the Elven captain and the Shining Warrior's Second Mate. Morien supplied an explanation now and then.

When they got down to the smaller items, he wasn't needed any longer. Morien went back on deck. It felt strange to be on an Elven ship again. A year wasn't really long in the life of an Elf, but so much had changed.

"What happens now? Are they planning on just keeping that thing on you forever?" A soft voice from behind him startled him as he looked out over the sea.

"No. *Shining Warrior* is headed back to the Empire to claim the reward for the crew and then the captain will sell *Demonfang*. She's hoping King Aran's Ambassador will offer her a reward for helping me get back to him. It probably won't be more than another month or so." Morien turned to face his questioner. He was a young man, who looked to have a fair bit of human in him. There was also a strong resemblance to *Golden Gull's* Captain. He might be a son, or a cousin.

"Wouldn't it be simpler just to hand you off to us? We'll be going back to the Kingdom of the Sun to make real repairs. We could get you home sooner."

Home. What did that mean? Home had been the *Sun Herald*. He had no family to go back to. It had all been aboard ship. He remembered the mix of suspicion and then pity he'd been greeted with. He didn't want more of that. But what else could he do? "I don't know. Those bastards from the *Demonfang* owe me a lot – more than I can ever hope to collect on. I'm hoping that they'll let me stay for the executions before they send me back to the Kingdom of the Sun." That thought brought a brief smile to his face.

"You want to watch Tengri executions?" The other man's face twisted in revulsion. "Do you know what kinds of things they do? They'll probably feed them to something that eats souls. I can't believe the King signed a treaty that sends people to that, even pirates. We should just kill them and be done with it."

Morien stared a moment in disbelief. How could he mean that? "You don't understand. That wouldn't mean anything to the pirates. They wouldn't even stay dead. Half of them have arrangements with Hell to get reborn there, and come back. Just killing them is no threat. As for what happens to this particular set, I hope they do get fed to something like that, and I want to be there." The hate Morien felt for his former crewmates on *Demonfang* was overpowering. He'd thought he had nothing left to live for, but now that he had options, the hope of revenge looked very sweet.

The other Elf took a step back. "You need a healer. You don't really mean that."

"I mean every word. You're probably right about the healer changing my mind eventually, but right now I'll enjoy every minute of it." Morien looked away across the sea at *Shining Warrior*. The man was right. The first thing they'd do when he went back to the Sun Kingdom was send him to a healer of minds. They'd haul out everything he'd lived through, and the things he'd done over the past year, all the accommodations he'd made to stay sort of sane.

They wouldn't blame him, of course. You couldn't hold someone responsible for anything they'd done when a compulsion invoking their Name was involved, but he'd still have to look at it all again. He couldn't face that. There would be no hope of ever getting revenge on the *Demonfang's* captain either. He needed to find another path.

Back aboard *Shining Warrior*, he sat late into the night considering options. Sounds of repairs drifted across the quiet water from *Golden Gull*. Now that they had materials, they would work night and day until they had maneuvering capability again. As long as the Elven ship was still there, the option for him to go with them was still open. The longer he considered it, the surer he was that he didn't want to go. He couldn't face tearing open his wounds for a healer, and imagining the healer's reaction to what he'd done was even worse. They'd try to put him back together as something like the man he'd been a year ago, and that man couldn't live with the events of the past year.

He needed a plan of his own to avoid that. He did have a valuable talent, and Captain Kithara already had his Name. Staying here might work. But was one set of pirates any better than another, really? They seemed to be. There were no good reasons he could think of for a Tengri pirate to pass up the chance to take the *Golden Gull* outright in favor of simply selling them repair material at exorbitant rates. The ship would fetch far more as salvage. The only answer he could find was that this Tengri pirate wasn't really a pirate.

There was no time like the present to test his theory. He went below and knocked at the door to the captain's cabin.

"Come in, sit down. " Captain Kithara gestured at a chair. "We should consider what you want to do now. Captain Fairwind has offered to take you back to the Kingdom of the Sun with them. "

"No!" The word burst from Morien before the thought about how to phrase his answer diplomatically. "Please. I don't want to go with them."

"Why not?"

"I," he stumbled over his words. "I don't want to go back to the Kingdom of the Sun at all. I know my weather talent is valuable. Could you use my skills here? You could give me more permanent defenses now that you have my Name." He bit his lip nervously.

"I could," the captain said slowly, giving him a measuring look. "It's very tempting. Your talent is rare, and very valuable. But I want to know why. This isn't a normal reaction to a chance to go home after being kidnapped and forced into slavery. For all you know, you're trading one kind of slavery for another."

"I hope not. The possibility had crossed my mind." He looked down. "I don't think I'll ever fit with the Elves again. I've done too many awful things in the past year. And more than anything else I want vengeance. If I go back to the Kingdom of the Sun, maybe a healer will succeed in making me back into someone who sort of fits there.. Assuming that they can do anything about the arrangements in Hell beyond simply helping me die in a way that avoids them. There aren't a lot experts on that there. Even if it all works, Zothar will have won completely, because he'll be beyond my reach forever"

"So why trust me?"

"I've spent a year seeing how real pirates act, and you're not doing that good a job of imitating one when looked at up close. A real pirate wouldn't have sold repair materials to the *Golden Gull,* she'd have just taken the whole ship. Your crew hasn't been playing with me, or with any of the prisoners. They've practically been treating me like a passenger. I don't think you're pirates – I think you're hunting pirates, and I want to be part of it. You know I can be useful."

"I do. I knew that even before you saved us from the storm." She tapped the pen she was holding thoughtfully on the desk. "I could do enough magic using your Name to give you some solid, long-term protections. We might even have a decent chance at replacing those arrangements with Hell with some of our own, if you wanted to make that commitment. You have to be willing though – I won't just rely on having your Name. And you have to be honest with me. Why are you afraid to go back to the Kingdom of the Sun? Were you a criminal before *Demonfang* took you? "

"No. It's just... " He hesitated. "I don't think I can face watching them try to deal with some of the things I've done in the past year, even though they wouldn't hold me responsible."

"What things? I need to know if you're going to be part of my crew." She held his eyes with her gaze.

He took a deep, shuddering breath. "You never asked how Zothar got my Name from me. My cousin had his two little girls on the ship. I gave him my Name, rather than watch him torture them."

"Gods damn him!" Captain Kithara's eyes flashed angrily, and the pen she'd been holding snapped in a suddenly clenched fist..

Morien looked up at her, startled.

"Most Tengri love children too. We have just as hard a time conceiving as Elves do." She sighed. "We didn't find them on *Demonfang* when we took her. What happened?"

Morien shuddered and forced himself to meet her gaze. "Nothing at first. He wanted to sell them as slaves, so he ordered the crew not to touch them. They'd be worth more that way. But I heard a lot of talk among the crew about what they'd like to do, and who he might sell them to. They had awful things ahead of them. He wasn't very careful about keeping me away from them – he had my Name after all. So a few weeks after he captured us, I was alone with them one night. I couldn't get them away from him, and I had to keep them safe from him and people like him, so while they slept, I killed them."

He expected some reaction from the captain – shock, horror, something. Her face was an unreadable mask. "I can't say you were wrong. Would the Elves not see that?" she asked softly.

"Not easily. Eventually I guess a healer would work past their own horror about the act and decide it was the right thing to do. But I don't want to be there while they do it. Will you have me?"

"Gladly, if you'll give me an oath of allegiance. "

He gaped a moment in surprise. An oath? Why was she

worrying about commitments when she already had his Name? What the Hell. He wanted to stay. An oath wasn't much to ask. "I'm willing to do that."

"This is writing off any chance of going back to the Sun Kingdom. They won't want you back after you do this."

"That doesn't matter. They probably don't really want me back as I am now anyway." He shrugged.

"Very well. I'll take your oath as crew now, and we'll get to work on those protections so we can get that collar off you first thing tomorrow. Repeat after me."

He stumbled his way through an oath which didn't bear much resemblance to any shipboard crew oath he'd ever heard. He almost stopped to question it when they came to a reference to the Empire, but he felt he was committed already, and went on,

When it was done, the captain smiled broadly at him. "You're quite right about us not being pirates. Welcome to His Imperial Majesty's Navy."

Kathryn Scannell makes her living doing database management, programming, and general IT support for an environmental consulting firm. She has a BA in German, a BS in Computer Science, and a head full of facts about odd things. She lives in NH with her wife Beth and their four cats. When not writing or reading, she participates in the Society for Creative Anachronism and a variety of role playing games.

You can find her on the web at http://www.kathrynscannell. com and http://kathryn-scannell.dreamwidth.org

Editor's Bio

Val Griswold-Ford is the author of the Dark Horseman novels *Not Your Father's Horseman*, *Dark Moon Seasons* and the upcoming *Last Rites*, all from Dragon Moon Press. She is also the co-editor of *The Complete Guide to Writing Fantasy: the Opus Magnus* (with Tee Morris) and *The Complete Guide to Writing Fantasy: The Author's Grimoire* (with Lai Zhao), also from Dragon Moon Press. She has published several short stories in various anthologies online and in print, and is owned by three cats. She and her husband live in New Hampshire with said cats.

Artist's Biogragphy

Bryan Prindiville spends his days as an Art Director for Catholic Relief Services (CRS) where he has worked since late 2000. In his free time he has had a hand in the creation of a number of comics including Bassetville and Hello with Cheese. Traditionally published work can be found in Rum and Runestones, Tee Morris' All a Twitter and others. Less traditionally he can be found as a member of the live art entertainment show Super Art Fight. More information and work are available at his sketch blog, bryanprindiville.com.

www.ingramcontent.com/pod-product-compliance
Lightning Source LLC
Chambersburg PA
CBHW032241010726
47494CB00002B/580